> That was the year my life fell apart,
> and that was the year I moved to Paris.

HARRY RICKS IS A MAN WHO HAS LOST everything. A romantic mistake at the small New England college where he used to teach has cost him his job, his marriage, and his relationship with his only child. And when the ensuing scandal threatens to completely destroy him, he votes with his feet and flees . . . to Paris. He arrives in the French capital in the bleak midwinter, where a series of accidental encounters lands him in a grubby room in a grubby quartier, and a job as a night watchman for a sinister operation. Just when Harry begins to think that he has hit rock bottom, romance enters his life. Her name is Margit, an elegant, cultivated Hungarian émigré, longtime resident of Paris, widowed, and, like Harry, alone. But though Harry is soon smitten with her, Margit keeps her distance. She will only see him at her apartment in the Fifth arrondissement for a few hours twice a week, and remains guarded about her work, her past, and her life. However, Harry's frustrations with her reticence are soon overshadowed by an ever-growing preoccupation that a dark force is at work in his life, and punishment begins to be meted out to anyone who has recently done him wrong. Before he knows it, he finds himself of increasing interest to the police and waking up in a nightmare from which there is no easy escape.

The WOMAN
in the FIFTH

The WOMAN *in the* FIFTH

A NOVEL

DOUGLAS KENNEDY

ATRIA PAPERBACK

New York   London   Toronto   Sydney

ATRIA PAPERBACK

A Division of Simon & Schuster, Inc.
1230 Avenue of the Americas
New York, NY 10020

First Atria Paperback edition July 2011

ATRIA PAPERBACK and colophon are trademarks of Simon & Schuster, Inc.

For information about special discounts for bulk purchases,
please contact Simon & Schuster Special Sales at
1-866-506-1949 or business@simonandschuster.com.

The Simon & Schuster Speakers Bureau can bring authors to
your live event. For more information or to book an event, contact the
Simon & Schuster Speakers Bureau at 1-866-248-3049 or
visit our website at www.simonspeakers.com.

Designed by Kyoko Watanabe

Manufactured in the United States of America

10   9   8   7   6   5   4   3   2   1

ISBN 978-1-4516-5956-6
ISBN 978-1-4516-0214-2 (ebook)

For Frank Kelcz

"Everything she had told the Superintendent was true, but sometimes nothing is less true than the truth."
—Georges Simenon, *La Fuite de Monsieur Monde*

The WOMAN
in the FIFTH

ONE

THAT WAS THE year my life fell apart, and that was the year I moved to Paris.

I arrived in the city a few days after Christmas. It was a wet, gray morning—the sky the color of dirty chalk; the rain a pervasive mist. My flight landed just after sunrise. I hadn't slept during all those hours above the Atlantic—another insomniac jag to add to all the other broken nights I'd been suffering recently. As I left the plane, my equilibrium went sideways—a moment of complete manic disorientation—and I stumbled badly when the cop in the passport booth asked me how long I'd be staying in France.

"Not sure exactly," I said, my mouth reacting before my brain.

This made him look at me with care—as I had also spoken in French.

"Not sure?" he asked.

"Two weeks," I said quickly.

"You have a ticket back to America?"

I nodded.

"Show it to me, please," he said.

I handed over the ticket. He studied it, noting the return date was January 10.

"How can you be 'not sure,'" he asked, "when you have proof?"

"I wasn't thinking," I said, sounding sheepish.

"*Évidemment,*" he said. His stamp landed on my passport. He pushed my documents back to me, saying nothing. Then he nodded for the next passenger in line to step forward. He was done with me.

I headed off to baggage claim, cursing myself for raising official questions about my intentions in France. But I had been telling the truth. I didn't know how long I'd be staying here. And the airplane ticket—a last-minute buy on an Internet travel site, which offered cheap fares if you purchased a two-week round-trip deal—would be thrown out as soon as January 10 had passed me by. I wasn't planning to head back to the States for a very long time.

How can you be "not sure" when you have proof?

Since when does proof ever provide certainty?

I collected my suitcase and resisted the temptation to splurge on a cab into Paris. My budget was too tight to justify the indulgence. So I took the train. Seven euros one-way. The train was dirty—the carriage floor dappled in trash, the seats sticky and smelling of last night's spilled beer. And the ride into town passed through a series of grim industrial suburbs, all silhouetted by shoddy high-rise apartment buildings. I shut my eyes and nodded off, waking with a start when the train arrived at the Gare du Nord. Following the instructions emailed to me from the hotel, I changed platforms and entered the metro for a long journey to a station with the aromatic name of Jasmin.

I emerged from the metro into the dank morning. I wheeled my suitcase down a long narrow street. The rain turned emphatic. I kept my head down as I walked, veering left into the rue La Fontaine, then right into the rue François Millet. The hotel—Le Sélect—was on the opposite corner. The place had been recommended to me by a colleague at the small college where I used to teach—the only colleague at that college who would still speak to me. He said that the Sélect was clean, simple, and cheap—and in a quiet residential area. What he didn't tell me was that the desk clerk on the morning of my arrival would be such an asshole.

"Good morning," I said. "My name is Harry Ricks. I have a reservation for—"

"Sept jours," he said, glancing up from behind the computer on his desk. *"La chambre ne sera pas prête avant quinze heures."*

He spoke this sentence quickly, and I didn't catch much of what he said.

"Désolé, mais . . . euh . . . je n'ai pas compris . . ."

"You come back at three PM for the check-in," he said, still speaking French, but adopting a plodding, deliberate, loud voice, as if I were deaf.

"But that's hours from now."

"Check-in is at three PM," he said, pointing to a sign next to a mailbox mounted on the wall. All but two of the twenty-eight numbered slots in the box had keys in them.

"Come on, you must have a room available now," I said.

He pointed to the sign again and said nothing.

"Are you telling me there isn't one room ready at this moment?"

"I am telling you that check-in is at three PM."

"And I am telling you that I am exhausted, and would really appreciate it if—"

"I do not make the rules. You leave your bag, you come back at three."

"Please. Be reasonable."

He just shrugged, the faintest flicker of a smile wandering across his lips. Then the phone rang. He answered it and used the opportunity to show me his back.

"I think I'll find another hotel," I said.

He interrupted his call, turning over his shoulder to say, "Then you forfeit tonight's room charge. We need twenty-four hours' notice for cancellation."

Another faint smirk—and one that I wanted to rub off with my fist.

"Where can I put my suitcase?" I asked.

"Over there," he said, pointing to a door by the reception desk.

I wheeled over my suitcase and also took off the computer knapsack slung over my shoulder.

"My laptop is in this bag," I said. "So please—"

"It will be fine," he said. *"À quinze heures, monsieur."*

"Where am I supposed to go now?" I asked.

"Aucune idée," he said. Then he turned back to his call.

At a few minutes past eight on a Sunday morning in late December, there was nowhere to go. I walked up and down the rue François Millet, looking for a café that was open. All were shuttered, many with signs: *Fermeture pour Noël.*

The area was residential—old apartment buildings interspersed with some newer ones from the ugly school of seventies brutalism. Even the modern blocks looked expensive; the few cars parked on the street hinting that this corner of town was upscale and—at this time of the day—lifeless.

The rain had quieted down to an insidious drizzle. I didn't have an umbrella, so I marched back up to the Jasmin metro station and bought a ticket. I got on the first train that arrived, not sure where I was heading. This was only my second trip to Paris. The last time I had been here was in the mideighties, the summer before I entered graduate school. I spent a week in a cheap hotel off the boulevard Saint-Michel, haunting the cinemas in that part of town. At the time, there was a little café called Le Reflet opposite a couple of backstreet movie houses on the rue . . . what the hell was its name? Never mind. The place was cheap and I seemed to remember that they were open for breakfast, so . . .

A quick study of the metro map on the carriage wall, a change of trains at Michel-Ange Molitor, and twenty minutes later I emerged at Cluny–La Sorbonne. Though it had been more than twenty years since I'd last stepped out of this metro station, I never forget my way to a cinema—so I instinctually turned up the boulevard Saint-Michel and into the rue des Écoles. The sight of the marquee of Le Champo—advertising a De Sica and a Douglas Sirk festival on their two screens—provoked a small smile. When I reached its shuttered doors and peered up the rue Champollion—the name of the street I had forgotten—and saw two other cinemas lining its narrow wet pavement, I thought, *Fear not, the old haunts still exist.*

But at nine in the morning, none of them were yet open, and Café Le Reflet was also shuttered. *Fermeture pour Noël.*

I returned to the boulevard Saint-Michel and started walking toward the river. Paris after Christmas was truly dead. The only working places nearby were all the fast-food joints that now dotted the streets, their neon fronts blotting the architectural line of the boulevard. Though I was desperate for shelter from the rain, I still couldn't bring myself to spend my first hours in Paris huddled in a McDonald's. So I kept walking until I came to the first proper café that was open. It was called Le Départ, located on a quay fronting the Seine. Before reaching it, I passed a nearby newspaper stand and scored a copy of *Pariscope*—the "what's on" guide for the city and my cinephile bible back in 1985.

The café was empty. I took a table by a window and ordered a pot of tea against the internal chill I felt coming on. Then I opened *Pariscope* and began combing the cinema listings, planning my viewing for the week ahead. As I noted the John Ford retrospective at the Action Écoles and all the Ealing comedies at Le Reflet Médicis I felt something that had been absent from my life for months: pleasure. A small, fleeting reminder of what it was like not to think about . . . well, everything that had so preoccupied me since . . .

No, let's not go there. Not today, anyway.

I pulled out a little notebook and my fountain pen. It was a lovely old red Parker, circa 1925: a fortieth-birthday gift, two years ago, from my ex-wife when she was still my wife. I uncapped the pen and started scribbling down a schedule. It was a blueprint for the next six days that would give me space in the mornings to set up my life here, and spend all other available waking time in darkened rooms, staring up at projected shadows. "What is it that people love most about a cinema?" I used to ask my students in the introductory course I taught every autumn. "Could it be that, paradoxically, it is a place outside of life in which imitations of life take place? As such, maybe it's a hiding place in which you cannot really hide because you're looking at the world you've sought to escape."

But even if we know we cannot really hide from things, we still try, which is why some of us jump planes to Paris on forty-eight hours' notice, fleeing all the detritus we've left behind.

I nursed the pot of tea for an hour, shaking my head when the waiter dropped by to ask if I wanted anything else. I poured out a final cup. The tea had gone cold. I knew I could have sat in the café for the rest of the morning without being hassled. But if I just continued to loiter without intent there, I would have felt like a deadbeat for hogging a table all that time . . . even though there was only one other customer in the café.

I glanced out the window. The rain was still falling. I glanced at my watch. Five hours to go until check-in. There was only one solution. I reopened *Pariscope* and found that there was a big cinema complex over at Les Halles that started showing movies at nine every morning. I put away my notebook and pen. I grabbed my coat. I tossed four euros down on the table and headed out, making a quick dash for the metro. It was two stops to Les Halles. I followed the signs to something called Le Forum, a bleak concrete shopping center, sunk deep into the Paris earth. The cinema had fifteen screens and was like any American multiplex in some nowhere suburban mall. All the big U.S. Christmas blockbusters were on show, so I chose a film by a French director whose work I didn't know. There was a screening in twenty minutes, which meant first sitting through a series of inane advertisements.

Then the film started. It was long and talky—but I followed most of it. It was largely set in some slightly run-down but hip corner of Paris. There was a thirtysomething guy called Mathieu who taught philosophy at a lycée but (surprise, surprise) was trying to write a novel. There was his ex-wife, Mathilde—a semisuccessful painter who lived in the shadow of her father, Gérard. He was a famous sculptor, now cohabiting with his acolyte Sandrine. Mathilde hated Sandrine because she was ten years her junior. Mathieu certainly didn't like Philippe, the info-tech business executive that Mathilde had been sleeping with. Mathilde, however, liked the lavish way Philippe treated her but found him intellectually exasperating ("The man has never even read Montaigne . . . ").

The film began with Mathieu and Mathilde sitting in her kitchen, drinking coffee and smoking and talking. Then it cut to Sandrine, who was posing naked for Gérard in his country atelier while Bach played on his stereo. They took a break from this modeling session. She put on some clothes. They went into his big country kitchen and drank coffee and smoked and talked. Then there was a scene in some expensive hotel bar. Mathilde was meeting Philippe. They sat at a banquette and drank champagne and smoked and talked . . .

On and on it went. Talk. Talk. More talk. My problems. His problems. Your problems. And, by the way, *la vie est inutile.* After around an hour, I lost the battle I was fighting against jet lag and lack of sleep. I passed out. When I came to, Mathilde and Philippe were sitting in a hotel bar, drinking champagne and smoking and . . . Hang on, hadn't they done this scene already? I tried to keep my eyes open. I didn't succeed. And then . . .

What the fuck?

The opening credits were rolling again—and Mathieu and Mathilde were sitting in her kitchen, drinking coffee and smoking and talking. And . . .

I rubbed my eyes. I lifted my arm. I tried to focus on my watch, but my vision was blurred. Eventually the digital numbers came into view: 4 . . . 4 . . . 3.

Four forty-three?

Oh, Jesus, I'd been asleep since . . .

My mouth was parched, toxic. I swallowed and tasted bile. My neck was rigid, nearly immobile. I touched my shirt. It was soaked through with sweat. Ditto my face. I put my fingers to my forehead. Intense heat radiated from my brow. I put my feet on the floor and tried to stand up. I didn't succeed. Every corner of my body now ached. My body temperature plunged—the tropical fever turning into a near-Arctic chill. My knees caved a bit as I attempted to stand up again, but I managed some sort of forward propulsion that moved me out of the aisle toward the door.

Everything got a little blurry once I hit the lobby. I remember negotiating my way out past the box office, then moving into a maze of walkways, then finding the elevator, then getting disgorged onto the street. But I didn't want to be on the street. I wanted to be in the metro. So why had I gone up when I should have gone down?

A smell hit my nose: fast-food grease. Check that: fast-food grease goes Middle East. I had emerged near a collection of cheap cafés. Opposite me was a tubby guy, deep-frying falafels at an outdoor stand. Next to him, on a rotating spit, was a blackened, half-carved leg of lamb. It was flecked with varicose veins (do lambs get varicose veins?). Beneath the lamb were slices of pizzas that looked like penicillin cultures. They provoked nausea at first glance. Aided by the falafel fumes, I felt as if I was about to be very sick. A moment later, I was very sick. I doubled over and heaved, the vomit hitting my shoes. Somewhere during my retch, a waiter in a café opposite me started shouting—something about being a pig and driving away his customers. I offered no reply, no explanation. I just lurched away, my vision fogged in, but somehow focused on the plastic ventilation shafts of the Pompidou Center in the immediate distance. Halfway there, I got lucky—a cab pulled up in front of a little hotel that was in the line of my stagger. As the passengers got out, I got in. I managed to give the driver the address of the Sélect. Then I slumped across the seat, the fever reasserting itself again.

The ride back was a series of blackouts. One moment, I was in a dark netherworld; the next, the driver was engaged in an extended rant about how my vomit-splattered shoes were stinking up his cab. Blackout. More hectoring from the driver. Blackout. A traffic jam—all spectral yellow automotive lights prismed through rain-streaked windows. Blackout. More yellow light and the driver continuing his rant—now something about people who block the taxi lanes, how he never picked up North Africans if he could help it, and how he would certainly steer clear of me if he ever saw me again on the street. Blackout. A door was opening. A hand was helping me out of the car. A voice whispered gently into my ear, telling me to hand over twelve euros. I did as ordered, reaching into my pocket for my money clip. There was some dialogue in the background. I stood up, leaning against the cab for ballast. I looked up at the sky and felt rain. My knees buckled. I began to fall.

Blackout.

And then I was in a bed. And my eyes were being pierced by a beam of light. With a click, the light snapped off. As my vision regained focus I saw that there was a man seated in a chair beside me, a stethoscope suspended around his neck. Behind him stood another figure—but he seemed lost in the encroaching shadows. My sleeve was being rolled up and daubed with something moist. There was a sharp telltale stab as a needle plunged into my arm.

Blackout.

TWO

THERE WAS A light shining in my eyes again. But it wasn't a piercing beam like the last time. No, this was morning light; a stark, single shaft landing on my face and bringing me back to . . .

Where am I exactly?

It took a moment or two for the room to come into definition. Four walls. A ceiling. Well, that was a start. The walls were papered blue. A plastic lamp was suspended from the ceiling. It was colored blue. I glanced downward. The carpet on the floor was blue. I forced myself to sit up. I was in a double bed. The sheets—soaked with my sweat—were blue. The candlewick bedspread—flecked with two cigarette burns—was blue. The headboard of the bed was upholstered in a matching baby blue. This is one of those LSD flashbacks, right? A payback for my one and only experiment with hallucinogenics in 1982 . . .

There was a table next to the bed. It was not blue. (All right, I'm not totally flipping here.) On it was a bottle of water and assorted packets of pills. Nearby was a small desk. A laptop was on top of it. My laptop. There was a narrow metal chair by the desk. It had a blue seat. (Oh no, it's starting again.) My blue jeans and blue sweater were draped across it. There was a small wardrobe—laminated in the same fake wood as the bedside table and the desk. It was open—and suspended from its hangers were the few pairs of trousers and shirts and the one jacket I'd shoved into a suitcase two days ago when . . .

Was it two days ago? Or, more to the point, what day was it now? And how had I been unpacked into this blue room? And if there's one color I hate, it's azure. And . . .

There was a knock on the door. Without waiting for a reply from me, a man walked in, carrying a tray. His face was familiar.

"Bonjour," he said crisply. *"Voici le petit déjeuner."*

"Thanks," I mumbled back in French.

"They told me you have been sick."

"Have I?"

He put the tray down on the bed. His face registered with me. He was the desk clerk who sent me packing when I arrived at that hotel . . .

No, this hotel. Le Sélect. Where you told the cabbie to bring you last night after you . . .

It was all starting to make sense.

"That is what Adnan said in his note."

"Who is Adnan?" I asked.

"The night clerk."

"I don't remember meeting him."

"He obviously met you."

"How sick was I?"

"Sick enough to not remember how sick you were. But that is just an assumption, as I wasn't here. The doctor who treated you is returning this afternoon at five. All will be revealed then. But that depends on whether you will still be here this afternoon. I put through payment for tomorrow, monsieur, thinking that, in your 'condition,' you would want to keep the room. But your credit card was not accepted. Insufficient funds."

This didn't surprise me. My Visa card was all but maxed out, and I'd checked in knowing that I had just enough credit remaining to squeeze out, at most, two nights here, and that there were no funds to clear the long-overdue bill. But the news still spooked me. Because it brought me back to the depressing realpolitik of my situation: everything has gone awry, and I now find myself shipwrecked in a shitty hotel far away from home . . .

But how can you talk about "home" when it no longer exists, when, like everything else, it has been taken away from you?

"Insufficient funds?" I said, trying to sound bemused. "How can that be?"

"How can that be?" he asked coolly. "It just is."

"I don't know what to say."

He shrugged. "There is nothing to say, except: Do you have another credit card?"

I shook my head.

"Then how do you propose paying for the room?"

"Traveler's checks."

"That will be acceptable—provided they are valid ones. Are they American Express?"

I nodded.

"Fine. I will call American Express. If they say that the checks are valid, you may stay. If not . . ."

"Maybe it would be better if I left now," I said, knowing that my budget couldn't really afford multiple nights in this hotel.

"That is your decision. Checkout time is eleven. You have just over two hours to vacate the room."

As he turned to go, I leaned forward, trying to reach for a croissant on the breakfast tray. Immediately, I fell back against the headboard, exhausted. I touched my brow. The fever was still there. So too was the pervasive sense of enervation. Getting out of this bed would be a major military maneuver. I could do nothing but sit here and accept the fact that I could do nothing but sit here.

"Monsieur . . . " I said.

The desk clerk turned around.

"Yes?"

"The traveler's checks should be in my shoulder bag."

A small smile formed on his lips. He walked over and retrieved the bag and handed it to me. He reminded me that the room cost sixty euros a night. I opened the bag and found my wad of traveler's checks. I pulled out two checks: a fifty-dollar and a twenty-dollar. I signed them both.

"I need another twenty," he said. "The cost in dollars is ninety."

"But that's way above the regular exchange rate," I said.

Another dismissive shrug. "It is the rate we post behind the desk downstairs. If you would like to come downstairs and see . . ."

I could hardly sit up, let alone go downstairs.

I pulled out another twenty-dollar traveler's check. I signed it. I tossed it on the bed.

"There you go."

"*Très bien, monsieur,*" he said, picking up it. "I will get all the details I need from your passport. We have it downstairs."

But I don't remember handing it over to you. I don't remember anything.

"And I will call you once American Express has confirmed that the traveler's checks are legitimate."

"They are legitimate."

Another of his smarmy smiles.

"On verra." We'll see.

He left. I slumped back against the pillows, feeling drained. I stared up blankly at the ceiling—hypnotized by its blue void, willing myself into it. I needed to pee. I tried to right myself and place my feet on the floor. No energy, no will. There was a vase on the bedside table. It contained a plastic floral arrangement: blue gardenias. I picked up the vase, pulled out the flowers, tossed them on the floor, pulled down my boxer shorts, placed my penis inside the vase, and let go. The relief was enormous. So too was the thought: *This is all so seedy.*

The phone rang. It was the desk clerk.

"The checks have been approved. You can stay."

How kind of you.

"I have had a call from Adnan. He wanted to see how you were."

Why would he care?

"He also wanted you to know that you need to take a pill from each of the boxes on the bedside table. Doctor's orders."

"What are the pills?"

"I am not the doctor who prescribed them, monsieur."

I picked up the assorted boxes and vials, trying to make out the names of the drugs. I recognized none of them. But I still did as ordered: I took a pill from each of the six boxes and downed them with a long slug of water.

Within moments, I was gone again—vanished into that vast dreamless void from which there are no recollections: no sense of time past or present, let alone a day after today. A small foretaste of the death that will one day seize me—and deny me all future wake-up calls.

Bringgggggggg . . .

The phone. I was back in the blue room, staring at the vase full of urine. The bedside clock read 17:12. There was streetlamp light creeping in behind the drapes. The day had gone. The phone kept ringing. I answered it.

"The doctor is here," Mr. Desk Clerk said.

The doctor had bad dandruff and chewed-up nails. He wore a suit that needed pressing. He was around fifty, with thinning hair, a sad mustache and the sort of sunken eyes that, to a fellow insomniac like me, were a telltale giveaway of the malaise within. He pulled up a chair by the bed and asked me if I spoke French. I nodded. He motioned for me to remove my T-shirt. As I did so, I caught a whiff of myself. Sleeping in sweat for twenty-four hours had left me ripe.

The doctor didn't seem to react to my body odor—perhaps because his attention was focused on the vase by the bed.

"There was no need to provide a urine sample," he said, taking my pulse. Then he checked my heartbeat, stuck a thermometer under my tongue, wrapped a blood pressure cuff around my left bicep, peered down my throat, and shined a penlight into the whites of my eyes. Finally he spoke.

"You have come down with a ruthless form of the flu. The sort of flu that often kills the elderly—and that is often indicative of larger problems."

"Such as?"

"May I ask, have you been going through a difficult personal passage of late?"

I paused.

"Yes," I finally said.

"Are you married?"

"I'm not sure."

"By which you mean . . . ?"

"I am legally still married . . ."

"But you left your wife?"

"No—it was the other way around."

"And did she leave you recently?"

"Yes—she threw me out a few weeks ago."

"So you were reluctant to leave?"

"Very reluctant."

"Was there another man?"

I nodded.

"And your profession is . . . ?"

"I taught at a college."

"You taught?" he said, picking up on the use of the past tense.

"I lost my job."

"Also recently?"

"Yes."

"Children?"

"A daughter, age fifteen. She lives with her mother."

"Are you in contact with her?"

"I wish . . ."

"She won't talk with you?"

I hesitated. Then: "She told me she never wanted to speak with me again—but I do sense that her mother has convinced her to say this."

He put his fingertips together, taking this in. Then:

"Do you smoke?"

"Not for five years."

"Do you drink heavily?"

"I have been . . . recently."

"Drugs?"

"I take sleeping pills. Non-prescription ones. But they haven't been working for the past few weeks. So . . ."

"Chronic insomnia?"

"Yes."

He favored me with a small nod—a hint that he too knew the hell of unremitting sleeplessness. Then: "It is evident what has happened to you: a general breakdown. The body can only take so much . . . tristesse. Eventually, it reacts against such *traumatisme* by shutting down or giving in to an intense viral attack. The flu you are suffering is more severe than normal because you are in such a troubled state."

"What's the cure?"

"I can only treat the physiological disorders. And flu is one of those viruses that largely dictates its own narrative. I have prescribed several *comprimés* to deal with your aches, your fever, your dehydration, your nausea, your lack of sleep. But the virus will not leave your system until it is—shall we say—bored with you and wants to move on."

"How long could that take?"

"Four, five days . . . at minimum."

I shut my eyes. I couldn't afford four or five more days at this hotel.

"Even once it has gone, you will remain desperately weak for another few days. I would say you will be confined here for at least a week."

He stood up.

"I will return in seventy-two hours to see what improvement you have made and if you have commenced a recovery."

Do we ever really recover from the worst that life can throw us?

"One last thing. A personal question, if I may be permitted. What brought you to Paris, alone, just after Christmas?"

"I ran away."

He thought about this for a moment, then said, "It often takes courage to run away."

"No, you're wrong there," I said. "It takes no courage at all."

THREE

FIVE MINUTES AFTER the doctor left, the desk clerk came into the room. He was holding a piece of paper in one hand. With a flourish, he presented it to me—as if it were a legal writ.

"La facture du médecin." The doctor's bill.

"I'll settle it later."

"He wants to be paid now."

"He's coming back in three days. Can't he wait . . . ?"

"He should have been paid last night. But you were so ill, he decided to hold off until today."

I looked at the bill. It was on hotel letterhead. It was also for an astonishing amount of money: two hundred and sixty-four euros.

"You are joking," I said.

His face remained impassive.

"It is the cost of his services—and of the medicine."

"The cost of his services? The bill's been written up on your stationery."

"All medical bills are processed by us."

"And the doctor charges one hundred euros per house call?"

"The figure includes our administrative fee."

"Which is what?"

He looked right at me.

"Fifty euros per visit."

"That's robbery."

"All hotels have administrative charges."

"But not one hundred percent of the price."

"It is our policy."

"And you charged me one hundred percent markup on the prescriptions?"

16

"Tout à fait. I had to send Adnan to the pharmacy to get them. This took an hour. Naturally, as he was not dealing with hotel business, his time must be compensated for . . ."

"Not dealing with hotel business? I am a guest here. And don't tell me you're paying your night guy thirty-two euros an hour."

He tried to conceal an amused smile. He failed.

"The wages of our employees are not divulged to . . ."

I crumpled up the bill and threw it on the floor.

"Well, I'm not paying it."

"Then you can leave the hotel now."

"You can't make me leave."

"Au contraire, I can have you on the street in five minutes. There are two men in the basement—*notre homme à tout faire* and the chef—who would physically eject you from the hotel if I ordered them to do so."

"I'll call the police."

"Is that supposed to frighten me?" he asked. "The fact is, the police would side with the hotel, once I told them that the reason we were evicting you is because you made sexual advances to the chef. And the chef would confirm this to the police—because he is ignorant and because he is a strict Muslim whom I caught *dans une situation embarrassante* with *notre homme à tout faire* two months ago. So now he will do anything I say, as he fears exposure."

"You wouldn't dare . . ."

"Yes, I would. And the police wouldn't just arrest you for lewd conduct, they'd also check into your background, and find out why you left your country in such a hurry."

"You know nothing about me," I said, sounding nervous.

"Perhaps—but it is also clear that you are not in Paris for a mere holiday . . . that you ran away from something. The doctor told me you confessed that to him."

"I did nothing illegal."

"So you say."

"You are a shit," I said.

"That is an interpretation," he said.

I shut my eyes. He held all the cards—and there was nothing I could do about it.

"Give me my bag," I said.

He did as requested. I pulled out the wad of traveler's checks.

"It's two hundred and sixty-four euros, right?" I asked.

"In dollars, the total is three hundred and forty-five."

I grabbed a pen and signed the necessary number of checks, and threw them on the floor.

"There," I said. "Get them yourself."

"*Avec plaisir,* monsieur."

He picked up the checks and said, "I will return tomorrow to collect the payment for the room—that is, if you still want to stay."

"As soon as I can stagger out of here, I will."

"*Très bien,* monsieur. And by the way, thank you for pissing in the vase. *Très classe.*"

And he left.

I fell back against the pillows, exhausted, enraged. The latter emotion was something with which I'd had extensive personal contact over the past few weeks—an ominous sense that I was about to detonate at any moment. But rage turned inward transforms itself into something even more corrosive: self-loathing . . . and one that edges into depression. The doctor was right: I had broken down.

And when the flu finally moved on, what then? I would still be wiped out, beaten.

I reached back into my shoulder bag and pulled out the traveler's checks. I counted them. Four thousand six hundred and fifty dollars. My entire net worth. Everything I had or owned in the world—as I was pretty damn sure that, thanks to the demonizing I'd been subjected to in the press, Susan's lawyers would convince the divorce judge that my wife should get it all: the house, the pension plans, the life insurance policies, the small stock portfolio we purchased together. We weren't rich—academics rarely are. And with a daughter to raise and an ex-husband permanently barred from teaching again, the court would rightfully feel that she deserved the few assets we once shared. I certainly wasn't going to fight that. Because I had no fight left in me—except when it came to somehow getting my daughter to talk to me again.

Four thousand six hundred and fifty dollars. On the flight over here, stuffed into a narrow seat, I had done some quick calculations on the back of a cocktail napkin. At the time I had just over five thousand bucks. At the current, legal rate of exchange, it would net me just over four thousand euros. If I lived very carefully, I estimated I could eke out three or four months in Paris—on the basis that I could find a cheap place to live as soon as I got there. But forty-eight hours after landing in Paris, I had already spent over four hundred dollars. As it looked as though I wouldn't be able to move from here for another few days, I could count on paying out another extortionate hundred bucks a night until I was fit enough to leave this dump.

My rage was dampened by fatigue. I wanted to go into the bathroom and strip off my sweat-sodden T-shirt and undershorts and stand under a shower. But I still couldn't make it off the bed. So I just lay there, staring blankly upward, until the world went blank again and I was back in the void.

Two soft knocks on the door. I stirred awake, everything blurred, vague. Another soft knock, followed by the door opening a crack, and a voice quietly saying, "Monsieur . . . ?"

"Go away," I said. "I don't want anything to do with you."

The door opened further. Behind it emerged a man in his early forties—with rust-colored skin and cropped black hair. He was dressed in a black suit and a white shirt.

"Monsieur, I just want to see if you needed anything."

His French, though fluent, was marked with a strong accent.

"Sorry, sorry," I said. "I thought you were . . ."

"Monsieur Brasseur?"

"Who's Monsieur Brasseur?"

"The morning desk clerk."

"So that's the bastard's name: Brasseur."

A small smile from the man in the doorway.

"Nobody likes Monsieur Brasseur, except the hotel manager—because Brasseur is very talented at *la provocation*."

"Are you the guy who helped me out of the cab yesterday?"

"Yes, I'm Adnan."

"Thanks for that—and for getting me settled here."

"You were very ill."

"But you still didn't have to get me undressed and into bed, or call a doctor, or unpack everything. It was far too kind of you."

He looked away, shyly.

"It's my job," he said. "How are you feeling tonight?"

"Very weak. Very grubby."

He stepped fully into the room. As he approached me, I could see that his face had grooved lines around the eyes—the sort of creases that belonged on the face of a man twenty years his senior. His suit was tight, ill-fitting, badly worn—and there was a serious tobacco stain on both his right index and middle fingers.

"Do you think you can get out of bed?" he asked.

"Not without help."

"Then I will help you. But first I will run you a bath. A long soak will do you good."

I nodded weakly. He took charge of things. Without flinching at its contents, he picked up the vase and disappeared into the bathroom. I heard him flush the toilet and turn on the bath taps. He emerged back into the bedroom, took off his suit jacket, and hung it up in the armoire. Then he picked up my jeans and the shirt and socks that had been placed on the desk chair and stuffed them in the pillowcase.

"Any other dirty laundry?" he asked.

"Just what I am wearing."

He returned to the bathroom. The water stopped running. Steam leaked out through the doorway. He emerged, his face glistening from the vapors, his right arm wet.

"It is hot, but not too hot."

He came over to the bed and sat me upright and placed my feet on the floor and then lifted my left arm and pulled it around his shoulder and hoisted me up. My legs felt as sturdy as matchsticks. But Adnan kept me vertical and walked me slowly into the bathroom.

"Do you need help with your clothes?" he asked.

"No, I can handle it."

But when I took one of my hands off the sink, I immediately lost balance and felt my knees warping. Adnan straightened me up and quietly asked me to keep one hand on the sink while raising the other above me. I was able to keep my arm aloft long enough for him to pull my T-shirt off my arm and over my head. Then he asked me to switch arms and inched the rest of it off. With a quick yank, he pulled my boxer shorts to the floor. I stepped out of them and allowed Adnan to walk me the two steps to the bath. The water was seriously hot. So hot that I recoiled when my foot first touched its surface. But Adnan ignored my protestations and gently forced me into the tub. The initial shock of the water gave way to a strange sense of scalded calm.

"Do you need help washing yourself?"

"I'll try doing it myself."

I managed to soap up my crotch, my chest, and underarms, but couldn't find the energy to reach down to my feet. So Adnan took the soap and dealt with them. He also brought over the shower hose and doused my hair and lathered it up with shampoo. Then he found a can of shaving cream and a razor among the toiletries he'd earlier unpacked, and knelt down by the bathtub and started covering my face in foam.

"You don't have to do this," I said, embarrassed by all the personal attention.

"You will feel better for it."

He took great care when it came to dragging a razor across my face. After he finished, he brought over the shower hose and rinsed off all the foam and the shampoo from my hair. Then he filled the sink with hot water, submerged a cloth in it, retrieved it, and, without squeezing out its excess water, placed it over my face.

"Now you will lie here, please, for a quarter of an hour," Adnan said.

He left the bathroom. I opened my eyes and saw nothing but the textured white of the cloth. I closed them and tried to empty my head, to concentrate on nothing. I failed. But the bathwater was balming, and it was good to be clean again. I heard occasional noises from the other room, but Adnan let me be for a long time. Then there was a soft knock at the bathroom door.

"Ready to get out?" he asked.

Once again, he had to help me up and wrapped me in one of the thin hotel bath towels before handing me two folded items of clothing.

"I found these in your things. A pajama bottom and a T-shirt."

He helped dry me down, then got me dressed and led me back to a bed that had been remade with fresh sheets. They felt wonderfully cool as I slid between them. Adnan positioned the pillows so I could sit up against the headboard. He retrieved a tray that had been left on the desk. He carried it over with care. On it was a tureen, a bowl, and a small baguette.

"This is a very mild bouillon," he said, pouring some into the bowl. "You must eat."

He handed me the spoon.

"Do you need help?" he asked.

I was able to feed myself—and the thin bouillon was restorative. I even managed to eat most of the baguette—my hunger overcoming the general lie-there-and-die listlessness I felt.

"You are being far too nice to me," I said.

A small shy nod.

"My job," he said and excused himself. When he returned some minutes later, he was carrying another tray—with a teapot and a cup.

"I have made you an infusion of *verveine*," he said. "It will help you sleep. But you must first take all your medicines."

He gathered up the necessary pills and a glass of water. I swallowed them, one by one. Then I drank some of the herbal tea.

"Are you on duty tomorrow night?" I asked.

"I start at five," he said.

"That's good news. No one has been this nice to me since . . ."

I put my hand over my face, hating myself for that self-pitying remark—and trying to suppress the sob that was wailing up. I caught it just before it reached my larynx—and took a deep steadying breath. When I removed my hand from my eyes, I saw Adnan watching me.

"Sorry . . ." I muttered.

"For what?" he asked.

"I don't know . . . Everything, I guess."

"You are alone here in Paris?"

I nodded.

"It is hard," he said. "I know."

"Where are you from?" I asked.

"Turkey. A small village around a hundred kilometers from Ankara."

"How many years in Paris?"

"Four."

"Do you like it here?" I asked.

"No."

Silence.

"You must rest," he said.

He reached over to the desk and picked up a remote control, which he pointed at the small television that had been bracketed to the wall.

"If you are lonely or bored, there is always this," he said, placing the remote in my hand.

I stared up at the television. Four pretty people were sitting around a table, laughing and talking. Behind them a studio audience was seated on bleachers, laughing whenever one of the guests made a funny comment—or breaking into loud applause when the fast-talking presenter encouraged them to cheer.

"I will come back and check on you later," Adnan said.

I clicked off the television, suddenly drowsy. I looked at the boxes of medicine again. One of them read, "Zopiclone." The name rang some sort of distant bell . . . something my doctor back in the States might have once recommended when I was going through one of my insomnia jags. Whatever the drug was, it was certainly creeping up on me quickly, blurring the edges of things, damping down all anxieties, diminishing the fluorescent glow of the room's blue chandelier, sending me into . . .

Morning. Or perhaps a moment just before morning. Gray dawn light was seeping into the room. As I stirred, I could sense that I was marginally better. I was able to put my feet on the floor and take slow, old-man steps into the bathroom. I peed. I splashed a little water on my face. I fell back into the blue room. I crawled into bed.

Monsieur Brasseur arrived with breakfast at nine. He knocked twice sharply on the door, then waltzed in without warning, placing the tray on the bed. No hello, no *comment allez-vous,* monsieur? Just one question: "Will you be staying another night?"

"Yes."

He retrieved my bag. I signed another hundred dollars' worth of traveler's checks. He picked them up and left. I didn't see him for the rest of the day.

I managed to eat the stale croissant and the milky coffee. I turned on the television. The hotel only had the five French channels. Morning television here was as banal and inane as in the States. Game shows—in which housewives tried to spell out scrambled words and win dry-cleaning for a year. Reality shows—in which faded actors coped with working on a real-life farm. Talk shows—in which glossy celebrities talked to glossy celebrities, and every so often girls in skimpy clothes would come out and sit on some aging rock star's lap . . .

I clicked off the television. I picked up *Pariscope* and studied the cinema listings, thinking about all the movies I could be sitting through right now. I dozed. A knock on the door, followed by a quiet voice saying, "Monsieur?"

Adnan already? I glanced at my watch. 5:15 PM. How had the day disappeared like that?

He came into the room, carrying a tray.

"You are feeling better today, monsieur?"

"A little, yes."

"I have your clean laundry downstairs. And if you are able to try something a little more substantial than soup and a baguette . . . I could make you an omelet, perhaps?"

"That would be very kind of you."

"Your French—it is very good."

"It's passable."

"You are being modest," he said.

"No—I am being accurate. It needs improvement."

"It will get it here. Have you lived in Paris before?"

"Just spent a week here some years ago."

"You picked up such fluent French in just a week?"

"Hardly," I said, with a small laugh. "I've been taking classes for the past five years back home in the States."

"Then you must have known you would be coming here."

"I think it was more of a dream . . . a life in Paris . . ."

"A life in Paris is not a dream," he said quietly.

But it had been my dream for years, that absurd dream which so many of my compatriots embrace: being a writer in Paris. Escaping the day-to-day routine of teaching at a nowhere college to live in some small but pleasant atelier near the Seine . . . within walking distance of a dozen cinemas. Working on my novel in the mornings, then ducking out to a

2:00 PM screening of Louis Malle's *Ascenseur pour l'échafaud* before picking up Megan at the bilingual school in which we'd enrolled her.

Yes, Susan and Megan always played a part in this Paris fantasia. And for years—as we took language classes together at the college and even devoted an hour a day to speaking to each other in French—my wife encouraged this dream. But—and there was always a *but*—we first had to get a new kitchen for our slightly tumbledown house. Then the house required rewiring. Then Susan wanted to wait until we both received tenured positions at the college. But once my tenure came through, she felt we had to find the "right time" to take a sabbatical, and the "appropriate moment" to take Megan out of her local school without damaging her "educational and social development." Susan was always obsessive about "getting the timing just right" on "major life decisions." The problem was, things never went exactly according to Susan's plan. There was always something holding her back from making the jump. After five years of "maybe in eighteen months' time," she stopped auditing the language classes and also ended our nightly conversations in French—two events that dovetailed with her withdrawal from me. I kept taking the classes, kept telling myself that, one day, I would get to live and write in Paris. Just as I also kept reassuring myself that Susan's distancing act was just a temporary thing—especially as she would never acknowledge that she had pulled away from me, and kept insisting that nothing was wrong.

But everything was wrong. And everything went from bad to catastrophic. And Paris didn't turn into a fantasia, but . . .

"Coming here was a way out for me," I told Adnan.

"From what?"

"Problems."

"Bad problems?"

"Yes."

"I'm sorry," he said.

Then he excused himself. He arrived back with the omelet and a basket of bread fifteen minutes later. As I ate, he said, "I will ring the doctor tonight to confirm that he will be seeing you tomorrow."

"I can't afford the doctor. I can't afford this hotel."

"But you are still very sick."

"I'm on something of a budget. A tight budget."

I was waiting for him to reply with something like, "I thought all Americans are rich." But Adnan said nothing, except, "I will see what I can do."

The sleeping pills did their chemical magic and sent me through the night. Brasseur arrived with the breakfast tray at eight and relieved me of another hundred-dollar traveler's check. I managed to make it to the bathroom again without aid—but only just. I spent the day reading and flipping mindlessly through the television channels. Adnan arrived at five.

"I called the doctor before I came to work. He said that he didn't need to see you as long as your condition hadn't deteriorated . . ."

Well, that was one bit of decent news.

"But he was also very adamant that you do not move for at least another forty-eight hours, even if you are feeling better. He said that there is a high incidence of relapse with this flu, so you must be prudent—otherwise you could end up in the hospital."

Where the damages would be a lot more than one hundred bucks a night.

"I guess I have no choice but to sit still," I said.

"Where will you go after here?"

"I need to find somewhere to live."

"An apartment?"

"A very cheap apartment."

A small nod of acknowledgment, then he asked, "Are you ready for your bath now, monsieur?"

I told him I could take care of it myself.

"So you are on the mend?" he asked.

"I'm determined to check out of here in two days. Any thoughts on a cheaper place to live?"

"My arrondissement still has lots of inexpensive places, even though people with money are starting to buy them up."

"Where are you?"

"Do you know the Tenth? Near the Gare de l'Est?"

I shook my head.

"Many Turks still live around there."

"How long have you lived there?"

"Ever since I came to Paris."

"Always in the same place?"

"Yes."

"Do you miss home?"

He looked away from me.

"All the time."

"Can you afford to get back there occasionally?"

"I cannot leave France."

"Why not?"

"Because . . ." He halted for a moment and studied my face, seeing if he could trust me. ". . . if I leave France, I will probably have difficulties returning. I do not have the appropriate papers."

"You're illegal here?"

A nod.

"Does Brasseur know that?"

"Of course. That's why he can get away with paying me nothing."

"How much is nothing?"

"Six euros an hour."

"And you work how many hours?"

"Five until one, six days a week."

"Can you live on that?"

"If I didn't have to send money back to my wife . . ."

"You're married?"

He avoided my eyes again.

"Yes."

"Children?"

"A son."

"How old?"

"Six."

"And you haven't seen him . . . ?"

"In four years."

"That's terrible."

"Yes, it is. Being unable to see your children—"

He broke off without finishing the sentence.

"Believe me, I know," I said. "Because I have no idea if I will ever be allowed to see my daughter again."

"How old is she?"

I told him.

"She must miss her father."

"It's a very difficult situation . . . and I find myself thinking of her all the time."

"I'm sorry," he said.

"As I am for you."

He acknowledged this with a small, hesitant nod, then turned and stared out the window.

"Can't your wife and son somehow visit you here?" I asked.

"The money doesn't exist for that. Even if I could somehow find a way for them to come, they would be denied entry. Or they would be asked to give an address at which they were staying. If the address didn't check out, they'd be deported immediately. And if it did check out, it would lead the police directly to me."

"Surely the cops have other things on their minds these days than busting one illegal immigrant."

"We're now all potential terrorists in their eyes—especially if you look like you come from that part of the world. Do you know about the system of being controlled here? The police are legally allowed to stop anyone and demand to see their papers. No papers, and they can lock you up, or if you have papers and no residency permit—*la carte de séjour*—it's the beginning of the end."

"You mean, if I stay on after my initial six-month visa and the cops stop me in the street . . ."

"You won't get stopped. You're American, white . . ."

"Have you ever been controlled?"

"Not yet—but that's because I avoid certain places, like the Strasbourg Saint-Denis or Châtelet metro stations, where the police often check papers. In wealthy areas I also try to stay away from the intersections of big thoroughfares. After four years, you get very adept at looking around corners, knowing just how far to walk down a certain street."

"How can you live like that?" I heard myself saying (and immediately regretted that I spoke without thinking). Adnan didn't flinch or bridle at such a direct question.

"I have no choice. I can't go back."

"Because . . ."

"Trouble," he said.

"Bad trouble?"

"Yes," he said. "Bad trouble."

"I know what that's all about."

"You can't return home either?"

"I suppose there's nothing legally stopping me," I said. "But there's also nothing for me to go back to. So . . ."

Another silence. This time he broke it.

"You know, monsieur, if you need somewhere cheap in a hurry . . ."

"Yes?"

"Sorry," he said, suddenly shy. "I shouldn't be interfering in this way."

"You know somewhere?"

"It isn't very nice, but . . ."

"Define 'not very nice.'"

"Do you know what a *'chambre de bonne'* is?"

"A maid's room?" I said, using a literal translation.

"What used to be a maid's room, but is now a tiny studio apartment. Maybe eleven meters square in size. A bed, a chair, a sink, a hotplate, a shower."

"But in bad condition?"

"Not good."

"Clean?"

"I could help you clean it. It is down the hall from my own *chambre de bonne.*"

"I see," I said.

"As I said, I don't want to intrude into your . . ."

"How much is it a month?"

"Four hundred euros. But I know the man who manages the building, and I might be able to get him to drop the price by thirty or forty euros."

"I'd like to see it."

Adnan smiled a shy smile.

"Good. I will arrange it."

The next morning, when Brasseur came in with breakfast, I announced that I would be checking out tomorrow. While arranging the tray on the bed, he casually asked, "So Adnan is taking you home with him?"

"What are you talking about?"

"Just what I heard from the chef, who lives down the corridor in the same building as Adnan: 'He has a new boyfriend—the American who has been so sick.'"

"You can think what you like."

"It is not my affair."

"That's right, it's not your affair—as there is no affair here."

"Monsieur, there is no need to reassure me. I am not your priest—or your wife."

That's when I threw the orange juice at him: without a pause for reflection, I made a grab for the glass and hurled the contents at him. It scored a direct hit on his face. There was a moment of stunned silence—as the juice dripped down his cheeks and pulpish bits lodged in his eyebrows. But then his shock turned into cold rage.

"Get out," he said.

"Fine," I said, jumping out of the bed.

"I'm calling the police," he said.

"For what? Baptism by fruit juice?"

"Believe me, I'll think of something unpleasant and damaging."

"You do that, I'll tell them about all the illegal workers you have here—and how you're paying them slave wages."

That stopped him cold. He pulled out a handkerchief and started mopping his face.

"Maybe I'll just fire Adnan."

"Then I'll make an anonymous call to the cops and tell them how you use illegal—"

"This conversation is finished. I'll call your 'petit ami' Adnan, and tell him to take you off to his place."

"You are a sick little bastard."

But he didn't hear the final three words of the sentence, as he was already out the door. When it slammed behind him, I slumped against a wall, stunned by what had just taken place and the crazed fury of it all.

But he started it, right?

I got dressed. I started packing. I fell into a guilty fugue, thinking how unnecessarily kind Adnan had been to me, and how I'd now put him in a difficult situation with his asshole boss. I wanted to leave him one hundred euros as a thank-you, but sensed that Brasseur would pocket it. Once I found another hotel, I'd come back here one evening and give it to him.

The phone rang. I answered it. It was Brasseur.

"I have spoken with Adnan at his other job. He will be here in half an hour."

Click.

I dialed reception right back. Brasseur answered.

"Please tell Adnan that I'll find a place on my own, that—"

"Too late," Brasseur said. "He's already en route."

"Then call him on his portable."

"He doesn't have one."

Click.

I thought, *Grab your bag and leave now.* Adnan might have been all nice and attentive while you were infirm (a little too attentive, if truth be told), but who knows what ulterior motive underscores his offer of a *chambre de bonne* down the corridor from his own. As soon as he gets you there, probably four of his friends will jump you, grab all your traveler's checks and what few valuables you have (your computer, your fountain pen, your dad's old Rolex), then cut your throat and dump your body in some large *poubelle,* where it will end up being incinerated along with half of Paris's rubbish. And yeah, this scenario might just sound a little paranoid. But why believe that this guy has any decent motives at all? If the last few months had taught me anything, it was that hardly anyone does anything out of sheer, simple decency.

I finished packing. I hoisted my bag and went downstairs. As I approached the reception desk, I noticed that Brasseur had changed into a fresh shirt, but that his tie was still dappled with juice stains. He said, "I've decided I'm keeping the twenty euros to cover my dry-cleaning costs."

I said nothing. I just headed to the door.

"Aren't you waiting for Adnan?" he asked.

"Tell him I'll be in touch."

"Lovers' tiff?"

That stopped me in my tracks. I wheeled around, my right hand raised. Brasseur took a step backward. But then, like any bully who realized that his provocation wouldn't result in instant retaliation, he looked at me with contempt.

"With any luck, I will never see you again," I said.

"Et moi non plus," he replied. The same to you.

I showed him my back and hit the street, where I ran straight into Adnan. It was hard to hide my surprise—and discomfort—in meeting him.

"Didn't Brasseur tell you I was coming?" he asked.

"I just decided to wait outside," I lied. "I couldn't stand being in there anymore."

Then I told him what had transpired in the room—after Brasseur had made his charming insinuations.

"He thinks all Turks are *pédés*," he said, using French slang for homosexuals.

"That doesn't surprise me," I said, also mentioning what he'd said about catching the *homme à tout faire* with the chef.

"I know the chef—Omar. He lives in the same building as me. He is bad."

And he quickly changed the subject, saying that Sezer—the manager of the building where he lived—would be expecting us within the hour. Then, taking the handle of my roll-bag (and refusing my protestations that I could wheel it along myself), he guided us a sharp right up the rue Ribera.

"Brasseur said he called you at your other job," I said as we headed toward the metro.

"Yes, I do a six-hour shift every day at a clothes importer near to where I live."

"Six hours on top of the eight at the hotel? That's insane."

"And necessary. All the money from the hotel job goes home to Turkey. The morning job . . ."

"What time does it start?"

"Seven thirty."

"But you only get off work here at one AM. By the time you get home . . ."

"It's about a half hour by bicycle. All the metros stop just before one. Anyway, I don't need much sleep, so . . ."

He let the sentence die, hinting he didn't want to keep talking about all this. Rue Ribera had a slight incline—and though it was one lane wide and lined with apartment buildings, the morning sun still found a way of beaming down on this narrow thoroughfare. In the near distance, a father—fortyish, well dressed, well heeled—walked out of some venerable building with his teenage daughter. Unlike most adolescent girls she wasn't in the midst of a vast, perpetual sulk. Rather, she laughed at something her dad said to her, and then made a comment that caused him to smile. The rapport between them was evident—and I could not help but feel a crippling sadness.

I stopped momentarily. Adnan glanced at the family scene, then back at me.

"Are you all right?"

I shook my head.

We moved on to the avenue Mozart and the Jasmin metro station. We took the line headed toward Boulogne. When the train arrived, I saw Adnan quickly scanning the carriage—making certain it was free of officialdom—before guiding us onto it.

"We change at Michel-Ange Molitor," Adnan said, "then again at Odéon. Our stop is Château d'Eau."

It was just two stops to our first change point. We left the metro and followed the signs for Line 10, heading toward Gare d'Austerlitz. As we walked down a flight of stairs, I insisted on taking my bag from Adnan. We reached the bottom of the stairs, then followed a long corridor. At the end of it were two flics, checking papers. Adnan froze for a moment, then hissed, "Turn around."

We executed a fast about-face. But as we headed back along the corridor, another two flics appeared. They couldn't have been more than thirty yards in front of us. We both froze again. Did they see that?

"Walk ahead of me," Adnan whispered. "And when they stop me, keep walking. You go to Château d'Eau, then to 38 rue de Paradis— that's the address. You ask for Sezer . . ."

"Stay alongside me," I whispered back, "and they probably won't stop you."

"Go," he hissed. "Thirty-eight rue de Paradis."

He slowed down his gait. But when I tried to stay by him, he hissed again, *"Allez rue de Paradis!"*

I started walking toward the flics, feeling the same sort of disquiet that comes over me on those rare instances when I have encountered the police or customs officers: an immediate sense that I must be guilty of something.

As I came into their direct line of vision, I could see the flics looking me over, their faces impassive while their eyes took in everything about my appearance. Five feet away from them, I expected the words, *"Vos papiers,* monsieur." But they remained silent as I passed by. I remounted the stairs, then stopped, loitering with intent as I waited in the futile hope that Adnan would follow right behind me. Five minutes passed, then ten. No Adnan. I decided to risk walking downstairs again. If the flics were there, I could plead that I was just a dumb American tourist who had lost his way. But when I reached the corridor again, it was empty.

There was a moment of awful realization: *They've nabbed him . . . and it's all your fault.*

This was followed by another awful thought: *What do I do now?*

Allez rue de Paradis.

Go to Paradise.

FOUR

PARADISE.

But before I got there, I had to first pass through Africa.

When I emerged from the Château d'Eau metro, I was in another Paris. Gone were the big apartment buildings and their well-heeled residents in their expensive casual clothes, loading well-groomed children into their shiny SUVs. Château d'Eau was dirty. There was rubbish everywhere. And grubby cafés. And shops that sold cheap synthetic wigs in garish colors like purple. And storefront telephone exchanges, advertising cheap long-distance rates to Côte d'Ivoire, Cameroun, Sénégal, and the Central African Republic and Burkina Faso and . . .

I was the only white face in sight. Though the mercury was hovering just above the freezing mark, the boulevard was crowded, with a lot of café conversations spilling out onto the street, and people greeting passersby as if they were in a small village, and merchants selling vegetables or exotic candy from carts. No one eyed me suspiciously. No one gave me a telltale look, saying I had wandered into the wrong corner of town. I was ignored. Even the elderly black man I stopped to ask for directions to the rue de Paradis seemed to look right through me—though he did point up a side street and uttered one phrase, *"Vous tournez à droite au fond de la rue,"* before moving on.

The side street brought me out of Africa and into India. A row of curry houses, and video shops with Bollywood posters in their windows, and more telephone exchanges—only this time the rates were for Mumbai and Delhi and they were also advertised in Hindi. There were also a lot of cheap hotels, giving me a fast, grim alternative for a few nights if the *chambre de bonne* turned out to be beyond bad, or if this guy Sezer was a trickster and I had walked into some class of setup.

I had to cross the rue du Faubourg Saint-Denis—a scruffy food market with more cheap shops, brimming with huddled people, their heads down against the cold wind that had started to blow through the streets. I turned right, then took a sharp left into rue de Paradis. At first sight, it looked bland. It was long and narrow—a hodgepodge of characterless nineteenth-century architecture and the occasional modern block. At street level, it seemed dead on arrival—no visible signs of life; just some large wholesale outlets for china and kitchen equipment. Then I began to pass by a place marked kahve. It was a large, faceless café—all fluorescent tubes and gray linoleum and the Istanbul Top Forty blaring on the loudspeaker systems. I peered inside. Men were huddled over tea and talking conspiratorially. A couple of late-morning drunks were asleep at the bar, and a low cloud of cigarette smoke hung over everything. The young, tough-guy bartender turned away from some soccer match on the television to look long and hard at me, wondering why I was loitering with intent outside this establishment. His hostile stare hinted that I should move on.

Which I did.

There were two more *kahves* on rue de Paradis. There were also a handful of Turkish restaurants and a couple of bars whose shutters were still pulled down at midday. I picked up my pace and stopped examining the street in detail. Instead, I started looking up to check numbers, noting the chipped paintwork on many of the buildings. Number 38 was particularly mangy—its façade blistered with chipped masonry and large yellow blotches, like the ingrained stains on a chain-smoker's teeth. The front door—a huge, towering object—was also in need of several coats of black gloss. I looked around for some sort of entry phone, but just saw a button marked PORTE. I pressed it and heard a telltale click. I had to put my entire weight against it to push it open. I pulled my bag in after me and found myself in a narrow corridor of battered mailboxes and brimming trash cans and a couple of fuse boxes from which loose wires dangled. Up ahead was a courtyard. I walked into it. Off it were three stairways—marked with the letters A, B, and C. The courtyard was a small dark rectangle, above which loomed four blocks of apartments. The walls here were as ragged as their exterior counterparts, only now adorned with laundry that draped from windows and makeshift clotheslines. The aroma of greasy cooking and rotting vegetables was omnipresent. So too was a sign that dominated the far side of the courtyard: SEZER CONFECTION (Sezer Ready-to-Wear). There was a separate stairway below this sign. I had to ring a bell to gain admittance. No one answered, so I rang it again. When there was still no answer, I leaned on the bell for a good fifteen seconds. Finally I heard footsteps on the stairs. The door opened and a young tough—dressed in a faded denim jacket with an imitation fur collar—opened the door. His upper lip boasted a meager mustache and he had a cigarette plugged between his teeth. His face radiated annoyance.

"What you want?" he asked in bad French.

"I'm here to see Sezer."

"He knows you?"

"Adnan told me—"

"Where is Adnan?" he asked, cutting me off.

"I'll explain that to Sezer."

"You tell me."

"I'd rather tell—"

"You tell me," he said, his tone demonstrative.

"He was controlled by the flics," I said.

He tensed.

"When was this?"

"Less than an hour ago."

Silence. He looked over my shoulder, scanning the distant corridor. Did he think this was a setup—and that I had brought "company" with me?

"You wait here," he said and slammed the door in my face.

I stood in the courtyard for the next five minutes, wondering if I should do the sensible thing and make a break for the street before he came back. But what kept me rooted to the spot was the realization that I owed it to Adnan to explain what happened—and to see if Sezer was the sort of connected guy who could pull strings and—

Oh sure. Just look at this backstreet setup. *Do you really think the boss here is chummy with the sort of high-up people who will spring an illegal immigrant for him?*

All right, what really kept me rooted to the spot was the realization, *Right now, I have nowhere else to go . . . and I needed a cheap place to live.*

The door was reopened by Mr. Tough Guy. Again, he glanced over my shoulder to make certain the coast was clear before saying, "Okay, you come upstairs to the office."

We mounted a narrow staircase. I pulled my suitcase behind me, its wheels landing with an ominous thud on each stair. I'd seen enough film noir to imagine what I was walking into—a dirty smoke-filled office, with a fat slob in a dirty T-shirt behind a cheap metal desk, a drool-sodden cigar in a corner of his mouth, a half-eaten sandwich (with visible teeth marks) in front of him, girlie calendars on the walls, and three lugs in cheap pinstripe suits propping up the background.

But the office that I entered bore no relation to any office I'd ever seen before. It was just a room with dirty white walls, scuffed linoleum, a table, and chair. There was no other adornment, not even a telephone—bar the little Nokia positioned on the table at which a man sat. He wasn't the Mr. Big that this clandestine buildup led me to expect. Rather, he was a rail-thin man in his fifties, wearing a plain black suit, a white shirt (buttoned at the collar), and small wire-rimmed glasses. His skin was Mediterranean olive and his head was virtually shaved. He looked like one of those secular Iranians who worked as a right-hand man to the Ayatollah, acted as the enforcing brain of the theocracy, and knew where all the infidel body parts had been buried.

As I was studying him, he was also assessing me—with a long cool stare that he held for a very long time. Finally: "So you are the American?" he asked in French.

"Are you Sezer?"

"*Monsieur* Sezer," he said, correcting me.

"*Mes excuses,* Monsieur Sezer."

My tone was polite, deferential. He noted this with a small nod, then said, "Adnan left his job to rescue you today."

"I am aware of that. But I didn't ask him to come to the hotel. It was the desk clerk, a total creep, who—"

Monsieur Sezer put up his hand, signaling me to stop this guilty-conscience rant.

"I am just attempting to assemble the facts," he said. "Adnan left his morning job to come to the hotel to bring you here because you were in some sort of trouble with the management. Or, at least, that is what he told me before he left. Adnan was very fond of you—and was looking forward to having you down the corridor from him. Were you fond of him?"

A pause. The question was asked in a perfectly level, unthreatening way—even though its subtext was glaringly obvious.

"I was very sick in the hotel—and he was very kind to me."

"By 'very kind' do you mean . . . ?"

"I mean, he showed me remarkable kindness when I could hardly stand up."

"What sort of 'remarkable kindness'?"

"I didn't fuck him, OK?" I said.

Monsieur Sezer let that angry outburst reverberate in the room for a moment or two. Then a small smile flashed across his thin lips before disappearing again. He continued as if he hadn't heard that comment.

"And when you left the hotel today with Adnan . . ."

I took him through the entire story, including Adnan telling me to walk ahead of him when we got caught between the two pairs of flics. He listened in silence, then asked, "You are married?"

"Separated."

"And the reason you are in Paris . . . ?"

"I am on sabbatical from the college where I teach. A sabbatical is kind of a leave of absence—"

"I know what it is," he said. "They mustn't pay much at the college where you teach, if you are interested in renting a *chambre*."

I could feel my cheeks flush. Was I such an obvious liar?

"My circumstances are a little tight at the moment."

"Evidently," he said.

"What I'm most worried about right now is Adnan," I said.

A wave of his hand.

"Adnan is finished. He will be on a plane back to Turkey in three days maximum. *C'est foutu*."

"Can't you do anything to help him?"

"No."

Another silence.

"So, do you want his *chambre*?" he asked. "It is nicer than the one I was going to show you."

"Is the rent high?"

"It's four hundred and thirty a month."

Thirty euros more than I had been quoted.

"I don't know," I said. "It's a little steep for me."

"You really are in a bad place," he said.

I gave him a guilty nod. He turned to the heavy who met me at the door and said something in Turkish. Mr. Tough Guy gave him an equivocal shrug, then murmured a comment that made Monsieur Sezer's lips part into the thinnest and briefest of smiles.

"I have just asked Mahmoud here if he thinks you are on the run from the law. He said that you seemed too nervous to be a criminal. But I know that this 'sabbatical' story is a fabrication—that you are talking rubbish—not that I really care."

Another fast exchange in Turkish. Then: "Mahmoud will take you to see the two *chambres*. I promise you that you will want Adnan's."

Mahmoud nudged me and said, "You leave bags here. We come back."

I let go of the suitcase with wheels, but decided to keep the bag with my computer with me. Mahmoud muttered something in Turkish to Monsieur Sezer. He said, "My associate wonders if you think all Turks are thieves?"

"I trust nobody," I said.

I followed Mr. Tough Guy down the stairs and across the courtyard to a door marked ESCALIER B. He punched in a code on a panel of buttons outside the door. There was the telltale click, he pushed the door open, then we headed up the stairs. They were narrow and wooden and spiral. The walls in the stairwell had been painted shit brown and were in an urgent need of a washing-down. But it was the smells that really got me: a noxious combination of bad cooking and blocked drains. The stairs were badly worn down. We kept heading upward, the climb steep. At the fourth floor, we stopped. There were two metal doors there. Mahmoud dug out a large bunch of keys and opened the door directly in front of us. We walked into a room that gave new meaning to the word *dismal*. It was tiny—with yellowing linoleum, a single bed. There was stained floral wallpaper, peeling and blistered. The length of the place was ten feet maximum. It was a cell, suitable for the suicidal.

Mr. Tough Guy was impassive during the minute or so I looked around. When I said, "Can I see Adnan's place, please?" he just nodded for me to follow him. We walked up a flight of stairs. There were another two metal doors on this landing and a small wooden one. Mr. Tough Guy opened the door directly in front of us. Size-wise, Adnan's *chambre* was no bigger than the dump downstairs. But he'd tried to make it habitable. There was the same grim linoleum, but covered by a worn Turkish carpet. The floral wallpaper had been painted over in a neutral beige—a crude job, as hints of the previous leafy design still poked through the cheap emulsion. The bed was also narrow, but had been covered with a colored blanket. There was a cheap generic boom box and a tiny television. There was a hotplate and a sink and a tiny fridge—all old. There was a baby-blue shower curtain. I pulled it aside to discover a raised platform with a drain (clogged with hairs) and a rubber hose with a plastic showerhead.

"Where's the toilet?" I asked.

"Hallway," he said.

There was a clothes rail in one corner, on which hung a black suit, three shirts, and three pairs of pants. The only decoration on the walls were three snapshots: a young woman in a headscarf, her face serious, drawn; an elderly man and woman in a formal pose, serious and drawn; and Adnan holding a child with curly black hair, around two years old, on his knee. Though Adnan also looked grave in this photograph, his face seemed around two decades younger than it did now . . . even though this snapshot must have been taken only four years ago. The last time he saw his son.

Staring at these photos provoked another sharp stab of guilt. It was such a sad, small room—and his only refuge from a city in which he was always living undercover and in fear. Mr. Tough Guy must have been reading my mind, as he said, "Adnan goes back to Turkey now—and he goes to prison for a long time."

"What did he do that made him flee the country?"

He shrugged and said nothing except, "You take the room?"

"Let me talk to your boss," I said.

Back in his office, Monsieur Sezer was still sitting at his bare desk, staring out the window. Mr. Tough Guy stayed by the door, and lit a cigarette.

"You take Adnan's room?" Monsieur Sezer asked me.

"For three hundred and seventy-five euros a month."

He shook his head.

"That's all I can afford."

He shook his head again.

"The other room is a dump," I said.

"That is why Adnan's room costs more."

"It's not much better."

"But it is still better."

"Three eighty."

"No."

"It's the best I can—"

"Four hundred," he said, cutting me off. "And if you pay three months in advance, I won't charge you four weeks' deposit."

Three months in that room? One part of me thought, *This is further proof that you've hit bottom.* The other part thought, *You deserve no better.* And then there was a more realistic voice that said, *It's cheap, it's habitable, you have no choice, take it.*

"OK—four hundred," I said.

"When can you give me the money?"

"I'll go to a bank now."

"OK, go to the bank."

I found one on the boulevard Strasbourg. Twelve hundred euros cost me fifteen hundred dollars. My net worth was now down to two thousand bucks.

I returned to Sezer Confection. My bag was no longer by the desk. Monsieur Sezer registered my silent concern.

"The suitcase is in Adnan's room," he said.

"Glad to hear it."

"You think we would be interested in your shabby clothes?"

"So you searched the bag?"

A shrug.

"You have the money?" he asked.

I handed it over. He counted it slowly.

"Can I have a receipt?"

"No."

"But how do I prove that I have paid the rent?"

"Do not worry."

"I do worry . . ."

"*Évidemment.* You can go to the room now. Here is the key," he said, pushing it toward me. "The door code is A542. You write that down. You need my associate to show you the way back to the room?"

"No thanks."

"You have problems, you know where to find me. And we know where to find you."

I left. I walked down the steps. I crossed the courtyard. I entered ES-CALIER B. I remounted the stairs. I came to the fourth landing. I opened the door facing me. The *chambre de bonne* had been stripped bare. Along with all of Adnan's personal effects, they had also taken the sheets, the blankets, the shower curtain, the rug, the cheap electronic goods. I felt my fists tighten. I wanted to run down the stairs and back into Monsieur Sezer's office and demand at least three hundred euros back to cover the cost of everything I would now have to buy to make the place habitable. But I knew he would just shrug and say, Tant pis. Tough shit.

Anyway, I knew that if I went back and made a scene, I'd be considered trouble. And right now, what I needed to do was vanish from view.

So I slammed the door behind me. Within five minutes I had unpacked. I sat down on the dirty mattress, the fever creeping back up on me again. I looked around. I thought, *Welcome to the end of the road.*

FIVE

LATE THAT NIGHT, Omar took a shit.

How did I know this intimate detail—and the identity of the gentleman moving his bowels? It didn't take much in the way of deductive reasoning. My bed faced the wall adjoining the crapper. Omar was my neighbor—something I knew already from Adnan, but which I rediscovered when he banged on my door just after midnight. I'd not met him before—but had already been briefed on his job as the chef at the Sélect, and how (according to Brasseur) he'd been caught in flagrante delicto with the hotel's handyman. I asked who was at the door before unlocking it.

"*Votre voisin,*" he said in very basic French.

I opened the door a few inches. A behemoth stood before me, his face seeping sweat, his breath a toxic cocktail of stale cigarettes and burped alcohol. Omar was big in every way—well over six feet tall and around three hundred pounds. He had a walrus mustache and thin strands of black hair dangling around an otherwise bald head. He was drunk and just a little scary.

"It's kind of late," I said.

"I want television," he said.

"I don't have a television."

"Adnan has television."

"Adnan is gone."

"I know, I know. Your fault."

"They took his television," I said.

"Who took?"

"Monsieur Sezer."

"He can't take. My television. Adnan borrow it."

"You'll have to talk with Monsieur Sezer."

"You let me in," he said.

I immediately wedged my foot against the door.

"The television isn't here."

"You lie to me."

He started to put his weight against the door. I got my knee up against it.

"I am not lying."

"You let me in."

He gave the door a push. I had never come up against a three-hundred-pound guy before. I pulled my knee out of the way just in time. He came spilling into the room. For a moment he seemed disorientated—in that way that a drunk suddenly can't remember where he is and why he has just slammed up against a hotplate. Then the penny dropped. He scanned the room for the television, but his disorientation quickly returned.

"This not same room," he said.

"It is."

"You change everything."

That wasn't exactly the truth—though I had made a few necessary design modifications since moving in that afternoon. The stained mattress, which sagged in five places, had been thrown out and replaced by a new one, bought in a shop on the Faubourg Saint-Denis. The shop owner was a Cameroonian. His place specialized in bargain-priced household stuff, so when he heard that I needed some basics for my *chambre,* he took charge of me. I came away with the mattress (cheap, but sturdy), a pillow, a set of light blue no-iron sheets, a duvet, a dark blue shower curtain, two lampshades, a neutral cream window blind (to replace the left-behind drape), some basic kitchen stuff, and (the best find of all) a small plain pine desk and a cane chair. The total price for all this was three hundred euros. It was a major dent in my remaining funds, but the guy even threw in a can of wood stain for the desk and got his assistant to load up everything in the shop's battered old white van and deliver it to my place on the rue de Paradis.

After everything arrived, I spent the rest of the afternoon putting my room together. The outside toilet was another matter. It was an old crapper—with a fractured black plastic seat—located in a tiny closet, with unpainted walls and a bare lightbulb strung overhead. The bowl was caked with fecal matter, the seat crisscrossed with dried urine stains. It was impossible to stay more than a minute inside this cell without wanting to retch. So I hit the street, finding a hardware shop further down the rue du Faubourg Poissonnière. Within five minutes I had bought a toilet seat, a toilet brush, and an industrial bleach *super fort* that the guy in the shop assured me would not just burn away all the residue stains, but would also remove two layers of epidermis if it came in contact with any exposed skin. So he insisted that I spend an extra two euros on a pair of rubber gloves as well.

Half an hour later, not only was a new seat installed, but the nuclear-powered bleach had also done its chemical magic. The bowl was virtually white again. Then I scoured down the toilet floor. After that was finished, I dashed out again to the rue du Faubourg Poissonnière and found an electronics shop. After a bit of haggling, the owner agreed to part with an old-model Sony boom box for fifty euros. I also picked up a baguette, some ham and cheese, and a liter of cheap red wine, and returned home. I hung the lampshades in my room and the toilet. Then, for the rest of the evening, I cleaned every inch of the *chambre de bonne,* while blaring the local jazz station on my newly acquired stereo. Halfway through my purge of every bit of grime from the room, I wondered, *Aren't you just being a little manic?* But I pushed aside such self-reflection and kept cleaning. By midnight the place was spotless, my laptop was set up on the desk, and I was making lists of things I still needed to buy. I felt my forehead. The fever was still there, but seemed low-lying. I took a shower—the hot water sputtering out in weak bursts. I dried off. I climbed into the narrow bed. I passed out.

Until Omar started taking a shit, then banged on my door and came spilling into the room.

"You change everything," he said, looking around.

"You know, it's kind of late."

"This nice now," he said.

"Thank you."

"You sell my television to buy all this?"

"Like I told you, Omar, Monsieur Sezer has the television."

"How you know my name?" he demanded, suddenly fixing me with a drunk/paranoid stare.

"Adnan told me—"

"You turn Adnan over to the police—"

"That's not what happened," I said, trying to stay calm.

"You want his room, you call the police, they catch him in the metro. And then you sell my television."

He shouted this last line, then looked bemused—as if he were a spectator at this event, suddenly surprised to hear himself yelling.

"Look," I said, trying to sound even-tempered, reasonable. "I was a hotel guest just until this morning. As you must have heard, I was sick for the past week. I didn't even know where Adnan lived until he told me about a *chambre de bonne* down the corridor from his own—"

"So that's when you decide to take it from him."

"My name's Harry, by the way," I said, hoping this change of conversational tack might throw him. He ignored my extended hand.

"Sezer has television?" he asked.

"That's what I said."

"I kill Sezer."

He burped. Loudly. He fished out a cigarette and lit it. I silently groaned. I hate cigarette smoke. But it didn't strike me as the right moment to ask him not to light up in my little room. He took a half-drag on his cigarette, the smoke leaking out of his nostrils.

"You American?" he asked.

"That's right."

"So fuck you."

He smiled as he said this—a crapulous smile, his eyes gauging my reaction. I remained impassive.

"Adnan a dead man. When they send him back to Turkey, he dies . . . in prison. Four years ago, he kills a man. A man who fucks his wife. Then he finds out the man does not fuck his wife. But the man still dead. Bad. Very bad. That's why he come to Paris."

Adnan—a killer on the run? It didn't seem possible. But, then again, nothing about this setup seemed possible . . . and yet, it was the reality into which I had slipped.

The cigarette fell from Omar's lips onto my just-cleaned floor. He ground it out with his shoe. Then, with another loud, aromatic burp, he abruptly left, reeling into his adjoining room. Immediately, my house-keeping instincts took over. I opened the window to air out the smoke. I picked up the cigarette butt and used kitchen paper to clean up the flattened ash on the linoleum. Then I went outside to use the toilet and found Omar's large unflushed turd greeting me in the bowl.

I pulled the chain—and felt myself tensing up into a serious rage. But I forced myself to pee and get back into my room before the rage trans-formed into something dangerous. When I was inside, I turned on the stereo and boomed jazz—in the angry hope that it might disturb Omar. But there were no bangs on the wall, no shouts of *"Turn that crap down."* There were just the edgy dissonances of Ornette Coleman, penetrating the Parisian night. Eventually, his grating riffs became too much for me, and I snapped off the radio and sat in the half-darkness of my room. I stared out at all the minor scenic adjustments I had made . . . and consid-ered the energy I'd expended to try to set up house in a place that could never be anything more than a grungy cell. That's when I started to cry. I had wept here and there over the past few weeks. But this was different. This was pure grief . . . for what I had lost, for what I had been reduced to. For a good fifteen minutes, I couldn't stop the deluge. I lay prostrate on the bed, clutching on to a pillow, as all the accumulated anger and anguish came flooding out. When I finally subsided, I felt drained and wrung out . . . but not purged. This kind of grief doesn't go away after a good cry . . . as much as I wished it would.

Still, the cessation of my sobs did force me to pull off my T-shirt and jockey shorts and stand under the sputtering showerhead for a few minutes, towel myself down, then drop a Zopiclone and finally surren-der to chemical sleep.

I didn't wake up until noon, my head fogged in, my mouth dry. When I went outside to use the toilet, I found the seat crisscrossed with urine. Omar, in true dog style, had marked his territory.

After brushing my teeth in the kitchen sink, I dressed, scooped up several invoices from yesterday, and went downstairs and rang the bell for Sezer Confection. Mr. Tough Guy answered the door, the usual scowl on his face.

"I want to speak with your boss," I said.

The door shut. Two minutes later it opened again. He motioned for me to follow him. *Comme d'habitude*, Sezer was sitting at the table, the cell phone on the desk, his gaze never leaving the window as I walked in.

"Tell me," he said.

"I replaced the seat and hung up a lampshade in the toilet on my floor."

"Congratulations."

"The seat, the brush, and the lampshade cost me nineteen euros."

"You expect reimbursement?"

"Yes," I said, putting the receipts on his desk. He looked at them, gathered them together, then crumpled them up into a ball and tossed it onto the floor.

"I don't think so," he said.

"The toilet seat was broken, there was a bare lightbulb—"

"No other tenants complained."

"Omar, that pig, would happily eat out of the toilet . . ."

"You do not like your neighbor?"

"I don't like the fact that he woke me in the middle of last night, demanding his television, which you took away."

"No, I didn't."

"All right, Joe Smoothie here took it away."

Sezer said something in Turkish to Mr. Tough Guy. He shrugged his shoulders in bemusement, then hissed something back.

"My colleague informs me that he didn't touch the television," Sezer said.

"He's lying," I suddenly said in English.

Sezer looked at me and smiled.

"Out of respect for your safety I won't translate that," he said back in perfect English. "And don't expect me to speak your language again, American."

"You're a crook," I said, sticking to my native tongue.

"Tant pis," he said, then continued on in French. "But now Omar is upset. Because I told him that you sold the television to buy the new toilet seat. And he is such an ignorant peasant that he believed such stupidity. My advice to you is: buy him a new television."

"No way," I said, returning to French.

"Then don't be surprised if he comes home drunk again tonight and tries to break down your door. He is a complete *sauvage*."

"I'll take my chances."

"Ah, a tough character. But not so tough that you couldn't stop crying last night."

I tried not to look embarrassed. I failed.

"I don't know what you're talking about," I said.

"Yes, you do," he said. "Omar heard you. He said you cried for almost a half hour. The only reason he didn't come looking for you this morning to demand his television money is because the idiot felt sorry for you. But, trust me, by tonight he will be in a rage again. Omar lives in a perpetual rage. Just like you."

With that last line, Sezer trained his gaze on me. It was like having a white-hot light shined in your eyes. I blinked and turned away.

"So why were you crying, American?" he asked.

I said nothing.

"Homesick?" he asked.

After a moment, I nodded. He took his gaze off me and returned it to the window. And said, "We are all homesick here."

SIX

L *A VIE PARISIENNE.*
Or, to be more specific about it: *ma vie parisienne.*
For my first weeks on the rue de Paradis, it generally went like this:

I would get up most mornings around eight. While making coffee I would turn on France Musique (or France *Bavarde*, as I referred to it, since the announcers seemed less interested in playing music than in endlessly discussing the music they were about to broadcast). Then I'd throw on some clothes and go downstairs to the *boulangerie* on the nearby rue des Petites Écuries and buy a baguette for sixty centimes before heading down to the market on the rue du Faubourg Saint-Denis. While there, I'd shop carefully. Six slices of *jambon*, six slices of Emmenthal, four tomatoes, a half-dozen eggs, 200 grams of haricots verts (I quickly learned how to calculate metrically), 400 grams of some sort of cheap white fish, 200 grams of the cheapest cut of steak that didn't look overtly rancid, three liters of vin rouge, a half-liter of milk, three liters of some generic bottled water, and I'd have enough food to live on for three days. And the cost of this shopping expedition would never be more than thirty euros . . . which meant that I could feed myself for around sixty euros a week.

On the days that I bought food, I'd be back in the apartment by twelve thirty. Then I would open my laptop and let it warm up while making another coffee and telling myself that it was just a matter of five hundred words. As in: two typed pages. As in: the daily quota I had set myself for writing my novel.

Two pages, six days a week, would equal twelve pages. As long as I kept up this output without fail, I'd have a book within twelve months. And no, I didn't want to consider the fact that I only had enough money to cover a pretty basic existence for the three months of rent I had paid. I just wanted to think about achieving the daily quota. Five hundred words . . . the length of many an email I used to bang out in less than twenty minutes . . .

Five hundred words. It was nothing, really.

Until you started trying to turn that five hundred words into fiction, day in, day out.

My novel . . . my first novel . . . the novel I told myself twenty years ago that I would write. It was going to be an Augie March for our times; a large, sprawling, picaresque bildungsroman about growing up awkward in New Jersey, and surviving the domestic warfare of my parents and the dismal conformism of sixties suburbia.

For months—during the worst of the nightmare into which I had been landed—I kept myself alive with the idea that, once I negotiated an escape route out of hell, I'd find a quiet place in which to get it all down on paper, and finally demonstrate to the world that I was the serious writer I always knew myself to be. *I'll show the bastards* is a statement uttered by someone who has suffered a setback . . . or, more typically, has hit bottom. But as a resident of the latter category, I also knew that, rather than being some EST-style rallying cry, it was a howl from the last-chance saloon.

Five hundred words. That was the quotidian task, and one that I knew I could fulfill . . . because I had nothing else to do with my time.

Nothing except go to the cinema. The majority of my free time outside my *chambre* was spent haunting all those darkened rooms around town that cater to film junkies like myself. The geography of Paris was, for me, defined by its cinemas. Every Monday I'd spend sixteen euros on a *carte orange hebdomadaire*—a weekly travel card, which gave me access to all metros and buses within the Paris city limits. The card let me whiz around town at will—all the travels outside my quartier largely pertaining to my cinema habit. Once the five hundred words were down on the computer, I'd be free to leave the room and begin the movie-going day. The Fifth was my preferred terrain, as there were more than fifteen cinemas in a square mile. Most of them specialized in old stuff. At the Action Écoles, there was always a director's festival in progress: Hitchcock this week, Kurosawa the next, alternating with a season of

Anthony Mann Westerns. Down the road at Le Reflet Médicis, I spent a very happy three days watching every Ealing Comedy ever made, finding myself in floods of tears at the end of *Whisky Galore* . . . more an indication of my fragile state than of the film's emotional headiness. A few streets away, at the Accattone, they were always showing one of Pasolini's stranger explorations of the out-there frontiers of human behavior. I could make it from the Accattone to Le Quartier Latin in about three minutes for a Buñuel season. I could stroll over into the Sixth to nose around the film noir rarities at the Action Christine. Or, best of all, I could jump the metro to Bercy and hide out at the Cinémathèque until midnight.

Every day, I'd spend at least six hours at the movies. But before heading out on this daily movie marathon, I'd check my email.

The Internet café was located on the rue des Petites Écuries. It was a small storefront operation. There were a dozen computers positioned on unvarnished wooden cubicles, fronted by grubby orange plastic chairs. Behind this was a small bar that served coffee and booze. It cost one euro fifty an hour to check email and surf the Net. There was always a bearded guy in his thirties behind the bar. He looked Turkish, but spoke good French—though our conversations were always limited to a few basic pleasantries and the exchange of money for an Internet password or a coffee. Whenever I showed up, he was always on his cell phone, deep in some rapid-fire conversation—a conversation that turned into a low whisper as I bought my password and settled down in front of a computer. I could always see him studying me as I logged on—and wondered if he could gauge my disappointment as I opened my AOL mailbox and found no news from my daughter.

I'd been writing Megan twice a week since arriving in Paris. In my emails I asked her to please try to understand that I never meant to hurt her; that she remained the most important person in my life. Even if she now hated me for what had happened, I would never cease to love her and hoped that communication could be somehow reestablished. At first, my emails all followed a similar line of argument. After three weeks, I switched tactics—writing to her about my life in Paris, about the room in which I was living, the way I passed my day, the movies I saw—and always ending with a simple statement:

I will write again next week. Always know that you are in my thoughts every hour of the day—and that I miss you terribly. Love . . . Dad

When no answer was forthcoming, I wondered if she was being blocked from writing to me by her mother—as I also knew that, by telling Megan details of my life in Paris, I was probably passing them on to my ex-wife as well. But I didn't care if she learned about my diminished circumstances. What further harm could she do to someone who'd lost everything?

But then, at the start of my sixth week in Paris, I opened my AOL account and saw—amid the usual detritus sent to me from loan sharks and penis-extension hucksters—an email marked: meganricks@aol.com.

I hit the READ button nervously, preparing myself for a "Never write to me again" letter . . . given that, the one time I called her after everything blew up, she told me that, as far as she was concerned, I was dead. But now I read:

Dear Dad

Thanks for all your emails. Paris sounds cool. School is still hard—and I'm still getting a lot of crap from people in my class about what you did. And I still find it hard to understand how you could have done that with one of your students. Mom told me I was to tell her if you made contact with me—but I've been reading all your emails at school. Keep writing me—and I'll make sure Mom doesn't know we're in contact.

Your daughter
Megan

PS I'm still angry at you . . . but I miss you too.

I put my face in my hands after reading this—and found myself sobbing. Your daughter. That said it all. After nearly three months of thinking that I had lost Megan forever, here was the response I had been hoping for. *I'm still angry at you . . . but I miss you too.*

Hitting the REPLY button, I wrote:

Dear Megan

*It was wonderful hearing from you. You're right to be angry
with me. I'm angry with me. I did something stupid—but
by the time I realized I had made a terrible mistake, things
started to spin out of my control and I found myself unable
to stop bad things from happening. However, you do need
to know that people took my mistake and used it for their
own aims. I am not trying to make excuses for what I did.
I accept responsibility—and will always feel terrible for
hurting you. I am simply so pleased that we are now back in
contact with each other—and promise to keep writing you
every day.*

*I'm sure that, very soon, things will get easier at
school . . . and that you will be able to put so much of this
behind you. I appreciate how difficult it is not telling your
mother that we're in touch. In time, I hope that your mom
and I will be able to be on friendly terms with each other—
because I'm sure that's what you want too. Always know
that I think the world of you and am here for you whenever
you need me. Meanwhile I promise to write you every day.*

Love
Dad

I read through the email several times before sending it, wanting to
double-check that it was devoid of self-pity, that it didn't come across
as a self-justification, and that—most of all—it communicated to my
daughter how much I loved and missed her.

As I stood up to leave, the man behind the desk looked up from his
newspaper and said, "Bad news?"

This threw me—and made me realize he'd been studying me while I
was reading Megan's email.

"Not at all."

"Then why are you crying?"

"Because it's good news."

"I hope there will be some more for you tomorrow."

There was no further word from Megan for the next few days—even though I emailed her every afternoon, keeping the tone anecdotal, filling her in on life in my quartier. After three days, I received the following:

Dear Dad

Thanks for the last couple of emails. I was on a school trip to Cleveland . . . b-o-r-i-n-g . . . and only got back yesterday. I went into your office at home last night, and found an old map of Paris, and looked up where you are. Rue de Paradis—I like the name. I had to be very careful about going into your office, as Mom told me it was off-limits, and Gardner hasn't taken it over yet . . .

Gardner. As in: Gardner Robson. The man who helped engineer my catastrophe and had also taken my wife away from me. The very sight of his name on the computer screen made me grip the sides of the plastic chair and try to control the rage that I still felt.

Gardner hasn't taken it over yet . . .

Why not take over my office when he's taken over everything else? I read on:

I find Gardner very hard to live with. You know he used to be in the Air Force and he keeps telling me that he likes things "ship shape." If I leave a jacket on the staircase when I come home from school, or if I've forgotten to make my bed, that's not "ship shape." He can be all right as long as you do things his way, and Mom seems totally in lurve *with him . . . but I'm still not totally sold on him as a stepdad. I keep thinking it would be cool to visit you in Paris, but I know that Mom would never let me . . . and, anyway, I'm still trying to sort out how I feel about what you've done. Mom said you wanted to end the marriage . . .*

She said what? Given that she had taken up with Robson well before my scandal hit the front pages—and given that I begged her repeatedly for a second chance—how dare she twist the truth and then feed our daughter this lie . . . a lie that Megan understandably interpreted as, in part, a rejection of herself.

I read on:

> . . . and that's why you cheated on Mom with that student and then fled overseas when everything got too hot. Is this true? I hope not.
>
> Your daughter
> Megan

I slammed my fist so hard on the desk that the guy behind the counter looked up in surprise.

"Sorry, sorry," I said.

"Bad news today?" he asked.

"Yeah. Very bad."

I turned back to the computer, hit the REPLY button, and wrote:

> Dearest Megan
>
> I have made many mistakes in my life, and have been guilty of all sorts of wrong calls. But I never—repeat: never—wanted to end the marriage to your mom. That was her decision—and one which I tried to talk her out of. If I had my way, I'd still be living at home with you and your mom. Please understand that your mom ended the marriage because she was angry with me for what I had done . . . but she wasn't exactly blameless for the way things turned out. But, once again, let me reemphasize the fact that being away from you—and being unable to see you on a daily basis—is so terribly hard. And my one great hope is that I'll be seeing you very soon indeed.
>
> Love
> Dad

*PS It's very important that you don't raise any of this with
your mother. If you start asking her questions about whether
she wanted to divorce me, she might get suspicious and
wonder if we're in touch. The last thing I want is to lose
contact with you.*

After hitting the SEND button, I turned to the guy behind the counter
and said, "Apologies again for punching the desk."

"You're not the first. A lot of bad news gets read here every day. But
maybe there'll be good news for you tomorrow."

The guy was right. When I returned the next afternoon, there was a
reply from Megan.

Hi Dad

*Thanks for writing what you did. I'm still confused by it
all. Like who's telling the truth here? But it's good to know
that you didn't want to leave us. That means a lot. And
don't worry about Mom. She'll never know we've been
writing each other. But do keep the emails coming. I really
like them.*

*Love
Megan*

The fact that she signed the email with "Love" . . . that was not simply
"good news." That was the best news I had received since this whole
nightmare started. And I immediately wrote back:

Dearest Megan

*It really doesn't matter who is telling the truth here. What
does matter is that we stay close. And as I said yesterday,
I'm sure that we will be seeing each other again very soon.*

*Love
Dad*

It was a Friday when I sent that email—so it didn't surprise me that I didn't hear from her over the weekend. As she had a computer in her room at home, I knew it might be dangerous if I emailed her on Saturday or Sunday . . . just on the off chance that her mother or Robson might walk into her room when she was opening her mailbox (yes, this was overly cautious on my part—but I wanted nothing to jeopardize our correspondence, let alone land Megan in trouble at home). So I resisted the temptation to write her—and just continued on with my usual routine. Wake up at eight, the morning shop, the morning write, lunch, out the door by 1:30 PM at the latest, movies, home by midnight, a Zopiclone sleeping tablet chased with herbal tea, sleep . . . and the inevitable 2:00 AM wake-up call when Omar came rolling in drunk (he did this nightly without fail) and proceeded to pee loudly. Though his loud bodily functions would always snap me into consciousness, the Zopiclone ensured that I'd pass out a few minutes after this wake-up call. As such, I gave daily thanks to that hotel doctor who had overprescribed me one hundred and twenty tabs of this knockout drug.

But every morning I awoke to the charming discovery that Omar had left the toilet a mess. After weeks of having to clean up after him, I finally hit the wall. It was the day after I had received my last email from Megan—and the large pool of urine on the floor sent me to his door. I banged on it loudly. He answered after a minute, dressed in stained boxer shorts and an AC Milan T-shirt that strained to make it over his vast gut.

"What?" he asked, looking half asleep.

"I need to talk to you," I said.

"You talk to me? Why?"

"It's about how you leave the toilet."

"How I leave toilet?" he said, getting a certain edge to his voice. I tried to adopt a reasonable tone.

"Look, we both have to share the toilet—"

"We share toilet?" he said, sounding outraged.

"We both use the same toilet at different times."

"You want we use it together?"

"I want you to lift up the seat when you pee, please. And I always want you to flush the toilet and use the scrubbing brush when—"

"Fuck you," he said and slammed the door.

So much for my attempts at diplomacy. The next morning I found Omar had pissed everywhere . . . not just on the toilet seat and its adjoining walls, but on my front door as well. For the first time since moving in, I ventured back to the offices of Sezer Confection. Mr. Tough Guy let me in with a scowl. Monsieur looked away as I spoke. In other words, business as usual.

"There is a problem?" Sezer asked.

I explained what had happened.

"Maybe it was a cat," he said.

"Yeah—and he happened to arrive on a magic carpet with a full bladder. It was Omar."

"You have proof?"

"Who else would piss on my door?"

"I am not Sherlock Holmes."

"You need to talk to Omar," I said.

"If I do not have proof that it was his piss on your door . . ."

"Can you at least get someone to clean it off?"

"No."

"Surely as the building manager—"

"We clean the corridors. We make certain that the *éboueurs* pick up the rubbish every day. But if you piss on a door—"

"I didn't piss on the door."

"That's your story. But as I said: since you have no proof, I must assume—"

"Forget it," I said and started walking out.

"One small thing," Sezer said. "I have had word about Adnan."

I stopped and turned around.

"And?" I asked.

"As predicted, he was arrested as soon as he stepped off the plane in Istanbul last month. They brought him to Ankara for formal sentencing—as he had been found guilty in his absence. He got fifteen years."

I heard myself say, "That's not my fault." I regretted the comment immediately. Sezer put his fingertips together and smiled.

"Who said it was your fault?" he asked.

I washed down the door myself that day. And the toilet walls. And scrubbed the bowl clean yet again. That night, after Omar had had his late-night piss, I found I couldn't get back to sleep. Though I did my best to rationalize what had happened—to tell myself that Adnan had been on the run for years and had simply been lucky to escape being controlled until that morning when he came to fetch me—I couldn't pardon myself. Another ruined life, courtesy of yours truly.

There is only one cure for a sleepless night: work. I wrote like a maniac: five pages before dawn. It was early days yet—page thirty-five of what would be a very big book—but already, my protagonist, Bill, was nine years old and listening to his parents tear each other apart while drinking highballs in their New Jersey kitchen.

I was writing this scene—and feeling very pleased with it—when I noticed the leak. It was coming from the little cabinet below the sink. A small pool of water had gathered on the scuffed linoleum. I stood up from the desk, went over, and opened the cabinet. The cause of the leak was immediately evident. A piece of tape, fastened to the waste pipe, had come loose. There were a few loose tiles at the bottom of the cabinet. An old roll of black duct tape was positioned on one of them. I picked it up. In doing so, the tile beneath it came away. There was a small piece of plastic protruding. I pulled at it—and discovered a little carrier bag hidden in a hole that had been dug crudely into the floor. Inside were tightly rolled wads of banknotes, around twenty of them—each individually secured with a rubber band. I undid the first wad. The currency contained within was a mishmash of five-, ten-, and twenty-euro notes. I counted out the twenty notes contained in the bundle. It came to a total of two hundred euros exactly. I unrolled a second wad. Another thirty notes totaling almost exactly one thousand euros. Another roll. The same setup. By the time all the wads were open and spread flat on the linoleum, I saw that I was staring at four thousand euros.

Outside, light was smudging the night sky. I carefully re-rolled all the banknotes and put them back into the bag. Then I pushed it back down into the hole and covered it with the loose tile before tearing off a piece of duct tape to plug up the leaking pipe. That done, I stood up and made coffee and sat at my desk, staring out at the dirty window and realizing that I had a major moral dilemma on my hands. Four thousand euros. At my current rate of expenditure, it would buy me almost another four months in Paris. And I knew how easy it would be to say nothing about my find. Especially with Adnan locked away in Ankara.

But if I said nothing—and I got my additional four months—then what?

Guilt, guilt, and more guilt. Though I'd probably get away with it, I wouldn't let myself get away with it.

I finished the coffee. I grabbed my notepad and scribbled the following note:

> *Dear M. Sezer*
>
> *I would like to make contact with Adnan's wife to inquire directly about his situation. Might you please have a postal or email address for her?*
>
> *Amicalement*

And I signed my name.

I went out and placed the note in the mailbox for SEZER CONFECTION. Then I returned to my room and rolled down the blind and set my alarm clock and pulled off my clothes and finally fell into bed. I slept straight through until 1:00 PM. When I awoke, I noticed a scrap of paper that had been slipped under my door. The writing was spindly, small:

> *Her name is Mme Z. Pafnuk. Her email is: z.pafnuk@ atta.tky. She knows who you are and what happened.*

The note was unsigned. Leave it to Monsieur Sezer to twist the knife at any given opportunity.

I went off to a movie. When I returned to my quartier after dusk, I stopped at the Internet café. There was one email awaiting me online:

> *Harry:*
>
> *The librarian at Megan's school noticed that she was spending excessive amounts of time on the computer. When*

challenged as to what she was doing, she said that she was merely surfing the Net—but appeared very nervous. The librarian informed the school principal, who called me, stating that he was worried she might be having an inappropriate correspondence with a stranger. When she got home, I insisted she tell me the truth. She refused, so I then demanded she open her AOL mailbox for me. That's when I discovered all your emails to her—which she had dutifully saved. Your attempts to wriggle your way back into her life—and play the caring father—are nothing short of disgusting. Just as your pathetic attempts to demonize me are contemptuous. You only have one person to blame for your disaster—and that is yourself.

I had a long talk with Megan last night and informed her, in graphic detail, why that student of yours killed herself. She knew most of it already—because her classmates in school haven't been able to stop hounding her about it. But what she didn't know was just how horribly you had behaved toward that unfortunate girl. And now Megan wants nothing to do with you. So don't write her again. I promise you she won't respond. And know this: if you make any other attempts to make personal contact with her, legal steps will be taken to make certain you are permanently barred from setting foot within a mile from where we live.

Don't bother to reply to this letter. It will be deleted upon receipt.

Susan

I found myself shaking so badly as I finished reading this email that I had to hold on to the cheap wooden table on which the computer rested . . . *what she didn't know was just how horribly you had behaved toward that unfortunate girl.* Another lie—and one perpetrated by Robson in his campaign to ruin me. *And now Megan wants nothing to do with you.* Pressing my fingertips against my eyes, I tried very hard to stop myself from crying. When I brought myself under control, I pulled away my hands—and saw that the young bearded guy behind the café counter was studying me. When our eyes met, he turned away—embarrassed that I caught him looking at me in such distress. I wiped my eyes and came over to the counter.

"A drink?" he asked me.

"An espresso, please," I said.

"More bad news?" he asked.

I nodded.

"Maybe things will change."

"Not this time."

He finished making the coffee and placed it in front of me. Then he reached for a bottle of Scotch and poured out a small shot for me.

"Here—drink," he said.

"Thank you."

I threw back the whisky. It stung going down, but I could also feel its immediate balming effect. After gulping the refill that he poured me, I asked him, "Do you speak Turkish?"

"Why do you want to know this?" he asked.

"Because I need to write somebody an email in Turkish."

"What sort of email?"

"A personal email."

"I am not a translator."

"It's only three lines long."

A pause. I could see he was sizing me up, wondering why I needed to write something in Turkish.

"What's your name?" he asked.

I told him and proffered my hand.

"I'm Kamal," he said. "And this translation—it is just three lines?"

"That's right."

He pushed a pad toward me.

"OK," he said. "Write."

I picked up the stub of a pencil that he placed on top of the pad and wrote, in French, the veiled communiqué I had been hatching in my head since waking up this afternoon:

Dear Mrs. Pafnuk

*I am the new resident of the room which Adnan used to
live in. I was just wondering if there was anything he left
behind that he needs to be sent on to him. Please send him
my best wishes, and tell him I remain grateful to him for his
kindnesses shown to me. I think of him often and would like
to offer my assistance if his family is in need of any help.*

Yours sincerely

And I signed it with my email address.

I pushed the pad toward the guy. He looked down at the message.

"It's eight lines, not three," he said, then flashed me the smallest of smiles.

"You have the email address?" he asked.

I handed over the scrap of paper slipped under my door.

"OK," he said. "I take care of it."

He disappeared over to a terminal. A few minutes went by. He finished typing and said, "It's sent."

"What do I owe you?"

"One euro for the coffee, the whisky is on the house."

"And for the translation?"

"Nothing."

"Are you sure?"

"I knew Adnan."

That threw me.

"Don't worry," he said quietly. "I know it wasn't your fault."

But so much is my fault.

I was tempted to send Megan one more email—but figured she would now report it immediately to her mother, and Susan would then make good on her threat to get a restraining order, and I wouldn't have the money to fight it, and any hope of ever seeing Megan again . . .

Abandon all hope of that. Your ex-wife has ensured that she'll despise you forever.

I spent the next few days in a depressed fog—going through the motions of my routine, but almost catatonic with grief as the realization hit home: my contact with Megan is over. Every day I checked my email, trying to convince myself that she mightn't have listened to her mother and decided to risk contact with me. But the mailbox remained empty . . . until, around a week later, when there was a reply waiting for me from Mrs. Pafnuk. It was written in Turkish and Kamal translated it for me.

> *Dear Mr. Ricks*
>
> *I was very pleased to hear from you. So too was Adnan, whom I visited yesterday. He said that the conditions are dreadful, but he can do nothing except try to stay sane and see the time out. He sends you his best wishes—and asks me to convey to you his feelings of friendship, and hopes that you will look around his room carefully and see if you can find a storage area where he kept something very special. He senses that you have already found it—and know its contents—but are being understandably cautious. Please contact me again by email to let me know if you have found what he hopes you have found. Once again, my husband thanks you greatly for your assistance and sends you fraternal greetings.*
>
> *Sincerely,*
> *Mrs. Z. Pafnuk*

When Kamal finished reading the email out to me in French, he pursed his lips and said, "She obviously hired the local scribe in her village to write this for her."

"How can you tell?" I asked.

"Adnan told me she could hardly read or write. He would come here twice a week to write her—and he would dictate to me what to write, because he also couldn't read or write that much either."

"So you're the local scribe here as well?"

"You run an Internet café in a quartier like this, you end up writing many emails for people. But by this time next year, this café will be no more. Our lease is up in nine months—and I know that the landlord will double the rent. Because the quartier is changing. The French are moving back."

"The wealthy French?" I asked.

"*Bien sûr*. The bobos. They're buying up all the loft spaces in the Tenth and pushing property prices way up. I promise you, eighteen months from now this café will be a chic restaurant or a boutique that sells expensive soaps. Within two years, the only Turks you will find around here will be the waiters."

"And what will you do?" I asked.

"Survive, *comme d'habitude*. Do you want to reply to this email?"

"Yes," I said and reached for a pad by the computer and scribbled:

> *Dear Mrs. Pafnuk*
>
> *I have found what Adnan left behind. How would you like me to transfer it to you?*
>
> *Yours sincerely*

I handed the note to Kamal.

"How much money did you find?" he asked.

"How do you know it was money?" I asked.

"Do not worry. I will not come to your room tonight and beat you over the head with a hammer and take it."

"That's nice to know."

"So it was a large sum?"

"A good sum, yes."

He looked at me with care.

"You are an honorable man," he said.

"No," I said. "I'm not."

Two days later, there was a return email from Mrs. Pafnuk. She asked me to send the "item" by Western Union telegraphic exchange to their office in Ankara. "I will be visiting Adnan on Sunday and can collect it then."

After translating her email, Kamal said, "There is a Western Union on the boulevard de la Villette, near the Belleville metro."

"I'll head there right after this."

"Come on, tell me. How much money did you find?"

I hesitated.

"OK, don't tell me. I was just curious."

"Four grand," I said.

He whistled through his teeth.

"You must be very rich to have decided to inform Adnan's wife about all that cash—"

"If I was rich," I said, cutting him off, "I would hardly be living in a *chambre de bonne* on the rue de Paradis."

"That is true," Kamal said. "Then you are evidently a fool."

I smiled.

"A complete fool," I said.

I returned to my room and crouched down by the sink and removed the tile and pulled out the plastic bag. Then I stuffed every pocket of my jeans and my leather jacket with the rolled-up money. I felt like a drug dealer. It was around 5:00 PM. Night was falling, and I moved quickly through the streets, terrified that irony might strike me at any moment, in the form of the first mugger I'd encounter in Paris—a thug who would have hit the jackpot had he decided I was a suitable target this evening. But my luck held all the way to the boulevard de la Villette. At the little Western Union branch, the clerk behind the grille—an African woman with an impassive face and eyes that showed her suspicion—said nothing as I dug out roll after roll of banknotes. When she had counted them all, she informed me that the cost of sending four thousand euros to Ankara would be one hundred and ten euros—and did I want this sum deducted from the four grand?

I did want it deducted, but . . .

"No," I said. "I'll pay for that on top of the four thousand."

After finishing the Western Union transfer, I returned to Kamal's café and had him email Mrs. Pafnuk with the reference number she required for collecting the money. When he finished sending this communiqué, he got up and went behind the bar and produced a bottle of Johnnie Walker Scotch, and said, "Come on, we drink to your honesty and your stupidity."

Over the next hour, we drained most of the bottle of Scotch. It had been a very long time since I had downed so much alcohol in one go—and it felt pretty damn good. Kamal told me he was born in Istanbul, but arrived in Paris three decades ago as a five-year-old. "My parents were legal immigrants, so there was no problem with the authorities. But being sent straight into a French school in Saint-Denis was a nightmare. I didn't speak a word of the language. Happily, nor did half the other children at the school. Still, I caught on to French quickly—because I had no choice. And now . . . now I have a French passport."

"But are you French?"

"I see myself as French. But the French still see me as an *immigré*. You are always an outsider here unless you are French. It's not like London, where everyone is an outsider—the English included—so the city is a big stew. Here the French keep to the French, the North Africans to the North Africans, the Turks to the Turks. Tant pis. It doesn't bother me. It is just how things are."

He didn't reveal too much information about himself. There was a wife, there were two young children, but he mentioned them in a passing sort of way, and when I asked their names, he steered off that subject immediately, turning it back to me, finding out what I did in the States, and discovering that my marriage had recently ended.

"Who was the other woman?" he asked.

"That's a long story."

"And where is she now?"

"That's another long story."

"You are being reticent."

"Like yourself."

A small smile from Kamal. Then: "So what do you do now?"

"I'm trying to be a writer."

"That pays?"

"No way."

"So how do you live?"

"With great care. Six weeks from now, my money will run out."

"And then?"

"I have no idea."

"Are you looking for work?"

"I have no *carte de séjour*—and it's very difficult for Americans to get work permits here."

"You could ask around at the various universities and colleges."

No, I couldn't—because that would mean them checking up on my background, and demanding references from the college where I taught for ten years. And once they found out what happened . . .

"That would be difficult," I said.

"I see," he said quietly, then reached for his cigarettes. "So you are in a bad place, yes?"

"That's one way of saying it."

"So . . . might you be interested in a job?"

"Like I said, I'm illegal . . ."

"That wouldn't matter."

"Why?"

"Because the job I'm proposing wouldn't be legal, that's why."

SEVEN

T HE "JOB" WAS an easy one.

"It is a night watchman's job," Kamal said. "You come into an office, you sit there, you read, you write, you can even bring a radio or television if you like. You show up at midnight, you leave at six. That's it."

"That can't just be 'it,'" I said. "There must be more to it than that . . ."

"There is nothing more to it except what I said."

"So what kind of a business is it?"

"That is of no concern of yours."

"So it's a completely illegal business then?"

"As I said, that is no concern of yours."

"Is it drugs?"

"No."

"Guns?"

"No."

"Sex slaves?"

"No."

"Weapons of mass destruction?"

"The business in question is nothing more than a business. But in order to keep you free of questions about this business, it is far simpler that you know nothing about it."

"And if the cops bust it?"

"That will not happen. Because they are unaware of its existence."

"Then why do you—*they*—need a night watchman?"

"Because *they* do. End of story. But listen, my friend, if you have any doubts, then you do not have to accept the offer—even though it does pay three hundred euros for a six-night week."

"Fifty euros a night?"

"Your math skills are impressive. It works out at a little more than eight euros an hour—and there's nothing to the work except sitting at a desk and picking up a telephone on the rare occasion that someone shows up, and then clearing them for entry. That's it."

Of course that wasn't it. I knew that there was something completely sinister about his proposition. I was certain that I might be landing myself in a situation which could be potentially dangerous, or could jeopardize my future freedom. But I found myself being won over by a bleak but consoling thought: *Nothing matters.* When everything that once mattered to you has been taken away, what's the point in worrying about a further descent into shit?

Nothing matters. What a liberating idea. Nothing matters, so everything can be risked. Especially when you need the money.

"I'd prefer sixty-five euros a night," I said.

A small smile from Kamal. He had me.

"I'm certain you would," he said.

"I really couldn't do it for less."

"You'll take the job no matter what," he said.

"Don't be too sure about that."

"You'll take it—because you're desperate."

There was no hostility in his voice, no smug triumphalism. Just a cool assertion of the truth. I said nothing. Kamal refilled my glass. The whisky went down without burning me—my throat having already been anesthetized by the half bottle of Johnnie Walker that had preceded it.

"Do not fret so much," Kamal said, lighting up a cigarette.

"I didn't realize I was fretting."

"You are always fretting. Go home, sleep off the whisky, then be back here at six tomorrow evening. I will have news by then."

I returned as requested the following night. When I arrived, Kamal was on the phone, but he motioned me toward a computer. There was one email awaiting me. It was from Adnan's wife. After hanging up, Kamal translated it for me.

Dear Mr. Ricks

The money arrived this morning. I was stunned by the sum involved—and once again send you manifold thanks for

*sending it to me. It has, literally, saved our lives. May God
bless you and those close to you.*

I have no one close to me.

"You have done a good thing," Kamal said. "And a good deed is
always rewarded."

"Not always."

"You are a very cynical man. But, in this instance, it is the truth. You
have gotten your sixty-five euros a night. The boss was reluctant at first."

"Who's the boss?"

"That information is of no interest to you."

"OK," I said. "When do I start?"

"Tonight, if that works for you."

"Fine."

"Be here at eleven thirty PM and I'll bring you over to the place."

"Is it far from here?"

"No."

"How will I get paid?"

"There will be an envelope waiting for you here every day after one
PM. You'll get off work at six AM, so you can pick up your wages when
you wake up. By the way, the boss said that you only need work six days,
but if you want the seventh day—"

"I want the seventh day."

"Done."

"Can I bring my laptop and books to work?"

"And a radio and anything else to keep you occupied. Trust me, there
won't be much to do."

When I left Kamal, I walked down to the Faubourg Saint-Martin
and dropped thirty euros on a small transistor radio. I returned to my
room. I opened a can of soup and cut up some cheese and a few slices
of bread, and ate a simple dinner while listening to a concert of Berg and
Beethoven on France Musique. Then I made myself a pot of coffee and
drank it all. It was going to be a long night.

When I arrived back at the Internet café, I was carrying a small day
pack containing my laptop, my radio, a pad and a pen, and a copy of
a Simenon novel, *Trois chambres à Manhattan*, which I was reading in

French. Kamal was closing up the place as I entered. He reached behind the bar and dug out two large bottles of Evian.

"You'll need these for the night ahead," he said.

He walked among the computers, making certain they were all shut down. Then he turned off all the lights. We stepped outside. He rolled down the large steel shutter, dug out his keys, sealed them with a formidable padlock, and motioned for me to follow him down the rue des Petites Écuries.

"We don't have far to walk," he said.

At the end of the street, we turned into the rue du Faubourg Poissonnière. We crossed it and passed a showroom for some line of men's fashions. I knew this small stretch of street well, as it was right around the corner from where I lived. I'd bought a sandwich once from the local greasy souvlaki bar (and lived to eat again). I'd even treated myself to the set seven-euro dinner at the little *traiteur asiatique* next door. But I hadn't noticed the tiny doorway just beyond this four-table joint—a doorway that was set back off the street by around ten feet. The alley leading to the door was so narrow that a man with a forty-inch waistline would have had trouble negotiating it. There was a steel door at the end of it. There was a small camera above the door and a spotlight trained on the area below the doorway. There was a keypad with a speakerphone beside it. Kamal punched in six numbers. As he did so, he told me, "The code is one six three two two six. Memorize it, but don't write it down."

"Why don't you want me to write it down?"

"Because I don't want you to write it down. 1–6–3–2–2–6. You got that?"

I repeated it out loud, then said it a second time, just to make certain that it had adhered to my brain.

"Good," he said as the door clicked open. We entered a hallway lit by a single naked lightbulb. The walls were unpainted concrete. Ditto the floor. There was a stairway in front of us. Around twelve feet away there was another steel door. Behind it I could hear the low hum of . . . was it something mechanical? . . . machinery, perhaps? . . . and the occasional raised voice? But the sound was muffled. As I strained to hear it, Kamal put his hand on my shoulder and said, "Up the stairs."

The staircase led to another steel door. This was opened by two keys.

Kamal had to put his weight on the door to finish the job and gain us access to a small room. Like the hallway, it had unpainted concrete walls. It was ten by ten, furnished with a beat-up metal desk, a straight-back chair, and nothing else. A closed-circuit television monitor sat on one corner of the desk. It was broadcasting a grainy image of the doorway outside. By the monitor was a speaker and a keypad. There were two doorways off this room. One was opened, showing the interior of an old-fashioned stand-up French toilet. You had to face front and squat as you took a dump. The toilet was also unpainted and seemed to lack a light. The other door was wooden and locked with a sliding bolt. There were no windows in the room—and the one radiator wasn't throwing off much in the way of heat.

"You expect me to work here?" I asked.

"That is up to you."

"This place is a shit hole—a cold shit hole with no light."

"The radiator can be turned up higher."

"I'll need some sort of other heat."

"OK, you can buy an electrical heater for the room—"

"And a desk lamp."

"Fine. Will you start tonight?"

I looked around, thinking, *He's looking for a deadbeat to do a deadbeat's job—and he's sized you up as the perfect candidate.*

"All right, I'll start tonight—but I want some cash to buy paint and stuff tomorrow."

"If you want to paint the place, you will have to do it during your work hours."

"Fine by me. But doesn't anyone use the room by day? Don't you have a sentry for the morning hours?"

"That is no concern of yours," he said, reaching into his pocket and pulling out a substantial wad of cash. He peeled off three fifty-euro notes and handed them to me.

"This should be sufficient for the paint, the brushes, the heater, the lamp. But provide receipts, please. The boss is finicky about expenses."

Kamal lit up a cigarette, then said, "So here is how the job works. You arrive here every night at midnight. You let yourself in. Once inside this room, you bolt the door behind you and padlock it shut. Then you sit down and do whatever you want to do for the next six hours, always keeping an eye on the monitor. If you see anyone in the alley who is loitering, you press the number 2–2 on the keypad. This will send a signal to someone that there is an unwanted stranger outside. They will take care of the problem. If a visitor approaches the doorway, he will ring a button which will sound up here on the desk speaker. You press 1–1 on the keypad and say one word, *"Oui?"* If he is legitimate, he will answer, "I am here to see Monsieur Monde." Once you have received this answer, you press the ENTER button on the keypad, which will activate the door. You then press 2–3 on the keypad, which will inform the people downstairs that a legitimate visitor is on his way to them."

"And what will 'the people downstairs' do?"

"They will 'greet' this legitimate visitor. Now if the person who rings the door doesn't say, 'I am here to see Monsieur Monde,' you press 2–4 on the keypad. This will send a signal that there is an unwanted presence in the alley. Once again, the people downstairs will take care of the problem."

"It sounds like the people downstairs worry about unwanted guests."

"I will say this once more. What goes on downstairs does not concern you—and it will never concern you. Believe me, my friend, it is better that way."

"And say the cops just happen to show up in the alley . . ."

"No problem," he said, walking over to the door next to the toilet and unbolting it. "This is never locked. If you see the cops on the screen, you exit here. There is a bolt—very strong—on the other side. It will buy you a few minutes' time, as the cops will have to break the door down. By the time they do that, you will be out of the building. The passage behind here leads down to a basement. There is another door there which leads to a passage into the adjoining building. When you come out of that building, you will be on the rue Martel. The cops will have no idea."

"This is insane," I heard myself say out loud.

"Then don't take the job."

"Promise me that whatever is going on downstairs isn't so morally reprehensible . . ." I said.

"No one is being involuntarily harmed," he said.

I paused, knowing I had to make a decision immediately.

"I will never have to directly meet anyone?" I asked.

"You come at midnight, you go at six. You sit in this room. You don't leave. You see the people who come here on the monitor. They don't see you. It is all very elegant."

"OK," I said, "we have a deal."

"Good," Kamal said.

After taking me again through all the various numbers I had to press, and handing me the assorted keys, he said, "There is just one thing. You must never come here before midnight, you must leave promptly at six. Unless you see the police on the monitor, you must never leave the room until six."

"Otherwise I'll turn into a pumpkin?"

"Something like that, yes. D'accord?"

"D'ac."

"So you are clear about everything?"

"Yes," I lied. "Everything is perfectly clear."

EIGHT

NOTHING HAPPENED THAT first night. I set up my laptop. I forced myself to work—my eyes straining under the single naked lightbulb. I pushed myself into writing five hundred words. I turned up the radiator and discovered that it gave off no more heat. I drank the two liters of Evian. I peed several times in the toilet and was grateful that I didn't need a bowel movement, as I couldn't have handled standing up to do it. I read some of the Simenon novel—a dark, sparely written tale about a French actor getting over the breakup of his marriage by wandering through the night world of 1950s New York. Around four in the morning, I started to fade—and fell asleep sitting up at the desk. I jolted awake, terrified that I had missed something on the monitor. But the screen showed nothing save the glare of a spotlight on a doorway—an image so grainy it almost seemed as if it was from another era, as if I was looking at the past tense just downstairs.

I read some more. I fought fatigue. I fought boredom. I drew up a list of what I'd buy this afternoon to fix the place up. I kept glancing at my watch, willing 6:00 AM to arrive. When it finally did, I unlocked the door. I turned off the light in the room. I closed the door behind me and locked it. I hit the light for the stairs. At the bottom of them, I stood for a moment, trying to hear any noises from the big steel door at the end of the ground-floor corridor. Nothing. I unlocked the front door. Outside it was still night—a touch of damp in the air, augmenting the chill that had crawled under my skin during those six hours in a badly heated concrete box. I locked the door, my head constantly turning sideways to scan the alleyway and see if anyone was waiting to hit me over the head with a club. But the alley was clear. I finished locking the door. I walked quickly into the street. No cops, no heavies in parkas and balaclava helmets, waiting to have a few words with me. The rue du

Faubourg Poissonnière was empty. I turned left and kept moving until I came to a little *boulangerie* that was on the rue Montholon. This took me a few minutes past my own street, but I didn't care. I was hungry. I bought two *pains au chocolat* and a baguette at the *boulangerie*. I ate one of the croissants on the way back to my *chambre*. Once inside I took a very hot shower, trying to get some warmth back into my bones. Then I changed into a T-shirt and pajama bottom, and made myself a bowl of hot chocolate. It tasted wonderful. So too did the second *pain au choco-lat*. I pulled the blinds closed. I set the alarm for 2:00 PM I was asleep within moments of crawling into bed.

I slept straight through. It was strange waking up in the early after-noon—and knowing that I wouldn't see bed again until after six the next morning. Still, I had things to do—so I was up and out the door in ten minutes. Much to my relief—because the paranoid part of me wondered if, indeed, I would get paid at all—an envelope was waiting for me at the Internet café. As agreed there were sixty-five euros inside it.

"Where's Kamal?" I asked the guy behind the counter—a quiet, sullen-looking man in his late twenties, with a big beard and the telltale bruise on his forehead of a devout Muslim who prostrated himself sev-eral times a day in the direction of Mecca.

"No idea," he said.

"Please tell him I picked this up, and say thanks for me."

I headed off to a paint shop on the rue du Faubourg Poissonnière, and bought two large cans of off-white emulsion and a set of rollers and a paint pan and a tin of white gloss and a brush and a large bottle of white spirit. I would have preferred bringing all the decorating gear to "my office," but I had to obey the "No Arrival Before Midnight" rule. So I made two trips back to my room with the gear, then headed out back to the Cameroonian dude who had sold me all the bedding and kitchen stuff. Yes, he did have an electric radiator in stock—all mine for a knockdown price of thirty euros.

Getting all the paint stuff to my office that evening proved tricky. Before setting out, I made a pit stop by the alley at around eleven and discovered that, at the start of this laneway, there was a large crevice in a wall: currently filled with rubbish and animal droppings. Never mind—it was perfect for my needs. I returned with two cans of paint and some old newspapers. As I bent down to place the newspapers on the ground inside the crevice—I wanted to avoid getting rat shit on my stuff—the fecal smell became overwhelming. I shoved the two cans of paint in, and returned to my room to bring the next load of stuff over. It took a further run after that to have everything in place.

Then I sat in a bar on the rue de Paradis, nursing a beer and waiting for midnight to arrive. The bar was a dingy joint—all Formica tables and a battered zinc counter, and a French-Turkish barmaid dressed in tight jeans, and a dude with serious tattoos also working the bar, and the jukebox playing crap French rock, and three morose guys hunched over a table, and some behemoth splayed on a barstool, drinking a milky substance that was obviously alcoholic (Pastis? Raki? Bailey's Irish Cream?) as he was smashed. He looked up when I approached the bar to order my beer—and that's when I saw it was Omar. It took him a moment or two for his eyes to register it was me. Then his rant started. First in English: "Fucking American, fucking American, fucking American." Then in French: *"Il n'apprécie pas comment je chie."* ("He doesn't like the way I take a shit.") Then he pulled out a French passport and started waving it at me, yelling, "Can't get me deported, asshole." After that he started muttering to himself in Turkish, at which point I didn't know what the hell he was saying. Just as I was about to finish my beer and bolt from the place before Omar got more explosive, he put his head down on the bar—in mid-sentence—and passed out.

Without my asking for it, the barmaid brought over another beer.

"If he hates you, you must be all right. *C'est un gros lard.*"

I thanked her for the beer. I checked my watch—11:53. I downed the *pression* in three gulps. I headed off.

At midnight precisely, I walked up the alleyway and unlocked the door. Then, in less than a minute, I made three fast trips to retrieve my hidden gear and bring it into the hallway. I bolted the door behind me. There was the same mechanical hum I'd heard yesterday emanating from the door at the end of the corridor. I ignored it and headed upstairs. A minute later, all the gear was in my office and the door locked. I was "in" for the night. I plugged in the electric radiator. I turned on my radio to Paris Jazz. I checked the monitor. All clear in the alley. I opened the first can of paint. I went to work.

That night, nothing happened again—except that I managed to give the office two coats of paint. I did my "job" as well—checking the monitor every few minutes to see if there was anyone lurking in the hallway. There wasn't. Before I knew it, my watch was reading 5:45 AM—and though it was clear that the second coat wouldn't sufficiently cover the chalky gray concrete walls, at least I knew that another night had passed.

I packed away all the gear. I washed the brushes in the sink. I left at 6:00 AM exactly. I took several deep gulps of Paris air as I walked down the still-dark street toward the *boulangerie*. My usual two *pains*. One eaten on the way home, the second with hot chocolate after a shower. Then— with the aid of Zopiclone—seven hours of void until the alarm woke me at two and a new day started.

That night, I finished painting the walls. I sanded down the woodwork. I left at six. The next night, I finished glossing all the woodwork. Again, there was no activity whatsoever on the monitor. At six that morning, I moved all the empty cans and paint gear out of the office and dumped the lot in the rubbish bins at the end of the alley. When I awoke that afternoon, I went straight over to the café to collect my wages. For the third day running, Mr. Beard with the Prayer Bruise was behind the counter.

"Still no Kamal?" I asked.

"He goes away."

"He didn't say anything to me about that."

"Family problems."

"Is there a number I could call him on?" I asked.

"Why you want to call him?"

"I liked him. We got on well. And if he's got some personal problems . . ."

"There is no number for him."

The tone of voice was definitive. It also didn't encourage further questioning. So I picked up my pay envelope and said nothing, except, "I want to buy a few more things for the office. Might you be able to get a message from me to the boss?"

"You tell me what you need."

"A small refrigerator and an electric kettle. It's very hard to work in that room all night without coffee or hot water. I'd also like a rug. The concrete floor still gives off a bit of damp—"

"I tell him," he said, cutting me off. Then he picked up a rag and started swabbing down the bar. Our conversation was over.

When I arrived at work that night, a fridge was awaiting me in a corner of the room. Though somewhat battered—with hints of rust on its hinges—it was still working. So too was the electric kettle positioned on top of it. It looked new. When I filled it with water, it boiled its contents in less than a minute. The only problem was, I didn't have any coffee or tea on hand. But, at least, I now knew that the man in charge was amenable to certain requests—even though there was still no rug.

But there was a change in my usual routine: a visitor in the alleyway. He arrived at 1:48 AM precisely. The phone rang on my desk, jolting me. I looked away from my Simenon novel and turned immediately to the monitor and saw a man of indeterminate age (the grainy image made it hard to discern his features) standing outside. I was instantly nervous. I picked up the phone and said, *"Oui?"*

His voice was raspy, and French was not his first language. But he still said, *"Je voudrais voir Monsieur Monde."*

I hit the 1–1 entrance code. Downstairs I heard the telltale click of the door opening, then the door being closed with a decisive thud. I pressed 2–3 to alert my "neighbors" that they had a legitimate visitor. There were footsteps on the downstairs corridor. There was a knock on another door. The door opened and closed. Then there was silence.

I didn't see or hear him exit, even though I kept scanning the monitor. There were no other visitors. There were no sounds from down below. My shift ended. I went home.

A few days later, the carpet finally arrived at work—and I began to bring my laptop in every night, forcing myself back into the novel. As there was no other work to do but this work—my quota of words per night—I kept at it. Days would pass when no one would ring the bell, demanding admittance. Then there would be a night when four separate callers came to the door, all men of indeterminate age, all asking to see Monsieur Monde. I'd hit the button, the door would open and close, there would be footsteps, another door opening and closing, end of story.

A month passed. February gave way to March. There was an ever-early lightening of the evening sky; the days still cold, but brighter. Had

I been in a normal state of mind, the thought would have struck me: *You have been working for more than five weeks now without a day off.* But I was still operating on some sort of weird autopilot: work, sleep, pick up cash, movies, work. If I took a day off, I might fall out of routine . . . and if I fell out of routine, I might start to reflect about things. And if I started to reflect about things . . .

So I stuck to the routine. Day in, day out, nothing changed.

Until something unsettling happened. I was nursing a post-cinemathèque beer in the little bar on the rue de Paradis. I picked up a copy of *Le Parisien* that had been left on a table and started flicking through its contents. There, on the bottom right-hand corner of page 5, under the headline, BODY OF MISSING MAN FOUND IN SAINT-OUEN, was a photograph of someone named Kamal Fatel. Though the photo was grainy, there was no doubt that it was the same Kamal who ran the Internet café and found me my current job. The story was a short one:

> The body of Kamal Fatel, 35, a resident of rue Carnot in Saint-Ouen, was found last night in an unused Dumpster near the Périphérique. According to the police at the scene, the body, though badly decomposed, had been identified through dental records of the deceased. The Saint-Ouen medical examiner issued a statement saying that, due to the state of the cadaver, the exact time and cause of death had yet to be ascertained. According to Inspector Philippe Faure of the commissariat de police in Saint-Ouen, Fatel's wife, Kala, had thought her husband was traveling in Turkey to visit relatives there. Fatel, born in Turkey in 1972, had been a resident in France since 1977 and had run an Internet café on the rue des Petites Écuries . . .

I downed the dregs of the beer in one go. I grabbed the paper. I walked with considerable speed toward the rue des Petites Écuries. Mr. Beard was behind the counter of the café. I dropped the paper in front of him and asked, "Did you see this?"

His face registered nothing.

"Yes, I saw it," he said.

"Aren't you shocked?"

"This morning, when I first saw the story, yes, I was a little shocked."

"A little shocked? The guy is dead."

"Like his wife, I had thought he had gone back to Turkey. But . . ."

"Who was behind it?"

"Why should I know such a thing? I worked with Kamal. He was not my friend."

"Was he in some sort of trouble with somebody?"

"Once again, you ask questions which I cannot answer. His life was not known to me."

I could tell he was lying—because his eyes kept darting away from mine whenever I tried to eyeball him. Or if he wasn't lying, he was working very hard at not appearing nervous—and failing badly.

"Will there be a funeral?"

"In Turkey."

"How do you know that?" I challenged.

He tensed, realizing he'd just let himself be caught out.

"Just a guess," he said, then stood up and said, "I am closing now."

"Do I have time to check my email?"

"No."

"Just give me five minutes, no more."

"Be fast."

I sat down at one of the computer terminals, clicked on Internet Explorer, and then typed in AOL. Within a minute, my mailbox covered a corner of the screen: with one actual email . . . from, of all people, my former colleague Doug Stanley. It read:

Harry:

Sorry to have fallen off the face of the planet during the past few weeks. I'm going to cut to the chase straightaway— because I've never tried to bullshit you about things . . . and I certainly won't start now. Now that the dust has started to settle here, Susan and Robson have gone public as a couple. The official version is that, in the wake of your disgrace, Susan was "emotionally shattered." Robson befriended her— and then they "became close" . . . nice euphemism, eh? As bullshit goes, this is truly choice. Everyone knew they were an

*item long before everything blew up in your face. And yeah, I
do realize now—especially after all that's gone down—that
I should have told you long ago what was happening between
them. I still feel damn guilty about that—thinking that, if
you had been aware of their involvement, things might have
turned out differently for you.*

*Anyway, you also need to know that Robson has been
spreading word around the college that you have hit the skids
in Paris. Worse, he's also let it be known that he gleaned this
information from Megan. In his version of things—and,
believe me, I know that it is simply his version (and, as
such, far from the truth)—you've been sending her this
series of self-pitying emails, playing up your impoverished
circumstances and trying to point the finger at Susan.
Again, let me reemphasize the fact that I know he's twisting
whatever you sent to Megan—just as the* sad, what a tragic
story *tone he adopts when relating this information makes
me want to punch out his lights. But, as you well know, the
man is the all-powerful Dean of the Faculty—which, in our
little world, gives him power over all of us . . . especially if
we don't have tenure.*

*I thought long and hard about whether I should burden
you with this ongoing horseshit—but eventually decided
that you did need to know. My advice to you is: consider
that chapter of your life closed, and do know that if things
in Paris are as bad as Robson described, they will definitely
get better . . . because you will make them better. And there
is one small bit of good news from this Ohio backwater:
word has it that Robson has decided not to proceed with the
college's lawsuit against you. The son of a bitch was finally
convinced that continuing to crucify you was pointless.*

*I'm certain the separation from Megan is an ongoing
agony. Trust me: she will come around. It might take some
time—but it will happen. She will want to see her father
again.*

Finally, let me know if you are totally strapped, as I'm

*happy to wire over a thousand bucks pronto. I wish it could
be more, but you know what they pay third-tier academics in
the Ohio sticks. I certainly don't want to see you on the street.*
    Bon courage.

*Best
Doug*

*PS Did you stay at the hotel I recommended in the
Sixteenth? If so, I hope you fared better than some friends I
sent there last month. It seems they had a run-in with some
creep at the front desk.*

Trust me: she will come around. I doubt that, Doug. Without question,
Susan and her new man had poisoned Megan against me—and there
would be no more emails from my daughter. That knowledge—and the
pervasive sense of loss that accompanied it—made Doug's other news
(*Robson has been spreading word around the college that you have hit the skids in
Paris*) seem unimportant. Let Robson tell everyone that I had fallen on
hard times. It no longer mattered what people thought of me. Because I
no longer mattered—to anyone else, let alone myself.

And hitting the REPLY button next to Doug's email, I wrote:

*It was very good to hear from you. Regarding Robson's
continued demolition job on me . . . my only response is:
you're right. That chapter of my life is finished, so I can't
really worry about what is being said about me around
a college to which I will never return . . . though I am
relieved that Robson has called off his legal thugs. But you
should know that I had managed to reestablish contact with
Megan—and she had seemed genuinely pleased to have a
running correspondence with her father—until Susan found
out about it and . . .*
    Well, you can guess what happened next.
    *As to my situation in Paris . . . no, I am not completely
down and out. But it isn't exactly a romantic setup either. I*

live in a small room in a grubby building in the Tenth. I am
working illegally—a non-event night watchman's job . . .
but one which gives me the opportunity to write until dawn.
I have no friends here . . . but I am making use of the city
and I am managing to keep my head above water. I was
immensely touched by your offer of a cash injection—as
always, you are a true mensch—but my straits aren't that
dire. I am managing to stay afloat.

And yes, I did spend several nights at that hotel in the
Sixteenth. And yes, your friends are right: the guy at the
front desk was a real little monster.

Keep in touch.
Best

As soon as I sent this email, I switched over to the *New York Times* website. As I scanned that day's paper, an Instant Message prompt popped
up on the screen. It was a return email from Doug:

Hey Harry

Glad to hear it's not that desperate for you over there . . . and
I'm really pleased you're writing. Got to dash to a class, but
here's a Paris tip: if you're in the mood to meet people—or
are simply bored on a Sunday night—then do consider
checking out one of the salons that are held around town. Jim
Haynes—one of life's good guys—holds a great bash up at
his atelier in the Fourteenth. But if you want a more bizarre
experience, then drop in to Lorraine L'Herbert's soiree. She's a
Louisiana girl—starting to look down that long barrel of the
shotgun marked sixty. Ever since she moved over to Paris in
the early seventies, she's been running a salon every Sunday
night in her big fuck-off apartment near the Panthéon. She
doesn't "invite" people. She expects people to invite themselves.
And all you have to do is ring her on the number below and
tell her you're coming this week. Naturally, if she asks how you

*found out about her salon, use my name. But she won't ask—
because that's not how it works.*
    Keep in touch, eh?

*Best
Doug*

On the other side of the café, Mr. Beard said, "I close now. You go."

I scribbled the phone number of Lorraine L'Herbert on a scrap of paper, then shoved it into a jacket pocket, thinking that—as lonely as I often felt—the last thing I wanted to do was rub shoulders with a bunch of expatriate types in some big-deal apartment in the Sixth, with everyone (except yours truly) basking in their own fabulousness. Still, the guilty man in me thought that I owed Doug the courtesy of taking the number down.

Mr. Beard coughed again.

"OK, I'm out of here," I said.

As I left, he said, "Kamal was stupid man."

"In what way?" I asked.

"He got himself dead."

That phrase lodged itself in my brain and wouldn't let go. For the next few days, I searched every edition of *Le Parisien* and *Le Figaro*— which also had good local Paris news—to see if there were any further developments in the case. Nothing. I mentioned Kamal's death once more to Mr. Beard—asking him if he had heard anything more. His response: "They now think it is suicide."

"Where did you hear that?"

"Around."

"Around where?"

"Around."

"So how did he take his life?"

"He cut his throat."

"You expect me to believe that?"

"It is what I heard."

"He cut his own throat while walking along a street, then tossed himself in a Dumpster?"

"I report only what I have been told."

"Told by whom?"

"It is not important."

Then he disappeared into a back room.

Why didn't I walk away then and there? Why didn't I execute an about-face and vanish? I could have gone home and cleared out my *chambre* in a matter of minutes, and pitched up somewhere else in Paris. Surely there were grubbier streets in grubbier quartiers, where it was possible to find another shitty room in which I could eke out a living until the money ran out.

And then? And then?

That was the question that kept plaguing me as I sat at the little bar on the rue de Paradis, nursing a *pression* and wishing that the barmaid was available. I found myself studying the curve of her hips, the space between her breasts that was revealed by her V-neck T-shirt. Tonight I wanted sex for the first time since Susan had thrown me out all those months ago. It's not that I hadn't had a sexual thought since then. It's just that I had been so freighted with the weight of all my assorted disasters that the idea of any sort of intimacy with someone else seemed like a voyage into a place that I now associated with danger. But never underestimate the libido—especially when it has been oiled with a couple of beers. As I found myself looking over the barmaid, she caught my appraising stare and smiled, then flicked her head toward a beefy guy with tattoos who had his back to us as he pulled a *croque* monsieur out of a small grill. The nod said it all: I'm taken. But the smile seemed to hint an "Alas" before that statement. Or, at least, that's what I wanted to believe. Just as I wanted to believe that Kamal "got himself killed" because he owed somebody money, or he was in on a drug deal that had gone wrong, or he'd been fingering the till at the café, or he'd looked the wrong way at some woman. Or . . .

A half-dozen other scenarios filled my head . . . along with another pervasive thought. Remember what Kamal told you when he first offered you the job: *That is of no concern of yours.* Good advice. Now finish the beer and get moving. It's nearly midnight. Time to go to work.

Later that night, I opened my notebook and a piece of paper fell out of one of its back pages. It was the scrap on which I had written Lorraine L'Herbert's phone number. I stared at it. I thought, *What can I lose?* It's just a party, after all.

"It's not a party," said the uppity little man who answered L'Herbert's phone the next afternoon. He was American with a slightly simpering voice and a decidedly pompous manner. "It's a salon."

Thanks for the semantical niceties, pal.

"Are you having one this week?"

"Comme d'habitude."

"Well, can I book a place?"

"If we can fit you in. The list is very, very tight, I'm afraid. Your name, please?"

I told him.

"Visiting from . . . ?"

"I live here now, but I'm from Ohio."

"People actually live in Ohio?"

"The last time I looked."

"What's your line of endeavor?"

"I'm a novelist."

"Published by . . . ?"

"That's pending."

He issued a huge sigh, as if to say, Not another would-be writer.

"Well, you know that there is a contribution of twenty euros. Please arrive with it in an envelope, on which your name is clearly printed. Take down the door code now and don't lose it, because we don't answer the phone after five PM on the day of the salon. So if you misplace it, you will not gain entry. And the invitation is for yourself only. If you show up with anyone else, both of you will be turned away."

"I'll be alone."

"No smoking, by the way. Madame L'Herbert hates tobacco. We like all our guests to arrive between seven and seven thirty PM. And dress is smart. Remember: a salon is theater. Any questions?"

Yeah. How do you spell *up your ass?*

"The address, please?" I asked.

He gave it to me. I wrote it down.

"Do come prepared to dazzle," he said. "Those who shine get asked back. Those who don't . . ."

"I'm a total dazzler," I said.

He laughed a snide laugh. And said, "We'll see about that."

NINE

A BIG FUCK-OFF APARTMENT near the Panthéon.
Those words came back to me that Sunday evening as I
walked up the boulevard Saint-Michel in the direction of the
Luxembourg Gardens. I had dressed carefully for the occasion: a black
shirt and black pants and a black leather jacket I had bought at that secondhand shop on the Faubourg Saint-Martin the previous day. It was
a cold night, and the jacket didn't put up much resistance against the
cutting wind. I was around fifteen minutes early, so I stopped in a nearby
café and ordered a whisky. Not a single malt or some other premium
brand. Just a standard Scotch. When the waiter deposited the little bill
with the drink and I turned it over and saw that it cost eleven euros, I
tried to stop myself from gasping. Eleven euros for a shot of whisky?
Welcome to the Sixth.

I would have spent a good hour nursing the whisky and reading the
Simenon novel *La neige était sale,* which I had just picked up. But mindful
of the seven thirty cutoff point, I finished the Scotch, placed the necessary money on the table, tried not to think too hard about how eleven
euros could buy me a day's food, and headed off to Lorraine L'Herbert's
salon.

The address was 19 rue Soufflot. *Très haussmannien.* You walk around
Paris, you see dozens of examples of Baron Haussmann's architectural
left-behinds. This one was no different from the others: a large, formidable building, around six stories tall, with the requisite small baroque
flourishes. Only given its location—just down the street from the Panthéon—and its elegant lobby, it was clear that this *immeuble haussmannien* was also a testament to imposing grand bourgeois values.

Which meant that, even before I had entered Lorraine L'Herbert's
building, I felt shabby and humbled by it.

I punched in the code. The door opened with a click. Inside was a speakerphone. I picked it up and pushed the button marked with her name. It was answered by the American who had vetted me on the phone. Voices could be heard in the background.

"Name, please . . . *Votre nom, s'il vous plaît,*" he said.

I gave it to him.

"One second, please . . . *un instant . . .*" Then: "Fourth floor left . . . *quatrième étage gauche.*"

The elevator was a small gilded cage. I took it to the top floor. Before it reached four, I could hear the sounds of loud conversation. When the elevator opened, I turned left and rang the bell. The door swung back. A short man dressed in black slacks and a black turtleneck was standing sentry. He had close-cropped hair and carried a stylish stainless-steel clipboard and an expensive pen.

"Monsieur Ricks?"

I nodded.

"Henry Montgomery. Madame L'Herbert's assistant. Your envelope, please."

I reached into my pocket and pulled it out and handed it over. He checked that my name was—as instructed—printed on its front. Having verified that, he said, "Coats in the first room down the corridor to your left, food and drink *dans la cuisine*. But after you've deposited your coat, you must come back here so I can take care of the introduction to Madame. D'accord?"

I nodded again—and followed Montgomery's pointed finger down the corridor. It was a very long corridor, with high ceilings. The walls were white. There was a big abstract canvas—in five sections—that covered much of the wall space. Each panel was a varying shade of green, the outer ones lightish in timbre, the inner ones amalgamating near-blackish hue. From my fifteen-second assessment, it looked like imitation Klein or Rothko, and was showing its thirty years badly.

But I decided that now was not the moment to proclaim such thoughts at the top of my lungs. Tourette's hadn't seized me yet.

Instead, I followed the corridor to the first door. It was already open. It was a small room with a double bed and one of those plastic blow-up chairs that were popular back at the end of the sixties, but now looked like something out of the Paleozoic era. Over the bed (in what I pre-sumed was the guest room) was a big garish nude of a blond, brassy woman with Medusa-like hair and a multicolored (maybe psychedelic?) menagerie of wild animals and exotic flora sprouting out of her ample bush of pubic hair.

I couldn't imagine having a decent night's sleep beneath such a painting. Still, its cheesy Summer of Love garishness did hold my atten-tion. I must have lingered a little too long for Montgomery's liking, as I heard his voice behind me.

"Monsieur Ricks . . . Madame awaits you."

"Sorry, I was just . . ."

I motioned toward the canvas.

"You approve?" he asked.

"Oh yes," I lied. "Especially as it's so representative of a certain epoch."

"You know the artist?"

"Peter Max?"

"Oh, please . . . he was so commercial."

And this guy isn't?

"So who's the artist?"

"Pieter de Klop, *bien sûr.*"

"Yeah, *bien sûr.*"

"And you know that Madame was his muse."

"That's Lorraine L'Herbert?" I asked, hearing the shocked tone in my voice.

"Yes, that is indeed Madame," he said.

He motioned for me to follow him. We walked back down the cor-ridor, then turned left into a large reception room. Like everywhere else I'd seen so far, it had white walls, a high ceiling, and bad pop art. This room, however, was also large. Around thirty by twenty. Though it was currently packed with people—most of whom seemed to be wearing black (at least, I wasn't going to stand out from the crowd)—I could see that there were white leather sectional sofas dotted around the place, and a few more blow-up plastic chairs, and two more nude studies of Madame by the same artist. But I was steered away from the paintings by Montgomery. His hand firmly on my shoulder, he spun me around toward a voluminous woman—ample in all physical departments. She was nearly six feet tall, and must have weighed well over two hundred and fifty pounds. Her fleshy face was Kabuki-like, courtesy of a pancake-based makeup that tinted her near white, offset by big red-rouged lips. There were gold zodiac symbols dangling from her neck, and every finger had a ring, all of which seemed New Age in design. Her hair—now silver—was braided, and stretched down the length of her back. She was dressed in a caftan and was holding a glass of champagne. With his hand still on my shoulder, Montgomery leaned over and whispered something into Madame's ear. She immediately burst into life.

"Well, hey there, Harry."

Her accent was thickly Southern.

"Madame L'Herbert . . ."

"Now, y'all got to call me Lorraine. You're some kind of writer . . . ?"

"A novelist."

"Have I read anything of yours?"

"Definitely not."

"Well, life's long, hon."

She quickly scanned the room, and reached out for a guy in his early forties. Black cord jacket, black jeans, black T-shirt, small beard, intense face.

"Hey, Chet—got someone you should talk to," Madame said loudly. Chet came over, eyeing me carefully.

"Harry, meet Chet. A fellow Yankee. He teaches at the Sorbonne. Harry's some kind of a writer."

With that, she left us alone. An awkward moment followed, as it was clear that Chet wasn't going to make the conversational opener.

"What subject do you teach?"

"Linguistical analysis."

He waited for me to react to this.

"In French?" I asked.

"In French," he said.

"Impressive," I said.

"I suppose so. And you write what?"

"I'm trying to write a novel . . ."

"I see," he said, starting to look over my shoulder.

"I'm hoping to have a first draft done in—"

"That's fascinating," he said. "Nice talking to you."

And he was gone.

I stood there, feeling truly stupid. *Harry's some kind of a writer.* Quite. I looked around. Everyone was engaged in conversation—looking animated and at ease and successful and interesting and everything else that I wasn't. I decided that alcohol was required. I went into the kitchen. There was a long table on which sat a dozen boxes of "cask" wine in the usual two colors. There were three large pans of half-burned lasagna and around a dozen baguettes in various states of disrepair. The cheap wine and the semi-scorched food hinted that—whatever about the big fuck-off apartment near the Panthéon and the twenty-euro entrance fee—Madame did the "salon" on the cheap. The outlay for the food and drink couldn't have been more than four hundred. Toss in an extra hundred for staff (there were two young women manning the "bar" and making certain all the paper plates and plastic forks got thrown away), and the weekly outlay was five hundred tops. But there were over a hundred people here tonight, each paying the demanded entrance fee. A little fast math and Madame was netting a fifteen-hundred-euro profit tonight. Say she did forty of these a year. A cool sixty grand. And as it was all cash . . .

So much for Montgomery's bullshit about shine-or-don't-get-asked-back. The salon was a business.

But, as I quickly noted, it had its *habitués*. Chet was one of them. So too was a guy named Claude. Short, sad-faced, with sharp features and a black suit with narrow lapels and dark glasses, he looked like a cheap hood from one of Jean-Pierre Melville's fifties gangster films.

"What do you do?" he asked me in English.

"You know I can speak French."

"Ah, but Lorraine prefers if the salon is in English."

"But we're in Paris."

"No, monsieur. We are in Madame's Paris. And in Madame's Paris, we all speak English."

"You're shitting me."

"I shit not. Madame does not speak much in the way of French. Enough to order dinner in a restaurant or scream at the Moroccan *femme de ménage* if her vanity mirror is dusty. Otherwise . . . *rien.*"

"But she's been living here for . . . ?"

"Thirty years."

"That's crazy."

"Paris is full of Anglophones who haven't bothered to learn the language. And Paris accommodates them—because Paris is very accommodating."

"As long as you are white."

Claude looked at me as if I was insane.

"Why should such things concern you? This salon . . . it is a wonderful *souk des idées*."

"And what *idées* are you peddling, Claude?"

"I peddle nothing. I am merely a pedagogue. Private French-language lessons. Very reasonable rates. And I will come to your apartment." He proffered me a business card. "If you are trying to improve your French . . ."

"But why improve my French when I can come here and speak English with you?"

He smiled tightly.

"Very droll, monsieur. And what is your profession?"

I told him. He rolled his eyes and gestured to the crowd in front of us.

"Everyone is a writer here. They all talk of a book they are trying to write . . ."

Then he drifted off.

Claude did have a point. I met at least four other would-be writers. Then there was the super-cocky guy from Chicago (I have never met a reserved, modest Chicagoan) in his early forties who taught "media studies" at Northwestern, and had just published his first novel with some obscurantist press (but—he told me—it had still merited a short mention in the *New York Times Book Review*) and was spending a year in Paris on some sort of fellowship, and went off into this extended monologue about how, in "decades to come," we'd all be recognized as a new "lost generation," fleeing the oppressive conformism of the Bush years, blah, blah, blah . . . to which I could only say . . . in a deadpan voice, "Yes, we are the totally lost generation."

"Are you being sarcastic?" he asked.

"What makes you think that?"

He walked away.

I started to drink heavily. I picked up a glass of the red cask wine. It tasted rough, but I still downed three of them in rapid succession. It didn't do wonders for my stomach—vinegar never does—but it did give me the necessary Dutch courage to continue mingling. I decided to try my luck with any available woman who crossed my path and didn't have the sort of face that would frighten domestic animals. So I got talking to Jackie—a divorcée from Sacramento ('It's a hole, but I won our six-thousand-foot ranch house from Howard in the settlement, and I've got a little PR firm there that handles the state legislature, and Lake Tahoe isn't far, and I heard about Lorraine's salon in a guidebook—the place where all the Parisian artists commingle every Sunday night—and you say you're a writer . . . Who publishes you? . . . Oh, right . . ."). And I got talking with Alison, who worked as a business journalist with Reuters—a large, flirty Brit who told me that she hated her job, but loved living in Paris ("Because it's not bloody Birmingham, where I grew up"), even though she did find it very lonely. She came to the salon most weeks and had made some friends here, but had still not found that "special friend" she'd been looking for.

"It's all because I'm too possessive," she said.

"You think that?"

"That's what my last boyfriend told me. I couldn't let go."

"Was he right?"

"His wife certainly thought so. When he wouldn't marry me—even though he promised twice that he was going to leave her for me—I waited outside his apartment in Passy all weekend. Then, when he still wouldn't come out, I smashed the windscreen of his Mercedes with a brick."

"That is a little extreme."

"That's what all men say. Because, like him, they're all cowards . . . and little shits."

"Nice meeting you," I said, backing away.

"That's right, run off, just like every other coward with a penis."

I threw back the fourth glass of wine and desperately wanted an-other, but feared that the mad man-hating Brit might still be at the bar.

I looked around the room again. The salon's volume was reaching high pitch now. Everyone seemed to be talking with strange animation. All I could feel was mounting despair—for the artificiality of this set-up, for the shrieking Southern Belle voice of Madame, which towered over the amassed hubbub, for the undercurrent of sadness that was so prevalent in every conversation I'd had, and for my own pervasive awkwardness. Here was proof (as if it was needed) that my isolated weeks in Paris had turned me into a real Oblomov—inept when it came to social niceties or even managing to sustain a simple dialogue with someone else. I hated it here—not just because it was a sham, but because it also exposed everything I hated about myself.

Feeling just a little tight, I decided that some air was needed. So I headed out of the kitchen, weaving my way through the throng in the living room, making a beeline for the balcony.

It was a clear, cold night. No stars, but a full moon over Paris. The balcony was long and narrow. I went to the edge of it, put my glass down on the top of the balustrade, and breathed deeply—hoping the winter chill would muffle the buzz in my head. But instead the night air just seemed to deepen my light-headedness; the sense that there was something faintly illusory about this salon, this balcony, this amazing fuck-off view. I glanced at my watch. It wasn't yet nine. I wondered if I could catch a screening of something around nine thirty at the Accattone or any of the half-dozen other cinemas located within five minutes from here. But if I did make a film that let out at 11.30 PM, I'd be cutting it very fine to get to work by midnight. And I didn't want to risk not getting to work on time, just in case this was the first night when a visitor for Monsieur Monde showed up right after twelve, and word would get back to Mr. Beard and the Boss that I had been negligent, and they might decide to let me go, and then I'd be back to square one in this city, and . . . shit . . . look at that view of the Panthéon from here . . .

"I'm certain you're thinking, 'I merit an apartment like this.'"

The voice caught me by surprise. It was a woman's voice—low, slightly husky, and emanating from a far corner of the balcony. I looked over. I saw a figure silhouetted in this dark nook, her body outlined in shadow, the red ember of a cigarette lighting up the darkness.

"You can't know what I'm thinking."

"True—but I can conjecture," she said, continuing on in French. "And having seen your discomfort during the salon this evening, it is clear you are not at ease here."

"You've been observing me all evening?"

"Do not flatter yourself. I have simply caught sight of you, from time to time, looking forlorn. A little-boy-lost who tries to chat up women without success, and then escapes to the balcony, and stares out at the Panthéon and thinks—"

"Hey, thanks for the searing psychological profile, but if you'll excuse me I think I'm out of here."

I started to leave.

"Do you always react so badly to a little gentle teasing?"

I turned back toward her, but could still only see the outline of her body and the glow of her cigarette.

"Bizarrely, I find teasing from a total stranger just a little odd."

"I think you find teasing from a woman difficult."

"Many thanks for another slap in the face."

"You see, my point entirely. I make a few passing comments and you are immediately defensive."

"Maybe because I don't like games like this one."

"Who is playing a game here?"

"You are."

"That is news to me—as all I think I am doing is engaging in banter . . . or flirtation, if you want to give it its proper name."

"This is your idea of flirtation?"

"Well, what's your idea of flirtation? Trying to have a reasonable discussion with a crazy woman like that Alison monster?"

"'Monster' is a slight exaggeration."

"Oh please, don't tell me you're going to defend her after she emasculated you . . ."

"She didn't exactly do that . . ."

"It certainly sounded that way to me. 'Coward with a penis' isn't exactly an ego-enhancing—"

"How did you know she said that?"

"I was in the kitchen at the time."

"I didn't see you."

"That's because you were so absorbed with that psychotic that you didn't notice I was standing nearby."

"And listening to everything we said?"

"Absolutely."

"Didn't your mother ever tell you that it was rude to listen to other people's conversations?"

"No, she didn't."

"I was being ironic," I said.

"Were you really?"

"Sorry."

"For what?"

"For making a dumb comment."

"Are you always so self-critical?"

"I suppose I am."

"That's because . . . let me guess . . . you have suffered a terrible calamity, and since then you have doubted everything about yourself?"

Silence. I gripped the balustrade and bit down hard on my lip and wondered, *Why am I so damn transparent?*

"I'm sorry," she said. "I obviously said the wrong thing."

"No—you scored a direct hit, a bull's-eye . . ."

The ember on the cigarette glowed one final time, then fell ground-ward. As it did, she moved out of the shadows and toward me. The moonlight brought her into focus. She was a woman who had some years ago traversed that threshold marked middle age, but was still *bien conservée*. Of medium height with thick chestnut-brown hair that was well cut and just touched her shoulders. She was slender to her waist, with just a hint of heft around her thighs. As the light crossed her face, I could see a long-healed scar across her throat . . . the remnant of some surgical procedure, no doubt. Twenty years ago, men would have called her striking, rather than beautiful. She was still handsome. Her skin, though smooth, had been gently cleaved by a network of lines around her eyes. But rather than diminish her attractiveness, they seemed to enhance it.

"You have been drinking," she said.

"My, my, you are *très perspicace*."

"No, I just know a drunken man when I see one."

"You want a written confession?"

"It is not a crime, you know. In fact, I approve of a man who drinks. Especially one who drinks to soften the past."

"Booze doesn't soften the past. It just blots it out . . . until the next morning. Nothing softens over time. Nothing."

"That's a very Manichean way of looking at the world."

"No—it's a very Manichean way of looking at oneself."

"You don't like yourself very much, do you?"

"Who the hell are you?"

She smiled an amused smile—her eyes brimming with mischief. And I suddenly wanted to sleep with her.

"Who am I? I am a woman standing on a balcony in the Sixth arrondissement, looking out at the Panthéon, while talking to an American who has clearly lost his way in life."

"May I kiss the hem of your *shmatte*, Dr. Freud?"

She lit up a fresh cigarette, then said, "*Shmatte*. Yiddish. Are you Jewish?"

"My mother was."

"Then that makes you Jewish. The mother carries the religion and passes it on—"

"Like the clap."

"And the other part of you?" she asked.

"Dreary Midwestern Congregationalist."

"So you considered your father a dull man?"

"You ask a lot of questions."

"You seem willing to answer them."

"I don't talk much about myself."

"All Americans talk about themselves. It's how they give themselves an identity."

"What an original thought."

"I'm glad you think so."

"So let me guess: you're a professor of semiotics at the Sorbonne who has written a doctoral thesis on Symbolic Nuance in American Cultural Life . . ."

"No," she said, "but I'm certain your doctoral thesis wasn't far off that title."

"How did you know I was a professor?"

"Just a hunch. And your field is . . . ?"

"Was film studies. I no longer teach."

"You lost your job?"

"Have we met before? Or do you have a file on me?"

Another smile.

"No to both questions. I'm just 'bullshitting around,' as they say in your country."

"And what's the word for bullshit in your country?"

"Two words: *buta beszéd*."

"You're Eastern European?"

"Bravo. Hungarian."

"But your French . . . it is perfect."

"If you have not been born French, your French is never perfect. But after fifty years in Paris, it is serviceable."

"Fifty years? You must have been a baby when you arrived here."

"Flattery is always pleasant . . . and utterly transparent. I was seven years old when I arrived here in 1957 . . . and now I have given away a vital piece of information: my age."

"You look wonderful on it."

"Now we move from flippant flattery to absurd flattery."

"Do you have a problem with that?" I asked.

She let two of her fingers touch the top of my hand.

"Not at all," she said.

"Do you have a name?"

"I do."

"And it is . . . ?"

"Margit," she said, pronouncing it *Mar-geet*.

"A last name?"

"Kadar."

"Margit Kadar," I said, trying it out. "Wasn't there some Hungarian bigwig named Kadar?"

"Yes," she said, "the Communist stooge whom the Soviets put in place to control us. We are not related."

"So Kadar is a pretty common name in Hungary?"

"Not particularly. Do you have a name?"

"You're still trying to change the subject."

"We'll get back to me. But not until I know your name."

I told her, then added, "And the H in Harry is not dropped, as every French person does it here."

"So you don't like being called 'Arry. But you do speak very impressive French."

"Impressive because I'm American . . . and everyone assumes that all Americans are ignorant and unworldly?"

"'All clichés are fundamentally true.'"

"George Orwell?"

"Bravo. He was a very popular writer in Hungary, Mr. Orwell."

"You mean, during the Communist years?"

"Yes, that's what I mean."

"But if you left in '57, you must have escaped all that Stalinist stuff."

"Not exactly," she said, drawing deeply on her cigarette.

"By which you mean . . . ?"

"Not exactly."

Her tone was quiet, but sharp. A hint that she didn't want to continue this line of questioning. So I dropped it and said, "The only Hungarian joke I know comes from Billy Wilder. He said, 'A Hungarian is the only person in the world who can enter a revolving door behind you and come out first.'"

"So you really are a professor of film studies."

"Was."

"And let me guess—you are trying to be a novelist . . . like half the people at this absurd salon."

"Yes, I'm a would-be writer."

"Why call yourself that?"

"Because I haven't published anything yet."

"Do you write most days of the week?"

"Every day."

"Then you are a writer. Because you write. You actually do it. Which separates the true artist from the poseur."

I put my hand on top of hers—briefly, but tellingly.

"Thank you for that."

She shrugged.

"Now I'm certain you're no would-be artist," I said, changing the subject.

"True. I'm not a would-be artist because I am not an artist. I am a translator."

"French into Hungarian?"

"Yes, and Hungarian into French."

"Does it keep you busy?"

"I get by. Back in the seventies and eighties, there was plenty of work . . . especially as the French couldn't get enough of modern Hungarian authors . . . and yes, that probably sounds comic . . . but one of the few things I have always respected about this society is their cultural curiosity."

"'One of the few things' . . . ?"

"That's what I said."

"So you don't like it here."

"Now I didn't say that. I just said—"

"I know what you said. But that hints at a deep antipathy toward this place."

"Not antipathy. Ambivalence. And what is wrong with feeling ambivalent toward a country, a spouse, your work, even a good friend?"

"Are you married?"

"Now, Harry—think carefully. If I was married, would I be wasting my time at this salon?"

"Well, if you were unhappily married . . ."

"I'd simply have a lover."

"Do you have a lover?"

"I might . . . if he plays his cards right."

I felt myself tighten. I met her smile and put my hand back on top of hers. She immediately pulled hers away.

"What makes you think I was talking about you?"

"Pure arrogance."

"Nice reply," she said, and now put her hand on top of mine.

"So you definitely don't have a husband?"

"Why do you need to know that?"

"Idle curiosity."

"I had a husband."

"What happened?"

"That's a somewhat involved story."

"Children?"

"I had a daughter."

"I see."

"No," she said. "You don't see. No one can ever see that."

Silence.

"I'm sorry," I said. "I can't imagine what it must be like to . . ."

She put a finger to my lips. I kissed the finger. Several times. But when I started moving down her hand, she gently pushed me away.

"Not yet," she whispered. "Not yet."

"OK," I whispered back.

"So when did your wife divorce you?"

"Talk about a mood-breaking question . . ."

"You asked if I had a husband, a child. I think that gives me the right to ask you . . ."

"She left me a few months ago. The divorce is in the works."

"And you have how many children?"

"How do you know that I have kids?"

"It's the way you looked at me when you found out that I had lost my daughter. I knew immediately that you were a father."

"You never get over it, do you?" I asked.

"Never," she whispered.

Then she turned and pulled me toward her. Within an instant, we were all over each other. I had my thigh between her legs, and my hand on one buttock as she unbuttoned my shirt and grabbed my chest. We fell up against the wall. Her free hand was now up against my crotch, my penis so hard it strained against the zip of my pants. But when I moved my hand up her dress, she suddenly disengaged, her hands dropping to one side as she sidestepped away from me.

"Not here," she whispered.

I came close again and gently kissed her on the lips, my hands away from her, even though I so wanted to hold her again.

"Then where?" I asked.

"I live nearby . . . but not tonight."

"Don't tell me you have another appointment?"

"Just things to do."

I glanced at my watch. It was just nine thirty.

"I wouldn't have been able to do tonight anyway. I go to work at midnight."

"Doing what?"

"I'm a night watchman."

"I see," she said, reaching into her purse for another cigarette.

"It's just to pay some bills."

"Well, I didn't think you did it for intellectual stimulation. What exactly are you watching over?"

"A fur warehouse," I said, knowing that there was one around the corner from me on the rue du Faubourg Poissonnière.

"And how did you land such an unusual post?"

"That's a long story."

"They always are," she said, igniting the cigarette with a small, old-fashioned lighter. "Where do you live?"

"The Tenth."

"Some bobo loft on the canal Saint-Martin?"

"If I'm doing a night watchman's job . . ."

"And if you are guarding a furrier's, then it must be somewhere near the rue des Petites Écuries."

"That's the rue running parallel to my own."

"Rue de Paradis?"

"I'm impressed."

"After forty-five years of nonstop residence in a city, you don't simply know . . . you start to haunt it."

"Or it haunts you?"

"Precisely. Do you have a *ligne fixe*?"

"No."

"So you live in a *chambre de bonne*?"

"You are a quick study."

"If you don't have a *ligne fixe*, you are generally hard up. But everyone has a portable these days."

"Except me."

"And me."

"A fellow Luddite?"

"I simply don't see the need to be contactable at all times. But if you do want to contact me . . ."

She reached into her purse, pulled out a card, and handed it to me. It read:

Margit Kadar
Traductrice
13 rue Linné
75005 Paris
01.43.44.55.21

"Mornings are bad for me," she said. "I sleep until the middle of the afternoon. Any time after five PM is good. Like you, I start work at midnight."

"It's the best time of the day to write, *n'est-ce pas?*"

"You write, I translate. And you know what they say about translation: it's about rendering morning words into evening words."

"I will call," I said.

"I look forward to it."

I leaned forward, wanting to kiss her again. But she put a hand up between us.

"*À bientôt . . .*" she said.

"*À bientôt.*"

And she turned and walked back inside.

I stood on the balcony alone for a long time, oblivious to the night air, the gusting wind, still lost in the strange and extraordinary encounter that had just taken place. I tried to remember a previous time in my life when I'd met a woman and was locked in a crazed embrace with her only a few minutes after first saying hello. I knew the answer to that question: this was a first for me. In the past, the sex always arrived a few dates afterward. I was never someone who could ever make a bold move. Too cautious, too circumspect. Until . . .

No, don't bring that up again. Not tonight. Not after what just transpired.

Montgomery suddenly walked onto the balcony.

"Hiding out here?"

"That's right."

"We do like our guests to mingle, you know."

"I was talking with someone out here," I said, hating myself for being defensive. "She just left."

"I saw no one leave."

"Do you watch every corner of the apartment?"

"Absolutely. Coming back inside?"

"I have to go."

"So soon?"

"That's right."

He noticed the card in my hand.

"Meet someone nice?" he asked.

I immediately slipped Margit's card into the pocket of my shirt.

"Maybe."

"You must say good-bye to Madame before you go."

That wasn't a request, but a directive.

"Lead the way."

Madame was standing in front of one of her nude triptychs—with arms of war sprouting out of her vagina, only to be enveloped by Eden-like flora and fauna. It was beyond stupid. She was holding an empty glass and looked decidedly tipsy . . . not that I was one to talk.

"Mr. Ricks must leave us," Montgomery said.

"Mais la nuit ne fait que commencer," she said, and started to giggle.

"I write at night, so . . ."

"Dedication to one's art. It is so admirable, isn't it, Montgomery?"

"So admirable," he said tonelessly.

"Well, hon, I hope you had a fabulous time."

"Yeah, fabulous," I said.

"And remember: if you need company on a Sunday night, we're always here."

"I'll remember that."

"And I just can't wait to read that book of yours."

"Nor can I."

"Monty, he's so witty! We must have him back."

"Yes, we must."

"And, hon," she said, pulling me close to her, "I can tell you're a real lady-killer, a total *dragueur.*"

"Not really."

"Oh, please. You've got that vulnerable-lonely-artist thing going, which women just love."

As she said that, I could feel her fleshy fingers slide into mine.

"You lonely, hon?"

I gently disengaged my hand from hers. I said, "Thank you again for a very interesting evening."

"You've got someone, don't you?" she asked, sounding sour.

I thought of the card in my breast pocket.

"Yes," I said. "I think I do."

TEN

L ATER THAT NIGHT, as I sat at my desk and tried to work, my brain kept replaying that scene on the balcony. Margit's face continued to fill my mind's eye. Six hours after our embrace, I could still discern the musky scent she wore, as it had adhered itself to my clothes, my hands, my face. Her taste was still in my mouth. Her low husky voice continued to reverberate in my ear.

I must have looked at her card a dozen times that night. I wrote down her phone number in a notebook and on a pad I kept on the desk, just in case the card was misplaced. I tried to grind my way through my new quota of one thousand words. I failed. I was too distracted, too smitten.

The hours dragged by. I was desperate to leave this room early and walk the streets and try to clear my head. But if I did leave here before the specified time . . .

Blah, blah, blah. I knew all the old arguments, and knew that I'd play the good employee and stay put until 6:00 AM arrived. And then . . .

Then I would call her and tell her that I couldn't wait until 5:00 PM tomorrow; that I had to see her now. And I'd hop in a cab over to 13 rue Linné and . . .

Completely blow this affair before it has started.

A little detached cool is demanded here, *mon pôte.*

So when I woke up at two that afternoon, I picked up my wages and ate *steak-frites* at a little café near the Gare de l'Est, and then took an extended midevening stroll along the canal Saint-Martin, and caught a 9:30 screening of Chabrol's *La Femme infidèle* at the Brady (they were doing a mini-festival of his films), and walked to my job, thinking at length about Chabrol's complex morality tale. The story is an old one: a husband discovers his wife's infidelity. He confronts and kills her lover, at which point . . .

110

But here's where Chabrol pulls a very interesting rabbit out of the hat. Upon discovering that her husband has murdered her *amant*, the wife doesn't become hysterical and hypermoralistic. Nor does she turn him over to the cops. Rather, the couple become collaborators in the crime—the notion being that, in any intimate relationship (especially one that has lasted many years), we are always complicit with the other person. And once the frontier of sexuality is crossed, we are, in some ways, hostages to fortune. You can compartmentalize, you can tell yourself that you know the person with whom you are sleeping is rational and playing on the same page as you . . . and then you discover one of life's great truisms: you can never really know the landscape of somebody else's mind.

But how desperate I was to cross that frontier with Margit.

Still . . . discipline, discipline.

So I didn't call her until the following afternoon—from a phone kiosk on the rue des Écoles. I inserted my France Télécom card. I dialed her number. One rings, two ring, three rings, four rings . . . oh shit, she's out . . . five rings, six . . .

"Hello?"

She sounded groggy, half-asleep.

"Margit, it's me . . . Harry."

"I figured that."

"Did I wake you?"

"I was just . . . dozing."

"I can call back if . . ."

"No need to be solicitous. I expected you to call now . . . just as I expected you not to call yesterday."

"And how did you figure that?"

"Because I knew, though you might be eager to see me again, you wouldn't want to seem too eager, so you'd wait a day or so before calling me. But not more than that, because that would indicate disinterest. The fact that you rang exactly at five PM . . . especially after I told you that I shouldn't be disturbed before that hour . . ."

"Shows how completely predictable men are?"

"Your statement, monsieur, not mine."

"So do you want to see me or not?" I asked.

"American directness. *J'adore . . .*"

"I've posed a question."

"Where are you exactly right now?"

"Near Jussieu."

"My metro stop. How convenient. Give me thirty minutes. You have my address?"

"I do."

"Here's the code: S877B. Second staircase, then third floor, right. *À plus tard.*"

Her place was a three-minute walk from the Jussieu metro. The area—seen in the half-light of a late-March afternoon—was a mixture of old apartment blocks and a clustered exercise in sixties concrete brutalism that turned out to be a branch of the University of Paris. For all my flâneur-ing around Paris, I had never ventured down this way (always stopping at the Grand Action cinema on the rue des Écoles, then turning left toward the river). So it was intriguing to happen upon the Jardin des Plantes. It was a surprisingly large and unexpectedly *sauvage* green space in the middle of the Fifth arrondissement. I wandered inside—following an inclining path up past tall trees and exotic flora until it reached a meadow-like area, slightly overgrown, with a stone cupola house in the midst of this Elysian field. Had I been a film director, out scouting a location for an urban update of *A Midsummer Night's Dream,* this would have won hands down. There was even a small hill—accessed by a winding path—the summit of which brought me into a pagoda-style viewing platform. The view from here wasn't wildly panoramic. Rather, it was a vista of rooftops and chimney pots and sloping windows. There was nothing monumental about this prospect. But seen in the declining afternoon light, it still looked monochromatic and painterly: an urban still life, and one that was, by and large, out of public view. Rooftops are romantic—not just because they are, metaphorically speaking, adjacent to the sky, but also because they are hidden away. Stand on a rooftop and you cannot help but have simultaneous thoughts about life's infinite possibilities and the omnipresent potentiality for self-destruction. Look to the heavens and you can think, *Everything is possible.* Look to the heavens and you can also think, *I am insignificant.* And then you can shuffle your way to the edge of the roof and look down and tell yourself, *Just two steps and my life would be over.* And would that be such a horrendous thing?

No wonder the Romantics so venerated suicide. Seen as a response to life's fundamental despair, it was regarded as a grand final creative act: an acceptance of tragedy through the ultimate embrace of tragedy.

But why think such tragic thoughts when the prospect of sex was just ten minutes away? Ah, sex: the great antidote to all despair.

I walked down off the hill and out of the Jardin. I crossed the street and found a small grubby corner shop that sold just about everything— including champagne. The Arab guy behind the till said that he had one bottle on ice in the back. I bought it. When I asked if he sold condoms, he avoided my eyes as he said, "There is a machine on the next street corner."

I walked down to the machine. I inserted a two-euro coin. I pulled open the metallic drawer and withdrew a three-pack of Durex, presented in a plastic case. I checked my watch. It was 5:28.

Thirteen rue Linné was an undistinguished building—early nineteenth century, of considerable width, with an imposing black door. There was a kebab place sharing its left flank; a reasonable-looking Italian restaurant its other side. The code pad was to one side of the door. I opened my notebook and punched the necessary combination of numbers and letters. There was the telltale click. I pushed open the door, feeling nervous.

As always, I was in a courtyard. But this courtyard was different from all the others I had entered in Paris: it was light and airy and leafy. Paved in cobblestones, it also looked clean and well maintained. There was no laundry hanging from the balconies—only flower boxes and trellises around which plants had been interwoven. There was no loud jungle music coming from open windows. Just absolute bourgeois silence. At the entrance to the first stairwell, there was a collection of professional plaques:

M. Claude Triffaux
Psychologue
2ᵉ étage, gauche

Mme B. Semler
Expert Comptable

1er étage, droite

M. François Maréchal
Kinésithérapeute
1er étage, gauche

I smiled at the thought of an accountant—a man who deals with the financial narrative of one's life (and the stressful business of paying taxes)—working across the hall from someone who dealt with trapped nerves and seized muscles and other physical manifestations of life's assorted vicissitudes.

The second stairwell was further along the courtyard. There were no plaques here, just a listing of apartments. I checked for Kadar, Margit, but didn't see it. This worried me. Had I missed the second stairwell? The address was right, as the code had worked. But why no name?

I walked up the three flights of stairs, noting that, unlike my own state-of-collapse building, the walls here were well painted, the stairs were made of polished wood and had a carpet running up the middle of them. When I reached the third floor, there were only two doors. The one to the left had a small nameplate by its bell: LIESER. The door to the right had nothing. I rang the bell, my hands now clammy, telling myself if some irate old lady answered, I'd do my dumb American act and apologize profusely and hightail it down the stairs.

But when the door opened, Margit was standing in its frame.

She was dressed in a simple black turtleneck that hugged her frame tightly and accented the fullness of her breasts. She also wore a loose peasant-style skirt made out of a muslinlike material: very feminine, very chic. Even in the harsh glow of the stairwell lights, her face seemed radiant . . . though the eyes expressed a sadness that would never leave her be. She favored me with a small smile.

"I meant to tell you that my name isn't listed on the chart downstairs."

"Yeah, I did have a moment when I thought . . ."

She leaned forward and touched my lips with hers.

"You thought wrong."

My hand went around her back, but she gently disengaged herself, saying, "All in good time, monsieur. And only after we rid you of your nervousness."

"Is it that obvious?"

"Manifestement."

I followed her inside. The door closed behind me. The apartment was made up of two reasonable-size rooms. The first was the bedroom—with a simple queen-size bed. In a corner nook there was a bathtub (with a shower hose) and a sink. We didn't stop here, but continued down past a small door (the toilet, I surmised) and into a large living area. A kitchen had been fitted along the near wall of this room—the appliances and cabinets all dating from the mid-seventies. There was a large sofa covered in deep red velour fabric, a divan in a maroon paisley velour, and a venerable chocolate leather armchair. There were two large floor-to-ceiling windows at the far end. They overlooked the courtyard and seemed to benefit from afternoon light. To the right of the windows was a beautiful old roll-top desk, on top of which sat one of those bright red Olivetti typewriters that were so popular thirty years ago. There were bookshelves lining all the walls, crammed largely with old volumes in Hungarian and French, though I did spot a few novels in English by Hemingway and Greene and Dos Passos. On three of the shelves stood a massive collection of records—classical mainly, and quite comprehensive in their historical and stylistic range. Her taste was very catholic: everything from Tallis to Scarlatti to Schubert to Bruckner to Berg. There were no compact discs . . . only a turntable and an amplifier. There was no television, just a large, old Telefunken shortwave radio. And there were framed yellowing photographs of Budapest in the shadows and of (I presumed) assorted family members clustered neatly on all free wall space. But what struck me most about the place was its immaculateness and its sober good taste. Though she hadn't updated it for several decades, its subdued, *mitteleuropa* style still lent it a certain consulting-room warmth. Freud would have been happy working out of such an apartment, I sensed. So too would an *immigré* writer . . . or an *immigré* translator.

"This is a lovely place," I said.

"If you don't mind things being a little on the old-fashioned side. There are times when I think I should update it, move into the modern world. But that's impossible for me."

"Because of your Luddite tendencies?"

"Perhaps."

"You actually work on an old manual typewriter?"

"I cannot deal with computers."

"Or with CDs?"

"My father had a fantastic collection of records, which was sent on after my mother and I left for Paris."

"Your dad didn't come with you?"

"He died before we left Hungary."

"A sudden death?"

"That is correct," she said in a voice that hinted I shouldn't press further. "Anyway, he was a music fanatic, so he had this huge collection. When we left Budapest, we traveled with just a small suitcase each. Later on, when we had *immigré* status here, we had to apply to the Hungarian government to get certain personal effects shipped here. Among the things that arrived from our old apartment was Papa's record collection. Over the years, I added to it myself—but then, when the compact disc arrived, I thought, I have all the music I will ever need, so why switch over?"

"You mean, you don't like that consumerist frisson called shopping?"

"Shopping is an act of despair."

"That's extreme."

She lit up a cigarette.

"But true. It's what people do with their time now. It's the great cultural activity of this epoch—and it speaks volumes about the complete emptiness of modern life."

I laughed . . . a little nervously.

"Well, I certainly need a drink after that homily," I said. "And in 'an act of total despair,' I bought you this."

I handed her the brown paper bag. She pulled the bottle out of the bag.

"I don't know if it's a good champagne . . . " I said.

"It will do just fine. Did you get it at the shop three doors up from here?"

"How did you know . . . ?"

"Because it's my local place. I even remember when Mustapha, the owner, opened it in the early seventies. He'd just arrived from Bône in Algeria . . ."

"Camus's birthplace."

"*Chapeau!*" she said. "Anyway, when he was new in Paris and had just opened the shop, he was timid and eager to please, and was also subjected to a lot of brusqueness, as the idea of a *commerçant* from the Maghreb in this corner of Paris offended many of the long-term residents of the quartier. Now, three decades later, he's fully assimilated— and subjects everyone who comes into his shop to the same sort of brusqueness he once received."

She found two glasses in the kitchen, then placed the bottle down on a countertop and undid the foil and gently levered the cork out of the bottle. There was the decisive pop and she filled the two glasses.

"That was very professional."

"I could say something very banal like . . ."

"'. . . if there's one thing you learn after three decades in Paris, it's how to open a bottle of champagne'?"

She smiled and handed me a glass. I downed it quickly.

"Precisely."

"But you would never indulge in banalities like that," I said.

"It would offend my Hungarian sense of the sardonic."

"Whereas Americans like me . . ."

"You toss back half a glass of champagne in one go."

"Are you saying I'm uncouth?"

"My, my, you're a mind reader."

She had her face up against mine. I kissed her.

"Flattery," I said, "will get you . . ."

"Everywhere."

Now she returned the kiss, then removed the champagne glass from my hand and set it down alongside her own on the kitchen counter. Then turning back to me, she pulled me toward her. I didn't resist and we were instantly all over each other. Within moments, we had collapsed on the sofa, and she was pulling down my jeans. My hands were everywhere. So were hers. Her mouth didn't leave mine, and it felt as if we were both trying to devour each other. The idea of using a condom went south. I was suddenly inside her, and responding to her ferocious ardor.

Her nails dug into the back of my skull, but I didn't care. This was pure abandon—and we were both lost within it.

Afterward I lay sprawled across her, half-clothed, completely spent. Beneath me, Margit also looked shell-shocked and depleted, her eyes closed, her arms loosely around me. Several silent minutes went by. Then she opened one eye and looked at me and said, "Not bad."

We eventually staggered up from the sofa, and she suggested we take the champagne and get into bed. So I picked up the bottle and the two glasses and followed her to the bedroom. As we took off our clothes I said, "Now this is a first for me: taking off my clothes after sex."

"Who says the sex is finished for the afternoon?"

"I'm certainly not proposing that," I said, sliding between the stiff white sheets.

"Good," she said.

I watched her finish undressing. She said, "Please don't stare at me like that."

"But why? You're beautiful."

"Oh, please. My hips are too wide, my thighs are now fatty, and . . ."

"You're beautiful."

"And you are in a postcoital stupor, where all aesthetic discernment goes out the window."

"I'll say it again: you're beautiful."

She smiled and crawled in beside me.

"I appreciate your myopia."

"And you say I'm hard on myself."

"After fifty, all women think: *C'est foutu.* It's finished."

"You barely look forty."

"You know exactly how old I am."

"Yes, I know your deep, dark secret."

"That is not my deep, dark secret," she said.

"Then what is?"

"If it's a deep, dark secret . . ."

"Point taken."

Pause. I ran my fingers up and down her back, then kissed the nape of her neck.

"Do you really have a deep, dark secret?" I asked.

She laughed. And said, "My God, you are terribly literal."

"All right, I'll shut up."

"And kiss me while you're at it."

We made love again. Slowly, without rush at first . . . but eventually it built up into the same crazed zeal that marked our first encounter on the sofa. She was still remarkably passionate, and threw herself into lovemaking with ravenous intemperance. I had never been with anyone like her—and could only hope that my own ardor came close to the level that she reached.

When we were finished, there was another long span of silence. Then she got up and returned a few moments later with her cigarettes and an ashtray. I refilled our glasses of champagne. As she lit up her cigarette, she said, "Living in Paris must have corrupted you."

"Why do you say that?"

"Because you don't criticize me for smoking. I mean, what sort of American are you, not playing the Health Fascist and telling me how passive smoking is rotting your lungs?"

"Not all of us are that anal."

"Well, any of the Americans I have met . . ."

"Have you ever been to the States?"

"No, but . . ."

"Let me guess. You've met the occasional anally retentive American at Madame's salon?"

"I go there very infrequently."

"So it was my lucky night then."

"You could say that."

"Why do you go there if you so dislike it?"

"I don't dislike it. Madame is absurd—and someone who thinks that her life is her ongoing work of art . . . whereas the truth is that she is a dilettante who had five minutes of fame back in the sixties as an artist's muse, and briefly married a rich man . . ."

"Does that explain the big apartment?"

"Of course. The husband's name was Jacques Javelle. He was a big-deal film producer back then—largely soft-porn junk, but it made him briefly rich. He married Lorraine when she was this sexy, flower-girl mannequin, and continued seeing his two long-standing mistresses. But

Madame's strange American morality wouldn't put up with such sexual compartmentalization and she exploded the marriage. She came out of the divorce with the apartment and nothing more. Her looks began to diminish and she did not adapt well to the changing times. So what did she do? Reinvent herself as a curator of people. She found her little niche in Paris, the salon brings in an income, and for a few hours every Sunday night, she can pretend she is important. *Et voilà*—the story of Madame L'Herbert and her salon. Twice a year I find it amusing, nothing more. Occasionally it is good to go out and meet people."

"You don't have a lot of friends in Paris?"

"Not really . . . and no, that doesn't bother me. Since I lost my daughter and husband . . ."

"You lost your husband as well?"

A nod. Then: "Since then I have largely kept to myself. I like it that way. There is much to be said for solitude."

"It has its virtues, sure."

"If you are a novelist, you must appreciate it."

"I have no choice but to deal with being alone. Anyway, writing fills the hours when I do my job."

"So what—besides writing—do you do all night?"

"I sit in a room, and make certain that no one is trying to break into the place, and also let in the staff who do all the shipping of furs."

"I never knew that furriers ran a twenty-four-hour operation."

"This one does."

"I see," she said. "And how did you get the job?"

I told her a bit about arriving in Paris, and the horrendous experience in the hotel, and the day clerk who was such a bastard, and Adnan's kindness, and him getting controlled, and all the other strange happenstantial events that led me to rent his *chambre de bonne* and find my current employment.

"It's all rather picaresque," she said. "A run-in with a classic Parisian *connard*—Monsieur . . . what was his name again?"

"Monsieur Brasseur at the Hotel Sélect on rue François Millet in the Sixteenth. If you know anyone you hate, send them there."

"I'll keep that in mind. But you do have fantastic material, *n'est-ce pas*? Getting milked by a horrid hotel desk clerk and then ending up in a *chambre* in *le quartier turc*. I'm certain, during all those years that you were practicing your French in . . . where was it that you lived . . . ?"

"Eaton, Ohio."

"Never heard of it. Then again, never having set foot in your country . . ."

"Even if you're an American, you've probably never heard of Eaton, Ohio . . . unless you happen to have heard of Crewe College, which is the sole reason to know about Eaton, Ohio, though it's not exactly a big-deal college to begin with."

"But it's where everything went wrong in your life, yes?"

I nodded.

"But that's another conversation, isn't it?" she asked.

"Maybe not. It's something I'd rather not talk about."

"Then don't," she said and leaned forward and kissed me deeply.

Then she stubbed out her cigarette and drained her glass and said, "And now, I must ask you to leave."

"What?" I said.

"I have things I must do."

"But it's not even . . ." I checked my watch. ". . . eight o'clock."

"And we've had a lovely *cinq-à-sept* . . . which was so lovely that it nearly became a *cinq-à-huit*."

"But I thought we'd spend the evening together."

"That cannot be."

"Why not?"

"Because, as I said, I have things to do."

"I see."

"You sound like a little boy who's just been told that he has to leave his tree house."

"Thanks for that," I said, sounding hurt.

She took my face in her hands.

"Harry, do not take this badly. You simply have to accept that I am busy now. But I do want us to have another afternoon together."

"When?"

"Say three days."

"That long?"

She put a finger to my lips.

"You should know better," she whispered.

"I just want to see you before then, that's all."

"And you will—in three days."

"But . . ."

Her index finger again touched my lips.

"Don't overplay your hand."

"OK."

She leaned forward and kissed me.

"Three days," she said.

"What time?"

"The same time."

"I'll miss you until then," I said.

"Good," she said.

ELEVEN

THE NEXT THREE days were difficult. I went about my daily
routine. I woke at two. I picked up my wages. I killed time at
the Cinémathèque. I ate dinner at the usual collection of cheap
traiteurs and cafés that I patronized. I went to work. I wrote. Dawn arrived. I picked up my croissants and returned home.

So far so normal. The difference now was that every waking hour
of every day was spent thinking about Margit. I replayed our afternoon
together, minute by minute, over and over again: a continual film loop
that kept running in the cinema inside my head and wouldn't pause
between showings. I could still taste the saltiness of her skin, still feel
her nails as they dug into me as she came, still relive the moment when
she threw her legs around me to take me deeper, still remember the long
deep silence afterward when we lay sprawled across each other and I
kept thinking how my ex-wife told me repeatedly what a bad lover I was,
and pushed me away for months, and how I always tried to get her to
talk about what I was doing that was wrong, and how she always shied
away from what she called "the mechanics," and how, when I discovered
that she was involved with the dean of the faculty, I knew I had lost her
completely, and . . .

*Stop. You're doing what you always do. You're harping back to the unpleas-
ant in an attempt to block out the happiness you feel . . .*

*Happiness? I'm being forcibly kept away from my daughter—so how could
I be at all happy?*

Anyway, this isn't happiness. This is infatuation.

But in my more rhapsodic moments, it also felt a bit like love.

*Listen to you, the lovesick teenager, head over heels after an afternoon of pas-
sion.*

Yes—and I'm counting down the minutes until I see her again.

123

That's because you are desperate.
She's beautiful.
She's pushing sixty.
She's beautiful.
Have a cup of coffee and sober up.
She's beautiful.
Have three cups of coffee . . .

I kept telling myself that I should brace myself for a disappointment . . . that, when I arrived at her place again, she'd show me the door, announcing that she'd changed her mind about continuing with our little adventure. It was all too good to be true.

When the third day finally arrived, I showed up in her quartier a good hour before our 5:00 PM rendezvous. Again I killed time in the Jardin des Plantes, then stopped in the same grocery store and bought a bottle of champagne. I loitered for three minutes outside her front door until it was exactly the hour in question. I punched in her code. I ascended the second *escalier*. Outside her front door I was hit by a huge wave of nervousness. I rang her bell. Once. No answer for at least thirty seconds. I was about to ring it again when I heard footsteps behind the door, then the sound of locks being unbolted.

The door opened. She was dressed in a black turtleneck and black pants, a cigarette between her fingers, a small smile on her lips. She looked radiant.

"You are a very prompt lover," she said.

I stepped forward to take her in my arms. But one of her hands came up in traffic-cop style and touched my chest, while her lips lightly touched mine.

"*Du calme*, monsieur," she said. "All in good time."

She took me by the hand and led me to the sofa. Music was playing on her stereo: chamber music, modern, slightly astringent. She relieved me of the champagne I had brought.

"You don't have to do this every time you come here," she said. "An inexpensive bottle of Bordeaux will do."

"You mean, you don't want huge bouquets of roses and stuffed cuddly animals and magnums of Chanel No. 5?"

She laughed and said, "I once had a lover like that. A businessman.

He used to send me mortifying presents: heart-shaped bouquets and earrings that looked like a Louis XIV chandelier . . ."

"He must have been mad about you."

"He was infatuated, that's all. Men really do have a little-boy streak. When they want something—you—they'll shower you with toys, in the hope that you will be sufficiently flattered."

"So the way to your heart is to be mean and ascetic. Instead of diamonds, a box of paper clips, perhaps?"

She stood up to fetch two glasses.

"I am glad to see your sense of irony is up and running this afternoon."

"By which you mean, it wasn't up and running when I last saw you?"

"I like you when you're funny, that's all."

"And not when I'm . . ."

"Earnest. Or a little too eager."

"You certainly put your cards on the table," I said.

She opened the champagne and poured two glasses.

"That's one way of looking at it."

I was going to say something slightly petulant like, I stuck to the rules and haven't called you once in three days. But I knew that would simply reemphasize my earnestness. So instead I changed tack, asking, "The music you're playing . . . ?"

"You're a cultured man. Have a guess."

"Twentieth century?" I asked.

"Very good," she said, handing me the champagne.

"Slight hint of Gypsy edginess," I said, sipping the champagne.

"Yes, I hear that too," she said, sitting down beside me.

"Which means the composer is definitely Eastern European."

"You're good at this," she said, stroking my thigh with her hand.

"Could be Janácek."

"That is a possibility," she said, letting her hand lightly brush the top of my crotch, making me instantly hard.

"But . . . no, he's Czech, you're Hungarian . . ."

She leaned forward and touched my neck with her lips.

"But that doesn't mean I listen exclusively to Hungarian music."

"But . . ."

Her hand was back on my crotch, unbuttoning my jeans.

"It's Bartók," I said. "Béla Bartók."

"Bravo," she said, reaching into my jeans with her hand. "And do you know what piece it is?"

"One of the String Quartets?"

"Thank you for that blinding glimpse of the obvious," she said, pulling my penis out of my pants. "Which one?"

"I don't know," I said, my body tightening as she began to run her finger up and down my erection.

"Have a guess."

"The Third, the slow movement?"

"How did you know that?"

"I didn't. It was just . . ."

I didn't finish the sentence as her mouth closed over my penis, and began to move up and down, her hand accompanying the movement of her lips. When I was close to climax, I uttered something about wanting to be inside her, but this just increased the rhythm of her sucking. I didn't so much come as explode. Margit sat up and downed her glass of champagne in one go, then lit a cigarette.

"Feeling better?" she asked.

"Just a bit," I said, reaching for her. She took my hand, but resisted my attempts to pull her down toward me. So I sat up and kissed her deeply. But when I began to slip my hand up the back of her top, she whispered, "Not today."

She disengaged from me and took a drag of her cigarette.

"Have I done something wrong?" I asked.

A small laugh.

"Your ex-wife must have played havoc with your self-esteem."

"That's beside the point."

"No, it's not. All I'm telling you is, I don't want to be made love to today, and your immediate reaction is to think that you've been 'bad.' Which leads me to conclude—"

"I was just wondering why—"

"I can give you a blow job but want nothing in return?"

"Well, if you want to put it in such a blunt way . . ."

"You see, you act as if I'm rejecting you . . . whereas all I'm saying is—"

"I'll shut up."

"Good," she said, topping up my glass.

"I have to tell you . . . that's the first time I've ever had a blow job with Bartók as the musical accompaniment."

"There's a first for everything."

"Did you blow your businessman to Bartók?"

"You are a jealous man, aren't you?"

"It was just a question."

"And I will give you an answer. As our affair went on while I was still married, we always met at a little apartment he kept near his office. His fuck pad."

"And all the gifts . . . did he send them here?"

"Yes. He did."

"Your husband didn't get upset about that?"

"You do ask many questions."

She stubbed out her cigarette, then reached for the packet, fished out another one, and lit it up.

"No," she said. "My husband wasn't suspicious. Because he was fully aware of the affair from the moment it started."

"I don't understand . . ."

"Then I will explain it to you. It was 1975. Due to budget cutbacks, my husband, Zoltan, had just lost his job as a monitor of Hungarian radio broadcasts for some international airwaves watchdog group that was funded by the CIA. Our daughter, Judit, was just two years old. I was getting very little work as a translator, so we were dangerously low on money. Then, out of nowhere, a job dropped into my life—translating desperately boring technical documents for a French company that was exporting Hungarian-made dental supplies."

"I never knew Communist Hungary specialized in that."

"Nor did I before I got this job. Anyway, I did the translation and was then called out to the company's offices—in some modern area near Boulogne—to explain a few technical points to the company's director. His name was Monsieur Corty: fiftyish, potbellied, puff-faced, sad eyes . . . archetypal. I could see him noticing me with care as soon as I came into his office. We spent half an hour going through the documents. He then proposed lunch. I hadn't eaten in a restaurant for a very long time, so I thought, *Why not?* He took me to a very nice place. He ordered an excellent bottle of wine. He asked about my husband and my daughter, and found out how hard up we were. Then he started talking: about how he was married to an impossible woman; how she had so pushed him away that he found it difficult 'performing' for her; how she had ridiculed him for that and essentially ended that part of their lives, and how he couldn't leave her—that traditional French Catholic thing of keeping the family together to maintain social respectability—but was looking for someone with whom he could have 'an arrangement.' He also said that he found me very attractive, he could see that I was intelligent, and liked the fact that I was married . . . which meant that I had responsibilities of my own. And he offered me three hundred francs a week—a small fortune to us back then—if I would meet him twice a week for two hours in the afternoon."

"You weren't shocked by this offer?"

"Of course not. It was made so graciously. Anyway, I told him I would have to think about it, and that night I went home and after we got Judit to bed, I sat down with Zoltan and explained what had transpired that afternoon. The next day I called Monsieur Corty and I told him that, yes, our arrangement would be acceptable—but the price would have to be four hundred francs per week. He agreed on the spot."

"Your husband didn't mind?"

"I know what you are thinking: How could he have agreed to let me whore for a fat middle-aged man? But his attitude, like mine, was very pragmatic. We were virtually penniless. The money he was offering was—to us—vast. And to me, it was just sex. Actually, the sex never lasted more than a few minutes—he was very fast. But what Monsieur Corty wanted more than anything was a bit of tendresse. Someone he could talk to for a few hours each week. So I would go to the drab functional little studio near his office that he had organized for our liaison. I would undress, he would take off his suit jacket and trousers, his shirt, but he'd remain clothed in his underwear. He would pull out his penis and I would spread my legs and—"

"I think I know how the act works," I said.

"Am I making you uncomfortable?"

"It's just more information than I need."

"Don't tell me you're a puritan, Harry."

"Hardly, but . . ."

"Surely the writer in you appreciates that, in storytelling, the significant detail is everything. And so, the very fact that Monsieur Corty would never make love naked with me, and that sex was merely a mechanical act for him, surely must tell you that—"

"It was a sad, sordid little arrangement?"

"It wasn't sordid and it wasn't sad. It was what he wanted it to be."

"How long did it last?"

"Three years."

"Good God."

"It was a very lucrative three years for us. The money allowed us to buy this apartment . . ."

"Where did your daughter sleep?"

"There's another room—a very small room . . ."

"Where exactly . . . ?"

"Over there," she said, pointing to a door on the left-hand wall, near one of the French windows.

"I hadn't noticed . . ."

"Never overlook the significant detail."

I wanted to ask, *What do you use the room for now?* but I held myself in check.

"What ended the affair?"

"Circumstances," she said.

"Your husband must have been a remarkably tolerant man."

"He was as complex as anyone else. He had some great strengths, some profound weaknesses. I loved him madly and often hated him . . . and I think it was the same for him with regard to me. And he was no saint when it came to other women . . ."

"He had mistresses?"

"Un jardin secret . . . avec beaucoup de fleurs."

"And you didn't object?"

"He was discreet, he never flaunted the fact to me, he never made me feel in any way less important to him. On the contrary, I think his many lovers kept him with me . . ."

I shook my head. She said, "You are amused by all this."

"Absolutely—because I could never imagine an American couple agreeing to this sort of arrangement . . ."

"I am certain there are many who do . . . but, of course, never breathe a word to anyone outside of their marriage . . ."

"Maybe—but the prevailing rule in American life is, *If you transgress, the punishment will follow.*"

"As you well know," she said.

"How do you know that?"

"It's written all over you. You got caught at something. And the other great rule of American life is, *Don't get caught.*"

"No," I said, "the rule is, *There is a price to everything.*"

"What a sad way of looking at the world: thinking that pleasure must be punished."

"Only illicit pleasure."

"Most pleasures are best when they are illicit, *n'est-ce pas?*" she said, tracing a line down my face and kissing me. This time she responded when I kissed her back deeply. But then, a few moments later, she ended the embrace.

"Like I said . . ." she whispered.

"I know," I said. "'Not today.'"

"But three days from now—absolutely. Now you must go."

"So soon?"

"I have things to do."

"OK," I said.

Ten minutes later I was on the street, walking quickly toward the metro, trying to sort through everything that had happened during the brief hour I had spent in Margit's apartment. Questions, questions. "Not today." But why? And also, what things did she have to do that made her turn me out of her apartment after sixty minutes? The story of her "arrangement" with the fat businessman strangely rankled—because it felt as if she was testing me, seeing what I would accept, and also letting me know (without much subtlety) that this "thing" (I couldn't yet call it an affair, let alone a liaison) would be conducted according to her rules, her limits. And if I didn't want it . . .

But the truth was, I did want it. As I descended into the Jussieu station, the letdown intensified. Three days was a long time from now.

While walking to work that night, all I could think was how I now had to spend the next six hours locked up in an airless room, and how I was tiring of the job, and wouldn't mind taking a sixty-five-euro loss if it meant getting one day off each week.

But when I posited this idea to Mr. Beard the next afternoon, his reaction was not positive.

"I do not think the Boss would like that," he said. "You are needed there every night."

"But when I was first offered the job, Kamal said I could work just six nights."

"Kamal is dead . . . and you are needed there all seven nights."

"Couldn't you get someone else to handle just one night of the week?"

"It will not be possible."

"Would you at least ask the Boss?"

"I will ask him, but I know what he will say: It will not be possible."

But the next afternoon, when I stopped by the café to pick up my wages envelope, Mr. Beard favored me with a scowly smile.

"I have spoken to the Boss. He is d'accord. 'Every man needs a day of rest,' he said. Yours will be Friday, but the Boss also wants you to work one evening shift: six PM to midnight, one day a week."

"But that means doing a twelve-hour shift . . ."

"You will not lose any money that way."

No, but if Margit will only see me at five PM every three days . . .

"Could I do six AM to twelve noon?"

"It will not be possible."

"Ask him."

When I returned the next day, Mr. Beard tossed me my envelope and said, "The Boss wants to know why you can't do those extra hours."

"Because I see a woman in the late afternoon."

That caught him by surprise—even though he tried hard not to look shocked.

"I will tell him that," he said, looking away from me.

And it was only three hours before I could see her again. With time to kill, I walked over to that little café near the Gare de l'Est where I ate *steak-frites* twice a week. The place was quiet. I sat down. The waiter approached me and took my order. I asked him if he had a newspaper I could read. He returned with *Le Parisien*. I opened it up and started flicking through its pages. I have to say that I liked the paper because it was full of the usual petty crimes and misdemeanors that inform the life of a city. Today's criminal reports included: Two teenage thugs caught trashing a car in Clichy-sous-Bois. An insurance executive killed instantly when his car swerved in front of a truck on the *autoroute* to Versailles (and the postmortem showed that he was, booze-wise, way over the limit). A feud between two families in Bobigny that got so out of hand that one of the husbands smashed the windshield of his neighbor's Renault Mégane. A desk clerk at a small hotel in the Sixteenth getting knocked down in a hit-and-run accident on the rue François Millet.

Hang on . . .

Hotel Clerk Left Paralyzed By Hit-and-Run Driver

Philippe Brasseur, 43, the morning desk clerk at the Hôtel Sélect, rue François Millet, has been left paralyzed from the neck down after being struck by a car yesterday afternoon in front of the hotel. Eyewitnesses say that the vehicle—a Mercedes C-Class—had been double-parked near the hotel, and pulled out suddenly as M. Brasseur left the hotel. According to Mme Tring Ta-Sohn, who operates a *traiteur asiatique* opposite the Sélect, "The driver of the vehicle appeared to deliberately target the man." Mme Tring Ta-Sohn also informed the police that the license plate of the Mercedes appeared to have been covered. According to the investigating officer, Inspector M. Guybet, this detail evidently indicated that this was a premeditated act. M. Brasseur remains in stable condition at the Hôpital de Saint-Cloud. The attending neurologist, Dr. G. Audret, said it was too early to tell whether the paralysis was permanent.

Good God. As much as I hated that bastard—and privately wanted to see him get some sort of comeuppance for his hideous behavior toward me—I still wouldn't have wished that fate upon him. The man must have made some serious enemies over the years.

Four hours later I was recounting this tale to Margit. We were in bed, sprawled naked across each other and talking for the first time since I had arrived. When she'd opened her front door, she'd immediately pulled me down onto the bed, yanking down my jeans, hiking up her skirt. Once I was inside her, she became immoderate—her legs tight around me, her moans increasing in volume with each of my thrusts.

Afterward, she said, "Take off your clothes and stay awhile."

I did as ordered while she went into the next room to retrieve two glasses. Then picking up the bottle of champagne I had brought ("I won't say, 'Again,' . . . but you really must stop such extravagance"), she opened it, the cigarette ash falling off onto the sheets as the cork popped.

"More work for the maid," I said.

"I am the maid. Just like you."

"You're beautiful," I said, stroking her thigh.

"You've said that before."

"It's the truth."

"You're a liar," she said with a laugh. "And you're continuing to evade my question . . ."

"What question?"

"The question I posed to you last time."

"Which was?"

"How badly did your wife damage you?"

"Badly," I finally said. "But ultimately it was me who damaged my-self."

"You only say that because you believe her rhetoric . . . because, all of your life, you've been told you're a bad boy."

"Stop sounding like a shrink."

"You have nothing to be guilty about."

"Yes, I do," I said, turning away.

"Did you kill anyone?" she asked.

"Don't try to soft-pedal this . . ."

"It's a legitimate question: Did you kill someone?"

"Of course I didn't kill anyone."

"Then what are you guilty about? Betraying your wife perhaps?"

"Maybe."

"Or was it really all about getting found out?"

Silence. I turned away.

"We all want to get found out," she said. "It's sadly human . . . and sadly true. Just as we all can't really cope with the guilt that—"

"Do you want to know about the sort of guilt I contend with, day in, day out? Well, listen to this . . ."

That's when I told her about the hit-and-run accident involving the desk clerk at the Sélect.

"It hardly sounds like an accident," Margit said when I finished recounting this story.

"That's what's nagging me, the fact that—"

"Now don't tell me that, because you thought ill of the bastard, the wrath of the gods came down upon him?"

"Something like that, yes."

"But he got what was coming to him. Somebody out there didn't like the way he was behaving toward others, and decided to settle the score. And even though you had no bearing whatsoever on this person's decision to run him down, you still feel guilt?"

"I wanted something bad to happen to him . . ."

"And that puts you at fault?"

"I have a fucked-up conscience."

"Clearly," she said, topping up my glass with champagne. "But I'm certain this self-loathing didn't simply arrive one day, out of nowhere. Did your mother—?"

"Hey, I really don't feel like talking about it . . ."

"Because she so disapproved of you?"

"Yeah, that—and because she was a deeply unhappy woman who told me repeatedly that I was the root cause of her problems."

"Were you?"

"According to her, sure. I screwed things up completely for her . . ."

"How, exactly?"

"Before I showed up in her life, she was this big-deal journalist . . ."

"How 'big deal'?"

"She was a court reporter . . ."

"A mere reporter?"

"For the Cleveland *Plain Dealer*."

"Is that an important newspaper?"

"It is . . . if you live in Cleveland, Ohio."

"So she was a self-important hack, covering trials . . ."

"Something like that. I arrived by accident. She was forty, a hard-bitten professional, someone who never married and lived for her work. But—and this I got from her later—she was starting to 'feel her age' . . . wondering if she'd end up alone in her early sixties; a dried-up spinster, living in some small apartment, on the way out at the paper, no one caring if she lived or died . . ."

"There was no husband in her life?"

"Not until she met Tom Ricks. Ex-army guy, built up a successful insurance business in the Cleveland area, divorced after the war, no kids, met my mom when she was covering an accident case in which he was testifying. She was lonely, he was lonely, they started seeing each other. It was 'pretty agreeable at first,' she later told me, especially as they both liked to drink . . ."

"And then she got pregnant?"

"Yeah, that's exactly what happened. It was all a big accident, she 'agonized' over what to do, whether to keep it . . ."

"She told you all this?"

"Yeah—when I was around thirteen and we'd just had a fight about my refusal to do something stupid, like take the garbage out. 'You know the biggest mistake of my life was not having you scraped out of my womb when I still had the chance.'"

"Charming," she said, stubbing out her cigarette.

"Well, she was pretty drunk at the time. Anyway, she found herself up the spout, Dad convinced her to keep it and promised her he wouldn't stop her working or anything. But then the pregnancy turned out to be a nightmare. She ended up confined in a hospital bed for around three months. As this was 1963, when maternity leave wasn't exactly a progressive concept, the paper let her go. It was the biggest blow of her life. All the time I was growing up, she always referred to the *Plain Dealer* as 'my paper' . . . talking about it in such mournful tones you'd think it was a man who jilted her."

"So you were vilified for being the person who ruined her life. Is she still alive?"

I shook my head. "The cigarettes got my father first—he died in '87. Mom went in '95—cigarettes and booze. Suicide on the installment plan. I'm pretty damn sure my mom started the slow process of killing herself the day the *Plain Dealer* let her go. And . . . could we drop this subject, please?"

"But it's so illuminating—and it so explains why you feel such guilt about nothing."

"Guilt has its own weird trajectory."

"Which is why you weirdly blame yourself for that desk clerk getting run over?"

"I don't blame myself . . . I just wish I hadn't wished him ill."

"Why spill tears over a shit? Anyway, don't you think that those who damage others deserve to be damaged themselves?"

"Only if you buy into an Old Testament view of things."

"Or if you do truly believe in retribution."

"But you don't believe in . . . ?"

"Retribution? Of course I do. It's a rather delicious concept, don't you think?"

She was smiling at me.

"You're joking, right?" I asked.

"Not really, no," she said, then glanced at the watch on my wrist.

"Don't tell me our 'allotted time slot' is over?" I said.

"Just about."

"Great," I said, then added, "And yeah, I know that sounds petulant, but . . ."

"See you in three days, Harry."

"Same time?"

She stroked my hair.

"You're learning," she said.

Learning what? I wondered.

TWELVE

I WAS DETERMINED TO break out of my daily routine. So I made the point of exploring new quartiers on foot, and even forced myself to jog three times a week along the Canal Saint-Martin—my one small nod to the idea of getting back into shape. And twice a week, I declared a "movie-free" day and loitered in museums instead of the Cinémathèque.

But, for me, all these extracurricular activities were secondary to my twice-weekly rendezvous with Margit. It wasn't just the sex. It was also the break from the quotidian—the sense that, for a couple of hours (if I was lucky), I would escape the banality of everything. No wonder we all respond to the idea of intimacy. It doesn't just allow us to cling to someone else and believe that we are not alone in the world; it also lets us escape from life's prosaic repetitiveness.

But with Margit, I always did still feel somewhat alone, as she continued to keep a certain distance from me. When I arrived for our fourth rendezvous, she led me to the sofa, opened my jeans, and proceeded to go down on me. But when I tried to touch her, she gently pushed my hand away with the comment I'd heard before, "Not today."

Three days later, however, she was a different woman—sexually voracious and passionate, delighted to see me, full of chat and—dare I say it—almost loving. So much so that when eight o'clock arrived and she hinted that it was time for me to leave, I said, "Listen, I know I'm probably pushing things here—but this has been such a wonderful afternoon, why don't we do something like go out to dinner or . . ."

"I have work. And so do you."

"But I don't have to be there until midnight, which gives us a couple of hours—"

She cut me off, asking, "You really just sit there all night, while the furs come and go?"

"That's it."

"And do you ever meet the people who employ you?"

"Just the grumpy bastard who runs the local Internet café and hands me my pay envelope every day."

"The middleman?"

"Something like that."

"Have you ever thought about what's really going on in that building?"

"I told you, it's a furrier's."

"And I know you're lying to me."

Silence. She said, "Don't tell me you're suddenly feeling guilty about not telling me the truth?"

"The truth is, I don't know the truth. Sorry."

"Why should you be sorry? All men lie."

"No comment," I said.

"Listen to your guilt. But let me guess: your ex-wife talked a great deal about the need for 'trust' in a marriage, and how without 'complete honesty,' there was 'no real basis for intimacy.'"

Once again, I found myself tensing—and trying to rewind my memory in an attempt to remember when I told her all that about Susan. She preempted me by saying, "How did I know that? It was simply a supposition—and one based on my rudimentary knowledge of American morality in all its hypocritical finery."

"Whereas the French way is . . . ?"

"Compartmentalize. Accept the Cartesian logic of two separate universes within one life. Accept the contradictory tug between familial responsibility and the illusion of freedom. Accept that—as Dumas said—the chains of marriage are heavy and, as such, they often need to be carried by several people. But never allow the two realms to meet—and never admit anything. Whereas you, Harry, confessed everything . . . didn't you?"

"Yes, I did. And yes, I was a fool to confess."

"But you had to share the guilt."

"I'd been caught . . ."

"Being caught and confessing are two different things. You know the story of the man who gets caught by his wife in bed with another woman. Immediately he jumps up, naked, and starts yelling, 'It's not me! It's not me!'"

"I'm afraid I've never had much in the way of 'sangfroid.'"

"No—you just feel uncomfortable about lying. You consider it reprehensible and morally wrong . . . even though it is the most common—and necessary—of human impulses."

"You consider lying necessary?"

"Of course. How else do we navigate the absurdities of life without falsehoods? And do you know what the biggest falsehood is? 'I love you.'"

"Didn't you love your husband?"

She reached for her pack of cigarettes. I said, "You always do that when I ask you something awkward."

"You are a very observant man. And yes, I did love my husband . . . sometimes."

"Just sometimes?"

"Now please don't tell me that you can love somebody all the time?"

"There's nothing I wouldn't do for my daughter."

"Even though she won't speak with you now?"

"Did I tell you that?"

"Harry, you always sound so shocked when I infer something about your life. But it's not as if I have psychic powers. It's just . . ."

"My story is so banal and obvious?"

"All lives are extraordinary. All lives are simultaneously banal and obvious. From what you've told me so far, it's not hard to deduce certain things about you and your situation from a few hints you've dropped here and there. But as you don't want to talk about it . . ."

"Any more than you want to talk about what happened to your daughter . . ."

"My daughter died."

"How?"

"Do you really want to hear this story?" she asked.

"Yes, I do."

She turned her gaze away from me, focusing her eyes on the window near her bed. After several long drags on her cigarette, she began talking.

"On June 22, 1980, Zoltan took our daughter Judit—who was just seven—for a walk in the Jardin du Luxembourg. I remember telling him, as he left this apartment, that I was planning to have dinner ready in an hour, and wouldn't it be easier if they spent time across the road in the Jardin des Plantes. But Judit was very insistent about riding the carousel in the Luxembourg, and Zoltan—who so adored Judit he would give in to anything she asked—told me, 'We'll take a taxi there and back. Anyway, it's midsummer's night, so why don't you come with us? We can splurge and go to a restaurant, and maybe even take Judit to see *Fantasia* afterward.' But I had already started cooking a spaghetti sauce, and I was rather inflexible back then about changing our domestic schedule once it had been planned for the evening. So I insisted that they come back within an hour, no more. Zoltan told me I was being rigid, '*comme d'habitude.*' I lashed back, saying that somebody had to be disciplined around here, in order to keep everything afloat. That's when he called me a bitch, and Judit got upset and asked why we had to fight all the time, and Zoltan said it was because I needed to control everything, and I told my husband that the only thing that was keeping me in this marriage was our little girl, because he was such a complete waste of time. Judit started to cry, and Zoltan yelled that he was sick of this marriage, and he grabbed Judit and told me that they would eat elsewhere tonight, and as far as he was concerned, I could drown in my fucking spaghetti sauce, and the door slammed behind them, and . . ."

She fell silent. Then, "Hours went by. Three, four, five hours. I figured that, after they had gotten something to eat, they'd gone to the movie. But the cinema was only ten minutes from our apartment by foot. When eleven PM arrived, I was worried. By midnight, I was scared. By one AM, totally panicked—and I started inventing scenarios in my head, telling myself that, in a fit of anger, he'd decided to check them into a hotel for the night . . . and that he wasn't letting me know their whereabouts to punish me for being such a bitch. But I knew that Zoltan would never do something so extreme. He mightn't have had much in the way of ambition, but he still didn't have a mean streak . . . something I always loved about him, even though I was often so stupidly critical about so much to do with him. It's terrible, isn't it, how we lash out at the most important people in our lives—often against our better judgment, but just because we are frustrated in our own lives and—"

She broke off again. Another long drag on her cigarette.

"The police arrived just before two. When I heard the voices on the stairs, I realized immediately that . . ."

Silence.

"The police were very quiet, very solicitous. They told me there had been an accident, and would I please accompany them to the Hôpital de la Pitié-Salpêtrière. I became immediately hysterical and demanded to know what had happened. '*Un accident,* madame,' one of them said, also explaining that they weren't able to discuss the circumstances of the incident or the condition of my husband and daughter. As the gendarme told me this, his colleague put his hand on my shoulder, as if to steady me. That's when I knew they were dead.

"I remember feeling as if I had walked into an empty elevator shaft— a long free fall. My legs buckled, but I somehow managed to make it into the bathroom and empty my stomach in the toilet. At that moment I wanted to stick my head into the vomit-filled water and not pull it out again. Death seemed like the only option. One of the policemen came into the bathroom and stood over me as I was sick. I sensed he knew I might do something self-destructive—and once, when I dipped my head in the bowl, he gripped my shoulder and said, 'You must somehow stay strong.'

"I finished getting sick. The policeman helped me up. I remember flushing the toilet and going to the sink and filling it with cold water and plunging my head into it and the policeman getting a towel and wrapping it around my head, and shouting something to his colleague, and being helped into my coat and down the stairs, and into the back of their car.

"At the hospital, they brought me into this small room. We waited almost a quarter of an hour for the 'officials' to arrive—but I didn't care. I knew that the longer 'they' stayed away, the longer I wouldn't have to face . . ."

She stopped in mid-sentence to light up another cigarette.

"I must have gone through six cigarettes in that fifteen minutes. Then the door swung open and two men walked in. They were both middle-aged, chubby, grim-faced. One of them wore a white coat, the other a suit. A doctor and a police inspector. The doctor pulled up a chair beside me. The cop hovered by the door, watching me with dark, middle-of-the-night eyes. The doctor forced himself to make eye contact with me. When he started to say, 'Madame, I regret to inform you . . .' I lost the fight I had been waging ever since the police had knocked on my apartment door. I must have cried for at least ten minutes—howling like some wounded animal. The doctor tried to take me by the hands to steady me, but I pushed him away. He offered something to calm me down. I screamed that nothing would deaden the pain. Eventually the doctor started explaining, 'Hit-and-run . . . killed while crossing a street . . . they were at a pedestrian crossing when the driver struck them both . . . your husband killed instantly, your daughter died just fifteen minutes ago . . . we tried everything we could to save her, but her neck was broken, her other internal injuries too severe . . .'

"The police inspector then began to speak, telling me that a passer-by had taken down the number of the car—a black Jaguar—and that they expected to trace the vehicle and apprehend the driver within the next twenty-four hours. 'We are treating this as accidental manslaughter . . . but I must ask you: Did your husband have any enemies who might have wanted him . . . ?' I started screaming again, telling him that Zoltan had been a wonderful dreamy layabout with no ambition whatsoever, so why would anyone want him dead? '*Très bien*, madame,' the inspector said. 'I am sorry to have posed such a difficult question at this time.'

"'I want to see them,' I started screaming. But they refused, informing me that their injuries were too severe. My screaming intensified. 'I don't care what they look like, I will see them.' But they still said no, the doctor telling me it would be too traumatic . . . that Zoltan's skull had been crushed by the wheels of the car and Judit had been dragged for several meters by the car, and her face . . .

"That's when I went crazy—kicking the desk, overturning the chairs, clawing at my face with my nails, and then trying to smash my head against the walls. I remember the policeman and the inspector attempting to hold me down, and me fighting against them, and the doctor running out of the room, and returning with a nurse, and me now shrieking that I wanted to die, and someone forcing my jacket off me and a needle penetrating my arm and the world going dark and . . .

"When I came back into consciousness, I was strapped down to a bed in the hospital's psycho wing. The nurse on duty said that I had been sedated for the past two days. She also told me the police wanted to speak with me. A few hours later, the inspector showed up. By this point, one of the doctors on call had decided I was calm enough to be freed from my restraints, so I was sitting up in bed, still being fed intravenously, as I refused all offers of food. The inspector was all business.

"'Madame, we have apprehended the driver . . .' he said. The man's name was Henri Dupré. He was an executive with a big pharmaceutical company and lived in Saint-Germain-en-Laye. They were certain that he was very drunk when he killed my husband and daughter—because when they arrested him the next morning at his house, the blood test showed he was still way over the limit . . . which meant that when he had struck them, he must have been completely *bourré*. Smashed beyond reason.

"The inspector also said that one of our neighbors had identified the bodies, and that they had been released to a mortician who had reconstructed their faces, and if I wanted to view them now . . .

"But I told the inspector that I didn't want to see them dead. Because I couldn't face . . ."

Silence.

"We didn't have many friends in Paris. But my businessman lover, Monsieur Corty, did come and see me. I was still being sedated, still under 'suicide watch,' but I could nonetheless tell that he was shocked by my appearance. His kindness was extraordinary. He spoke in a very quiet voice and told me that he would be taking care of all funeral expenses, and that he had spoken with the mortician and that he could hold off for a week or so with the burial until I was well enough to leave the hospital.

"But I said that I didn't want to be present at the funeral . . . that I couldn't bear the sight of their bodies . . . that they should burn them straightaway. I didn't care what they did with the ashes, because they were just fucking ashes and had no meaning now that my daughter and husband were dead. Monsieur Corty tried to reason with me, but I would hear none of it. 'Burn them now,' I hissed, and eventually Monsieur Corty nodded quietly and said that, with regret, he would carry out my wishes.

"A few days later, I was discharged from the hospital. Monsieur Corty sent a car for me. I went home to an empty apartment—yet one in which everything seemed completely frozen in that moment in time just before they died. The spaghetti sauce I had been making was coagulated in the pot on top of the stove. Judit's drawing books and dolls were scattered in front of the fireplace. Zoltan's reading glasses were still balanced on the arm of the easy chair where he always sat. So too was the book he was reading: a Hungarian translation of Moravia's *Contempt*. Do you know the novel?"

"Of course," I said. "It was filmed by Godard."

"We saw it when our marriage was in a happier place. When things started to go wrong, Zoltan became obsessed with both the film and the novel. Because he identified with the central character. Like Moravia's protagonist, he had lost the respect of his wife. Until he was dead—and every moment of every day was spent mourning him and my wonderful daughter."

"You felt guilt?"

"Of course. Especially when, a few days after being released from the hospital, I was called into the *commissariat de police* of the Sixth arrondissement. The inspector needed to formally interview me for the dossier of the case. That's when I found out that the same bystander who managed to get the vehicle's registration number had also seen Zoltan and Judit right before the accident. Zoltan had seen a taxi on the far side of the road, and ran across with Judit to hail it. Halfway there . . ."

"Surely you didn't blame yourself for . . ."

"Of course I fucking blamed myself. If it hadn't been for me insisting that they rush home for dinner . . ."

"That's absurd, and you know it."

"Don't tell me what's absurd. Had I been more flexible about things, about my stupid spaghetti sauce . . ."

Another silence, only this time I didn't dare fill it. Finally she said, "It's time you left."

"OK."

"You think me rigid, don't you?"

"I didn't say that."

"No—but I know you hate the fact I shoo you out of here after a few hours and insist that I only see you every three days."

"It's OK, Margit."

"Liar. It's not OK. You tolerate it, but you don't like it."

"Well . . . if this is the way it has to be . . ."

"Stop being so reasonable . . . especially when I know it's an act."

"Everyone acts in relationships . . . especially ones as strange as this one."

"There! You said it. A strange relationship. So if you find it so strange, why don't you abandon it? Tell me I'm a rigid, controlling bitch and . . ."

"What happens after I leave here?"

"I work."

"Bullshit."

"Believe what you want."

"So what are you translating right now?"

"That's my business."

"In other words, nothing."

"What I do after you leave is my business."

"Is there another guy?"

"You think me that energetic?"

"No, just completely cryptic."

"Do yourself a favor, Harry. Walk out of here now and don't come back."

"Why the melodrama?"

"Because it won't end well. It never does with me."

"Maybe that's because you've never been able to get over—"

"Don't play the psychiatrist here. You know nothing about me. Nothing."

"I know . . . what you just told me . . . that terrible story . . ."

"What? It 'touched your heart.' Or maybe it brought out your long-dormant protective instincts which you didn't extend to your wife and daughter—"

"That was a shitty thing to say."

"So leave and don't come back."

"That was the point of that comment, right? See if you could really alienate me and make me never want to come back here. But maybe if you stopped blaming yourself—"

"That's it!" she said, standing up. "Get dressed and get out."

But I grabbed her and violently yanked her back onto the bed. When she struggled, I pinned both her arms down and climbed on top of her legs.

"Now you can answer two questions for me."

"Fuck you," she said.

"That scar on your throat . . ."

She spat in my face. I ignored that and increased my pressure on her hands and legs.

"That scar on your throat. Tell me . . ."

"A botched suicide. Happy now?"

I let her arms go. They lay motionless on the bed.

"Did you try to kill yourself right after you were released from the hospital?"

"Two days later. In the apartment where I fucked Monsieur Corty."

"He asked you to fuck him forty-eight hours after . . . ?"

"No. I proposed the idea. He was hesitant, telling me there was no need to rush things. But I insisted. After he'd given me his usual two-minute in-and-out, I excused myself and went into the kitchen and grabbed a bread knife and . . ."

"You really wanted to punish him, didn't you?"

"Absolutely—even though he was always so good to me. Or as good as anyone could be to a whore."

"But the very fact you did it when he was in the next room . . ."

"No, it wasn't a cry for help. If you cut your throat the right way, you die on the spot. I botched it . . . and Monsieur Corty somehow managed to stop the bleeding and call an ambulance and . . ."

"You lived."

"Unfortunately . . . yes."

"And Monsieur Corty?"

"He visited me twice in the hospital, then sent me a check for ten thousand francs—a small fortune back then—with a short note, wishing me well in the future. I never heard from him again."

"And the driver of the car?"

"He was a man with many connections—so he managed to keep everything out of the papers, and the magistrate investigating the case somehow decided to drop the charges from manslaughter to something punishable by a slap on the wrist and a fine. His people offered me compensation. Fifty thousand francs. I refused the offer—until my lawyer reasoned with me and said that I would be spiting myself if I didn't take his money . . . especially as he could get it increased by fifty percent. Which he did."

"So you accepted the payment?"

"Seventy-five thousand francs for the lives of the two people who meant most to me in the world."

"And the driver just vanished from view?"

"Not exactly. The world sometimes works in strange ways. Three weeks after the accident, there was an attempted burglary at the home of Henri Dupré. It was the middle of the night, Dupré surprised the burglar, there was a tussle, and Dupré was stabbed in the heart. Fatally."

"And you felt avenged?"

"It counted for something, I suppose—especially as Dupré showed little remorse for the murder of my family. His lawyers did all the dirty work for him—but I never even received a card apologizing for the terrible thing he had done. All I received was a check."

"So revenge has its virtues?"

"The standard moral line on revenge is that it leaves you feeling hollow. What bullshit. Everyone wants the wrongs against them redressed. Everyone wants to 'get even.' Everyone wants what you Americans call 'payback.' And why not? Had Dupré not been killed, I would have lived my life thinking that he'd gotten away with it. That burglar did me a huge favor: he ended a life that was worth ending. And I was grateful to him."

"But did it in any way balm the wound?"

"Hardly. You might come to terms with the loss of a husband—no matter how much you miss him—but you never get over the death of a child. Never. Dupré's death didn't mollify my grief—but it did give me some grim satisfaction. And I'm certain that shocks you."

"Part of me wants to say, 'Yes, I am appalled . . .'"

"And the other part?"

"Understands exactly why you felt that way."

"Because you too want revenge?"

"I haven't suffered anything like you have."

"True, no one died. But you did suffer the death of your marriage, your career. And your child will not speak with you . . ."

"As you reminded me earlier."

"As you remind yourself every hour of every day. Because that's how guilt works."

I stood up and started to get dressed.

"Leaving so soon?" Margit asked, sounding amused.

"Well, it is close to the 'witching hour,' isn't it?"

"True—but unusually you're the one leaving without a shove for a change. Now why might that be?"

I said nothing.

"Answer this question honestly, Monsieur Ricks. The person—I presume it is a man—who did you harm . . . Wouldn't you want harm to befall him?"

"Absolutely. But I'd never perpetrate it on him."

"You're far too ethical," she said.

"Hardly," I said, then added, "three days from now?"

"You are a fool to be pursuing this."

"Yes, I am."

"Three days then," she said, reaching for her cigarettes.

Later that night, as I sat at my desk in my windowless office, Margit's story continued to rattle around in my head. The sheer terrible randomness of it all—the way life can come completely asunder in a moment—nagged at me all night. It also explained plenty about Margit's emotional reticence and the way she kept a certain distance from me. The longer I dwelled on it, the more I realized just how haunted she was by this appalling calamity, and how the grief would only end with her own death. Margit was right: there are certain tragedies from which we never recover. We may eventually adjust to the sense of loss that pervades every waking hour of the day. We may accept the desperate sadness that colors all perception. We may even learn to live with the loss. But that doesn't mean we will ever fully cauterize the wound or shut away the pain in some steel-tight box and consider it vanquished.

I finally got back to work, cranking out the usual thousand words. But when 6:00 AM finally showed up, I couldn't break free of my confinement, as this was the first night when I agreed to a twelve-hour marathon in exchange for a day off. The extra six hours dragged by. I forced myself to write another thousand words. I read another fifty pages of Simenon's *La neige était sale*, gripped by his account of France under German occupation. Eventually I found myself pacing the room and actually doing sit-ups on the concrete floor in an attempt to keep blood circulating and my brain awake. There were a few callers in daylight. Their images were clearer on camera. They were all men of seemingly Turkish origin, and they all kept their heads turned downward as they uttered the necessary password into the speakerphone. Who, I often wondered, *was Monsieur Monde? Someone you don't need to know.*

When noon arrived, I found myself blinking into the sunlight and needing to take in extended lungfuls of air and staggering home without the usual croissants and remembering to set the clock for 7:00 PM that night, and falling into a vast empty sleep, and waking with a jolt, and thinking how strange my existence was now: an all-night non-job, a sort-of girlfriend who would only see me every three days, and the realization that—even though this was allegedly my "day off"—I would be staying awake all night, as I couldn't suddenly break the sleep-by-day schedule I had been living since starting this idiotic, wretched job.

So when I came to during the early evening, I hurried off to the Cinéma Grand Action on the rue des Écoles, where a new print of Kubrick's *Spartacus* was being shown at 8:15. When it let out at 11:30 I kept thinking, Margit's apartment is just a five-minute walk from here. But I turned away and found a Mexican place off the boulevard Saint-Germain that did very authentic guacamole (or what I took to be authentic guacamole) and even better margaritas, and wonderful enchiladas washed down with Bohemia beer. The meal cost me fifty euros and I didn't give a damn, because I had just worked twelve hours, and this was my first night off in almost two months, and I was determined to throw financial caution to the wind tonight and get a little smashed and fall about Paris like a pinball. So when I finished my meal, I stopped in a *tabac* and bought a Cohiba Robusto and sauntered across the Seine, puffing happily on this absurdly expensive Cuban cigar and eventually reached Châtelet and a string of jazz clubs on the rue des Lombards. As it was almost 1:30 in the morning, the guy on the door let me into Sunside without hitting me for the usual twenty-euro cover charge. I threw back a couple of whiskies and listened to a so-so local chanteuse—thin, big frizzy hair, a reedy voice that still somehow managed to swing with the Ellington and Strayhorne standards, which she sang with her backing trio. When the set finished and the club emptied, I found myself on foot toward the Tenth arrondissement. It was well after two. This corner of Paris was deserted, bar a few entangled couples, and the street people who would once again be sleeping rough tonight, and the occasional drunk like myself. I followed the boulevard de Sébastopol most of the way home. As I got to Château d'Eau the smattering of Africans on the street looked at me as if I were a cop, taking a step back as I strode by. The rue de Paradis was shuttered—the Turkish workingmen's cafés long closed. Ditto the bobo restaurants. The occasional streetlamp cast an oblong shaft of light on the pavement. There was no traffic, no ambient urban noise—just the percussive click of my heels punctuating the night . . . until I heard the tinny beat of shitty pop music up ahead, and saw that my local dingy bar was still open.

The barmaid—the same Franco-Turkish one I had seen there before—smiled as I entered. Without me asking, she poured me a beer, set it in front of me, and then turned and retrieved two glasses and a bottle and poured out two shots each of a clear liquid. Reaching for a pitcher, she added a drop of water to both drinks. As the liquid went murky, she raised a glass to me and said, "*Serefe.*"

Turkish for *cheers.*

I raised my glass and clinked it against hers and, following her example, downed the shot in one go. As it traveled down my throat, all I could taste was its pastis-like flavor. But as soon as it hit my stomach, the alcoholic content kicked in: a one-hundred-and-ten-percent proof burn that made me grab the beer and drain it. The barmaid saw my discomfort and smiled.

"Raki," she said, pouring us two more shots. "Dangerous."

Her name was Yanna. She was the wife of the owner, Nedim, who was back in Turkey helping bury some uncle.

"You marry a Turk, you find out they are always burying some fucking uncle, or sitting in a corner with a bunch of their friends, conspiring against someone who dared to make some pathetic slight against their family, or—"

"You're not Turkish?" I asked.

"Supposedly. Both my parents came from Samsun, but they emigrated in the seventies and I was born here. So yes, I am French—but if you are born into a Turkish family, you are never really allowed to escape its clutches. Which is why I ended up marrying Nedim—a second cousin and a fool."

She clicked her glass against mine and threw back the raki. I followed suit and accepted the bottle of beer she handed me.

"Raki is good for just one thing," she said. "Getting smashed."

"And every so often," I said, "we all need to get smashed."

"Tout à fait, monsieur. But I have a question. Omar—*le cochon*—tells me you are American."

"Absolutely."

"So why do you have to live in his proximity?"

"Ever heard the expression 'a struggling artist'?"

"I've never met an artist. In this work, the only people you meet are assholes."

"Artists can be assholes too."

"But they are probably interesting assholes."

Then, over three rakis—interrupted by the final orders of the two drunks semi-passed out in a corner—she gave me a rambling version of her life. Raised in this "shitty arrondissement" when it was still primarily Turkish, always getting crap in school for being the child of *immigrés*, working in her father's little *épicerie* when she was seventeen, very strict parents, pushed into this arranged marriage with Nedim three years ago ("My twenty-first birthday present from my fucking parents").

"It could be worse," she said. "At least it's a bar, and not a *laverie*."

But Nedim was a slob who expected her to play the traditional wife when it came to picking up after him. "I am also duty-bound to spread my legs and fuck the idiot twice a week . . . a disgusting experience as the fool always burps just before coming . . ."

We kept throwing the rakis back, and she kept lighting up cigarettes and coughing. Finally she told the two drunks to beat it. When they had both staggered out, she looked at the mess around her—the dirty glasses, the brimming ashtrays, the tables and counters that needed wiping down, the floor to be swept and mopped—and shuddered.

"This," she said, "is the sum total of my life."

"I should go," I said.

"Not yet," she said, standing up. She walked to the front door, locked it, then pulled down an inside set of shutters. She returned to where I was sitting, flashing me a drunken smile, took my hand, and pulled me up from the chair, then placed the same hand under her short skirt and inside her *petite culotte*. As my index finger touched her slit, it became wet and she uttered a small groan before grabbing my head and shoving her tongue down my throat. I might have been drunk, but I was also cognizant of the fact that I was engaged in an insane activity. But my finger pushed deeper inside her. And her smoky, raki-coated mouth tasted . . . well, smoky and raki-coated. And the rational side of my brain was being trumped by the intoxicated moron with a hard penis. Before I knew it we were staggering into a dingy back room where there was a cot bed and a sink with rust stains (the small shitty details one notices while locked in a drunken carnal embrace), and she was unbuckling my jeans and I pulled down her panties and she kicked off her shoes, and we collapsed half-clothed on the cot, and I smelled damp from the grungy blanket covering the mattress, and the cot creaked under our combined weight, and when I hesitated from entering her she whispered, "It is safe." As soon as I was deep within her, she started doing mad, violent stuff like pulling my hair and lacerating my buttock with her nails, and pushing her free hand between us and aggressively rubbing her clitoris as I thrust into her. She must have woken two neighboring arrondissements as she came, then bit down hard on my tongue and wouldn't let go until I detonated inside of her.

Immediately she stood up and said, "I have to clean up now."

A minute or so later, after I had pulled up my jeans and spat blood into the sink (she had really done a number on my tongue), she hustled me out onto the street without a good-bye—just a fast guilty glance in either direction along the rue de Paradis to make certain no one she knew was about. The shutters came down. I walked a few steps along the street, then leaned against a wall, trying to fathom if what had just happened in the last ten minutes had just happened. But my brain was still too addled from all the booze and the sheer madness of it all. The blood in my mouth was flowing freely now and my tongue suddenly hurt like hell. So I staggered home and went back to my room and ran the tap and gargled with salt water for around two minutes, and spat out the bloodied water, and stripped off my clothes, and took three extra-strength ibuprofen tablets and a Zopiclone. The chemicals did the trick, but when I jolted awake at two, I found that I couldn't speak.

I discovered this because my wake-up call this morning wasn't my clock radio; rather, several loud knocks on my door. As I staggered out of bed, my tongue touched the roof of my parched mouth and immediately recoiled in agony. I went to the little mirror hanging by the kitchen sink and opened my mouth. I shuddered when I saw what was inside. My tongue had taken on a general blue-black appearance and was grotesquely distended. The banging on the door increased. I opened it. Outside stood Omar—in a dirty T-shirt and a pair of cotton drawstring pants with fresh urine stains around the crotch. The first words out of his mouth were, "You give me one thousand euros."

"What?" I said, sounding as if my mouth was filled with dental cotton wool. That's when I realized that speech was virtually impossible.

"You give me one thousand euros today. Or else you are dead man."

"I don't understand," I said, though the sentence came out all muffled and distorted. As in: *jenecomprendspas.*

"Why you can't speak?"

"Bad cold."

"Liar. She bit you, yes?"

Now I was very awake and scared.

"I don't know what you're talking about."

"I see you this morning. Very early. Leave bar."

"I wasn't in a bar . . ."

"Bar closed. Shutters down. Shutters then open. She looks out, looks both ways. Coast clear. You come out. Shutters close. Got you."

"That wasn't me."

"Bullshit. I am coming down street. I see her open bar. When she gives nervous look, I duck into doorway. Hidden. I see you. Now I tell Nedim—when he comes back next week—that you fucked his wife. How you like that, American? Nedim will cut off your balls. Unless you pay me to keep my mouth closed."

I slammed the door in his face. He immediately began to pound on it.

"You pay me one thousand euros by end of the week, or you are man who will lose his balls. You no fuck with me."

There are moments in life when you feel as if you are in free fall. This downward spiraling motion is underscored with the knowledge that you have stumbled into something so potentially dangerous and maniacal—all because you have engaged in that most commonplace of male displacement activities: thinking with your prick.

I forced myself into the shower and into some clothes and out onto the street. Mr. Beard glowered at me when I came into the café to collect my pay packet—did he already know what had happened as well?—but we exchanged no words, which was no bad thing just now; as any verbal utterances caused immense pain. My stomach was rumbling, I knew that solid food would also be a problem. So I hit upon a grim option: a chocolate milkshake at the McDonald's by the Gare de l'Est. It was raining as I entered its portals. At three on a wet afternoon, there were a handful of travelers grabbing fast-food provisions before catching a train. Largely, however, the people huddled at the plastic tables eating plastic food were those who lived on the streets. Or they were immigrants—a mélange of African and Middle Eastern faces—who saw this dump as nothing more than a cheap meal. Looking at my fellow diners, all I could feel was a curious solidarity with these people who lived in Paris and yet really lived outside of it; who had few opportunities here; who were quietly ignored or despised by everyone doing better than just "getting by." But in expressing camaraderie with my fellow outsiders, I knew I was playing the hypocrite. After all, I longed for the other side of the Parisian divide: a nice apartment, an intellectual (yet chic) cinephile girlfriend, dinners in good restaurants, drinks at the Flore (and not worrying about the exorbitant prices they charged), a little bit of literary fame and its attendant fringe benefits (invitations to *salons du livre*, being asked to write the occasional reflective article for *Libération* or *Lire*, more women). Instead I was a self-marginalized loser—and currently a fearful one, as I wondered if Omar really would shop my ass to Yanna's husband.

The catastrophist in me invented ten different ruinous scenarios, all of which centered around sexually transmitted diseases and grievous bodily harm being meted out by a gang of angry Turkish gentlemen.

But once the thousand euros was handed over to Omar, then what? Paying a blackmailer does not guarantee the cessation of threats. From my extensive knowledge of film noir and dime-store mysteries, I knew that, au contraire, it usually signaled the start of an intensive campaign of menace. And Omar was stupid enough to think that he was smart enough to get me cornered and keep the hush-money game going for as long as I lived in fear of disclosure.

Which meant that I couldn't give in to the slob in the first place. But how to cut him off at the pass?

Margit would have an interesting answer to that question. But Margit was the last person to whom I could tell any of this . . . for obvious reasons. I lived in dread of seeing her in two days' time, as all sorts of questions would be raised about my distended tongue and the scratch marks on my ass from Yanna's exceptionally sharp nails.

For the next forty-eight hours, time flowed like cement. Everything seemed interminably long, overshadowed by my fears of disclosure and disease. However, I did do something sensible: I took myself off to a walk-in medical clinic on the boulevard de Strasbourg. The doctor on duty was a thickset man in his midfifties with thinning hair and an indifferent seen-it-all countenance. He looked at my tongue and appeared impressed.

"How did this occur?"

I told him.

"*Ça arrive,*" he said with a shrug, then explained that there was little he could do to cure a badly bitten tongue. "Keep rinsing it in salted water to keep the wound clean. Otherwise it must heal on its own. Within a week the swelling will diminish. I would also suggest to your '*petite amie*' that she doesn't demonstrate her ardor in such an aggressive way the next time you make love."

"There isn't going to be a next time," I said.

Another indifferent shrug. "*Très bien,* monsieur."

I then detailed my worry about having unprotected sex with Yanna.

"She is French?" he asked.

"Yes, but her husband is Turkish."

"But he lives here?"

"Yes."

"Is she an intravenous drug user?"

"I don't think so."

"Her husband?"

"He's a drunk."

"Do you think she sleeps with other men? More specifically, Africans?"

"She's a racist."

"In my experience, you can be a racist and still have sex with those you allegedly despise. Are you having unprotected sex with anyone else?"

"Yes, but . . . I do not think there is any risk involved."

"A final question then," the doctor asked. "Might you have any cuts or wounds in or around your genitalia?"

"Not to my knowledge. But if you wouldn't mind taking a look."

Another shrug—this time accompanied by a bored sigh. He reached behind him and grabbed a small bag from an easy-to-reach pile, opened it, and began to pull on surgical gloves, while motioning me to stand up. I dropped my trousers and underwear. The doctor took my limp penis between his latexed fingers and then, using a small pen flashlight, peered around my testicles and crotch. The entire inspection only lasted around thirty seconds and should have been humiliating, but was carried out in such a dispassionate way that he might as well have been examining a turnip.

"Generally, female-to-male HIV transmission needs some sort of open wound or sore in order to enter the immune system. Yes, it allegedly can swim up the urethra, but you would have to be profoundly unlucky."

"I can be profoundly unlucky, Doctor."

"The odds are still very small . . . Still, if you want to be absolutely certain, we can do a blood test now and also screen you for other STDs. And then we can do another in six months' time—to give you the complete 'all-clear.'

"I'd like the test."

"*Très bien*, monsieur . . ."

Ten minutes later, I was out on the street, a small card in my pocket with a number to ring tomorrow to get the results of the test. I knew that, privately, the doctor regarded me as a man suffering nothing more than a surfeit of guilt. Just as I also knew that when I saw Margit later that afternoon, I would have to make a clean breast of everything. There are certain things about which you can lie. And others . . .

Forty-five minutes later I was walking obsessively around the Jardin des Plantes, trying to work out how I'd tell Margit what had happened, terrified about how she'd react, and cursing myself for, yet again, detonating a relationship thanks to sexual transgression—a relationship I definitely didn't want to lose. Do we ever learn anything from our mistakes? Not when it comes to sex. That's the one arena of bad behavior in which we are recidivists, over and over again.

As I mounted the stairs to Margit's apartment, I told myself, *As long as you're prepared for the worst, there's really nothing to fear.* But I couldn't embrace such advice. I was guilty—guilty of so much.

I knocked on the door. A minute went by. She opened it. She was wearing a black dressing gown and smoking a cigarette.

"Hi there," I said, leaning forward to kiss her and wondering if she could hear the blurriness of my speech. She accepted the kiss. I stepped inside. She led me by the hand past the bedroom and into her front room. I sat down in an armchair. Without saying anything she went to the little table where she kept a few bottles of booze and poured me a whisky. She handed it to me. I sipped it and flinched, the alcohol burning my wounded tongue. She sat down opposite me. She smiled. Then she said, "So who have you been fucking, Harry?"

THIRTEEN

"I DON'T KNOW WHAT you're talking about," I said.

"Liar," she said with a laugh.

I sipped some whisky and winced again.

"What's wrong with your mouth?"

"I bit my tongue."

"Liar."

"Haven't you ever bitten your tongue?" I asked.

"What was her name?"

"I'm telling you—"

"You are telling me shit. Which is fine by me. I don't care. Any more than I care if you slept with someone else—which I know you did. So what was her name?"

Pause. Then, "Yanna."

"Turkish?"

"Half-French, half-Turkish."

"How did you meet her?"

I explained.

"And how did the fuck happen?"

I explained.

"Did she did bite you before or after penetration?"

I explained.

"And when you were finished?"

"She threw me out."

"And let me guess—you didn't use a condom . . ."

"I'm sorry."

"But why?"

"Because now . . ."

"Now what?"

"Now perhaps you won't want . . ."

"To have sex with you?" She laughed again. "Sometimes, Harry, you become infantile."

I hung my head . . . and felt infantile.

"Surely that doctor you consulted . . ."

I looked up at her.

"How did you know I consulted . . . ?"

"Here we go again. Harry, you are so charmingly predictable. And you are so American when it comes to your need to feel bad about everything to do with sex. So let me guess: the doctor told you there's nothing to worry about. But you're still worried—still calculating the million-to-one possibility that you might have contracted—"

"Stop," I said.

"But why, *chéri*? You feel guilt about fucking someone else. But instead of properly hiding it, you wear it on your sleeve. And when I call you on it, you admit all—and hand the guilt on to me."

"That wasn't my intention."

"I don't care what you did. I don't care into which of her orifices you shoved your penis. All I care about is being treated as an adult by an adult. But when you enter my apartment, cowering—"

"It's not just the sex," I said, cutting her off.

"Even though the doctor gave you the virtual all-clear?"

"I am being blackmailed."

"By whom exactly?" she asked

I gave her the complete run-down on Omar, then said, "The guy has a certain animal cunning. He thinks he's got me cornered . . ."

"But he does have you cornered."

"So what do I do?"

"You don't pay him the money."

"But he will make good on his threat . . ."

"Let him. You can always deny it. And believe me, Madame Teeth Marks will deny it too."

"That won't change his mind. At best, I'll get my face smashed in."

"The thing to play for is time. Tell Omar you will give him the money, but you don't have the cash right now. Tell him you'll get it to him in a few weeks. If he pushes you, be firm. What's he going to do? Go ahead and tell her husband? If he does that he doesn't get the money. That's all he's after—the thousand now and whatever he can bilk from you later. So keep him on the long finger. Meanwhile, I think you should make contact with Madame Teeth Marks and let her know what's going on. She can definitely help you contain things. Suggest to her that she tells her husband that Omar tried to make a pass at her late one night while he was away burying his uncle. Suggest to her that she gives him graphic details of the pass he made . . . how he attempted to touch her everywhere. She really needs to make it sound as grubby as possible. Once she's done that, Omar's credibility will be zero. He can tell him anything about you, and the husband won't believe it. Because he'll think Omar is simply trying to off-load blame on you."

I looked at her, impressed.

"That's a very elegant, nasty solution to the problem."

"It comes with a price, however."

"Which is what?"

"I want to know what happened to you in the States—what you did that was so shockingly terrible that you had no choice but to flee over here."

A long pause—I downed the whisky, even though the alcohol burned into the wound and hurt like hell.

"You owe me this, Harry," she said.

"Because of my transgression?"

"No—because I've told you so much about my past. Whereas you . . ."

"You'll think it such a banal story."

"If it destroyed your life, it's hardly banal. Anyway, you want to tell me."

"Could I have another shot of that whisky?" I asked.

"Dutch courage?"

"What other courage is there?"

She poured me out a hefty shot. I downed half of it, my eyes watering up as it went down.

"*On y va,* monsieur," she said. "Get on with it."

I finished the whisky. I took a deep breath. I started to talk.

"I suppose I should first tell you about my wife. I met Susan in grad school in Michigan. She was doing drama—and had all these great plans for becoming a professional theater director. I was getting a doctorate in film studies and wanted nothing more than a nice secure tenured job at a nice secure university which wouldn't be too taxing, would allow me to teach something I genuinely liked, and would also give me plenty of time to write 'the novel'—check that: 'the novels'—that I knew I was destined to write. From the moment I met her, Susan struck me as the ideal 'life partner.' She was attractive . . . in a very wholesome Midwestern way. She certainly wasn't chic—that would have been anathema to her. But yes, she was genuinely cute."

"A horrible word, *cute*. And let me guess: she always wore jeans and hiking boots and crème-colored sweaters and a ski parka and . . ."

"Do you want to tell this story?"

"I'm right, am I not?"

"Yes, you're right. And yes, we got married before we both got our doctorates. And yes, we both found jobs at the same middle-ranking small college—Crewe, in Ohio. No mean feat that, considering how hard academic jobs are to come by. I was an instant hit with my students. . . ."

"And Susan? Was she too a hit in the realm of 'student drama'?"

"Susan—as it turned out—had difficulty fitting in at the college. Everyone saw that she was a very talented director—great creative vision and all that—but she wasn't the easiest of teachers, and several students complained that she was too demanding on them, that she expected standards far higher than those kids at Crewe College could obtain . . ."

"Was she hypercritical of you as well?"

"Yes, she could be rather finicky around the house. And yes, she did push me very hard professionally—as we both came into the college as assistant professors, and both had to get enough articles and the like published in order to get tenured."

"Let me guess what happened next. You got tenured and she was turned down?"

"That is precisely what happened. The thing that decided it against her wasn't her lack of professional accomplishment—it was her inability to relate to her students."

"So suddenly she was out of a job, and you had the permanent post you wanted, which meant that you were stuck in this little town—which was the original master plan, except that now that your wife had nothing to do . . ."

"Well, she did get a few more small directing gigs at some small regional theaters—but again, there would always be some blowup with the cast, some dispute with the scenic designer, or she would rub management the wrong way . . ."

"An endlessly angry woman?"

"I'm afraid so."

"So the next obvious plot twist of this story is . . . like your mother, she gets pregnant?"

"Bravo."

"Well, what else would she do, being now out of work and thirty . . . ?"

"Thirty-two to be exact. And yes, within two months of not getting tenured she was pregnant. Though we both adored Megan straightaway, it was Susan who was around the house most of the time—and within a year or so, the strain started to show."

"Didn't she try to get other work?"

"Of course she did. The problem was, with all her regional theater opportunities dried up, the only directing jobs around Eaton, Ohio, were high school productions. Totally rinky-dink stuff which further played into her growing despair."

"And that despair continued to grow for the next . . . how old is Megan now?"

"Fifteen."

"So for the ensuing thirteen years, she floundered?"

"Well, she did have our daughter, and she was a very attentive mother. But as Megan got older and entered school, not only was there less and less for Susan to do, but she also hinted from time to time that she resented being a mother and wife . . . telling me several times during a squabble that, if she wasn't rooted to Eaton because of her husband and daughter, she'd be having a proper high-flying career in a big city like Chicago, where they would naturally appreciate her high professional standards and wouldn't get offended by her acerbity."

"Such a happy woman. How did you deal with all that?"

"I chose to ignore it . . . especially as it always came out when she'd had a few glasses of wine."

"So she was drinking heavily?"

"Hey, we were living in a small town with not much to do at

night—and she was, for all intents and purposes, depressed. So what else do you do but drink? Like I started to hit the hard stuff a bit as well. Largely because her own negativity was beginning to corrode things between us . . ."

"So you decided that the only way to combat this negativity was to have an affair?"

"It was actually she who had the first affair . . . though I didn't know that until some time later."

"And who was the lucky man?"

"Around two years ago, the college got a new dean of the faculty—a true smoothie named Gardner Robson."

"They actually name people such things in the States?"

"White Anglo-Saxon Protestants do. This guy was a real Mr. Preppie. Ex–air force. Ex–management consultancy. Early fifties. Superfit. Superstraight. Supercorporate—and brought in by the Board of the College to 'streamline management,' whatever the fuck that meant. There was a reception for Robson when he became dean—and, having already met him briefly at some administrative thing, I remember telling Susan on the way over to the party that she was bound to loathe him—as he stood for everything Republican and conservative that she hated about Bush's America.

"There were a lot of people swirling around Robson that night, but Susan did manage to spend some time talking with him. Only later did I realize that there was a moment when I saw their eyes meet . . ."

"How romantic."

"I thought nothing of it at the time. On the way home, Susan's only comment about him was, 'He's not bad . . . for a Republican.'

"Around a week or so later, she came home and told me she now had a private drama student—some local high school junior who was trying to get into the Juilliard acting program. She said she'd be doing intensive dramatic training with her every Tuesday and Thursday from four to six."

"And you didn't suspect anything?"

"No. Maybe that was completely naive of me, but there you go. I was simply happy that Susan had something to do with herself."

"My, my, you were so trusting."

"I just wanted my wife to stop being so bitter and self-loathing and, in turn, critical of me. The thing was, once she started to 'teach' this private course, her spirits began to improve. Susan even began to sleep with me again. On the surface, things were better between us. Until something curious happened. Out of nowhere, the woman who replaced Susan in the Drama Department left to take a job offer at another college. Susan was offered a one-year contract to replace her."

"Engineered by the dean of the faculty."

"Once again, I suspected nothing. Susan was naturally thrilled. Once back to teaching she seemed to mend her ways. No more of the old aggression or perfectionism toward her students or the other faculty members. Instead, she was a real 'team player' . . ."

"A transformation also brought about under the tutelage of the dean of the faculty."

"Well, all tracks were so carefully covered that I still had no knowledge that she had a *jardin secret.* Even the following year, when she was suddenly promoted and actually became a tenured professor, I still didn't suspect . . ."

"Did others?"

"Being a small college, I'm sure there was a lot of talk about this promotion—because it's absolutely unprecedented for someone who has been denied tenure to suddenly get a second chance. Still, I heard nothing of this talk—because the rule of gossip is that you don't tell the person being gossiped about that they are the subject of whisper-whisper talk. But, as I found out from a faculty friend much later on, their liaison didn't become official until well after my—"

"Downfall?" she asked, finishing the sentence.

"Yes—after my downfall."

"And that came about . . . ?"

"When I met a student named Shelley. But before I turn to that . . ."

"Susan gets her tenured job—and suddenly the domestic balance of power shifts again? She becomes arrogant and very preoccupied and busy, and begins to push you away?"

"Bull's-eye. Now that she too was a tenured professor, Susan started playing the arrogance card. As in, telling me that her time was now more important than mine, and that I had to be at home every day at four when Megan got home from school. And she stopped wanting to have sex with me. Or we'd be in the middle of the act and she'd push me away and say something like, 'You're useless.'"

"Charming."

"That was one of the milder things she hurled at me. One night, mid-act, she grabbed my head in both her hands and looked up at me and said, 'Do you have any idea how boring this all is?'"

"Did you think it boring?"

"Not particularly—but she let it be known that I now turned her off."

"So she made you feel unwanted, unloved, and all that. And you still didn't suspect . . . ?"

"Of course I suspected something. I even came out one night and asked her if she was having an affair. You know what her response was: 'I should be so lucky.'"

"And you still—still!—didn't suspect?"

"I was naive, OK? Or maybe I just didn't want to really see what was going on."

"And then this Shelley student came into your life?"

"Shelley Sutton. From Cincinnati. Super-bright, super-precocious. A complete film nut and very pretty—if you like the artsy intellectual type."

"Long black hair, little Lenin-like glasses, black jeans, a black leather jacket, and a dreadful family background?"

"And someone who was far too bright to be at Crewe College—but was a self-admitted screwup in high school . . ."

"And she was in one of your lectures and came up to you afterward and started talking about . . ."

"Fritz Lang."

"How romantic."

"Listen, it's not every day that you meet a very attractive freshman student who knows everything there is to know about Lang's Hollywood noirs."

"So it was a *coup de foudre*?"

"Not exactly—especially as all American colleges have insanely strict rules these days not just against student/professor relationships, but even doing something mild and innocent like having a meal with a student of the opposite sex. At Crewe, we were even sent directives by some faculty committee on 'sexual ethics,' informing us that, if we had a student in our office, we had to keep the door open and that we should always maintain at least three feet of physical distance between ourselves and them."

"No wonder America is insane."

"Anyway, after that first lecture, Shelley and I had coffee in the café on campus—and I have to say that there was this absolute instant rapport between us. She might have been nearly thirty years my junior— but within a few meetings it was clear to me that her worldview was so considerably more mature than her age."

"Isn't that always the cliché with the significantly younger woman? Yes, she might just have stopped playing with Barbie dolls, but her insights into Dostoyevsky are extraordinary."

"OK, I do realize I was acting out certain Humbert Humbert fantasies—"

"But Lolita was only in her early teens."

"Still, we had to be fantastically careful. So we started meeting at a coffee shop downtown. When the woman who ran the place noticed we'd been there around three times too often, we arranged that I would pick her up on a backstreet far from the college and then we'd drive to a small shitty city named Toledo—"

"Like Toledo in Spain?"

"Like Toledo—the rubber-tire capital of America."

"When did you finally have sex with her?"

"Around two months after—"

"Two months!" she said, interrupting me. "What took you so damn long?"

"I was nervous as hell. Naturally I was smitten with her—but I also knew I was playing an insanely dangerous game."

"What made you finally decide to sleep with her?"

"Susan kept pushing me away at home, and Shelley kept telling me how wonderful I was . . . and how we should 'give ourselves to each other' . . . even if it was just for one time."

"And you believed that?"

"After two months of flirtatious chat, I thought I knew her. The thing was, I kept trying to patch up things at home."

"So what triggered you finally sleeping with her?"

"I came home one night from the college and walked into Susan's study and put my arms around her and told her how much I loved her and how I wanted things to be put right between us again. Know what her response was? 'If you think that's going to ever make me want to fuck you again, you're completely deluded.'"

"Charming."

"No—it was anything but that. The next day I saw Shelley again for coffee. She put her hand on mine and told me she wanted me, and that we had to stop being so damn cautious and . . ."

I fell silent.

"Where did you go?" Margit asked. "A hotel?"

"A grim little place called Motel 6 in Toledo. It's a chain in the States, and only twenty-four ninety-nine if you check out of the room by six PM. Twenty-four ninety-nine meant I could pay cash, as I didn't want the motel stay clocking up on my credit card. We really didn't care about the look of the place, we just wanted—"

"To fuck each other."

"Well, that's a crude way of putting it, but—"

"Completely accurate."

"Absolutely."

"And the sex was wonderful?"

"I was in love with her. I know that sounds inane—and probably strikes you as yet another example of male midlife stupidity. But it's the truth. I fell completely for her—and she for me. Truth be told, I'd never been in this sort of realm before . . . never really felt this sort of . . . OK, I'll say it . . . completeness with another person. She might have been several decades my junior, but there was no sense of gulf between us. She was so damn smart—and not just when it came to movies and books and jazz and all the other things I also loved to talk about. She was just so wise about everything . . ."

"Very touching," Margit said.

"Haven't you ever been so smitten by another person you couldn't stand being out of their presence?"

"Once," she said quietly.

"Zoltan?"

"Someone else."

"What happened?"

"This is your story, remember? So you were madly in love with your 'student.' And you kept meeting twice a week at the same *autoroute* motel?"

"No—after that first tryst in the Toledo motel, I ended it."

"Out of guilt?"

"Absolutely. As smitten as I was, once we crossed that line I knew it had to stop immediately. Because—"

"You feared for your job, your career?"

"Yes, that. But also because I kept telling myself that things with Susan and I would eventually improve . . . that her disaffection with me was just one of those temporary dips that happen in a long marriage."

"Why couldn't you have simply arranged to see your student discreetly a few times a week? That's what she wanted, wasn't it?"

"Once we finally did the deed, Shelley was head over heels. And she couldn't understand why I wouldn't sleep with her again. I tried to explain—many times—that I simply couldn't continue to be her lover . . . that as much as I was taken with her, this simply had no future . . ."

"She took it badly, of course."

"Who could blame her? Especially as I'd been stupid. Wildly stupid—in the way that only a man can be stupid. I'd carried on an everescalating two-month flirtation with a very impressionable student, and then—once we finally consummated it—I broke it off."

"But why was that stupid? All right, you enjoyed a quasi-platonic relationship with this girl. Then you both decided to become lovers. Then you decided that it was not wise to continue as lovers. Surely, had she been emotionally more mature, she would have accepted your decision—"

"The thing was, she was eighteen—"

"There are emotionally mature eighteen-year-olds. She wasn't."

"All during those months of holding hands in cafés, and staring dreamily into each other's eyes, I knew that if I kept seeing her, it was all going to blow up in my face. But the thing is, I couldn't bear the thought of not keeping it going."

"That's because you were in love. That's also why you ended it—

because you knew that, once you started sleeping with her regularly, you wouldn't be able to stop."

"Perhaps. But don't you see how my thinking was so completely contradictory? I so desperately wanted her. Then when I'd finally had her . . ."

"Why shouldn't you have thought that way? And why can't you accept that when it comes to matters of the heart, we all do contradictory things? You know that line from Pascal—'The heart has its reasons which reason itself does not know.'"

"You're trying to tell me it's 'all right,' when the truth is—"

"You resisted temptation, you acceded to temptation, then you decided to resist temptation again. End of story. But because Americans equate sex with risk and potential disaster, it wasn't the end of the story, was it?"

"No, it wasn't."

"So what happened to the girl, Harry?"

"The story goes a little haywire here. In the days after that afternoon in the motel, she started sending me love notes all the time—five a day on colored paper in my office mailbox at the college. There were just as many emails. And they all said the same thing: 'You are the love of my life . . . I can't bear to be apart from you for more than another day . . . can we go to the motel tomorrow?'

"I was just a little unnerved by all this instant emotional excess. When we were just meeting over coffee, she was always romantic . . . but I never got the idea that, once we'd slept together, she'd get so clingy."

"You can never predict another person's emotions . . . especially the postcoital ones."

"Too damn true. When I found Shelley loitering outside one of my classes two days after Toledo, I decided to take immediate action. I suggested we go for a drive out into the country. Once we got to the place by a lake, I quietly explained that, as much as I cared for her, the affair had to end. She was devastated—and told me that she would never have slept with me if she knew it was going to end straightaway. I tried to patiently explain that, as crazy as I was about her—"

"You were a man with a conscience . . ."

"Something like that, yes. It's amazing, isn't it, how you agonize over crossing a dangerous threshold. Then, when you finally summon the courage to make that move, you instantly regret it."

"Another of those large contradictions, Harry. So did she cry when you broke her the news?"

"She simply wouldn't accept it . . . simply couldn't believe that I had changed my mind. Again, I tried to explain. Yes, I had feelings for her . . . yes, I'd loved all our conversations, and thought she was a fantastic person . . . and yes, if I wasn't married and wasn't her professor . . .

"She didn't take the news well—and started to plead with me, telling me she'd do anything to keep it going between us."

"Was she a virgin?"

"No—there had been a big high school love affair . . . which ended when she came to college. But as far as she was concerned, we were Tristan and Isolde: destined to be together from here to eternity. Try as I did to persuade her that, in time, she'd just see this as a passing blip in her romantic life, she remained devastated . . . and determined to somehow keep things going between us. There were constant notes in my mailbox, at least a half-dozen emails every day, and she made a point of hanging around every class I taught."

"Surely your colleagues began to realize that one of your students was a bit obsessed about her professor?"

"Of course. Doug Stanley—my one close friend on the faculty—took me aside and asked me directly if I had been involved with Shelley. Naturally I told him everything—and wondered out loud if I should go to the dean of the faculty, Gardner Robson—and make a clean breast of everything. He was adamant that I confess nothing. Because once I did that, I was finished. He also emphasized that, until Shelley went public about the affair, I was in the clear. His hope was that she would soon calm down—and he even offered to speak to her and see if she might agree to seek help from the college psychotherapist."

"Knowing you, the guilt must have been massive."

"It was nonstop. I wasn't sleeping and lost about fifteen pounds in less than two weeks. I couldn't teach, couldn't concentrate. Even my wife, who was totally ignoring me, noticed that I was in rough shape, and asked me what was wrong. I said I was depressed—and that's when she told me that, as far as she was concerned, I had been in a gloomy place for years. 'And the only time you'd lightened up was during the last few months—when it was clear to me that you were having an affair.' I didn't deny it, nor did she hint that she knew who my lover might be. But when I came back from the college the next night, I found her in my office, on my computer, reading my email files."

"Don't tell me you hadn't deleted everything you'd written to your friend—and she to you."

"I'd deleted it from my AOL account, but not the recycle bin. A bad oversight on my part, as that's where Susan found them all."

"Your wife had the password to your computer?"

"I'm pretty certain she once heard me tell our daughter that it was her name: Megan123. Whatever way she had managed to get into my files, the fact was, she had managed to get into my files. When I walked in and found her sitting in my desk chair, and staring at an email that Shelley had sent me, she said—in a voice so low and cold it sounded like a frozen whisper—'Pack a bag and leave right now. Otherwise I'll call the police and tell them you've assaulted me.'"

"And you bowed to this threat . . . this blackmail?"

"I thought it best to let the initial shock she was feeling—"

"Harry, she was fucking some guy before you even hooked up with Shelley—"

"I still didn't know that—"

"But she betrayed your privacy—"

"True. And she also evidently emailed all this evidence against me to her lover, the dean. Because, the next day, I had a visit from representatives of the firm that looks after security for the college. Two of their goons showed up at my office around ten that morning, telling me that they were escorting me off the premises and that I was now legally barred from setting foot on the campus again. They brought me downtown to the office of the law firm which handled all the college's legal stuff. There, some flinty small-town lawyer—bow tie, blue serge suit, suspenders—read me a document, informing me that, as I had contravened several college codes of professional conduct, I was being summarily dismissed from my tenured position 'without pay or any subsidiary benefits.' He also said that if I made trouble, the case would go public and—"

"You didn't get a lawyer yourself?"

"The college's legal eagle said that if I signed an agreement he'd prepared, in which I promised not to contest this dismissal, they would announce that I had 'resigned' for health reasons. 'You might just be able to rebuild your career,' he told me. So I signed the damn document . . . not knowing that Susan's lover, the dean, had another denouement in mind for me. The next day I woke up on the sofa in the house of Doug Stanley, to find I was being laid siege to by assorted regional television stations, not to mention a couple of local newspaper reporters."

"All over a brief fling with a student?"

"Being dismissed for sexual misconduct is a big thing in small-town America. As it turned out, somebody had forwarded to the Ohio press the salient details of my correspondence with Shelley. Doug was certain that Gardner Robson had tipped them off and also told them where I could be found—because Doug had run into Robson on the campus, and the dean had started spewing this bullshit of how it 'genuinely injured' him to have to let me go, and how he wondered if Doug knew of my whereabouts. When Doug made the innocent mistake of telling Robson that he was harboring me, do you know what that sonofabitch told my friend? 'I really feel for him right now.'

"Doug managed to keep the reporters from invading his house—and I essentially took refuge in the rec room in his basement until . . ."

Pause. I looked away.

"Until . . . ?" Margit asked.

"Until Shelley killed herself."

FOURTEEN

L ATER THAT NIGHT, before going to work, I stopped by my room to pick up my laptop computer and a book I was reading. When I arrived home, the note I was dreading was stuck under my door:

I GET 1000 EUROS TOMORROW OR YOU FUCKED.

The handwriting was scrawly. I turned over the scrap of paper and wrote:

YOU WILL GET YOUR MONEY IN A COUPLE OF DAYS. IF YOU REVEAL ANY-THING BEFORE THEN, YOU WILL GET NOTHING.

I shoved this note under Omar's door, then entered my room and sat down on my bed and tried to sift through everything I had told Margit tonight, and how good it felt to finally unburden myself of this secret, and how I felt simultaneously exposed and self-belittled for having admitted the terrible shame that haunted my every waking hour.

But Omar's blackmailing note also emboldened me. En route to work I walked directly into the little bar on the rue de Paradis. Yanna was serving the usual crew of drunks (many of whom were her husband's chums). Her eyes grew wide when I entered her establishment—a case of the guilty jitters, which she tried to temper with a tight smile as she pulled me a *pression* and simultaneously filled a shot glass with bourbon.

"What brings you here?" she said in a low whisper, glancing at the half-cocked clientele, wondering if they were picking up on her nervousness.

"We need to talk," I whispered back.

"Bad time."

"It's somewhat urgent."

"I can't leave the bar with all these creeps watching us."

"Make an excuse. I'm going to finish these drinks and leave. Meet me in ten minutes up on the corner of the rue de Paradis and the rue du Faubourg Poissonnière. What I need to say can't be said here right now."

Then I threw back the whisky and drained the beer and left—all the other clientele glaring at me as I hustled myself out the door. As expected, Yanna did show up ten minutes later at my proposed rendezvous spot. She had a cigarette going when she arrived and appeared hyper-tense.

"Are you out of your fucking mind?" she hissed at me. "Everyone in the bar saw you were trying to talk to me."

"It was an emergency," I said. "Omar . . ."

And I told her how he saw us and what he was now threatening.

"Oh fuck," she said. "My husband will first kill you, then me . . ."

"Not if you do what I tell you."

That's when I outlined the idea that Margit gave me (though not telling her that another party had cooked up this scheme). Yanna didn't seem convinced.

"He'll still believe that fat slob," she said, "because he's a fucking Turk. It's an idiotic Turkish male code-of-honor thing. If the slob tells you that your woman is a slut, then, without question, she is a slut."

"If you go to your husband crying, saying how Omar forced himself on you, how he had his hands everywhere, how he was so drunk he obviously didn't know what he was doing, but still did vast amounts of improper things to you—"

"He'll still beat me."

"Not if you sell it properly to him."

"He'll do it anyway—even if he totally believes me. And his justification will be that—as it was me acting like a slut which prompted Omar's 'attentions'—I deserve to have my eyes blackened."

"You should get out of this marriage."

"Thank you for such intelligent advice. My husband gets back tonight. If you value your life I would lay low for a few days—just in case he does believe his fellow Turk and decides to come looking for you with a sickle."

"I'll make myself scarce."

"One last thing: don't come into our bar again. I want to erase you from my life."

"The feeling is entirely mutual," I said, then turned on my heel and left.

Some hours later, at work, the thought struck me: "laying low" was not going to be the easiest of tasks, especially in an area where everybody knew each other and in a job where an unexplained absence from work wouldn't be tolerated. There was a part of me that wanted to return to my room, pack up all my possessions (a process that would take no more than ten minutes), and vanish into the night. But once again, I was plagued by the question: Then what? I also knew that if I did do a bunk, I'd severely disappoint Margit. Earlier that evening—after I had finished telling her what had happened to Shelley—she had returned to the subject of Omar's threat, saying, "It would be far simpler for all concerned if Omar simply disappeared from view before the husband got home."

"Sure it would. But from what I've heard, he has no family back in Turkey, and no life to speak of outside of his job and his *chambre de bonne*. And he's completely legal here. Even flashed his French passport in my face."

"A pity, that. Had he been illegal, you would have been easily able to turn the tables on him. One phone call to the Immigration Authorities—"

"But he could have ratted on me too. After all, I am working here without a *carte de séjour*."

"But your job doesn't really exist, does it? You live beneath the usual Social Service radar that would get you found out if you were legitimately working. Anyway, if forced to choose between the story told by an educated American and an illiterate greasy Turk, who do you think they are going to believe?"

"Racism has its virtues, I guess."

"Absolutely. And you're just as racist as the cops."

"Or as you."

"That's right. But remember this: though an immigrant like Omar, living on the margins in this city, might despise all the people here having plush, proper lives, his real scorn and despair are aimed at those in closest proximity to him. Zoltan always used to say, 'Never trust another *immigré*. They wish for your downfall in order to reassure themselves there is someone lower than themselves.' So, yes—Omar will rat you out. Which means you should go home right now and pack a bag and flee the rue de Paradis. But if you do that—"

"I'm running away again."

"As you ran away after your friend's suicide . . . even though you weren't to blame for what she did."

"I will always blame myself for what happened."

"As a way of hating yourself. But suit yourself. You haven't finished the story, Harry. So . . . tell me about the suicide."

Margit poured me another glass of whisky. I tossed it back. Even though I had already downed half the bottle, I still felt nothing.

"First I have to tell you about the abortion business," I said.

"Your friend had to have an abortion?"

"No. It was alleged that I was trying to talk her into having an abortion . . . which was certainly news to me. That day—the day I woke up on Douglas's couch to find his front lawn under siege by reporters—all hell broke loose. By six that evening, it was a major story across Ohio: PROFESSOR TRIES TO FORCE FRESHMAN STUDENT TO HAVE ABORTION AFTER AFFAIR.

"Now, you have to understand that I never, never, spoke with Shelley about an abortion. Nor was I even aware that Shelley was pregnant. In fact, it struck me as virtually impossible that she was carrying my child, as I had used a condom when we slept together."

"So how did this fantastic story about you trying to talk her into a termination go public?"

"It seems that Shelley had kept a journal since we'd started seeing each other. When all the shit hit the fan, the proctor in her dormitory—a real little goody-goody born-again Christian type—carried out her own raid on Shelley's room, found the journal, and dutifully turned it over to the dean of the faculty. As it turns out, Shelley's journal was full of crazy romantic stuff: about me being the love of her life, about me telling her that I had never felt so passionate about anyone before—something I never said—and also promising her that I'd leave my wife and daughter to marry her—another complete fabrication. This romantic fantasia went on and on for pages, and recounted, in prurient detail, the afternoon we spent together in that Toledo motel—something the press leaped upon after the diary was leaked to them . . ."

"Leaked by Robson?"

"As I found out later. But though the media loved all the graphic stuff in the diary about our afternoon of love—Shelley's exact words— they really went crazy when they read a long sequence of entries about her wanting to be the mother of my baby. Then, after I decided to break it off with her, her imagination went wild. Suddenly there were statements in the diary like, *How could he do this to me when he knows I'm pregnant?* and, *All I want is to have our child, but Harry tells me he will never allow that.* And then there was the kiss of death: *I got the results of the pregnancy test today. I am a Mom-to-Be! I raced to Harry's office to tell him the good news. But his reaction was horrible and absolute: the baby must die. And he picked up the phone and called an abortion clinic in Cleveland and made us an appointment in three days' time. But there's no way I will kill our baby.*

"Margit, I swear to you, I never had any of those conversations with Shelley. It was pure invention on her part."

"And one which the dean must have looked upon as a gift from God."

"Not just the dean, but every right-wing press commentator in the country. The story played right into their hands: 'progressive' professor seduces young student and then insists on 'murdering' their baby. I was held up as an example of everything that was degenerate and sordid about the so-called liberal elite . . . while Shelley was considered a heroine for saving the life of her unborn child.

"All the television stations staked out my house—and showed my wife and daughter being ambushed by the press as they left our home. One of the journalists actually asked Megan, 'What do you think of your father having a girlfriend who is only three years older than you?' She burst into tears and I wanted to kill that bastard.

"They also showed footage of some greasy lawyer for Shelley's father—an ex-marine whom she loathed—telling the cameras that he was filing, on behalf of his client, a hundred-million-dollar lawsuit against the college for allowing a degenerate like me to teach there. There was also a sound bite with Robson, where he put on this face of gravitas and concern, saying how it was horrible that 'this poor young woman' had been victimized by me, and how he would personally ensure that I never entered a center of higher education again."

"And where was Shelley during all of this?"

"Her parents had taken her home to Cincinnati—where she was kept locked away from the press."

"And meanwhile . . ."

"I stayed in Douglas's basement and ignored all knocks on the door and all phone calls. But I did email a statement to the press, in which I categorically denied that I had ever demanded the abortion, as she had never told me that she was pregnant. And as we had practiced safe sex . . .

"Well, this created a new feeding frenzy. The next day the television crews caught Shelley and her family en route to church, and started hurling questions at her like, 'Are you lying about being pregnant? Did you make it all up . . . ?' Shelley looked like a deer caught in the headlights. Later that afternoon, the family lawyer issued a statement, saying that I was being even more of a monster by calling Shelley a liar . . . and how they would have certified medical substantiation of her pregnancy within forty-eight hours.

"In the middle of all this madness, Doug was fantastic. He ran interference for me, keeping all intruders at bay and screening all phone calls . . . except for one from Megan, which came right after Shelley's lawyer appeared on TV, saying that I was a beast. Megan must have gotten the number from Susan—who, in turn, had to have been told by Robson where I was hiding out. Anyway, when I got on the line, I started saying something lame like, 'Megan, darling, I know this is awful. And I know you must hate me for all this. But I just want you to know—'

"She cut me off. 'I never want to talk to you again,' she said, crying. Then she hung up.

"Naturally I called her straight back. Susan answered—and said, her voice completely calm, 'You will never see—or hear from—your daughter again.' And then she added, 'If I were you I'd kill myself.'

"But it was Shelley who did that. Late that night, while everyone was asleep, she left her parents' house. Around two hours later, she jumped off a highway overpass a mile from where they lived. She landed right in the path of an oncoming truck. The cops said someone saw her standing on the overpass for several minutes before she jumped. This led them to surmise that she was waiting for some large vehicle to approach."

"Or maybe she was trying to find the courage to jump."

"She left no note, or any hint that she was planning to . . ."

I fell silent and reached for the whisky bottle, pouring myself another substantial slug.

"Do you think she jumped because she was about to be revealed as a fantasist?"

"Perhaps. Or maybe her father had been making her life hell for her. And if her obsessive behavior was anything to go by, she was certainly not in the most balanced and reasonable state . . . which, in turn, was all due to me breaking it off with her."

"Harry—if the diary proved anything, it's that she lived in a fantasy world. She didn't reveal the extent of her compulsions while you were getting friendly with each other . . . which means she was either very good at disguising her manias or you were completely blind to them. But knowing you, I sense it was the former. Had she shown telltale signs of obsessiveness—"

"I would have ended it well before we slept together."

"My point entirely. But instead, she wove this fiction about 'having your baby.' Robson went public with it. You countered, saying she was making it up. When faced with probable exposure as a fantasist, she killed herself."

"That's one interpretation."

"Was it your friend Douglas who found out all the details of the suicide?" Margit asked.

I nodded.

"And did he inform you about Robson and your ex-wife?"

"Doug finally did tell me about the rumors going around. He also admitted that he had known about them for the past few months—but felt uneasy about telling me, in case it blew over. I understood—especially as I never told Doug that I knew that, a couple of years earlier, his ex-wife had been sleeping with the college librarian . . . who was also a woman.

"Anyway, Doug was also unable to accuse Robson of leaking both the story and Shelley's diary to the press. He was coming up for promotion in a few months and, if he crossed Robson, he was finished. Still, privately, he was appalled—and encouraged me to simply disappear. 'You start exposing Robson now, and it's going to look like you're trying to deflect responsibility. It's really best if you just vanish.'

"The next day, the Cincinnati medical examiner revealed that Shelley hadn't been pregnant when she killed herself. Within an hour, the family lawyer issued a statement saying that it was medically plausible that her period had been several weeks late—and that the pregnancy test might have been faulty. 'Whether or not she was actually carrying Professor Ricks's child,' he said, 'is less important than the fact that she thought she was pregnant—and that Ricks, upon hearing the news, dropped her and insisted on the abortion . . . a demand that sent her fragile psyche into a downward spiral, eventually resulting in her suicide. Ricks, in essence, murdered this poor young woman.'

"Well, this spin on the story played everywhere—and I decided to take Doug's advice. I got him to go over to my house when Susan wasn't there to collect my passport and laptop. I went downtown to my bank. When I walked in, the manager told me that my patronage was no longer welcome here. I said, 'Fine by me, because I'm closing my account.' I had twenty-two thousand dollars in a savings account. I transferred fifteen of that into a mutual fund for Megan. I took the rest in cash—and grabbed my things at Doug's and got into my beat-up Volvo and left town. Eight hours later I was in Chicago. I found a cheap hotel—four hundred and fifty dollars a week—off Lake Shore Drive. I parked my bags and drove out into the 'burbs and stopped at the first used-car lot I found and accepted three grand in cash for my Volvo. Then I caught a cab back to the subway, returned to the hotel, and began a life of . . . well, nothing, really. My room was shabby, but adequate. It had a lumpy bed, and an old television, and a toilet that flushed, if you were lucky, on the third go. But the management asked no questions, and I paid my weekly bill on time, and didn't ever complain or say much to them during the weeks I was there."

"How many weeks?"

"Six."

"What did you do during that time?"

"I forget."

"I see."

"It's the truth. I remember sleeping until noon every day and always having breakfast in the same little luncheonette, and never buying a newspaper or magazine because I was afraid of reading something about the case. I never checked my email. I spent a lot of time at the movies. I bought paperbacks in secondhand shops, I drank in down-at-heel bars near the hotel, then watched shit television half the night. I suppose I was in total shock. I never had any sort of emotional highs or lows. I just dragged myself through the day like the walking dead. Until, one evening, I came home from an all-day session at the same multiplex cinema. The night porter on duty told me that a guy had come by that morning, asking for me. 'He looked like some sort of process server to me,' he said, and added that he was certain to come back very early the next morning, 'because that's what those assholes all do.'

"I went upstairs and called Doug. He asked me why the hell hadn't I answered any of the emails he'd sent me, and did I know that Shelley's father had made good on his threat to sue the college? The college, in turn, had decided (at Robson's urging) to sue me for defamation of their public reputation, gross professional negligence, and so forth, and had hired a private detective to find me. 'If you're calling me, the gumshoe has obviously tracked you down,' Doug said. When I explained that it seemed I was about to be served papers, he told me to flee immediately. 'Get out of the country now, otherwise prepare to be destroyed in the courts.'

"So I said, 'OK, I'll get the next flight to Paris.'"

"And once you got here?"

"I did manage to get back into contact with Megan—and we actually started a correspondence until her mother found out and put an end to it. I haven't heard from my daughter since then. But after they reached some sort of smallish payoff arrangement with Shelley's dad, the college did decide to drop its threatened action against me. According to Doug, the college's board of directors overruled Robson, who wanted me pursued to the ends of the earth."

"That man really has it in for you."

"Yes. It's not enough that I have been ruined. He won't be happy until he sees me completely crushed."

"And if you could be revenged against him . . . ?"

"I don't want revenge."

"Yes, you do. And you deserve it. So does Shelley. Had he not leaked any of this to the press, she would probably still be alive today. So what do you think would be an appropriate payback for all the harm he perpetrated?"

"You want me to fantasize here?" I asked.

"Absolutely. The worst thing that could happen to the bastard."

"You mean, like discovering that he had a huge collection of kiddy porn on his computer?"

"That would do nicely. And say you wanted to devise an appropriate punishment for your ex-wife . . . ?"

"Now let's not get ridiculous here . . ."

"Go on, it's just loose talk."

"If she lost her job—"

"You'd feel vindicated then?"

"Why are you playing this game?"

"To help you."

"Help me . . . what? Psychologically?"

"The talking cure is a good one—especially when it comes to articulating your anger, your grief. But it doesn't fully close the wound."

"Then what does?"

She shrugged and said nothing. Except, "You need to be on your way now. We will continue talking in three days' time, if that's fine with you."

"Of course."

"We might even have sex the next time . . . as you might be feeling less guilty about fucking that barmaid. You will definitely tell her to go crying to her husband about Omar's horrible assault on her."

"I'm dreading the idea—"

"You will dread a beating even more. *À très bientôt . . .*"

Having now done what Margit had demanded—having spoken to Yanna and hatched my plan with her—I felt strangely calm. Though there was a part of me that wanted to go to Mr. Beard and make up some story about having to leave town for a few days on "personal business," I decided to stay put and see just how things played out . . . like someone playing Russian roulette, who was certain it was worth staying in the game because the odds were six to one that he wouldn't get his brains blown out.

Back in my office later that night, I opened my laptop and went to work. My novel was now more than four hundred pages in length. The doubts that haunted the early months of writing had been replaced by a fierce momentum—and the sense that the novel was starting to write itself. This was another reason why I was loath to run away from this small nocturnal cell. Its claustrophobic bleakness had become almost talismanic to me; the place where, free from all outside distraction, I pounded out the words and moved the story on. And I feared if I suddenly left this room, the writing would stop. So despite all the creeping doubts about everything to do with this job, this quartier, I was determined to stay working here until the novel was finished. Then, one day, I'd simply pack up my things and slip away. Until then—

Why is somebody screaming downstairs?

The scream was loud, shrill, alarming. It had an almost animalistic intensity—like that of a wild beast caught in a trap and howling in torment. After a moment it fell silent. Then I could hear the same voice engaged in loud supplications, followed by other voices shouting him down, and then . . .

The scream this time was agonizing. Pain was being inflicted in a merciless manner. When a further howl pierced the concrete walls of my room, I found myself on my feet and unbolting the door. But as soon as I yanked it open, the howling stopped. I peered downstairs into an empty corridor. I walked down several steps and stared at the door at the end of the corridor on the ground floor. A voice in my head whispered, *Are you out of your fucking mind?* I dashed upstairs, closed the door and bolted it again, trying my best to secure it quietly. But it still made a decisive thwack when I pushed it home. After a minute, the howling started again. This time, the other voices started to shout, the howls became hysterical, a word—*Yok! Yok! Yok!*—was repeated over and over again by the man who was screaming. There was further shouting, then one final appalling screech . . . then a deep, eerie silence.

I sat at my desk, chewing on a finger, feeling helpless, terrified. *Don't move, don't move. But if you hear footsteps coming up the stairs, grab your laptop and make a dash for the emergency exit* (not that I had any idea where that exit might actually bring me).

Ten, fifteen, twenty minutes went by. I kept staring at the television monitor. No one appeared on its fuzzy screen. Twenty-five minutes. Silence. Then, suddenly, I heard the downstairs door open and footsteps in the corridor. The front door opened. A man came out into the lane. He appeared short—but it was hard to discern anything about him, as he had the hood of his parka pulled up around his head to conceal his face. He also had a broom in one hand. *What the hell is he doing with that?* I wondered—until he thrust the broom handle at the camera hanging above the door. I flinched—because the image that appeared on the monitor made it seem like he was jabbing the broom handle directly at me. With the first blow the camera just shook. With the second, he scored a bull's-eye on the lens and the screen went black. Then I could hear whispered voices and low grunts accompanied by the sound of something heavy being dragged along the corridor. The dragging sound stopped, there were more whispers—*Were they checking that the coast was clear before hoisting the body?*—then the sound of further dragging before the front door closed with a dull thud.

Don't panic. Don't panic . . .

But say they come back for you . . . ?

If I left now, they could be waiting for me outside. I'd see who they were . . . and that would be, at best, unfortunate. If I waited here, at least I'd be sending a signal that I was playing by the rules. I wasn't going to ask questions, go to the cops, make trouble.

I was desperate to flee. I couldn't flee. But as soon as my watch read 6 AM, I was gone. Though I wanted to take a long walk by the Canal Saint-Martin to try to calm down, I sensed that it was best to stick to my usual routine, just in case somebody might be watching my movements. So I hung on until 6 AM, went to the *boulangerie* and bought my *pains au chocolat,* then returned to my room, where I found a new note stuck under my door:

I GIVE YOU TWO MORE DAYS, NO MORE. 1000 EUROS OR I TELL.

I crumpled up the note and shoved it into my pocket. Then I went inside and took a Zopiclone and crawled into bed.

Up as usual at two. At the Internet café thirty minutes later. But as soon as I walked in, I could tell that Mr. Beard knew all about last night. Because he came out from behind the bar and locked the front door, then motioned for me to follow him into a back room. When I hesitated, he said, "You do not leave here until we have a talk."

"Let's talk here," I said, thinking if some stooges emerged from the back room, I'd have some minor chance of throwing myself through the glass of the front window and getting away with mere major lacerations.

"It's quiet in the back."

"We'll talk here," I said.

A pause. I could see him staring out at the street, looking just a little paranoid.

"What you see last night?" he asked.

"I saw some vandal smash the television camera."

"Before that?"

"Nothing."

"Nothing?"

"That's right: nothing."

"I don't believe you. You opened the door. They heard you."

"They heard wrong."

"You lie. They heard. They know."

"I didn't hear a sound all night. I never left the room all night. The only thing out of the ordinary was the clown who threw something at the camera—"

"You see his face?"

"He had a hood pulled up over his head, so it was hard to—"

"Why you think he broke the camera?"

"How should I know?"

"You lie."

"Lie about what?"

"You know what happened. And if the police ask you what you heard?"

"Why would the police do that?"

"If the police ask you . . ."

"I'd tell them what I told you: I heard nothing."

Silence. He reached into his jacket pocket and tossed my pay envelope on the floor. I decided not to raise objections to this little act of aggression, and instead played the subservient role demanded of me and leaned over to pick up the envelope. As I stood up again he said, "They know you heard the screams. They know you left the room—because they heard you leave the room. You don't do that again. Understand?"

"Yes," I said quietly.

I tried to go about my business that day. But as I sat down in a restaurant for lunch, as I took the metro out to Bercy for a screening of Kazan's *Splendor in the Grass,* as I sipped a coffee afterward in the little brasserie opposite the Cinémathèque, I couldn't help but wonder, *Is someone watching me?* I kept scanning people near me to see if I noticed the same recurring face. Walking down a street, I'd stop and spin around in an attempt to catch the man tailing me. But I saw no one. Still, I was taking no chances. I resisted the temptation to use a phone kiosk and call the walk-in clinic to get the results of my HIV test—out of fear that someone would report back to them that I was seen on the phone and, ergo, to the cops. So I decided to go there myself, my apprehension about the result somewhat tempered by everything else that had happened in the past twenty-four hours.

The clinic was open until eight. I arrived half an hour before closing time. The doctor I had seen was in the reception area as I walked in.

"What brings you back here?" he asked.

"I just came by for the test results."

"You could have phoned."

"I'd rather hear them in person."

He shrugged, as if to say, *If you insist.* Then he turned to the receptionist and told her my name (I was impressed that he remembered me). She riffled around an inbox until she found the necessary file and handed it to him. He motioned for me to follow him into his office. I shut the door behind us. He settled into his desk chair and opened the file and started to read. I studied his face—in a manner similar to a defendant staring at the foreman of a jury as he returns holding the verdict envelope in his hand.

"Please sit down, Mr. Ricks," the doctor said.

"Bad news?"

"No need to be a fatalist, monsieur. The HIV test came back negative. However, I must inform you that you did test positive for another sexually transmitted disease: chlamydia."

"I see," I said.

"It is not a serious condition, and can easily be treated with antibiotics . . ."

"I thought only women got chlamydia."

"Think again."

He started scribbling something on a script pad.

"You will need to take these four times a day, and drink at least three liters of water daily. And no unprotected sex for three weeks."

Three weeks! Margit would be thrilled to hear this—though the fact that I might have also given her a sexually transmitted disease would probably overshadow that minor detail.

"It is also advised that you do not drink alcohol during this course of antibiotics. It diminishes their efficacy."

Better and better. Three weeks without booze. How could I get through this life of mine without booze?

"Naturally, you will also need to inform all your sexual partners of this condition."

How do you know that I have "partners" and not just a partner? Or is my ever-growing sleaziness that apparent?

"I would also strongly advise you to return after the course of antibiotics for another blood test—just to be certain that there is no ongoing ambiguity."

Doctor, there is always ongoing ambiguity . . . not to mention ongoing worry, as the past few days have shown.

"Fine," I said. "Just fine."

After stopping off at a late-night pharmacy on the boulevard de Sébastopol and handing over an exorbitant thirty-eight euros for the prescribed tablets, I decided to get the first bit of nasty business over with. I returned to the rue de Paradis and walked into Yanna's bar. It was a slow night. There were only three other customers there—and they were conveniently installed in a table toward the back. Yanna's eyes grew wide as I sat down at the otherwise empty bar.

"I thought I told you not to come here anymore," she hissed.

"Did you speak to your husband?"

"He was delayed. He comes back tomorrow."

She glanced nervously at the customers at the back table.

"Order a drink," she whispered, "otherwise they will get suspicious."

"Water."

"Water?"

"Not my idea of a good time, believe me. But I am on antibiotics."

"For what?" she asked.

That's when I told her. She turned several shades of white.

"You fucker," she hissed. "You gave me—"

"I gave you that? Think again, madame. It's a female condition that's passed on to the male." I had no idea if this was true. "And since I haven't been sleeping around—"

"Liar."

"I caught this from you. And who knows where you caught it. Maybe your husband—"

"Get out," she said.

"Not before you see this," I said, and passed her the crumpled note that Omar had left under my door. She opened it up, glanced at it, then handed it back to me.

"*Cochon,*" she said.

"You've got to tell your husband as soon as he arrives."

"Believe me, I will. And I'll also tell him that Omar raped me and gave me this condition."

"Now hang on . . ." I said, thinking if she told her husband that, it would result in an automatic death sentence for Omar.

"I hope he kills him," she said. "And if you don't get out now, I'll also tell him that you tried to interfere with me as well."

I stared at her furious face—and knew that I should not pursue this discussion any further.

Some hours later, staring at the screen of my laptop, ticking off the hours until 6:00 AM, I wondered, *Why do I have this singular talent for making women angry at me?* Or, to cut to the heart of the matter, *Why do I always seem to fuck it up?* But this was superseded by a larger concern: Omar. The sonofabitch was a blackmailer and a moron who wouldn't think anything of selling me down the river. Still, the scheme that Margit devised for tripping him up would now result in . . . well, a fast death might be the mildest of punishments once Yanna's husband and his collection of goons got their hands on the man who had "raped" his wife and given her a disease (even though Yanna's husband probably picked it up from one of the whores he frequently slept with). The twisted morality of all this—do I endanger somebody who is threatening to endanger me?—preoccupied me all night. Then dawn came and I was out in the street, walking back to my *chambre de bonne,* a bag of *pains au chocolat* in hand.

I mounted the stairs to my room. When I reached my floor, my bladder felt full from all the water I had been drinking that night (doctor's orders), so I turned toward the hallway toilet.

I opened the door and suddenly jumped back in horror, a scream leaping out of my throat. There before me was Omar. He lay slumped on the toilet seat. His throat had been cut. There was blood everywhere. And a toilet brush was sticking out of his mouth.

FIFTEEN

INSPECTOR JEAN-MARIE COUTARD was a flabby man. He was in his fifties and short—maybe five foot six—with a double chin, a large gut, and a red face that made him look self-basting. His clothes were a jumble of contrasting styles and patterns: a checkered sports jacket, gray trousers, a striped shirt dappled with food stains, a paisley tie. His lack of sartorial interest mirrored his general air of unhealthiness. He had a cigarette screwed into his mouth, and he seemed to be puffing away on it in an attempt to wake himself up. It was only seven fifteen in the morning, and he looked like he had been summoned directly from his bed to this crime scene.

When he arrived, there was already a crowd of people around the tiny bathroom. Three plainclothes policemen, two forensic guys in white coats and latex gloves, a photographer, and a medical man examining the grotesque mess that was Omar. Two plainclothes inspectors then showed up, one of whom was Coutard.

The uniformed cops had been the first on the scene. They came within ten minutes of me racing downstairs and calling them from the phone kiosk at the end of rue de Paradis. Running out to phone them had been an instinctual reaction—and one made in the complete shock of the moment. As soon as I had done so, the thought struck me, *They are going to ask where I was when the crime took place.* As I couldn't tell them about my "work," I raced back to my room and "unmade" my bed, hoping that it looked like I had slept there that night. Then I started thinking fast, trying to construct the alibi I would give the cops when they arrived.

I charged downstairs again to let the police in: two young officers who followed me upstairs and tried hard not to blanch when they saw the bloody state of Omar in the toilet. Within moments they were calling for backup. One of them posted himself outside to make certain nobody left the building. The other stepped into my room with me and asked to see my papers. When I handed over the American passport, he looked at me quizzically.

"Why do you live here?" he asked.

"It's cheap."

Then he began to ask me some basic questions. What time did I find the body? Where was I last night? ("I couldn't sleep, so I went out for a walk.") What time was that? ("Around two.") And where did I go? ("I just walked along the canal Saint-Martin, then eventually crossed the river and followed the Seine as far as Notre-Dame, then headed back here, stopping at the local pâtisserie for *pains au chocolat*.") Did I know the deceased? ("We were merely passing acquaintances.") Did I have any idea who might have done this? ("None at all.")

After this brief Q&A, I was told to wait here in my room until the inspector arrived. The cop held on to my passport—and left me alone to my thoughts. My alibi sounded flimsy, full of holes . . . though, at least, they'd be able to confirm with the guy at the pâtisserie that I was there around six this morning. I lay down on my bed and shut my eyes and tried to expunge every grisly detail of Omar on that toilet: the splatter-effect crimson blood, the deep oozing gorge around his throat, the fact that his trousers were down and he must have been in mid-bowel movement when the attack happened. Two people must have killed him: one held him down while his partner shoved the toilet brush in his mouth to stifle his screams before slitting his throat. Had Yanna somehow managed to call her husband that night in Turkey to tell him about the "rape," and then he phoned some friends who . . . ?

No, that was completely implausible—as Yanna told me he was on the night flight back to Paris yesterday. Which meant he would have been out of contact. So rule out Yanna's husband. But knowing Omar—and how he pissed off everyone who ventured into his path—he must have had a lot of enemies.

That was Inspector Coutard's first question to me.

"Did the deceased have any ongoing disputes with anyone?"

I had figured this question would arise and decided to play dumb.

"I didn't know the man."

"Even though he lived next door to you?"

"We didn't speak."

"You shared the same floor, the same toilet."

"You can share a communal toilet and still not speak with someone."

Coutard reached into his jacket pocket and pulled out my passport. I tried not to look surprised. He flicked through its pages, stopping at the two sole entry stamps.

"You entered France on December 28 of last year, via Canada."

"That's right. My connecting flight was from Montreal."

"From where?"

"Chicago."

"That is where you last lived in the United States?"

"No, I lived in . . ."

And I named the town in Ohio.

"And what made you come to France on December 28 of last year?"

I was prepared for this.

"My marriage had fallen apart and I had lost my job at the college where I taught, and I decided to flee my problems, so . . ."

"There are no direct flights from Chicago to Paris?" he asked, and I could see the subtext behind that question: if you flew here via another country, perhaps you weren't just fleeing a failed marriage.

"The Air Canada flight via Montreal was the cheapest option."

"What sort of work do you do, Monsieur Ricks?"

"Novelist."

"What is the name of your publisher?"

"I don't have one."

"Ah, so you are an aspiring novelist."

"That's right."

"And you have lived on the rue de Paradis since . . . ?"

"Early January."

"An intriguing place for an American to live—but I'm certain you have been asked this question already today."

"Yes, I have."

"And your neighbor, the late Monsieur Omar Tariq. He was a good neighbor?"

"We had little contact."

"Do you know anything about him?"

"Nothing at all."

He nodded, taking this in. Then, "No sense whatsoever of who might have done this to him?"

"Like I said, I stayed out of his way."

He tapped my passport against his hand, looking directly at me. Then he slipped the passport in his pocket.

"You will be required to make a statement about all this—so if you wouldn't mind, I ask that you present yourself at the *commissariat de police* for the Tenth arrondissement at two this afternoon."

"Fine. I'll be there. And what about my passport?"

"I'll keep it until then."

He left my room. I sat down on the bed and suddenly felt very tired and just a little worried that I was playing it a bit too dumb about having had no contact with Omar. But if I told the truth, I might put myself under suspicion, and they also might start demanding to know what I did with my nights. And if they found out I was working illegally . . .

My guess was that Omar owed somebody money or had done something grievous enough to be bumped off in such an unpleasant manner. No doubt, the cops would question everyone in the building. No doubt, someone would tip them off as to who was the assailant.

My lack of sleep—it was now 9:00 AM—somehow managed to override the nightmarish image of Omar in death. I nodded off for a few hours, waking with a jolt when I heard something bang against my door. I jumped up from the bed, opened the door, and found four ambulance attendants trying to maneuver a stretcher with the now bagged body of Omar down the stairs. The ambulance guys looked up at me as I stood, half awake in the doorway. Then, with several audible groans, they continued attempting to inch this stretcher containing a very overweight dead man down the narrow, circular stairs.

I went back inside and checked the time: 12:48 PM. I showered and shaved and dressed, choosing conservative clothes for my interview with the police. When I went out into the hallway, there were several technical guys still working on the toilet and Omar's room, picking up every microfiber in the vicinity. Downstairs, a uniformed cop was still posted outside the door.

"No one is allowed to leave the building," he said.

"But Inspector Coutard asked to see me at the *commissariat de police* at two PM."

"Your name?" he asked me. I gave it to him. He picked up his walkie-talkie and spoke into it. I heard him mention "Monsieur Harry Ricks." There was a static-filled pause, then a voice coming over the speaker. The cop lifted it to his ear, then said, "D'accord," and turned to me.

"Yes, you are expected at the *commissariat de police* at two PM sharp. Do not be late, monsieur."

I nodded and hurried off to the Internet café. Once inside, Mr. Beard immediately shut the front door, locking it behind him.

"What have you told the police?" he asked.

"News travels fast."

"What have you told the police?"

"I've said nothing."

"Nothing?"

"I told them Omar was my neighbor, I didn't know him, I had no idea who might kill him, and that's all."

"They ask you about your work?"

"Not yet."

"Not yet?"

"I have to go to the *commissariat de police* now and make a statement."

"You must tell them nothing about your work."

"Believe me, I won't."

"You must tell them nothing about what you saw the other night."

"As I told you at the time, I saw nothing."

"If they ask you what you do—"

"I will continue to tell them I am a writer. That's it. Happy now?"

"If you say anything else, we will find out. And then—"

"There is no need to threaten me. I certainly don't want to be exposed as someone working illegally here. So don't worry. I'm not going to give the game away."

"I don't trust you."

"You have no choice but to. Just as I have no choice but to trust you . . . even though I don't either. Now may I have my money, please?"

He reached into his jacket and handed me the usual envelope.

"You say nothing, life will continue as before," he told me.

"That sounds good to me."

"Omar was a pig. He deserved his death."

I felt like saying, *No one—not even gross-out Omar—deserved that sort of gruesome finale.* But I held myself in check.

"See you tomorrow," I said.

"Yeah," Mr. Beard said, "tomorrow."

The *commissariat de police* for the Tenth arrondissement was located on the rue du Louis Blanc. It was an ordinary squat building—three stories high—which didn't stand out amid the other squat shabby buildings along this street. There was a man behind the reception desk as I came in. I told him I was here to see Inspector Coutard and gave him my name. He told me to take a seat. The chairs were cheap plastic ones. The walls of the reception area were painted an institutional beige. There were ceiling tiles gone yellow from extended exposure to cigarette smoke, and fluorescent tubes, and posters taped to the walls, exhorting all citizens to be vigilant about bags left on the metro, and to not drink and drive. A framed photo of Chirac hung in a discreet corner of the room. After a few minutes, a youngish man in shirt-sleeves—his gun and holster exposed for all to see—popped his head through the door.

"Monsieur Ricks?"

I stood up. The cop introduced himself as Inspector Leclerc. He ushered me inside and down a flight of steps. We came into an open area, where two men sat shackled to a bench. (I quickly noticed there were two other empty shackles at the far end of this long bench awaiting new customers, as well as a man locked into a small cell adjacent to the bench.)

"Busy afternoon?" I asked the inspector.

"It's always busy here," he said.

I followed him down a corridor and into a cramped office with two desks. Leclerc took a seat at the first one, pushed aside some papers, lit up a cigarette, and explained that he would take my statement from me. He then talked me, point by point, through everything that had happened when I discovered Omar, and also asked me (as Coutard had done) about my relationship with my neighbor.

"I saw him from time to time in the corridor of our building," I dictated to Leclerc. "I saw him from time to time in the street and around the quartier. Beyond that, we had no additional contact."

When Leclerc finished typing, he reread the statement to me and asked if I agreed with it. When I nodded yes, he hit a button on his keyboard and a copy whizzed out of an adjoining printer.

"Please read it, then sign and date it."

After I had done so, he said, "Now we need to fingerprint you."

"I thought I was just being called in to make a statement."

"You must be fingerprinted as well."

Am I a suspect here? I felt like asking. But I knew the answer to that question, just as I also knew that if I refused to be fingerprinted, I would be acting guilty.

"Lead the way," I said.

He escorted me to another room—where a technician rolled each of my fingers in ink and then made the necessary imprints. I was pointed to a sink and told I could wash my hands there. As I finished, Leclerc said, "You will need to wait outside while I get your statement to Inspector Coutard. If he needs to interview you further, you'll be summoned to his office."

"How long might that be?"

"It is a busy afternoon . . ."

He stood up and escorted me to the bench where the two men still sat shackled to its steel frame.

"You can wait here," Leclerc said.

"You mean, you're not going to shackle me down?" I asked.

A sour smile from Leclerc.

"Not unless you insist."

The two men on the bench eyed me up and down. When I met the gaze of one of them—and saw a druggy aggression in his dilated pupils—he hissed, "What are you staring at, asshole?"

"Nothing," I hissed back.

"You trying to start something?"

I just shook my head. But when he jumped up to confront me, the chain on his hand stopped his trajectory and caused him to yelp in pain.

"I'll get you later," he said.

"Don't count on it."

I sat at the far end of the bench and pulled out a new book I was plowing through—a collection of Jacques Prévert's *Paroles*. Though I greatly admired his wordplay and imagery, I wished I had brought something more narrative-driven to read. I tried to ignore the clown at the end of the bench. Having been, in his mind, "provoked" because I'd looked at him the wrong way, he continued to jeer at me, until one of the uniformed cops came along and told him to shut up. When he back-talked the cop—"You think you scare me, flic?"—the officer took his nightstick and slammed it down a few centimeters away from where he was sitting. The guy jumped in fright.

"Keep shooting off your mouth, the next time it will land between your legs."

I pulled the volume of Prévert higher up around my face.

Either Coutard was truly busy or he was deliberately ignoring me, as half an hour passed without a word from him. I stopped a uniformed officer and asked him if he could find out whether or not Coutard wanted to see me. Twenty more minutes passed, during which time the thought struck me: *This is the law-enforcement version of "passive aggressive."* I stopped another officer.

"Might you please find out if Inspector Coutard—"

"He will call you when he's ready."

"But I have been waiting nearly an hour—"

"So? An hour is nothing. Sit down and he'll call you when—"

"Sir, please—"

"Sit!" This wasn't a request; rather, an order. I did as told. The thug—still chained to the bench—glowered at me.

"They've got you by the balls, asshole."

"And you're the guy chained to the bench."

"Fuck you."

The uniformed cop—halfway out of the room—spun around and pointed his baton at me. "You—no talking."

"This guy started it—"

"I said, no talking."

I nodded, looking meek. The psycho laughed. I tried to sink back into Prévert's verses. Psycho Boy continued cackling to himself and occasionally whispering to the other shackled guy. Fifteen minutes passed, then twenty, then . . .

This is crazy. Just get up and leave—and let them try to stop you.

But as I was seriously considering this stupid idea, Coutard stuck his head around the door.

"Monsieur Ricks . . ."

He motioned for me to follow him. As we left the holding area and headed down a corridor, he said, "I am sorry they kept you waiting with the local trash."

I said nothing—pretty damn certain that I was placed next to Psycho Boy to unnerve me . . . which, truth be told, he succeeded in doing.

"Just in here," he said, steering me into a more substantial office than the one occupied by Leclerc. There were two functional armchairs facing a large desk, several framed citations, the ubiquitous photograph of Chirac, and a brimming ashtray next to his computer terminal. He lit up a fresh cigarette and picked up a pair of bifocal glasses and placed them on his nose.

"So, Monsieur Ricks . . . I have read your statement. Interesting."

"Interesting?" I asked cautiously.

"Yes, interesting. In fact . . . very interesting."

"In what way?"

"In your statement, you repeat what you told me in your *chambre* yesterday—that you only had minimal contact with Monsieur Omar. And yet, the gentleman who rented you the room, Monsieur Sezer, made a statement to us, where he stated that you had an ongoing war with Monsieur Omar over his sanitary habits . . . specifically, the condition of the toilet you both shared."

"That's true, but—"

"The fact that Monsieur Omar was found dead with a toilet brush in his mouth—"

"Now hang on a minute—"

"You have an unfortunate habit of interrupting me, Monsieur Ricks."

"Sorry," I mumbled.

"I repeat: according to Monsieur Sezer, you repeatedly complained to him about Monsieur Omar's lack of hygiene. Couple this with the fact that a toilet brush was found lodged in Monsieur Omar's mouth, and this leads one to presume that the murderer was making some sort of symbolic point about the gentleman's disregard for communal cleanliness. So . . ."

I raised my hand. Coutard peered down at me over his bifocals.

"You have a question?" he asked.

"More of a statement."

"You have already made a statement."

"But I want to add to that statement."

"You have signed that statement."

"All I want to say is—"

"You wish to amend your statement."

"I didn't kill Omar."

A shrug from the inspector.

"You expect me to accept that as truth?"

"Consider this: I called you to report the crime."

"In sixty-five percent of the murders I have investigated, the actual killer reported the crime."

"I am part of the thirty-five percent."

"Sticking a toilet brush down your victim's throat while cutting his jugular . . . It is most original."

"I didn't—"

"You say you didn't, but you had a motive: rage at his disgusting habits. Let me guess: he never flushed the toilet after taking a shit, and then mocked you when you tried to get him to amend his vile ways. Americans, I know, have a thing about cleanliness . . . and smoking."

He exhaled a small cloud as he said that.

"I have nothing against cigarettes."

"I applaud you for such open-mindedness. You also have no objections to living in cramped conditions. In fact, I would posit that you might be the only American living on the rue de Paradis in a *chambre de bonne.*"

"It's cheap."

"We do know how you found the room. A certain Adnan Pafnuk, who worked at the Hôtel Sélect on the rue François Millet in the Sixteenth. You were a guest at this hotel from December 28 of last year for a period of ten days, during which time you fell sick with the flu and had a dispute with the day clerk—a Monsieur Brasseur . . ."

His face was impassive as he said this, but I could see him simultaneously studying mine . . . and registering my growing nervousness as the revelation hit me: I am the prime suspect here.

"Brasseur was a deeply unpleasant man."

"So we have learned from anyone who worked with him. Nonetheless, it is also intriguing to note that—just as you had a little war with Monsieur Omar and he was found dead on his beloved toilet—so you also had a little war with Monsieur Brasseur and he was struck down by a car—"

"You don't think that I—"

"What did I tell you about interrupting me, monsieur?"

I hung my head and wished a hole would open up in the floor and whisk me out of this nightmare. Coutard continued, "We have, of course, checked the motor vehicle records. You do not own a car, nor did you rent a car on the day that Monsieur Brasseur was run down. He remains paralyzed—and it appears that the condition is permanent. But who's to say that you didn't hire somebody to mow him down?"

"My motive being . . . ?"

"Wasn't there a dispute about money?"

"He overcharged me for the doctor who came to see me when I was ill."

"Voilà: the motive."

"I am not in the habit of running down people who cheat me, any more than I cut the throats of neighbors who treat the communal toilet like an open sewer."

"Perhaps. But the fact that your fingerprints are all over the toilet brush that had been shoved down Monsieur Omar's throat—"

I now knew why I had been kept waiting over ninety minutes. They were running a computer check, comparing my prints with those found at the crime scene.

"I used that brush to clean the toilet," I said.

"And you've just interrupted me again."

"Sorry."

"So you quarreled with Monsieur Brasseur. You quarreled with Monsieur Omar. But you befriended Monsieur Adnan. Was your friendship just a friendship?"

"What are you implying?"

"Once again, the peculiarity of the story is fascinating. Consider: an American comes to Paris and falls sick in a hotel. Nothing unusual about that. But then the same American meets a young Turkish gentleman in the hotel—and before you know it, he takes over his *chambre de bonne.* Now that is an unusual narrative twist, *n'est-ce pas?*"

I raised my hand. He nodded that I could speak.

"If I could explain . . ."

"Off you go."

I took him through everything that happened at the hotel, and how Adnan had looked after me, and how hearing that I was short on funds—

Now Coutard interrupted me.

"Because you had lost your job and had to flee the States after your tragic affair with your student?"

A long pause. I wasn't surprised that he knew this—but hearing him confront me with this fact still unnerved me.

"Your detective work is most impressive," I said.

"It must have been a great tragedy for you, losing your professorship, your family, your *maîtresse.*"

"Her death was the worst aspect of it all. The rest—"

"I saw all the press coverage—courtesy of Google. May I say something which is perhaps beyond my professional concern? As I read about your downfall, I actually felt sorry for you. So what if she was your student? She was over eighteen. She was not coerced. It was love, yes?"

"Absolutely."

"The fact that everyone accused you of trying to make her have an abortion—"

"I never even knew she was—"

"You do not have to plead your case with me, monsieur. As far as I'm concerned, you were a victim of a very American inability to accept moral complexity. It all must be black and white. Right and wrong."

"Isn't that what a police officer deals with all the time?"

"All criminal action is fundamentally gray. Because everyone has a shadow . . . and everyone is haunted. Which leads me to another curiosity about this case: your whereabouts at night. Monsieur Sezer told us you were usually out until dawn, and slept in most days until the early afternoon."

Sezer was evidently doing his best to shop me—for reasons best known to him. Did he have Omar bumped off? Was that why he was trying to pin it on me?

"I'm a night owl, yes."

"So what do you do all night?"

"Often I simply walk, or stop in an all-night café and write on my laptop. But many nights I am at home."

"But the owner of the *boulangerie* on the rue Montholon informed us that you arrive every morning just after six to buy two *pains au chocolat*. You do this without fail six mornings a week."

"I am a man who likes to stick to a fairly strict routine."

"Do you work somewhere at night?"

"Only on my novel."

"The novel that has yet to find a publisher?"

"Yes, I am an unpublished writer."

"Perhaps that will change."

"It will."

"I admire your self-belief. But I can't wholly believe that you simply walk all night or spend time writing in a twenty-four-hour café. Which café might that be, by the way?"

"I use several," I said, wondering if he could hear the lie in my voice.

"So which ones exactly?"

"There's this place in Les Halles called Le Tambour. And there's also the Mabillon on the boulevard Saint-Germain—"

"That's a long way from your quartier."

"Half an hour on foot."

"If you walk fast."

"All right, forty-five minutes if you're limping. As I told you, I like to wander at night."

"You're a flâneur?"

"Absolutely."

"Might you also be a flâneur who holds down a full-time job?"

"I don't have a *carte de séjour*."

"That has never stopped the vast majority of *immigrés* from working here. Professionally speaking, I don't care at all if you are holding down illegal employment or not. I am investigating a murder. As you are 'of interest' to us, I simply want to find out your whereabouts on the night of the murder."

"As I said, I was—"

"Yes, yes, strolling the streets of Paris like Gene Kelly. May I say that I don't believe you. I know you are hiding something. Clarity, monsieur, is essential now."

Why didn't I tell him about the all-night job? Because I might also be implicated in whatever was going on downstairs. And it still wouldn't clear me of suspicion in the death of Omar. Who would vouch for me being in full-time employment?

Nobody.

"I am hiding nothing, Inspector."

His lips tightened. He tapped two fingers on the desk. He reached for the phone. He swiveled around in his chair and spoke in a low voice. Then he hung up and swiveled back toward me.

"You are free to go, monsieur. But I must inform you that we will be keeping your passport . . . and that I advise you not to leave Paris."

"I'm going nowhere."

"We'll see about that."

SIXTEEN

THEY'RE FOLLOWING ME.

Now I was sure of this. Just as I was also sure that it was only a matter of time before they found out where I worked at night, and raided the place.

Someone's on your tail.

Had an innocent passerby seen me on the street, he would have thought, *That man is mad.* Because I had developed the paranoid habit of turning around every two minutes or so to see who was behind me. This was no neurotic knee-jerk response that only lasted a few hours after I was allowed to leave the *commissariat de police*. No, this became a full-blown tic—and one that was difficult to control. Every two minutes—one hundred and twenty seconds exactly (I was counting it down in my head)—I had to spin around and try to surprise the gumshoe who was shadowing me.

But no one was ever there.

That's because they know how to make themselves vanish . . . to duck into a doorway as soon as they see you twirling around.

Several times, this abrupt pirouette nearly landed me into trouble. An elderly African woman—using a walker to help her negotiate the Faubourg Saint-Martin—screamed when I spun around. I apologized profusely, but she still glared at me as if I was delusional. The second time, the victims were two young toughs. They were both around twenty, of Arab origin, dressed in tight leather jackets and wearing cheap sunglasses. Their initial shock was quickly replaced by umbrage and aggression. Immediately they grabbed me and shoved me into a doorway.

"What you fucking doing?" one of them hissed.

"I thought you were the cops."

"Stop talking shit," the other said. "You thought we were following you, right?"

"I honestly didn't think—"

"Racist asshole, thinks we're a couple of sand niggers, wanting to jump him for his cheap watch."

"I meant no disrespect. I—"

"Yes, you did," the first said, then spat on me. Simultaneously the other guy shoved me hard, knocking me off my feet.

"You do that again to us," he said, "we cut you the next times."

But as soon as I had picked myself up and wiped that man's spittle from my jacket and headed off down the street, I still found myself turning around every two minutes.

I'm sure they're there. I'm sure they're watching me at all times.

When I left the *commissariat*, I decided to do what I always do whenever life overwhelms me: I hid in a movie. (Come to think of it, I hide in a movie even if I am finding things moderately cope-able.) There was a Clint Eastwood festival at the Action Écoles—so I caught *The Beguiled.* (Wounded Civil War veteran ends up in a house of spinster women, starts sleeping his way through them, and pays a horrible price for his sexual profligacy . . . I must have been insane to have chosen this movie—especially as I had seen it twenty years earlier and therefore vaguely remembered what I was letting myself in for.)

Afterward, it was time for work. Now I turned around every minute, reducing this to thirty seconds as I approached the alleyway and the steel door, behind which . . .

I spun around. No one there. I walked back to the intersection of the alley and the street. I looked both ways. No one there. I walked back down the alley, turning one last time. No one there. I opened the door and locked it behind me. I went up to my office, knowing that tonight I wouldn't get a single word written . . . that I would be watching the monitor nonstop, just in case anyone suspicious poked their head into the alleyway, looking around.

My eyes hardly left the monitor for the entire six hours of my shift. Somewhere toward the end of the night, the thought struck me, *You're a little unhinged by all this.* To which the only reply could be, *Being under suspicion for murder does strange things to one's psyche.*

When I left my work at six, however, I did discover someone waiting at the end of the alley for me. It was Sezer's stooge, Mr. Tough Guy. He blocked my path as I approached him.

"Monsieur Sezer wants to see you," he said.

"At this hour?" I said, trying to appear cool—even though I was suddenly anything but cool.

"He is awake."

"I need to sleep."

"You sleep afterward."

"I'd like to stop by the *boulangerie* and pick up—"

He had me by the arm.

"You come now," he said.

So back we went to my building and up the stairs to Sezer Confection. Himself was seated behind his desk, sipping a demitasse of coffee.

"You keep early hours," I said.

"I don't need much sleep," he said. "Unlike you."

"How do you know that?"

"You come home every morning at six ten, six fifteen the latest, after stopping at the pâtisserie for two *pains au chocolat*. You sleep until two PM. You pick up your wages at the Internet café on rue des Petites Écuries. You generally eat at a café near the canal Saint-Martin or the Gare de l'Est. You spend most of your days at the movies—though every few days, you pay a visit to someone on the rue Linné in the Fifth. A woman, I presume?"

"You've had someone following me?" I asked, my voice just a little shrill.

"We simply like to monitor our employees' movements . . ."

"Our employees. Am I working for you?"

"Put it this way: we are all working for the same organization."

"And what organization might that be?"

"You surely don't expect me to tell you that."

"Well, how about telling me why you told the cops that I killed Omar?"

"I never said such a thing. I simply informed them, under interrogation, that you'd had an ongoing dispute with Monsieur Omar about the condition of the toilet."

"Under interrogation? You make it sound like they were beating you with a rubber hose."

"Like most people, I am not at ease when in conversation with the police."

"You tried to set me up . . . tried to finger me as the killer as a way of deflecting attention from—"

He raised an index finger and said, "I would stop right there if I was you, monsieur. I dislike accusations."

"Even though you think nothing of making false accusations against other people."

"The police have nothing whatsoever on you—"

"Except a motive—courtesy of you—and my fingerprints all over the toilet brush."

"Fear not. The evidence is weak."

"I'm their prime fucking suspect."

"There will be no problem—this I can assure you—as long as you do what you are told."

"By which you mean . . . ?"

"You tell the police nothing about your work, no matter how hard they press you—"

"I wouldn't dream of—"

He raised his finger again to silence me. Why was everybody doing this?

"And you also don't do anything idiotic like try to run away."

"The cops have taken my passport."

"That has never stopped anybody from fleeing. False passports can be bought in this quartier for two hundred euros maximum."

"I'm going nowhere."

"I'm pleased to hear that. Because it would be very problematic for you if you did try to vanish. Not that we would allow you to vanish . . . unless, of course, you made us make you vanish."

A small tight smile from Monsieur Sezer. I could feel the sweat cascading down my neck.

"Do you understand what I am telling you, Monsieur Ricks?" he asked.

I nodded.

"Very good. Then if you understand that, you must also understand that your movements are known to us at all times. Continue with your life as it is—your bookshops, your movies, your cafés, your woman in the Fifth, your work at night—and, I assure you, there will be no problem. Try to make a run for it—head to some railway station or attempt to purchase false documents—and the response will be fast and brutal. Are we clear about that?"

I nodded again. He said, "I need to hear you say, 'I understand.'"

"I understand."

"Very good. I also want you to assure me that, if the police approach you again, you will inform me immediately about their line of questioning."

"You have my assurance," I said, sounding like a complete flunky. Though I wanted to add, *If you're so worried about me going to the cops, why the hell did you finger me as the prime suspect?* But I knew the answer to that question: By putting me under suspicion, he could appease the police and also keep me in his control.

"Then we are in complete understanding?" he asked.

"Yes," I said.

"Excellent. One last thing: regarding that idiot you fucked—Yanna. I'm afraid that her husband has been informed of her infidelity with you. He has also been informed that you visited a walk-in medical clinic a few days ago and were diagnosed with a sexually transmitted disease—"

"You asshole," I heard myself say.

"Intemperate remarks like that cannot but upset me. And I do not like to be upset. Yes, Yanna's husband will kill you . . . but only if we tell him to. He's like Omar—stupid, bestial. But he also knows his place in the pecking order of things. So, once again, fear not: he won't hurt you, unless ordered to."

"I don't want trouble," I heard myself say.

"Then you won't have any . . . unless you make trouble. Good day to you, Monsieur Ricks."

He motioned to Mr. Tough Guy, who tapped me on the shoulder and pointed toward the door. I exited through it and down the stairs. Though part of me wanted to hurry across the courtyard, out the door, and down to the *commissariat,* I knew I'd just be playing into everybody's hands if I did that. Sezer would find some way of providing definitive evidence that I murdered Omar, and the cops would happily buy it. As far as they were concerned, this case needed a denouement—and my conclusive guilt was it.

Think, think.

But all I could do right now was think about how tired I was, and how bed was the only logical place for me right now.

So I went to my room and drugged myself, as I knew sleep wouldn't arrive without massive chemical help. I didn't set the alarm. The next thing I knew there was a loud banging on my door.

"American! . . . American!" a familiar voice shouted.

It took me several moments to work out where I was, and to squint at my watch. Four thirty. Shit, shit, shit. I was due at Margit's in thirty minutes.

"American! . . . American!"

More banging.

I staggered out of bed, my head still fogged in, and opened the door. Mr. Beard was standing outside, looking pissed off.

"Where the fuck were you?"

"What?" I asked.

"You always pick up your money at two thirty PM. Today you're not there . . ."

"Overslept."

"You no oversleep again," he said, tossing my pay envelope on the floor. Then he turned and left.

I picked up the envelope. I went back inside. My grogginess had suddenly vanished, replaced by a deeper, unnerving realization: They really are following me now. Any moves out of the ordinary will be jumped upon in a nanosecond.

I forced myself into the shower. I was dressed and heading out the door ten minutes later. I turned around three times as I hurried toward the metro. No one there. But they were there. They knew my every move.

I was back on the street by 5:15, hurrying down the rue de Paradis. I passed the joint that Yanna co-owned. I made the mistake of glancing in as I passed by. Yanna was behind the bar. Our eyes met—and immediately I could tell that something was very wrong. Within moments, she was out on the street, screaming at me. With good reason. Her face looked like it had come under extended assault. Both eyes were blackened, her lip had been split open in two places, there were gashes above her eyebrows, and her right cheek had turned an inky purple.

"You stupid bastard," she shouted. "I follow your advice, I tell him what Omar did, and look what he does to me. Starts telling me someone informed him you'd been fucking me too."

"I'm so sorry—"

"Sorry?" she shouted. "The bastard nearly killed me . . . and now he's going to kill you. So much for your brilliant 'plan'—"

"You have to go to the police—"

"And really end up dead? You understand nothing, American. Nothing. You better run away now. Far away. Otherwise you'll end up dead. Like Omar."

"He killed Omar?"

"Impossible. I didn't tell him until the morning he got in. Omar was dead by then. But he knew about Omar's death by the time he walked in here. Just as he also knew I'd been stupid enough to fuck you. That's the part I can't figure out . . . how he found out about us . . ."

Because Sezer must have called him in Turkey before his departure and told him. Maybe he also threw Omar into the mix, and Yanna's husband made a phone call before boarding the plane and Omar received his mid-bowel movement tracheotomy that night.

". . . and why he hasn't killed you yet."

"I'll make myself scarce," I said.

"Shit really follows you around, doesn't it?"

I couldn't argue with that.

"I'm sorry you're in such bad shape," I said.

"As soon as I feel better, I'm planning to beat him to death."

It was five forty by the time I reached Margit's apartment. She was not pleased.

"You cannot be late like this," she said as soon as she opened the door. She was wearing a black silk robe. It was half open.

"I can explain."

"Don't explain," she said, pulling me inside. "Fuck me."

"I can't do that," I said, dodging her grasp.

"Playing hard to get?" she said, reaching for me and thrusting her crotch against mine.

"It's not that . . ."

"Shut up then," she said, pulling her head toward mine and trying to kiss me. But I broke free.

"I just can't," I said.

"Yes, you can," she said, reaching for my crotch.

"Will you stop!"

My tone made her freeze. Then she shrugged and walked away from me, past her bed and onto the sofa in her living room. She lit up a cigarette and said, "Let me guess: you're in love . . ."

"I have a sexually transmitted disease."

She considered that for a moment, puffing away on her cigarette.

"The fatal kind?" she finally asked.

"Chlamydia."

"Just that?"

"I'm sorry . . ."

"For what?"

"I might have infected you."

"I doubt it."

"Why's that?"

"Because . . . I just doubt it. Anyway, chlamydia is not the end of civilization as we know it."

"I'm aware of that. Still . . ."

"Ah yes. Guilt, guilt, and more guilt. It's nothing, Harry."

"How can you say that?"

"Because I've had chlamydia myself. Courtesy of my husband. He gave it to me around a week before he was killed. Picked it up from some Sorbonne hottie he was fucking. I was rather aggrieved at the time— mainly because it hurt like hell every time I peed. In fact, on the night he and Judit were killed, our fight started with me telling him I now understood why he wasn't that interested in sex with me . . . courtesy of his little girlfriend. He became outraged that I would mention this in front of Judit. He stormed out with her. And that's the last time I ever saw them alive . . ."

She poured herself a whisky and sipped it.

"So, to tell the truth," she said, "chlamydia is no big deal for me."

"That's a terrible story," I said.

"All stories are fundamentally terrible," she said. "But you're not just worried about a sexually transmitted disease, Harry. It's more than that, isn't it?"

"I'm in a lot of trouble," I said, and the entire story came pouring out. When I finished she was stubbing out her second cigarette.

"This Monsieur Sezer . . . you think he set you up?"

"Think? I'm sure of it."

"So he murdered Omar?"

"Sezer would never grubby his hands like that. But he does have this resident thug who probably does all his dirty work for him."

"Any thoughts on why he wanted Omar dead?"

"Everyone hated Omar."

"You especially."

"I didn't want him dead."

"True. But you did intimate you wanted him out of your life. Now he's out of your life. The problem is, Sezer is now in your life . . ."

"Not just that—he's having me tailed everywhere."

"I think he wants you to think that."

"If he knows where I eat lunch, if he knows I come here every three days . . ."

"True, maybe he has a couple of flunkies who have tailed you. But all the time? That's a bit labor-intensive, don't you think? He's relying on his powers of intimidation to keep you in place. Anyway, if he wanted you dead . . . you'd probably be dead by now."

"It's Yanna's husband who will probably beat me to death with a hammer if Sezer gives him the go-ahead."

"But Sezer evidently wants you alive . . ."

"For the time being."

"How badly was Yanna beaten?"

I gave her the full picture. Her face tightened as I explained the extent of the injuries inflicted on Yanna.

"Bastards," she said. "That's what they did to my mother."

"Sorry?" I said.

"The secret police . . . when they came to kill my father, they also beat the shit out of my mother. Actually beat her around the face."

"When did this happen?" I asked.

"May 11, 1957. I was seven years old. My father was a newspaper editor—a one-time Party member who turned very anti-Communist after the 1956 Uprising was crushed by Russian tanks. Since martial law was declared, he had gone underground and was publishing a samizdat newspaper—very anti-Kadar and his regime—which was being run from a variety of safe houses around Budapest. Father was never at home—he was essentially on the run all the time—but I remember these men in suits or leather jackets frequently waking us up in the middle of the night, and sometimes ransacking the apartment and even pulling me from bed to see if Father was hiding underneath it.

"This went on for months. I kept asking Mother, 'Why are these men after Papa? When do I get to see Papa again?' Mother simply told me to be patient . . . that we would be reunited with Papa soon . . . but that I should stop asking questions about his whereabouts and that, if anyone at school asked me where he was, I was to say that I had absolutely no idea.

"Then, one Friday, Mother said, 'I have a nice surprise. We're going away for the weekend.' But she wouldn't tell me where exactly we were heading. So we got into our little car and drove off after dark. Hours later—I had no idea how long we'd been on the road, as I'd fallen asleep in the back—we turned off down a dirt road and eventually stopped at this tiny cottage in the woods. There, inside the cottage, was Papa. I ran into his arms and wouldn't let go of him . . . even when Mother, who was crying with happiness to see him, tried to hug him. Papa was mine . . . until I got tired and they put me to bed on the lumpy sofa in the front room. I remembered waking once or twice in the middle of the night when I heard groans from the bedroom—not knowing what they were doing at the time—but then falling back to sleep again . . . until, suddenly, there was this loud pounding at the door. The next thing I knew, there were loud voices and Mother came running out of the bedroom and I turned around and saw Papa trying to scramble out of the bedroom window. Then the front door burst open, and several policemen and two men in suits came marching in.

One of the cops went running into the bedroom and pulled Papa back from the window and started beating him with his stick. My mother began to scream—and a plainclothes officer grabbed her while his colleague repeatedly punched her in the face. Now I started to scream, but the other cop held me down while his colleague dragged my father outside. The officer who was beating Mother stopped, and pushed her onto the sofa. Her face was a bloody pulp and she was evidently unconscious. Now he started shouting orders and dashed to join the cop who pulled Papa outside, then ducked back in once to grab a chair. His colleague—certain that Mother wasn't moving—ran out as well. There was more shouting—then the cop holding me lifted me up and frog-marched me outside.

"First light was in the sky—and what I saw there I will never forget. My father—his hands behind his back, a rope around his neck that had been suspended from a tree—was being forced to climb on top of a chair placed right under the tree. When he refused, one of the plainclothes cops grabbed him in the crotch and squeezed so hard that Papa doubled over and the two men forced him on the chair, and I was crying and trying to turn away, and the same officer who'd grabbed Papa in the crotch shouted to the cop holding me, 'Make her watch.' So he grabbed my ponytail and forced me to see the other plainclothes guy kick the chair, and Papa wriggling and jerking and coughing up blood as . . ."

Margit stopped and sipped her whisky.

"It must have taken him a good two minutes to die. And do you know what one of the plainclothes officers—they were Secret Police—told me? 'Now you know what we do to traitors.'"

"Jesus Christ," I said. "I never knew . . ."

"Because I never told you."

"How the fuck could they have done that to you . . . a little girl . . . ?"

"Because they were bastards. And because they could do this. They had the power. They made the rules. They could force a seven-year-old girl to watch her father being lynched."

"What happened after?"

"They bundled me into a car and took me off to a State orphanage. A hellhole. I was there for three weeks. Refused to leave my bed, except to go to the bathroom. Refused to speak to anyone. I remember they sent doctors to see me. I said nothing. They were always talking in whispers to the nurses and the orphanage people, saying things like, 'She's traumatized . . . She's in shock . . . She has to be fed.' But I refused to eat. So they eventually tied me down to a bed and stuck needles in my arms and fed me that way.

"After three weeks, one of the matrons of the orphanage came in and said, 'Your mother's here. You're leaving.' I didn't feel elation. I didn't cry with happiness. I felt nothing but numbness.

"Mother was waiting for me in the director's office. Her face had only half-healed. One eye was half closed, the other . . . she was never able to use that eye again. She came over and put her arms around me, but there was no strength to her hug, no comfort. Something had been killed in her. She was accompanied by two men in suits. When I saw them I immediately recoiled—and hid behind my mother—because I was certain they were the same sort of men who had killed my father. Even they were embarrassed by my fear of them, and one of them whispered to my mother who then whispered to me, 'They want you to know they will do you no harm.'

"But I still refused to come up and face everyone until Mother crouched down beside me and said, 'We have been given permission to leave Hungary. These men will drive us to the Austrian border, and there we will be met by other men who will bring us to a city called Vienna. And we will start a new life there.'

"Again, I said nothing. Except, 'Those men who killed my father . . . will they hurt us again?'"

"One of the suits crouched down and spoke to me. 'No, they will never hurt you again,' he said. 'But I can promise you they will pay terribly for what they did.'

"As I found out from my mother some years later, those men with her at the orphanage were also from the Secret Police. My father's death had been something of a big deal. One of the uniformed officers who had been on the scene when he was murdered had a crisis of conscience, and made contact with the Reuters correspondent in Budapest. The story went everywhere—especially the bit about me being forced to watch Papa's execution. The fact that the cop who yanked my ponytail to make me keep my eyes open was the same one who ratted out his colleagues and went to the Western press . . . well, I suppose it shows that even the police sometimes have a conscience."

"What happened next?"

"There was a small international cause célèbre. It was the height of the Cold War, and the press outside of Hungary jumped on the story— Communist savagery and all that. Anyway, the Kadar government was under a lot of pressure to 'solve the problem.' So they offered my mother and me free passage out of the country and a little money to start a new life in the West."

"And what happened to the two plainclothes officers?"

"Their names were Bodo and Lovas. After we left Hungary they were put on a big public trial and sentenced to many years of hard labor. But through sources in the country, I found out that, after the trial, they were secretly transferred out to the intelligence division of the Hungarian Embassy in Bucharest . . . which, I suppose, was a prison sentence of sorts. Two years later, they were back working in Budapest in big jobs."

"And since then . . . ?"

"Dead."

"You know that for a fact?"

She nodded.

"And the cop who ratted on his comrades?"

"After he leaked everything to the Reuters man, he did what every true soldier would do who betrayed his cause. He went home and blew his head off. The ethical ones among us often pay a very high price."

Silence. She finished her cigarette. I topped up her whisky glass. She didn't touch it. I tried to take her hand in mine. She pushed me away.

"You expect me to accept your sympathy?" she asked.

I ignored her anger—as I knew she would want me to—and instead asked, "How could you have ever gotten over something like that?"

"You can't—and I didn't. But to those bastards, it was war. And when it's war you can do whatever you want. And I don't really want to say anything more about this, except . . . now you know why I hate any man who hits a woman in the face."

Then, "You are going to have to kill Yanna's husband."

"Are you insane?" I said.

"He will kill you."

"Only if Sezer tells him to. And if Sezer has me bumped off, the cops will immediately know that he was behind it—"

"If the cops even care. You could 'disappear' and who would notice?"

"I'm not killing Yanna's husband," I said. "I could never kill anyone."

"Everyone is capable of murder, Harry. You must remember that Yanna's husband is a thug—and one whose pride has been damaged by the fact that you fucked his wife. Where he comes from, that's up there with genocide and pedophilia in the catalog of human horrors. Sezer might hold him off for a while . . . but he is going to kill you. Be absolutely certain about that."

After leaving Margit's apartment, I took the metro over to Les Halles and a sporting goods shop that I passed once in that subterranean shopping center, and was open late this evening. I stopped a clerk and said, "I know this probably sounds very American, but you wouldn't happen to sell baseball bats by any chance?"

"Straight ahead, then turn right," he said.

So much for me thinking I'd have to explain what a baseball bat is.

Ten minutes later, I walked back into the metro at Les Halles, carrying a full-size Louisville Slugger. Yes, several passersby did stare at me—no doubt wondering what I was doing with such a threatening object in a metro—but I didn't care. If Yanna's husband—or any of his goon friends—did try to jump me, at least the baseball bat would give me a fighting chance (unless, of course, he used a gun).

As I walked out of the metro at Château d'Eau—baseball bat in hand—several people actually crossed the road when they saw me coming toward them. I took a different route to work, dodging the rue de Paradis, cutting down some small back alleys, and always carrying the bat up against my chest, while spinning around every twenty paces to see who was following me.

I reached work. I bolted the door behind me. I drank coffee all night and kept my eyes glued to the screen. An image kept filling my head: the seven-year-old Margit being frog-marched out by the cop. No wonder she tried to cut her throat after the death of Zoltan and Judit. How much tragedy can one person bear? How do you get up in the morning and negotiate the day, knowing that you have twice lost—in horrible circumstances—the people closest to you?

My admiration for her had increased sevenfold. But so too had my unease with her cut-and-dried solutions to things: *You must kill Yanna's husband.*

No, I must dodge Yanna's husband and somehow hope the police work out who really killed Omar and get my passport back and . . .

Vanish.

Because now—after Sezer's threats and Margit's warnings about the inevitable—I knew that I had few choices open to me.

But I couldn't just disappear right now. Not with my movements being so closely observed, and with my passport in the pocket of Inspector Coutard.

Say the cops followed me here tonight? How would I explain that one? 'Fess up—"All right, I do have a job"—and hope whatever they found downstairs wasn't so gruesome that . . . ?

You can work out that one once they've arrested you. And maybe getting arrested is the safest option going right now.

But if they arrest you, they can pin everything on you. And they will. Better to tough it out, get the passport returned, and skip town.

You could buy false documents . . . and be elsewhere tomorrow.

And be on the run for the rest of my life? And never see my daughter again? And always be looking over my shoulder? And . . .

You'll never see your daughter again. And you'll always be looking over your shoulder . . . unless you kill Yanna's husband.

You're talking melodrama. If you flee to the States . . .

You'll still never rest easy. Get rid of him.

Shut up.

You know you can do it.

Says you. Look what happened when Omar was silenced. His dirty little secret—with which he attempted to blackmail me—was still whispered into the ear of Yanna's husband. So if I kill Yanna's husband, then I also might as well kill Sezer and Mr. Tough Guy and Mr. Beard . . . since they all could still get me . . . all could want me dead.

When 6:00 AM came, my brain felt fried. My all-night anxiety had left me feeling as if I had overdosed on Dexedrine or some other form of high-octane speed. As I walked down the stairs to the front door, the entire grubby concrete hallway seemed to blur and take on a certain strange liquidity, as if it could form another shape or dimension around me. I hoisted the bat, holding it against me the way a soldier on inspection might keep his rifle crossed against his chest. At the pâtisserie, the Algerian guy behind the counter gave me a scared look when he saw the weapon.

"It's just a precaution," I told him. "Just self-defense in case they try to get me."

"Monsieur, do you want your *pains au chocolat, comme d'habitude?*" he asked.

"You see them, you tell them I used to be a pinch hitter on my high school baseball team, so I really know how to swing one of these—"

"Monsieur, please. There is no need to . . ."

That's when I realized I was brandishing the bat and also talking in English.

"Sorry, sorry," I said, switching back into French. "Very overtired. Very . . ."

"No problem, sir," he said, handing me the usual bag with the *pains au chocolat.*

"Don't know what's wrong. Don't—"

"Two euros, sir," he said, still proffering the bag.

I threw five on the counter and took the bag and headed off.

"Don't you want the change?"

"I want sleep."

Did I sound spooked, maybe a little insane? Absolutely. But I knew that things would all look a lot better after eight hours of sleep.

Actually, things wouldn't look better at all.

I turned the corner into the rue de Paradis. I reached my doorway. I punched in the code and went up to my room. I passed the toilet. It was still sealed off with police tape, forcing me to always use the toilet on the upper floor. I opened my door, leaned the bat against a wall, undressed, climbed beneath the sheets, and—

There was a loud pounding on the door, followed by one uttered word, "Police!"

I blinked and looked at the bedside clock: 6:23 AM. Great. I'd been asleep for maybe ten minutes.

"Police!"

More heavy knocking. Part of me wanted to play dumb and hope they'd go away and let me sleep.

"Police!"

I was about to say something, but the door burst open and two uniformed officers came charging in. Before I knew it, they'd forced me to put on a pair of pants and a jacket and had handcuffed me and frog-marched me downstairs and into a car that had now pulled up in front.

Ten minutes later, I was in the *commissariat de police* of the Tenth arrondissement, sitting in front of Inspector Leclerc. My hands were no longer cuffed behind my back. Instead, one of my wrists had been chained to the metal chair where I had been placed . . . and the chair itself bolted to the floor. The two arresting officers had brought me in here, attached me to the chair, and left me to my own devices for around twenty minutes. Then Leclerc arrived, carrying my baseball bat in one hand.

"Good morning, Monsieur Ricks," he said, sitting down behind his desk. "I presume you know what this is?"

"Why am I here?" I asked.

"Please answer the question."

"A baseball bat."

"Very good. And I presume you also know that we just found this bat in your *chambre.*"

"Can you search somebody's place without a permit?"

"Answer the question, monsieur. Is this your bat?"

"I'm answering no questions until I know why I'm here."

"You don't know why you're here?" he asked, studying my face with care.

"No idea."

"Do you know a Monsieur Attani?"

"Never heard of him."

"He runs a bar on the rue de Paradis—a bar where you have been seen to drink on several occasions."

I tensed. Leclerc noticed this.

"Do you know his wife, Madame Yanna Attani?"

I felt a sweat break on my forehead. I said nothing.

"I take your silence to mean—"

"I know her," I said.

"Then you must also know Monsieur Attani?"

"We've never been formally introduced."

"Even though you were formally introduced to his wife. In fact, word has it that you were intimately acquainted with his wife . . . that Monsieur Attani was made aware of your intimate acquaintance upon his return from Turkey a few days ago, and was heard publicly to say that he was planning to kill you. So . . . were you aware of these threats?"

I went silent again.

"We need to know your whereabouts last night."

"Why?"

"Because we have reason to believe that you assaulted Monsieur Attani with this bat."

"He was assaulted?"

"He is currently in the hospital, fighting for his life."

"Oh, my God . . ."

"Why are you sounding shocked, when it was clearly you who assaulted him?"

"I didn't—"

"You have a motive—he threatened to kill you. Perhaps you were so madly in love with his wife—"

"I didn't—"

"And now we have found the weapon used to smash his head in—"

"His head was smashed in?"

"He is in intensive care with a crushed cranium, a crushed face, and two crushed kneecaps. He is brain-dead and will not survive the day. The assailant was very violent and used a hefty circular object, like a baseball bat."

"I swear to you—"

"Where were you last night?"

"I only bought the bat to protect myself after Omar was found—"

"Where were you last night?"

"If you run forensic tests on the bat, you'll see it's clean."

"Where were you last night? And I will not repeat the question again. Answer it or I will call an examining magistrate and have you formally charged with murder."

Silence. I could feel the sweat now cascading down my face. I knew there was only one alibi I could give—and that she might hate me for implicating her in all this, but she'd still cover for me.

"I was at my girlfriend's place," I said.

Leclerc pursed his lips. He didn't like that one bit.

"Her name?"

I told him.

"Address?"

I gave him that too.

He picked up the phone. I heard him read out Margit's name and her address in the Fifth. Then he hung up and said, "We will be keeping you here, pending further inquiries."

"I'd like to talk to a lawyer."

"But why? If your girlfriend vouches for you, you get to walk out of here."

"I'd like to talk to a lawyer."

"Do you have a lawyer?"

"No, but . . ."

He hit an intercom button on his desk, spoke briefly into it, then stood up.

"My superior, Inspector Coutard, will, no doubt, be speaking with you before too long."

Then he left. A few moments later, two uniformed officers came in. They unshackled me from the chair, recuffed my hands behind my back, then marched me down several flights of stairs, through a maze of corridors. Then we emerged in that holding area in which I had waited for Coutard yesterday. Only this time I wasn't going to be left unshackled on the bench. No, this time I was being placed directly in the cell located next to this bench. I started to protest, saying something like, "I want to talk to a lawyer," but one of the cops pulled hard on the cuffs, making certain they dug deep into my skin.

"Shut up," he said as his colleague unlocked the cell door. I was shoved inside. I was ordered to lie facedown on the concrete bed located in one corner of this tiny cell. The bed had a bare dirty mattress, a pillow that was a blotchy canvas of dried blood and snot, and a thin dirty blanket. I did as requested. The cop uncuffed me, while also informing me that if I did anything stupid—like taking a swing at him—his colleague had his nightstick in his hand and would think nothing of beating me senseless.

"A taste of your own medicine, after what you did to your lover's husband."

"I promise you I'll behave."

"Smart boy," he said, removing the cuffs, then added, "You can get up from that bed once we have left the cell and the door has been closed. Understood?"

"Yes, sir."

After the cell door closed behind him, however, I didn't get up. Rather, I gripped the thin mattress and buried my head against the filthy pillow, thinking, *I'm dead.*

I reached down for the blanket. I pulled it over me. The only good thing about not yet having slept was that, finding myself in a horizontal position, exhaustion overtook me and I was vanished from this terrible world in moments.

And then a voice said, "Get up."

The voice came from a metal slit in the cell door. I glanced at my wrist and remembered they had earlier taken my watch off me, along with my belt and shoelaces. I felt stiff all over and grubby and parched.

"What time is it, please?"

"Five twenty."

I had been asleep all day.

"Get up," the voice said again. "Inspector Coutard wants to see you."

"Can I use the toilet first?" I asked, pointing to the stainless-steel commode next to the bed.

"Make it fast."

After I finished peeing, the officer opened the cell and cuffed my hands behind my back and started leading me back up through the maze of corridors we'd traveled earlier that morning. Coutard was seated behind his desk when we entered. A lit cigarette was in his mouth. He was reading a file and looked up at me over his half-moon glasses.

"You can uncuff him," he told the officer. When this was done, Coutard motioned for me to sit in the metal chair facing his desk. The cop was about to recuff me to the chair, but Coutard said, "No need."

Then looking at me again, he added, "You look like you could use a coffee."

"That would be nice."

He motioned to the cop who disappeared into the corridor. Then he returned to studying the file, deliberately ignoring me for the moment. The cop returned with a small white plastic cup and handed it to me. It was hot to the touch, but I still downed it in one go.

"Thank you," I said to both the cop and the inspector. Coutard put down his file. He now faced me square on.

"Inspector Leclerc informed me that you said you spent last evening at the apartment of a woman friend . . . a Madame Margit Kadar, resident of thirteen rue Linné, Fifth arrondissement. Is that correct?"

"Yes, sir."

"Naturally, we investigated this. We sent several of our men to Madame Kadar's apartment. And I regret to inform you that we discovered that Madame Kadar is dead."

The news was like a mule kick to the stomach.

"That can't be true," I finally said.

"It is, I am afraid, completely true," he said.

I put my head in my hands. *Not Margit. Please, not Margit.*

"What happened?"

"Madame Kadar killed herself."

"What?" I whispered.

"Madame Kadar took her own life."

"But I saw her yesterday. When did this happen?"

Coutard stared right at me. And said, "Madame Kadar killed herself in nineteen eighty."

SEVENTEEN

"WHAT DID YOU just say?" I asked.

"Madame Kadar killed herself in 1980," Coutard said.

"Very funny."

"It is not at all funny. Suicide never is."

"You expect me to believe—?"

"Monsieur, the question should be rephrased: 'You expect me to believe that you spent yesterday evening at the apartment of a woman who has been dead for twenty-six years?'"

"What proof do you have that she died in 1980?"

"I ask the questions here, monsieur. You tell me you were at her apartment last night."

"Yes," I said, deciding fast that, under the circumstances, it was better to maintain the lie than to backpedal.

"How long have you been involved with Madame Kadar?"

"Several months."

"You met her where?"

I explained about Lorraine L'Herbert's salon. Coutard noted this on a pad and asked for her address.

"And you've regularly seen Madame Kadar since that first meeting?"

"Twice a week."

"And you were 'intimate' with her?"

"Absolutely."

"You are being serious here?"

"I am completely serious."

He looked at me and shook his head. Slowly.

"Have you suffered hallucinations like this in the past?"

"Inspector, I am telling you the truth."

"Have you ever been hospitalized—committed—for psychotic disorders? I can—will—run a complete check on your medical history and—"

"I am not delusional, Inspector."

"And yet you insist that you've been having an affair with a dead woman. That certainly exceeds the definition of *delusional*."

"Show me some proof that she is dead."

"In time," he said quietly. "Describe Madame Kadar to me."

"Late fifties. Striking face, sharply etched features, not much in the way of age lines, a shock of black hair—"

"Stop. Madame Kadar was thirty when she died in 1980. So the woman you were allegedly seeing was over twenty-five years older."

But if she was thirty in 1980, wouldn't she be in her late fifties now?

"Do you have a photograph of her in 1980?" I asked.

"In time," he said again. "Anything else you wish to tell me about her physical appearance?"

"She was—is—beautiful."

"Nothing else? No distinguishing marks or characteristics?"

"She had a scar across her neck."

"Did she tell you how she received such a scar?"

"She tried to cut her own throat."

Coutard seemed thrown by my answer, but was simultaneously trying to mask his bemusement.

"Tried to cut her own throat?" he asked.

"That's right."

"The suicide was not successful?"

"Well, evidently not, if she was telling me about it."

He reached for a file in front of him. He opened it. He turned several pages, then looked up at me again.

"Did she explain why she tried to kill herself?"

"Her husband and daughter were killed in a hit-and-run accident."

Coutard stared down at the file again. His eyes narrowed.

"Where exactly did this accident take place?"

"Near the Luxembourg Gardens."

"When exactly?"

"1980."

"What month?"

"June, I think."

"And what were the circumstances of the accident?"

"Her husband and daughter were crossing the road—"

"The husband's name?"

"Zoltan."

"The daughter?"

"Judit."

"How do you know this?"

"She told me."

"Madame Kadar?"

"Yes, Madame Kadar told me. Just as she told me the driver of the car—"

"What was the make of the car?"

"I forget. Something big and flashy. The guy was a businessman."

"Why do you know all this?"

"Because Margit is my lover. And lovers tell each other their pasts."

"Did your 'lover' tell you what happened to the driver of the black Jaguar—"

"That's right—she said it was a Jag . . . and the man lived in Saint-Germain-en-Laye."

Again he glanced down at the file, then looked up at me. His cool was cracking. He now seemed angry.

"This game is no longer amusing. You have obviously engaged in some sort of warped research about a dead woman who murdered the man who ran over her husband and daughter and then—"

"Murdered?"

"That's what I said. Murdered."

"But she told me he was killed by a burglar."

"How was he killed?"

"Knife wound, I think."

"When?"

"Around three months after the accident."

"You're right. Henri Dupré—"

"That's the name she mentioned. A pharmaceuticals executive, right . . . ?"

"Correct. And Monsieur Dupré—a resident, as you said, of Saint-

Germain-en-Laye—was murdered at his home on the night of September 20, 1980. His wife and children were not at home at the time. In fact, his wife had just filed for divorce. The man was a hopeless alcoholic and the hit-and-run accident which killed Madame Kadar's husband and daughter also ended Dupré's marriage. However, Dupré was not killed by a burglar. He was killed by Madame Kadar."

"Bullshit."

He reached into the file and pulled out a faded Xerox copy of a newspaper article. It was from *Le Figaro* and dated September 23, 1980. The headline read:

EXECUTIVE MURDERED

AT HOME IN SAINT-GERMAIN-EN-LAYE

BEREAVED WOMAN SUSPECTED

This story outlined the facts of the murder—how Dupré had been surprised in his bed in the middle of a Saturday night; how the attack had been very frenzied; how the murderer had used a shower in the house, then left a note in the kitchen: FOR JUDIT AND ZOLTAN. A neighbor who had been up early saw a woman leaving the house around 5 AM and heading to the metro—and the police now wanted to question Margit Kadar, whose husband and daughter had been killed by Dupré in a hit-and-run accident several weeks earlier.

"This is unbelievable," I said.

Coutard reached into the file and pulled out an eight-by-ten photograph and pushed it across his desk. It was a police photo—black and white, but still shockingly lurid. Dupré was shown strewn across a blood-stained bed—huge black blotches surrounding him—his chest ripped open in several places; his face and head gashed horribly.

I sucked in my breath and pushed the photograph back to Coutard.

"To call this attack 'frenzied' would be to exercise understatement," Coutard said. "This was a murder committed in white-hot rage; the killer unable to desist even after the fatal blow was struck. What most intrigued the investigating inspector at the time were two interrelated aspects to the case: its meticulous planning and the fact that the murderer clearly wanted the police—and the public—to know that she was responsible. The police checked Madame Kadar's phone records after the attack. It seems she had rung the Dupré household the night before the attack. In his report, the inspector presumed that she was calling on a pretext—perhaps using a false voice to ask for his wife and simultaneously finding out that he was at home that weekend. How did the police work this out? Because Madame Kadar's phone records also show that she called Madame Dupré on the same Friday evening at the apartment in Saint-Germain-en-Laye to which she had moved with her son, having first obtained this new number from Directory Enquiries. Madame Dupré remembered the call when she was questioned by the police—a woman, sounding very French, telling her that she got this number from her husband, and that she was working for a company selling holiday apartments near Biarritz and she would like to send Madame some information, and should she use her husband's address? Madame Dupré then informed her that she no longer lived with her husband, and that she wasn't interested in a holiday apartment near Biarritz, and hung up the phone.

"So Madame Kadar now knew that Dupré lived alone and was at home that weekend. The attack happened the following night around four. Madame Kadar had visited Saint-Germain-en-Laye earlier that day. The same neighbor who spotted her leaving the Dupré home at five that morning saw someone looking carefully at the house the previous afternoon—walking around it, inspecting every aspect of it. But as Dupré had it on the market, the neighbor thought it was just a prospective buyer. When Madame Kadar returned that night, she entered through a window that had been left open on the ground floor. She evidently made no noise, as Dupré was surprised by her in bed. We have no idea whether she briefly woke him before beginning the attack or murdered him while he was asleep . . . though the medical examiner postulated that Dupré must have woken up as soon as the first blow was struck and was therefore aware of his assailant. The police were fairly certain that Madame Kadar wanted Dupré to see it was her—as this was an obvious act of revenge.

"Afterward, Madame Kadar stripped off her clothes and used Dupré's bathroom to have a shower. She left her blood-splattered clothes on the bathroom floor and the knife by the bed. She had evidently arrived with a small suitcase containing a change of clothes—and after dressing, she went down to the kitchen and made coffee and waited—"

"She made coffee after knifing him like that?"

"The first train doesn't leave Saint-Germain-en-Laye until five twenty-three AM. She didn't want to be waiting outside the station—so, yes, she made coffee and wrote that simple note, FOR JUDIT AND ZOLTAN. It sounds like a book dedication, doesn't it? Besides being an act of revenge perhaps she considered this murder to be a creative act. Certainly her planning was most creative. She left the house around five. It was a fifteen-minute walk to the station. She boarded the first train and changed for the metro at Châtelet. There she proceeded to the Gare de l'Est and bought a first-class ticket to Budapest. She even paid for a separate sleeping compartment. She had to give her own name when booking the first-class compartment. This she did. But she evidently gambled that no one would be stopping by the Dupré house on Sunday . . . or that if it was discovered, it would still take the police most of the day to figure out she was the murderer, and to alert Interpol that she was now on the run. In other words she had, at a minimum, a clear twenty-four hours to get to Budapest. As it turned out, she gambled right. Dupré's body wasn't discovered until late Monday afternoon when he failed to show up for work, and his employers called his wife. She went back to his house and came upon the crime scene. Of course, she was immediately considered the prime suspect—the spouse always is in a case of a murder in the home—until the forensics showed that Madame Kadar's fingerprints were on the murder weapon and that the bloodstained clothes left behind were not Madame Dupré's."

"How did you have her fingerprints on file?"

"All resident aliens are fingerprinted. Also, in 1976, Madame Kadar became a French citizen—so she was re-fingerprinted. However, as she was traveling as a Frenchwoman, she had to apply for a visa at the Hungarian Embassy here in Paris. At the time, the Communist regime didn't allow foreigners to obtain an entry permit at their border . . . especially former citizens. Madame Kadar applied for this visa fourteen days before she murdered Dupré, stating that she wanted to visit family members there."

"But she hated Hungary . . . especially after what had happened to her father."

"What had happened to her father?"

I told him everything Margit had told me. Several times during this recitation, he looked down at the file, as if he was comparing the story I was telling with that which he had inside this battered, thick manila folder. When I finished, I asked, "Does that correspond with the information you have?"

"Naturally the Hungarian police—who cooperated with us during our investigation—also informed us of the findings of their investigations into the two murders that Madame Kadar committed on her return to Budapest."

"She killed Bodo and Lovas?"

Long silence. Coutard glared at me. He put down the file. He lit a cigarette. He took several deep thoughtful drags, never once taking his eyes off me. Finally: "I am trying to discern the game you are playing, monsieur. You are under investigation for two murders, and you simultaneously show extensive knowledge of a sequence of murders carried out here and in Budapest by a woman who killed herself in Hungary shortly after murdering her second victim there."

"She cut her throat after killing Bodo?"

"No, after killing Lovas. But let us not digress from the issue of concern to me: why you know so much about this case. Please do not repeat that preposterous alibi that she told you all about this. I will not accept such absurdities. So how and why did you garner all this information? You are a writer, yes? Perhaps someone told you about this case—it got quite a bit of publicity at the time. You were intrigued, and using the Internet, you found out all the details of the case. And now, under suspicion for two murders yourself, you spin this absurd tale of an affair with a dead woman in an attempt to—"

"Were there any reports in the Hungarian papers about the reason why she returned to Budapest to murder Bodo and Lovas?"

"You interrupted me again."

"Sorry."

"You do that once more, I'll send you back to the cells for twenty-four hours."

Won't you be sending me back there anyway?

Coutard reopened the file and spent several minutes studying some more old photocopied pages.

"We have a selection of the Hungarian press clippings about the case, and a French translation provided for us. Given the nature of the regime back then, the official reason given as to why she murdered Bodo and Lovas was, 'These two brave defenders of Hungary had arrested Madame Kadar's father when he was spreading "seditious lies against the homeland"' . . . that's an exact quote. According to the State media, he subsequently killed himself while in prison after it was revealed he was an agent working for the CIA. There is no mention in any report—either police or in the press—of the incident you describe, in which Madame Kadar was forced, as a seven-year-old girl, to watch her father's hanging. Then again, the Hungarian police in 1980 would never have shared such information with us. Instead, in their reports—and in the State press—Madame Kadar was depicted as a mentally unbalanced woman who, having recently lost her husband and daughter in a tragic accident, was on a rampage of revenge. The State newspaper printed all the French reports about Dupré's murder. They also intimated that the attacks on Bodo and Lovas were savage ones."

"Did the Hungarian police let you know how she tracked the two men down?"

"Of course not. According to the inspector's report at the time, the police in Budapest only nominally cooperated with us. And no, they didn't inform us that Bodo and Lovas were members of the security services—though in all the Hungarian press reports, they constantly referred to the two men as 'heroes' who had 'given their lives to protect the security of the homeland' . . . which is usual State double-speak for members of the Secret Police."

"And Margit killed herself after murdering the two men?"

He opened the file and found a document, glanced at one page, then turned to those stapled beneath it.

"This is a translation of a telex—remember the telex?—sent to us from the police in Budapest. First victim, Béla Bodo, age sixty-six, was found dead in his apartment in a residential district of Pest on the night of September 21, 1980. He was found bound and gagged to a chair in front of his kitchen table. His hands had been taped to the table using heavy duct tape, of the type generally employed for patching leaky pipes. The victim's ten fingers had been severed from his hands, his eyes had been gouged out, his throat cut."

"Jesus Christ," I whispered.

"There was nothing frenzied about such an attack. One must surmise that the murderer was very slow and deliberate in her maiming of her victim, in order to inflict maximum pain and terror on him. The coup de grâce when his throat was cut must have been a desperate relief to him."

"Did the police tell you how she had managed to bind and gag Bodo in the first place?"

"No, but like us, they too intimated that she must have entered his apartment carrying a firearm—thus forcing him to 'assume the position' at the kitchen table while she bound and gagged him. Had he known what was awaiting him, I've no doubt he would have tried to escape. Being shot to death is so much cleaner than the torment he suffered."

"And Lovas?"

"The same treatment. Only in this instance, a neighbor heard Lovas scream something—probably before Madame Kadar gagged his mouth—and decided to call the police. They took their time arriving— maybe thirty minutes after the call. When they got there, they banged on the door and announced themselves and insisted whoever was there should open the door immediately. There was no reply. So they got the concierge to open the door. As the door swung up, a spray of blood hit the officers. Madame Kadar had just cut her throat . . . and judging from the blood still pumping from Lovas, Madame Kadar had sliced his jugular right before her own."

"They tried to save them both. They both died."

He reached into the file, pulled out two aging black-and-white photos, and pushed them across the table to me. The first showed the bloodied head of a man lying limp, his torso also covered in blood, his hands taped to a table and so mutilated that they appeared to be gory stumps.

The second showed a woman sprawled on a linoleum floor, lying in a pool of blood, her clothes sodden, a kitchen knife in one hand, a gash across her throat. I studied the face. Without question, it was a younger version of Margit. I looked at her eyes. Though frozen, they seemed to glow with an exultant rage—the same sort of heightened fury that I saw in her eyes when she talked about the death of her father, or the accident that took Zoltan and Judit from her. I stared at her postmortem eyes again in the photograph. It was as if Margit had taken this rage with her from the past life into eternity.

The past life? But she was here, in this life. Now.

I pushed the photograph back toward the inspector. I bowed my head, not knowing what to say, what to think.

"Given the monstrousness of the attacks," Coutard said, "it is obvious that the murderer was not of sound mind. Yet she might not have committed suicide if the police hadn't shown up while she was slowly maiming Lovas to death."

"But she is not dead," I said.

He tapped the crime-scene photograph of Margit.

"You insist that the woman shown here is alive?"

"Yes."

He handed me another document from the file. It was in Hungarian and looked official. Toward the top of it was a space in which Margit's name had been written.

"This is the death certificate from the medical examiner in Budapest—signed after he performed the autopsy on Madame Kadar. The investigating inspector in Saint-Germain-en-Laye closed the case on the murder of Monsieur Dupré upon receiving this certificate from the Hungarian authorities, as he had proof that the individual who perpetrated this crime was dead. But you still insist that Madame Kadar is alive?"

"Yes."

"Do you understand the seriousness of your position, Monsieur Ricks?"

"I didn't kill Omar. I didn't kill Yanna's husband."

"Even though all the evidence points to you. Not just evidence . . . but motive as well."

"I had nothing to do with their deaths."

"And your alibi—at least in the case of the murder of Monsieur Attani—is that you were at the apartment of the woman whose death certificate you have just read?"

"You have heard me tell you, in detail, essential aspects of her life—"

"And these details could have been easily researched by you using a search engine . . ."

"Ask yourself, Inspector, please, the same question you posed to me:

Why would I be interested in such an old murder case? How would I have found out about it in the first place? And how would I know more intimate details of Madame Kadar's past than you do?"

"Monsieur, I have been doing this job for over twenty years now. And if there is one thing I comprehend about human behavior, it is this: the moment you think you can predict its pattern is the moment when it changes, and you discover that other people's realities are often divorced from the one you exist in. You say a dead woman is alive. I say, the man sitting in front of me seems rational and lucid and intelligent. And yet, when shown proof that his lover left this life twenty-six years ago . . ."

He opened his hands, as if to say, *And there it is.*

"So you must understand, monsieur . . . I am not interested in why you have created this invention in your head, or how you gleaned your facts, or whether or not you embellished the story with tales of your lover being forced to watch her father's execution. Naturally, I am intrigued by such detail. Naturally, I am curiously impressed by your forceful certainty that Madame Kadar exists. But as a police inspector, such interest is overshadowed by empirical facts. And the empirical facts of the case are profoundly empirical. The facts point to your culpability. Just as the fact that you use a dead woman as an alibi . . ."

Another shrug.

"I do suggest that you reconsider your story, monsieur."

"I am telling you the truth," I said.

He let out a deep, frustrated sigh.

"And I am telling you that you are either a compulsive liar or an irrational liar or both. I am now sending you back to the cells so you can reflect on your situation, and perhaps come to your senses and end this mad self-deception."

"Am I not allowed some sort of legal representation at this stage?"

"We can hold you for seventy-two hours without contact with the outside world."

"That's not fair."

"No, monsieur . . . that's the law."

He picked up the phone and dialed a number. Then he stood up and went over to the window and peered out.

"This morning we visited the address you gave my colleague of the apartment where you were having your 'assignations' with Madame Kadar. The concierge said that he wasn't aware of your visits. So how did you gain access to it?"

"Madame Kadar let me in."

"I see."

"How else would I have gotten inside? I mean, the apartment I described to you is exactly the one you saw, isn't it?"

Coutard continued to stare out the window as he said, "Madame Kadar did live in that apartment until her death in 1980. Since then, it has been empty . . . though it has remained in her estate. A small trust that was left behind after her death continues to pay, by *prélèvement automatique*, the service charge. But no one has occupied it in over twenty-five years. Can you describe the apartment to me, please?"

I did. In detail. He nodded.

"Yes, that is the apartment as I found it . . . including the 1970s décor. There was one major difference, however. The apartment I saw hadn't been cleaned or dusted in years."

"That's nonsense. It was always spotless when I visited it."

"I'm certain that's how you saw it, monsieur."

A uniformed officer knocked on Coutard's door and came inside.

"Please take Monsieur Ricks back to his cell. He will be spending some more time with us."

The officer approached me and took me by the arm. I turned to Coutard and said, "You have to try to believe me."

"No, I don't," he said.

They locked me up in the same cell. I was left alone there for hours with no reading material, no pen or paper on which to write, nothing but my thoughts to preoccupy me.

Am I insane? Have I been imagining all this? During the past few months, have I been acting out a strange, warped reverie? And if it is true that Margit has been dead for all these years, what sort of alternative reality have I been living in all these months?

A tray of cold tasteless food arrived around seven that evening. I was famished, so I ate it. Around nine, sleep began to overtake me. I stripped off my now rank jeans and crawled under the grubby blanket and quickly drifted into unconsciousness. Only tonight I did not sleep the dreamless sleep I craved. Tonight the nocturnal screening room in my mind played out a horror show where there was a trial, and I was in the dock, and everyone kept pointing fingers at me and shouting in French, and there was a judge calling me a danger to society and condemning me to life imprisonment with no chance of parole, and being locked up in this cell for twenty-three hours a day, and me continuing to swear blind that they had to find this woman Margit . . . that she would explain it all . . . and the walls of the cell closing in around me . . . and me huddled in a corner on the concrete floor, my head leaned up against the toilet, my eyes as frozen as Margit's in the crime-scene photograph . . . and . . .

That's when I jumped awake, my body drenched, my teeth biting in the filthy pillow. For a moment I didn't know where I was. Then the realization hit: *You're incarcerated.*

I had no watch, so I didn't know what time it was. I had no toothbrush, so I couldn't rid my mouth of the disgusting aftertaste of my nightmare. I had no change of clothes or access to a shower, so I was now feeling totally ripe. After emptying my bladder in the toilet and finishing what little water was left in the bottle, I stretched out on the bunk and shut my eyes and tried to empty my brain and blank out the present and tell myself to somehow stay calm.

But it's hard to vanquish negative thoughts when you're about to be charged with two murders, and when you're living in a hall of mirrors where nothing is as it seems . . .

The cell door opened. Morning light filtered in. An officer stood there with a tray of food.

"What time is it?" I asked.

"Eight thirty."

"Is there any chance I could have a toothbrush and toothpaste, please?"

"We're not a hotel."

"How about something to read then?"

"We're not a library."

"Please, monsieur . . ."

He handed me the tray. The cell door closed behind him. There was a plastic cup filled with weak orange juice, a hard roll, a pat of butter, a small plastic mug of coffee, plastic utensils. Five minutes later the cell door briefly opened and a hand shot in, holding a copy of yesterday's *Le Parisien*.

"Thank you," I said as the cell door clanged shut. Having devoured the breakfast—I was famished—I now devoured the newspaper, reading it cover to cover, trying to lose myself in its reports of petty crimes, of disputes between neighbors, of road accidents, of more internal problems with some local football team, of new movies opening this week, and the bust-up of a French pop star marriage. The obituaries, as always, gripped me. How do you summarize an entire life—especially one that doesn't merit a big journalistic splash? Beloved husband of . . . Adored husband of . . . Much admired colleague of . . . A respected employee of . . . Sadly missed by . . . Funeral Mass held tomorrow at . . . In lieu of flowers, please make a donation to . . . And that's that. Another life vanished.

That's the thing about the obituary page. You always know there is a story behind a story—all the hidden complexities that make a life a life. You also know that, one day, your life too will be summarized in a few hundred words . . . if you're lucky. Death is the great leveler. Once you've crossed over into that realm of nothingness, your story only really stays in the minds of those closest to you. And when they too vanish . . .

Nothing matters. And because of that, everything matters. You have to counter the insignificance of what you do with the belief that, somehow, it does have import. Otherwise what can you do but despair and think, *When I'm dead, none of the forces that drove my life—the anger, the neediness, the ambition, the search for love, the regrets, the terrible mistakes, the futile pursuit of some sort of happiness—will count for anything.*

Unless death isn't the end of everything.

This is the death certificate from the medical examiner in Budapest—signed after he performed the autopsy on Madame Kadar . . . But you still insist that Madame Kadar is alive?

I didn't know the answer to that question anymore.

The cell door opened again. A new officer entered.

"The inspector wants to see you now."

I pulled on my jeans and ran my hands through my grubby hair. The officer coughed loudly, a signal for me to hurry up. Then he took me by the arm and led me back upstairs.

Coutard was seated by his desk, smoking. My passport was next to the ashtray. Inspector Leclerc was standing by the window, in conversation with Coutard. The talk stopped as soon as I was brought into the room. Coutard motioned for me to take a seat. I did so.

"Sleep well?" he asked.

"No," I said.

"Well, you won't have to spend another night as our guest."

"Why is that?"

"Because you are no longer a suspect."

"I'm not?"

"It's your lucky day: we found the murderer of Monsieur Omar and Monsieur Attani."

"Who was it?"

"A certain Monsieur Mahmoud Klefki . . ."

"Never heard of him."

"A diminutive man with what seems to be a permanent scowl. He works for your landlord, Monsieur Sezer. Perhaps you met him?"

Of course I did. Many times. Only I knew him as Mr. Tough Guy.

"Once or twice, in passing."

"We found the knife used to murder Omar in Klefki's *chambre*, as well as the hammer with which he attacked Monsieur Attani. The blood of both victims matched that found on the respective weapons."

"Did Klefki confess?"

"Of course not—and he cannot begin to explain why the hammer and the knife were hidden beneath the sink in his room."

Leclerc came in here: "Murderers can often be overconfident—or stupid—when it comes to disposing of the weapons. Especially if they are arrogant enough to believe they can escape detection."

"Did he give you any reason for the attacks?"

"How could he—as he continues to deny them? But we did discover that his employer, Monsieur Sezer, was having a long-running dispute with Attani over the protection that Sezer charged for the bar Attani owned. And in the case of Monsieur Omar, we have heard rumors that he had borrowed a significant sum from Monsieur Sezer—which he was supposed to be paying back, at an exorbitant rate of interest, on a weekly basis. So we will also be charging Sezer with ordering the two murders.

With any luck, we can turn Klefki against his employer—in exchange for a fifteen-year sentence, rather than life imprisonment . . .

"So, Monsieur Ricks—you are free to leave. But if you could tell us anything else about Monsieur Sezer and his various business enterprises . . ."

"Why would I know about such things?"

"Because we know you work for him."

"That's not true."

"There is an alleyway on the rue du Faubourg Poissonnière, near the corner of the rue des Petites Écuries. You have been spotted going in there most nights."

"By whom?"

"As I told you yesterday, I ask the questions here."

"I use the place as an office."

"Yes, we found your laptop when we raided it yesterday."

"You raided it?"

"Another question, monsieur. If it is merely your office, why is there a television monitor on the table where you work? A monitor connected to a television camera on the street."

"Yeah, that was there when I rented the office."

"Rented it from whom?"

"Sezer," I said, knowing full well that if I mentioned Kamal's name, they would start asking questions about how I knew the late owner of my local Internet café and whether I had any thoughts on why his body was discovered some months back in a Dumpster near the Périphérique. Anyway, Sezer would back me up here, because he didn't want it known what went on downstairs . . . though I was certain that the cops had already raided the place and were now trying to see how much I knew.

"What did you pay Sezer for the office?" Coutard asked.

"Sixty euros a week."

"Not much for an office."

"Well, it's not much of an office."

"And you worked there on your novel . . ."

"Most nights from midnight until dawn."

"But on the night that Omar was murdered . . ."

"I was having writer's block, so I went for an all-night stroll."

"You didn't mention this when I first questioned you."

"Mention what?"

"Mention that you were at your 'office' before taking your all-night stroll."

"That's because you didn't ask me."

Pause. A quick glance between Leclerc and Coutard.

"It's rather convenient, you being 'out walking' the night Omar was murdered."

"I thought you'd found your murderer already?"

"Yes, we have. It was just a passing comment, that's all. But I would like to know if you were acquainted with your neighbors in the building where you maintained your 'office.'"

"No, I wasn't."

"Do you have any idea of what sort of business was going on in the 'office' on the ground floor?"

"None whatsoever. Do you?"

Another look from Coutard to Leclerc.

"We raided the place last night," Leclerc said. "The downstairs office—it was more like a small warehouse space—was empty. But it looked like it had been cleared out, with haste, only a few hours before we got there. Our forensic team did discover traces of blood in the wood floors and the walls, as well as several large electrical cables . . . the types often used for cinema lights. There was also a stage-like area in the center of the space, with a few pieces of furniture and a bed. The mattress had vanished, the headboard on the bed had been washed, but there were still microscopic particles of blood imbedded in the wood grain."

Coutard came in here.

"Our belief is that the downstairs premises were used to front several activities—including the making of pornographic and snuff films. You know what snuff films are, don't you?"

I nodded—and remembered the night the body was dragged out as I peered out of my doorway. But if I had been the night watchman for a snuff film operation, why didn't I hear other bodies being carted away?

"We have been aware, for some time, that these sorts of films have been shot in this quartier. We just didn't know where. Now we have reason to believe it was in the same building where you were writing your novel."

"That's news to me."

"And that is bullshit, monsieur," Coutard said. "You were the guard on the door; the man who vetted everyone who came and went there. That's why you had the monitor on your desk."

"I never knew what was going on downstairs. I never used the television monitor. As far as I was concerned the building was empty."

"We also found traces of cocaine and laxative in the kitchen area of the downstairs space," Leclerc said. "So a drugs operation was also working out of the same premises. And forensics turned up traces of gelignite as well."

"Gelignite is a plastic explosive," Coutard said. "A favorite of bomb makers. And still you had no idea of the activities taking place directly below you?"

"Absolutely none."

"He's a liar, isn't he?" Coutard asked Leclerc.

"I've no doubt he was the night watchman," Leclerc said, "but he could have been kept in the dark as to what was going on downstairs."

"I think he knew everything."

"I knew nothing," I said.

"We weren't speaking to you."

"You have no proof I knew anything," I said.

"Monsieur," Coutard said, "I can legally hold you for another twenty-four hours . . . which I will be most willing to do if you are disrespectful to us again."

"I mean no disrespect," I said.

"Curious man, Monsieur Ricks," Coutard said to Leclerc. "You know about the circumstances that brought him to a *chambre de bonne* in our quartier?"

"I read the dossier, yes."

"And do you remember from the dossier that there was a man in authority at the mediocre college who orchestrated Monsieur Ricks's downfall?"

"Wasn't that the same man who ran off with Ricks's wife?"

"Absolutely. And during the course of my further investigations into Monsieur Ricks's background yesterday, I discovered a fascinating new twist to the extraordinary narrative that is Monsieur Ricks's life. I typed in the name of the college at which Monsieur Ricks used to teach. What was it called again?"

"Crewe College," I said.

"That's it. Anyway, among the many entries listed was a news report from a local paper. It seems that the dean of this college—a Monsieur Robson—was dismissed from his job just a few days ago when it was discovered that he had an extensive child pornography library on his computer at work."

"What?" I said loudly.

"You heard me. According to the paper, it's quite the *scandale*. Your ex-wife must be appalled."

I put my head in my hands.

"He looks upset," Leclerc said.

I wasn't upset. I was suffering from a massive dose of disbelief and horror as I recalled the remnants of an exchange I had had with Margit only a few days earlier.

So, she said to me, *what do you think would be an appropriate payback for all the harm he perpetrated?*

"You want me to fantasize here?"

"Absolutely. The worst thing that could happen to the bastard."

"You mean, like discovering that he had a huge collection of kiddy porn on his computer?"

"That would do nicely."

"Oh my God," I said under my breath.

"I thought he'd be pleased to hear such news," Coutard said to Leclerc.

"Yes, you would have expected him to applaud such a downfall."

"Unless he feels guilty about it."

"But why would he feel guilty?"

"Perhaps he himself planted the pornography on the gentleman's computer."

"Unlikely . . . unless he's one of those highly skilled hackers who can tap into somebody's hard drive."

"Maybe he asked a friend to do it for him?" Coutard said.

"Yes—maybe he has a very malicious friend."

"It makes sense, doesn't it?" Leclerc said. "I mean, the man is also sleeping with a dead woman, so why shouldn't he also have an avenging angel?"

"I bet he also believes in Santa Claus."

"And the Easter Bunny."

"And Snow White . . . who was once his mistress."

Coutard began to laugh. Leclerc joined in. I didn't look up at either of the inspectors. I kept my head in my hands.

"The man has no sense of humor," Leclerc said.

"Don't you find any of this funny, Monsieur Ricks?"

"Am I free to go now?" I asked.

"I'm afraid you are."

Coutard pushed my passport across the desk.

"You need help, monsieur," he said.

To which I felt like saying, *I've got all the help I don't want.*

But instead I picked up my passport and gave the two inspectors a quick nod of good-bye.

"We'll meet here again," Coutard said as I turned to leave.

"How do you know that?" I asked.

"Trouble is your destiny, monsieur."

EIGHTEEN

I HIT THE STREET. I hailed a cab.

"Rue Linné," I said.

As soon as I reached Margit's address, I punched in the code and charged up the staircase to her apartment. When I reached her door I held down the buzzer. No reply. I banged on the door. No reply. I banged again and called her name. No reply.

"Goddamnit, Margit—open the fucking door."

Without thinking I threw my entire weight against it. There was a bit of give around the lock, but it still wouldn't open. I stepped back and attempted another flying tackle. No further give, but my right shoulder suddenly hurt like hell. I ignored the pain and charged at the door again. There was a loud crunch as it splintered free of the lock. Gravity carried me into the apartment. I stumbled and landed on the bed, breaking my fall with my hands. I immediately began to cough, courtesy of the thick layer of dust that covered everything. I raised up my hands. They were coated with gray powder. I looked at the bed, upon which I had made love so many times with Margit. Soot enveloped the pillows, the blanket, the sheets. I stood up, dusting off my jeans. I walked into the front room. All the furniture was buried under dust. Ditto the little kitchen. The windows were opaque with grime. There were cobwebs in every corner of the room. The carpet was covered with rodent droppings. And when I opened the door of the side room—the room that Margit's daughter called her own—I jumped back in horror. Three rats were huddled together on the floor, picking at the corpse of a dead mouse.

Then, suddenly, from behind me came a voice.

"Get out."

I spun around. Standing in the living room was a diminutive man of around sixty-five. He was gray, stooped, and holding a hammer in one hand. He glared at me with a mixture of anger and fear. His hand started to shake as he raised the hammer.

"What are you doing here?" he demanded.

"Who lives here?" I asked.

"No one."

"Do you know Margit Kadar?"

"She's dead."

"That can't be—"

"Get out now."

The hammer trembled again.

"Margit Kadar lives here," I said.

"She lived here. Until 1980, when she went back to Hungary and died."

"No one has lived here since then?"

"Look around you. Do you actually think someone lives here?"

"I have been coming here twice a week for months."

"I've never seen you—and I see everybody who comes through the front door."

"You're lying."

The hammer trembled again.

"I'm calling the police," he said.

"What sort of fucked-up game is going on here?"

"You're crazy."

He turned around and started to walk quickly toward the door. I chased after him. When I grabbed his shoulder, he spun around and swung the hammer at me. I just managed to duck out of its path, catching the concierge by the other wrist, then yanking it up behind his back. He squealed in pain.

"Drop the hammer," I said.

"Help me," he yelled to no one in particular. I yanked his arm harder. He squealed again.

"Drop the hammer now or I'll break your fucking arm."

The hammer fell from his hand. The concierge began to whimper.

"There's forty euros in my wallet, if that's what you're after."

"All I'm after is the truth," I said. "Who lives here?"

"Nobody."

"When did you last see Margit Kadar?"

"In 1980."

"Liar."

"You have to believe me—"

"The apartment is always clean, always—"

"What are you talking about?"

"Why haven't you seen me before? Why?"

"Because I never have. Now will you please let me go."

"Did you know about the murder she committed?"

"Of course. It was in all the papers. The man who ran over Zoltan and Judit."

"You know their names."

"Naturally I know their names. They lived here."

"With Margit?"

"I don't know why you are asking these mad questions. This was Margit's apartment. When she lost her husband and daughter, she went crazy and killed the driver of the car that killed her family. Then she fled back to Hungary, and the next thing I heard she was dead."

"And since then . . . ?"

"Since then? Nothing. The apartment remains unused. The bills get paid, but no one has ever come in here. Until this afternoon. Please, monsieur . . ."

I suddenly felt as if the world was spinning in front of me. I was in a reality that might not be a reality that still might be real. Dust and cobwebs and mouse shit and rats. And yet, just a few days ago when I was here . . .

"I don't understand," I heard myself saying.

"Please, monsieur, you're hurting me."

"I just want the truth."

"I've told you the truth. You must believe me."

I can't believe anything right now.

"If I let you go, do you promise not to start yelling for help or reaching for the hammer?" I asked.

"I promise."

I pulled my hand away from his arm.

"I'm leaving now," I said, taking one last bewildered glance around the room. "If you do anything . . ."

"You have my word, monsieur. Just go now. Please."

"I'm sorry if I hurt your arm. I'm just . . ."

"Go, monsieur, go . . ."

". . . lost."

I raced down the stairs and out into the street, wondering, *What now?* I saw a cab. I flagged it down. I climbed inside.

"Where are you going, monsieur?" the cabbie asked.

"I don't know."

"You don't know? Monsieur, this is a taxi. I need a destination."

One suddenly arrived in my head.

"The Panthéon. Rue Soufflot."

"*Très bien,* monsieur."

He dropped me in front of Lorraine L'Herbert's apartment building. There was no intercom speaker on the front door, but I got lucky. An elderly woman with a small dog was going inside as I approached. After she punched in the code, I held the door open for her and followed her inside. She thanked me, though I could see her looking over my bedraggled state and wondering if she did the right thing by letting me in.

"Are you visiting someone, monsieur?"

"Madame L'Herbert."

That reassured her. I excused myself and headed up the stairs. When I reached L'Herbert's apartment, I rang the bell. No answer. I rang it again, holding it down a long time. From inside, I heard L'Herbert shouting, "All right, all right, I'm coming." After a minute, the door opened. She was in a long silk bathrobe. Her face was covered in some black substance—a makeup mask—which she was attempting to rub off with a handful of tissues.

"Who are you?" she asked.

"My name is Harry Ricks and I was at your salon a couple of months ago."

"You were?" she said, staring at my unkempt state.

"I met somebody here—a woman named Margit Kadar . . ."

"And you came by to get her phone number? Hon, we're not a dating service. Now if you'll excuse me . . ."

I put my foot in the door as she tried to close it.

"I just need to ask you—"

"How'd you get in here?"

I told her.

"Well, the salon's on Sunday night, and you know the rules: you have to call up and reserve your place. Coming by like this, unannounced . . ."

"You have to help me. Please."

She looked me over with care.

"You're American, right?"

"You don't remember me?"

"We have fifty to one hundred people every week, so, no, I don't remember everyone. Something wrong, hon? You look like you've been sleeping in the park."

"Margit Kadar. The name doesn't ring a bell?"

She shook her head.

"You sure?" I asked, then described her. Again L'Herbert shook her head.

"Why is this so important? You in love or something?"

"I just need to verify that she was here the night I was here."

"Well, if you met her here, then she was here."

"Please, could you get your assistant to check your records?"

"He's out right now. If you phone him in about two hours—"

"I don't have two hours. Don't you have a database or something where you could look her up?"

She stared down at my foot in her door.

"You're not going to go away until I do this, are you?"

"No, I'm not."

"If you agree to let me shut the door, I'll see if I can help you."

"You will come back?"

"Fear not," she said with an ironic smile. "'Cause if I don't, y'all are going stand here, beating on my door till I do come back. Am I right, hon?"

"Absolutely."

"Back in a jiffy."

I removed my foot. She closed the door. I sat down on the stairs and rubbed my eyes, and tried to get that image of Margit's apartment under dust out of my brain. I failed. No doubt the concierge had called

250 • DOUGLAS KENNEDY

the cops by now. No doubt they were probably searching for me. If they couldn't pin two murders on me, they could still have me arrested for assault and general lunacy. By the end of the day I could be locked up in some madhouse, awaiting deportation back home. Imagine what will happen if word gets out that I was thrown out for insisting that I was romantically involved with a dead woman. Then again, compared with the scandal that had engulfed Robson . . .

But it wasn't just Robson. It was also Omar—because I'd mentioned to her how I despised his toilet habits. And then there was Yanna's husband: ". . . now you know why I hate any man who hits a woman in the face."

Then: "You are going to have to kill Yanna's husband."

But surely she didn't take it on herself to beat him with a hammer . . . any more than she ran over that desk clerk at Le Sélect. But again, I had told her of the harm these people had done—or were threatening to do—to me. And then . . .

Brasseur was a deeply unpleasant man, I informed Inspector Coutard during my first interrogation.

To which he said, *So we have learned from anyone who worked with him. Nonetheless, it is also intriguing to note that—just as you had a little war with Monsieur Omar and he was found dead on his beloved toilet—so you also had a little war with Monsieur Brasseur and he was struck down by a car . . .*

There was a pattern. I talk about someone who has done me wrong, she responds with . . .

No, that's so out of left field . . .

But her being dead is just a little out of left field too.

I don't get it . . .

There's only one way of "getting" it. Show up for your rendezvous with her today at five.

The apartment door opened. Lorraine came out. The remnants of her black makeup mask had gone. She was now holding a printout and a small card.

"OK, hon. I checked our guest list for the night you were there, and as you'll see . . ."

She handed me the page.

". . . you're on the guest list, but Margit Kadar isn't. I ran her name through our system—which only goes back ten years. Nothing. Then I checked our Rolodex, where we always kept the names of anyone who had ever come to the salons prior to 1995. And guess what I found . . . ?"

She handed me the Rolodex card. On it was written Zoltan and Margit Kadar, their address on the rue Linné, and a date: May 4, 1980 . . . just a few weeks before the accident.

"So she did come to the salon?" I asked.

"Once—with her husband . . . but I don't remember much about them. Hell, how could I, considering the amount of human traffic that comes through here every week. She and her husband never came back. So they were filed away as One-Offers."

"And there's absolutely no way she could have snuck in here on the night I came?"

"None at all. We're pretty strict on security for the salon. You don't get past this door unless you're on the list. And we certainly don't like it when people show up unannounced. But let me ask you something, hon. If you think you met her here, and I have proof that you didn't . . . well, what sort of conclusion do you expect me to draw from that?"

"Thank you for your time," I said and headed quickly down the stairs.

Outside there were no taxis. Rain was falling. I ran down the boulevard Saint-Michel to the Line 4 metro. I hopped on, my clothes now sodden with the rain. I started to shiver—the same sort of feverish shakes that had hit me on my first day in Paris. As always, no one was speaking in the metro, and the passengers in my carriage were avoiding eye contact. But several of them stole glances at this derelict man with wet, grimy clothes and several days' growth of beard and sunken eyes and chattering teeth.

At Château d'Eau I got off the metro and went back out into the rain. By the time I reached the Internet café, the febrile shakes had escalated into a sense of total depletion. Mr. Beard looked me over with cold anger as I walked in. Without saying anything, he went to the front door and locked it.

"You didn't go to work last night."

"That's because I was a guest of the police in one of their better cells."

"You told the cops . . ."

"Nothing."

"Why did they arrest you?"

"I was under suspicion . . ."

"For the murder of Omar . . . ?"

"Yes," I said, deciding it was best not to mention anything about Yanna's husband.

"Did they also tell you about the man whose wife you fucked?"

"They did."

"And did you tell them it was Monsieur Sezer and Mahmoud who did it?"

"Of course not."

"They've arrested them . . . but they've let you go. Why?"

"I'm not the cops, but the cops generally don't arrest people unless they have evidence—"

"You planted the evidence—"

"You're crazy."

"We know it was you—"

"Why would I—"

"Because you killed Omar and Monsieur Attani, that is why, and then you put the weapons—"

"My fingerprints weren't on the weapons. Mahmoud's were—"

"Ah, so the cops did tell you they arrested Mr. Sezer and Mahmoud."

"If I allegedly 'planted' the weapons, then why were Mahmoud's fingerprints on them?"

"You could have left them somewhere obvious in Mr. Sezer's office. Mahmoud might have picked them up to hide them—"

"Mahmoud would have seen the blood on them and thrown them out. But maybe Mahmoud isn't the cleverest guy to have walked the face of the earth. Maybe, having killed Omar and Attani on the orders of Sezer, he simply threw the weapons into some back room, some attic, not thinking that the cops would—"

"The weapons were found below the sink in Mahmoud's room. They were placed there, the police were called—"

"And I was in police custody at the time—"

"You could still have put them there. Did you also tell them about where you worked?"

"Absolutely not."

"Liar. They raided the building last night, pulled everything apart. Fortunately, after the arrests of Monsieur Sezer and Mahmoud, we had a little time to clear out—"

"Were you making snuff movies and bombs there?"

"Stop asking questions. You are in enough trouble right now—"

"Trouble for what? I kept my mouth shut. I showed up every night at midnight. I never asked questions. I never interfered—"

"But you saw—"

"I saw nothing."

"Liar."

"Think what you like. I didn't send the cops to you, I played by the rules you set."

Pause. He stared at me for a very long time. Then: "You go back to work tonight."

"But what is there to guard?"

"That is not your business."

"Surely the cops are treating downstairs as a crime scene. Surely they'll have men guarding the place."

"The cops are no longer there. They have finished all their 'tests.' They are gone."

"Did you pay them off or something?"

"They are gone. And you must return to your work tonight."

I knew that if I now said, "No damn way," I wouldn't be allowed off the premises. I also knew that if I did show up for work tonight, I might not ever walk out of there alive. The fever was now making me shiver. I clutched myself tightly.

"You sick?" he asked.

"Didn't get much sleep in the cell . . ."

"Go home, get some rest, be at work on time tonight."

Then he opened the door and motioned for me to leave.

On the way back to my room, I thought, *They are going to kill me.* They just want to do it in an enclosed environment where they can make me disappear with minimal detection. There was only one thing to do: flee.

But before I did that, I had to go see Margit at the agreed hour of five. I had to convince myself I hadn't gone completely crazy. I had to know the truth.

I also needed to lie down for a couple of hours, before this fever overwhelmed me. I would take a nap, then pack a bag, then arrive at the rue Linné, then run to the Gare du Nord and get the last Eurostar out to London. God knows what I would do there once I arrived, but at least it would be away from all this. That's all that mattered to me now: disappearing from view.

But when I reached my room, I found the door half open, the lock dangling from its hinges, everything trashed. Shelves had been ripped from the walls, drawers pulled out, their contents dumped. All my clothes had been rifled through, many of them torn. The bed had been over-turned, the sheets and duvet ripped apart, the mattress split down the middle. I stood in the doorway, stunned. Then I was immediately on my knees by the sink. Everything in the cabinet had been pulled out, but whoever rampaged through my room didn't notice the loose linoleum covering the floor. Pulling it up, I reached into the same hole that Adnan once used as a safe and found the money I had been storing was still there. I pulled out the Jiffy bags in which I had placed twenty euros a day from my wages. I quickly counted the three separate wads. Twenty-eight hundred euros—the total savings from all my nights of work.

My relief was enormous. But there was a possible stumbling block from my newly hatched escape plan: the backup disk for my novel. I kept it hidden in a paperback copy of Graham Greene's *This Gun for Hire*. Scouring the debris on the floor, I found the book and riffled through its pages. The disk was gone.

Don't panic . . . don't panic . . . it has to be here somewhere.

But I did panic. I rummaged again through all the debris, getting more frantic as I couldn't find it. I must have spent the better part of a half hour combing every corner of the room, my anxiety growing as it dawned on me that the disk had been taken.

But why take the disk and nothing else? It wasn't as if it contained secret codes or some revelation that would overturn the foundations of all Judeo-Christian faith. It was just a backup copy of my novel— insignificant to anyone but myself.

The thief—having found nothing of value here—probably pocketed it as a way of saying "Fuck You" for not leaving anything for him to steal.

Or maybe it was Sezer's henchmen. They knew I was writing something in my "office" at night. Maybe they decided to really stick it to me by lifting the only backup copy of the novel I had.

But it wasn't my only copy . . . as I had hidden another disk in a crevice above the "emergency exit" in my office. To retrieve it, however, would mean returning to that building . . . and I knew that was impossible now. The ransacking of my room—and Mr. Beard's menacing belief that I had set up Sezer and his stooge to take the fall for those murders—heightened my belief that the only thing to do was disappear. But with my laptop still impounded by the cops, I was in a quandary. If I left Paris now, I would be doing so without a copy of the novel I had worked on for the past four months. Though the police might send on my laptop computer at some future date, they also might decide to hang on to it. Which would leave me with nothing to show for all those midnight-to-dawn stints in that claustrophobic room. I had nothing else in my life right now but that novel. I couldn't . . . wouldn't . . . leave Paris without it.

The fever was spreading. Every joint in my body pained me. But I couldn't afford to give in to exhaustion. The longer I stayed in Paris, the more chance I would have of ending up like my room: broken into pieces. Time was of the essence. They could be coming for me any minute.

I scrambled through the debris. I found my suitcase. Amid the torn clothes, I discovered a pair of jeans, a shirt, underwear, and socks that had not been shredded. I reached into the shower stall and grabbed soap and shampoo and a toothbrush and toothpaste from the medicine cabinet. My portable radio—though badly dented by having been tossed from my bedside table—still worked. Along with everything else I'd rounded up, I dumped it into the suitcase, stuffed the cash and my passport into my jacket pocket, and slammed the broken door on my *chambre de bonne*, thinking, *I'm never coming back here again.*

Out in the street, I scanned the rue de Paradis to see if anyone was on the lookout for me. It seemed clear. I wheeled my bag down to the Faubourg Saint-Martin. Five minutes and several turns later, I walked into the *commissariat de police*. I asked to see Inspector Coutard. The man on the desk told me he was out of the building. I asked to see Inspector Leclerc. A phone call was made. I was told to take a seat. Leclerc came downstairs ten minutes later. He nodded hello and immediately noticed my suitcase.

"Planning to move back into your cell?" he asked.

"Very funny," I said.

"Leaving Paris then?"

"A short break to London," I said. "And I need my laptop computer."

"What laptop computer?"

"The one you confiscated when you raided the office."

"I wasn't part of that assignment. It was another division. If they have the laptop—"

"Inspector Coutard told me they did have the laptop—"

"Then you should speak to Inspector Coutard."

"But he's not here now."

"He should be back tomorrow—"

The man on the desk came in here.

"No, he's taking four days off."

"He didn't bother to tell me," Leclerc said.

"Is there any chance you might still be able to locate the laptop?" I asked.

"If it is part of an ongoing investigation . . . no. I cannot interfere with evidence. And as the inspector in charge is not here to approve its return to its alleged owner—"

"I am the owner."

"So you say. But without Inspector Coutard here to verify—"

"Couldn't you phone him on his cell phone?"

"While he is on his *vacances*? Impossible. More to the point, he would tell you the same thing. If the computer is part of an investigation, it stays with us until we have finished the investigation."

"But couldn't I copy something off the hard disk?"

"That would be tampering with evidence."

"It's just my novel."

"Your novel could be part of the evidence."

"But how?"

"As it is not my investigation—"

"I need a copy of my novel so I can continue writing it."

"You didn't make a backup copy?"

"I lost it," I said, not wanting to tell Leclerc about my trashed room, which might lead to more questions and him insisting that I stay around for a few more days in Paris . . . which I simply wasn't prepared to do.

"Too bad," he said. "Surely a proper novelist makes more than one copy of his work in progress."

"I'm just a goddamn amateur."

"No need to get touchy, monsieur. And if you don't mind me saying so, you are looking very unwell and smelling rather ripe."

"You didn't exactly provide me with an en suite bathroom."

"Be pleased that you were released . . . with your passport. The inspector could still be legally detaining you."

"You could watch me make the copy."

"It would still be tampering with evidence."

"That novel is my life."

"Then I can't understand why you didn't duplicate 'your life' many times over."

And he turned and walked back toward his office.

I sat slumped in a chair, trying to figure out my next move. The cop behind the desk spoke.

"Monsieur, if you have no further business here, I must ask you to leave."

"Ok, Ok," I said, standing up. "Any chance I could leave my bag here for a couple of hours?"

The cop looked at me as if I had lost all reason.

"Monsieur, this is a *commissariat de police,* not a *vestiaire.*"

"Sorry, sorry," I said as I wheeled my suitcase toward the door.

Outside I checked my watch: 1:23 PM. Just under four hours to go before I could cross the threshold again at rue Linné. I needed shelter before then. So I walked down the first side street to my left and saw a cheap hotel—Le Normandie—directly in front of me. It looked shabby from the outside and had a one-star rating pasted onto its doorway. It looked shabby on the inside. The lobby was narrow, with peeling paint, scuffed linoleum, fluorescent lighting. I rang the bell on the desk. No answer. I rang it again. An elderly African man came out, rubbing his eyes.

"I need a room, please," I said.

"Check-in is at three."

"Is there any chance . . . ?"

"Three PM, monsieur."

"I'm not well. I'm . . ."

He studied me for a moment, trying to see if I was telling the truth or just trying to get an extra ninety minutes free of charge.

"How many nights?" he asked.

"Just one."

"With shower?"

"Absolutely."

He turned to the box of keys and pulled out one. It had a wooden tag on it marked 7.

"Forty-five euros, payable now."

I handed him the cash.

"Second floor, turn right."

"Thank you."

He just shrugged and disappeared back through the door behind the front desk.

The room was a dump. I didn't care. It was shelter. I stripped off my filthy clothes. I dug out the soap and shampoo and stood under the drizzle that passed for a shower. I dried myself off with the tiny towel that had been provided, amazed that it was clean. I set the clock on my radio to wake me up in two hours. I climbed between the sheets. I shut my eyes. I felt as if I were falling. Within seconds the bed was drenched with sweat. My teeth were chattering, and I clutched the pillow as if it were a life preserver. I blacked out. I woke up again to the sound of France Musique playing Berlioz. The Symphonie fantastique. 3:45 PM. Back into the shower. Clean clothes. My body still ached with fatigue, but the fever had broken. I put my jacket back on, tapping the pocket where my money and passport were stored. A voice in my head whispered, *Just leave now. You can get the laptop back from the cops some other time. You can walk away from all the questions about Margit and write it off as . . .*

As what? My insanity. A four-month delusion that I sleepwalked through?

Call it whatever you like. Quit while you're ahead.

I will quit—as soon as I've confronted her and found out what I need to know.

And what is that?

Am I insane?

No comment.

Down the crumbling stairs of the hotel, out into the street, a left turn, and an abrupt stop at an Internet café on the boulevard de Sébastopol. I checked my watch again: 4:07 PM. I had to be out the door and on the metro toward the Fifth in under ten minutes. I was going to check the local Ohio papers to find out more about the alleged downfall of my nemesis . . . but first I opened my mailbox. There was only one email waiting for me—from my former colleague Doug Stanley. It explained the entire scandal breaking around Robson; how the dean's computer crashed last week and a technician was called in to remedy the problem and discovered:

> . . . *something like two thousand pornographic images of children on his hard drive. The technician informed the college authorities, the authorities called the cops, the cops called the Feds, and Robson is now being held in a slammer near Cleveland, trying to raise the $1 million bail that has been set. Ever since this went down, he's been protesting his innocence, saying that somebody "planted" these images on his computer. But the Feds released a statement yesterday, saying their experts had conclusive evidence that he had downloaded all this stuff himself.*
>
> *The man is in total shit—of the type that simply won't wash away. The college has dismissed him, the scandal has been picked up by all the usual tabloid media, and rumor has it that he's under suicide watch in jail. The prosecutor on the case has announced that he plans to make an example of Robson—"horrible breach of public trust, especially for an educator"—and demand a minimum twenty years . . . as Robson was trading these images with other like-minded perverts. Unlike trading baseball cards, trading in child*

260 · DOUGLAS KENNEDY

pornography can be classified as "trafficking in obscene material," which is a Federal offense. The DA also stated that he had proof that Robson was the ringleader for this ring of kiddy porn collectors, as they also found some credit card account he'd set up for collecting payment for this stuff. It's unbelievable . . . and further proof that you can never really know the dark side of other people.

There has been another victim of Robson's downfall, and that is Susan. In studying every document on the hard drive of Robson's computer, the Feds found a sequence of emails he sent her several months before he drove you out of your job. The emails were love letters—and, I hate to tell you this (but you need to know), very graphic when it came to intimate stuff between them. This has provoked a subsidiary scandal, which has just broken in the press. And the college has suspended Susan without pay while it conducts an investigation into whether she received tenure because she was Robson's mistress.

I called Susan last night. She sounded terrible— appalled about the revelations about Robson and pretty convinced that it was just a matter of time before the college permanently dismissed her. She was also worried about how Megan would take all this, and how she was going to meet the bills, since the scandal was also going to make her unemployable as a professor. I'm going over to see her this afternoon. Without wanting to unsettle you any further, Susan really struck me as shaky—and on the verge of some sort of breakdown. I'll report back by email later.

As you can well imagine, the entire college is reeling. In the wake of all these revelations, many faculty members have told me that they now felt guilty about voting for your dismissal. Because among the "love letters" he sent Susan, they also found ones in which he talked about how he was going to "go public" on your affair with Shelley, and decimate you. I'm afraid that Susan's email reply was not pretty: "Let him have it," or words to that effect.

*Sorry to have to lay this all at your feet . . . but I did
think you should hear it from a friend rather than read about
it or get a call from some hack journalist, wanting to know
how you were taking the news.*

*Be grateful you're in Paris, and away from this shabby
Peyton Place. I'll be at home this evening if you want an
update.*

*Best
Doug*

I put my head in my hands, and actually felt appalled at what had befallen my ex-wife. Yes, the "Let him have it" comment did rankle. But I
still feared for her now.

I signed off the computer and decided to hop a cab to the rue Linné.
The traffic was light. We made it there in less than twenty minutes. I
checked my watch: 4:58 PM. I walked up and down outside her doorway
for two minutes, then took in a deep steadying breath and punched in
the code.

The door clicked open. I entered the building. I scanned the courtyard. Nothing different. But when I turned toward the concierge's lodge
I saw the man with whom I had scuffled yesterday. He was sitting in
his chair and staring out at me. But he also seemed to be looking right
through me. So I walked over to his window and tapped three times on
it. No response from him. His face was blank—as if he was in some sort
of catatonic state. I tapped again on the window. Nothing. I opened
the door. I put my hand on his shoulder. His flesh was warm to the
touch—but still no recognition that someone was now shaking him,
trying to rouse him from his stupor. I shouted, "Can you hear me?" His
eyes remained frozen, his body immobile. I felt a chill run through me.
I backed away from the lodge, spooked. *Get out . . . get out now.* But when
I tried the main door in the courtyard, it was locked. I must have spent
five minutes struggling to open it. *You can't open it, because you can't leave.*
I looked for other ways out. There were none. I stared up the staircase
leading to Margit's apartment. *You have no choice now. You have to go up
there.*

On the way up to her apartment, I tried knocking on every other door en route. Not one answer. Had I ever heard any neighbors before? Had I ever been cognizant of other life in this place? Had I . . . ?

As I approached her floor, her door opened. She stood there in her usual black lace nightgown, a sardonic smile on her lips.

"What did I tell you about not coming here other than at our agreed-upon time?"

Her voice was calm, quiet. Her smile grew. I approached her, saying nothing. I grabbed her and kissed her fully on the lips.

"You taste real," I said.

"Do I?" she said, pulling me inside the apartment. She took my hand and stuck it between her legs. "And do I feel real?"

I pushed a finger inside her. She groaned.

"It seems so," I said, putting my free hand through her hair and kissing her neck.

"But there's one big difference between us, Harry."

"What's that?"

With one sudden movement, she pushed me off her. As I stumbled, I saw the flash of a cut-throat razor in her spare hand. It headed toward me, slicing me lightly across the hand.

"Fuck," I screamed as blood began to pour from the wound.

"The difference is . . ."

She took the razor and slashed her throat. I screamed again . . . but then stood there, dumbfounded, as nothing happened.

"You get it, Harry?" she asked.

Now she took the razor and sliced her left wrist, cutting deep into the skin. Again, not a single sign of injury.

"The difference is: you bleed, and I don't."

NINETEEN

"SO WHAT DO you want to know?" she asked.

"Everything," I said.

"Everything?" she said after a sharp laugh. "As if that would explain—"

"Are you dead?"

"Have another drink, Harry."

She pushed a bottle of Scotch toward me.

"Fuck your Scotch," I said. "Are you dead?"

We were sitting on her sofa. It was a few minutes after her razor attack. My hand was now bandaged. She insisted on dressing the wound and wrapping it in gauze moments after cutting her own throat. I was in such shock—both from the pain of the sliced hand and her bloodless suicide—that I allowed her to lead me to the sofa and pour me a steadying whisky (I downed it in one go) and play nurse on the hand she had cut with such swift deftness.

"How's the pain?" she asked, pouring me a second whisky and handing me the glass.

"It hurts," I said, throwing back the whisky, and not thinking too much about how the alcohol would deaden the effects of the antibiotics I was taking.

"I don't think any of the tendons were damaged," she said, taking my hand and checking its mobility.

"That's wonderful news. Are you dead?"

She refilled my glass. I drank.

"What did the police tell you?" she asked.

"That you slashed Dupré to death and left a note: FOR JUDIT AND ZOLTAN. Is that true?"

"It is."

"And then you fled to Hungary and hunted down Bodo and Lovas."

"That is correct."

"They also showed me Hungarian police reports. They said you mutilated both men before killing them."

"That is also correct."

"You cut off their fingers and gouged out their eyes?"

"I didn't gouge out Lovas's eyes because I didn't have enough time. But yes, I did cut off all their fingers and I did blind Bodo before cutting his throat—"

"You're insane."

"I was insane. Insane with grief. With rage. With an absolute need for revenge. I thought if I killed the men who killed the most important people in my life, somehow the fury that consumed me would cease."

"But you just didn't kill them. You butchered them."

"That is also correct. I butchered them in a completely premeditated way . . . and with great malice aforethought. I was determined to make them pay for what they did to me."

"But to cut off their fingers?"

"Dupré didn't suffer that fate. I stabbed him repeatedly in the stomach and arms and made him look me in the face—so he could hear me tell him how he destroyed my life—before I plunged the knife into his heart and then cut his throat."

"And then you left a note and took a shower and left all your clothes behind."

"They did get very bloody during the attack. But yes, I had planned it all out. And yes, after administering the coup de grâce I used his bathroom to shower. I left the note. I made myself some coffee, as I had some time to kill before the first train left at five twenty-three . . . funny how I can still remember all such exact details. I reached the Gare du Nord forty minutes later. I collected my bag and bought my ticket and boarded the train. I splurged on a first-class *couchette*—so I had a compartment to myself. I remember giving the porter my passport and a large tip and telling him I didn't want to be woken up at the German or Austrian borders. Then I took off my clothes and got into the *couchette* and slept soundly for the next eight hours, by which time we were somewhere near Stuttgart—"

"You slept soundly after murdering a man?"

"I had been up all night. I was tired. And the adrenaline rush . . . well, it did exhaust me."

"Did you feel better after killing Dupré?"

"A crazed numbness best describes it. Ever since I had decided on this course of action, I had been operating like an automaton. You do this, you do that, you go here, you go there. It was all carefully plotted out in my mind. Point by point."

"Including your own suicide?"

"That wasn't part of the plan."

"So you are dead?"

"I'll get to that—but only after I tell you about Bodo and Lovas."

"I don't want to hear about how you tortured them."

"Yes, you do—and you have no choice but to listen. Otherwise you won't find out what you want to know."

I reached for the Scotch, poured myself two fingers, and threw it back.

"Tell me then," I said.

"Some weeks before I set my plan in motion, I contacted a friend in Budapest—a man who, like my father, was part of the entire samizdat newspaper brigade that operated for a time in the fifties. He was now in his seventies . . . and had done time in prison for his crimes of talking back to the State. He had been 'rehabilitated'—though he'd also been tortured so badly during his 'reeducation' that he could no longer walk. I had made one journey back to Budapest in 1974, right after I had become a French citizen. I had a need to see it again, I suppose, as an adult—and had taken tea with this gentleman at his apartment. We couldn't talk openly—he was certain the place was bugged—but he did ask me if I'd push him out in his wheelchair in a nearby park. Once we were outside, I asked him if he could find the whereabouts of the men who executed my father in front of me. He said, 'It's a small country . . . everybody can be found. But are you sure you want to find them?'

"I said, 'Not now. But one day, perhaps . . .' He told me that when that day arrived, I should inform him by mail that 'I would like to meet up with our friends,' and he would take care of the rest.

"So, six years later, when I decided to *régler les comptes,* I sent him a letter. He wrote back, saying, 'Our friends are alive and well and living in Budapest.' I made my plans, deposited my bag at the Gare de l'Est, and cut Henri Dupré's throat. When I arrived in Hungary I went directly to this gentleman's apartment. He was now a very old man, very infirm. But he smiled when he saw me and told me he'd like to head out to the park. Once I had wheeled him outside, he handed me a piece of paper and said, 'Here are their addresses. Is there anything else you need?' I told him, 'A gun.' He said, 'No problem.' When we went back to his apartment, he sent me rummaging around an attic storage room for a shotgun that his father used for hunting back when Charles I was our king. He even provided me with a saw to shorten the barrel. As I left the apartment—with the gun in my bag—he pulled me toward him and whispered in my ear, 'I hope you kill them slowly.' Then he sent me on my way.

"I checked into a hotel. I went to an apothecary—they still had such things in Budapest—and bought a cut-throat razor. I went to another shop and bought tape. I took the metro over to the Buda Hills, where Lovas had his flat. I found it, no problem. I even rang the intercom and put on a funny voice and asked him if the woman of the house was in. 'She died five years ago. Who is this?' I said I was a member of the local Party committee for Senior Activities, and apologized for the mistake. Then I went over to Bodo's flat in some ugly modern block in Pest. This time there was no intercom. But he answered the door himself: a hunched man around seventy in a dressing gown and wheezing while he smoked a cigarette. Of course he didn't recognize me. 'What do you want?' Is the woman of the house in? 'She left years ago.' I said, 'I'm from the Party committee on Pensioners and we want to see . . .' and I spun some lie about looking into the needs of the elderly. 'Well, the woman you want isn't here . . . but if you want to talk about the needs of the elderly . . . you can come in now and hear an earful.'

"Now, I hadn't expected to carry out my plan so quickly—but I did have everything I needed with me, so I let him usher me into his small, depressing flat. Crap furniture, crap wallpaper, a nasty little kitchen, brimming ashtrays, empty bottles of cheap booze.

'So who are you again?' he asked.

"I told him my name.

'Kadar . . . like our Party chairman?' he asked me.

'No . . . Kadar like Miklos Kadar. You remember Miklos Kadar, don't you?'

'I'm an old man. So many people have come and gone in my life.'

'Yes, but Miklos Kadar must hold a special place in your memory . . . as you executed him in front of his daughter.'

"By this point we were seated in his little bed-sitting room. I opened the bag. I pulled out the shotgun. He gasped, but I put my finger to my lips and he didn't say another word.

'Surely you must remember his little girl, Margit? You ordered one of your police stooges to keep her eyes open while you lynched him two meters from where she stood.'

"At that point, he started to feign ignorance. 'I don't know what you're talking about . . . I don't remember such things.' I hit him on the side of the head with the gun and told him that if he didn't tell me the truth I'd shoot him on the spot. That's when he started to cry, to plead, to say how sorry he was, how he was 'only following orders' . . . Yes, he actually used that expression.

"I told him, 'My mother and I were whisked out of the country afterward and even paid a pittance of a recompense by the government, because they were ashamed of what had happened. So please do not tell me you were only following orders. The cop who held me, he was only following orders—because you barked at him on several occasions when he let me shut my eyes. You, sir, wanted a seven-year-old girl to witness her father's death. You wanted that scene burned on my memory forever. You succeeded. I've spent the ensuing decades trying to wipe that image away—but it simply will never leave me . . . a trauma which you inflicted on me out of sheer malice and cruelty—'

'You're right, you're right,' he cried. 'I was so wrong. But they were terrible times and—'

"That's when I hit him again on the head and ordered him to sit down at his kitchen table. The fool complied. When I told him to lay his hands flat down on the table, he didn't resist . . . even though he could have made a break for it when I had to put down the gun to start taping him. I used three rolls of tape—making certain he couldn't move his arms and couldn't get out of the chair.

"When I had finished I said, 'You dare to tell me, "They were terrible times." You were one of the perpetrators of those terrible times. You were an essential part of a repressive regime—against which men like my father had the courage to raise their voice. And how did you respond to his criticisms of your tyrannical methods? You strung him up in front of his daughter and forced her to watch him jerk and twist as he slowly strangled to death. How can you justify such a thing? How?'

"He didn't answer. He just sat there weeping. Much later, I was certain the reason why he didn't put up a fight when I started taping him down was not just because of the gun within reach of me. It was also because part of him knew he merited this . . . that what he had done was so monstrous he deserved a terrible retribution."

"But what you did to him . . . that wasn't monstrous?"

"Of course it was. And after I wound the tape around his mouth and head—ensuring that he couldn't scream or breathe—I did tell him, 'In a few moments, you will wish I'd shot you and ended your life quickly.' Then I reached into my bag and pulled out the razor and opened it and severed his right thumb. It's not easy, severing a finger. You have to work your way through bone and tendon and—"

"Enough," I said.

"I told you, if you don't sit through my story you don't get to hear the truth—"

"The truth? You expect me to believe there's any truth to any of this?"

"Where are you right now, Harry? In some dream?"

"I haven't a fucking idea anymore . . ."

"In dreams you might get your hand cut, but it doesn't bleed. This is real. It's simply a different version of real. But again, you're interrupting my story. And until I finish the story—"

"You're sick, you know that?"

"Sick because I cut off all of Bodo's fingers? Without doubt, it was a sick thing to do. Even through the tape around his mouth I could hear his screams. But I was very systematic. Every finger on his right hand. A short pause. Every finger on his left hand. Then I started on his eyes. The police were wrong, by the way. I didn't gouge them out. I simply sliced across them. You remember that Buñuel exercise in surrealism: *Un chien andalou*, where a woman gets her eye cut by a razor. It approximated that. And yes, you can think me mad and twisted for inflicting such horror . . . but surely you can grasp the madness that overtakes someone when they have been so wronged that—"

"Don't try to justify it. Don't."

"I'm trying to justify nothing, Harry. I am simply relating to you what happened."

"Did it settle the score? Did doing that to Bodo in any way make you feel better about your father's death?"

"At the time, all I could think was, *Do what you must do . . . Be systematic . . . Then get out of this dreadful country.* So after blinding Bodo, I made a small incision in the side of his throat—to let him slowly bleed to death . . . though within moments I could hear gurgling and gasping behind his taped nose and mouth: a sign that he was starting to drown in his own blood. I had packed a spare set of clothes in the bag—so it was the same drill as with Dupré. I stripped everything off and had a shower. Only this time, I cleaned up all the evidence. I wanted everyone in France to know what I did. I also wanted everyone to know in Hungary . . . but only after I was out of the country. So I scrubbed down every surface I touched and bundled up my bloody clothes and waited until Bodo was no longer gasping and gagging.

"Then I left and took the metro back across the city to Buda. I returned to the shop where I had purchased the duct tape and bought four more rolls. I walked over to Lovas's apartment and rang his bell. He said, 'Go away, I want to see nobody.'

"I said, 'But I am the woman from the Party's senior services. I have come with a special present for you. You must let me deliver it.'

"Once I had talked myself inside his apartment and revealed who I was and brought out the gun, he began to scream. I told him to shut up, but he kept screaming. That's when I slammed him on the head with the gun. It knocked him out cold. I taped him down, I gagged him as I had done with Bodo. But just as I started working on him, there was a banging at the door. It was some neighbor who'd evidently heard his screaming, as she kept shouting, 'Mr. Lovas, are you all right? Is someone there with you?' If I had been sensible, I would have cut his throat right there and hightailed it out of the kitchen window—his apartment was on the ground floor. But I wasn't sensible. I was deranged. So deranged that I convinced myself I had to dismember all of his fingers and blind him as well. The pain caused Lovas to wake up when I was cutting off his right pinky, and I'd been sloppy when it came to taping his mouth, as I left a small gap. So he started to scream again. The neighbor heard this and told him she was going to call the police. But I still didn't make a run for it. I just continued my grim work—"

"You wanted to get caught—"

"I don't know what I wanted at the time. When you're deranged you don't think logically. You just tell yourself, *Get the next finger off . . ."*

"Jesus . . ."

She smiled and lit up a cigarette.

"It gets worse. The police arrived. They pounded on the door, demanding to be let in. I worked super-fast, making certain all his fingers were severed. By this time, their pounding was replaced with the boom-boom sound of a battering ram they were using against the door. As it began to give, I grabbed Lovas by the hair. As soon as the door burst open and the cops fell in, I cut his jugular. Then, as they watched in complete horror, I drew the razor across my own throat."

"And then?"

"And then . . . I escaped arrest, detention, trial, and probable execution by a regime I loathed."

"By dying?"

"Yes. I died."

Silence. She continued to puff on her cigarette.

"And then?" I asked.

"Death is death."

"Which means?"

"I no longer existed in a temporal form."

"But what happened after you died?"

Another smile. Another deep lungful of smoke.

"That I cannot say."

"Why not?"

"Because . . . I can't."

"The cops showed me your death certificate. And you yourself have confirmed that you slit your throat and you died. So why . . . why . . . are you here?"

"Because I am."

"But that doesn't make sense. How can I believe you when I know what you're telling me is impossible?"

"Since when has death ever made sense, Harry?"

"But you've been there. You know."

Another smile.

"True—and I'm saying nothing."

"You have to tell me—"

"No, I don't. And no . . . I won't. Any more than I have to explain my work on your behalf."

"Your work on my behalf. Now I know you are insane."

"Think what you like, my sweet. But consider this: every person who has recently done harm to you has, in turn, been punished."

"You ran over Brasseur outside the hotel?"

"Yes."

"How?"

"How else do you run a man down? I got into a car that I borrowed on the street. A Mercedes C-Class—not the best Mercedes, but still a car with considerable kick. I waited for him to emerge from Le Sélect. When he stepped off the pavement, I hit the accelerator and ran right into him."

"He said he couldn't see the driver, but he thought it was a woman."

Another smile.

"And you cornered Omar when he was on the toilet?" I asked.

"You were right about him. His shit truly stank. And I'll let you in on a small revolting secret: when he wiped himself he only used a minimal amount of paper, so the shit was everywhere on his hands. A disgusting bastard. And I'd seen how he had treated you, how he left that communal toilet in such a grim state—"

"You saw? How?"

She stubbed out a cigarette and lit another.

"Do you know what I like best about being dead? You can smoke without guilt."

"But even in death you still age, just like the rest of us."

"Yes, that is rather ironic, don't you think? But that's how it works . . . for me, at least."

"And the others?"

A shrug.

"So you didn't go to heaven after you—?"

"Killed myself? Hardly."

"To hell then?"

"I went . . . nowhere. And then, somehow, I was back here. I was ten years older, but the apartment was here . . ."

"Who paid the bills?"

"Before I left for Hungary, I saw my lawyer and told him to set up a trust with the money I received as compensation from Dupré. I left my estate to no one. And I made certain in my will that no one could sell the apartment from under me. You see, I knew what I was going to do in Budapest . . . and I also knew that I would have to disappear for a very long time afterward . . ."

"So you weren't planning to kill yourself?"

"Not until the police burst in. It was a completely impulsive decision. But, like I said, I was crazy then."

"And you're not crazy now? Beating men to death with a hammer—"

"He kicked the crap out of his wife, and he also threatened to kill you."

"That was never established."

"I heard it."

"When?"

"In his bar. When he didn't think I was there."

"And Robson?"

"I asked you what you thought was the worst thing that could befall him. You said—"

"I didn't think you'd actually download kiddy porn onto his computer."

"It's what you wanted, Harry. That man systematically destroyed your life. His punishment struck me as . . . apt. His life is now completely shattered. And before the week is out, he'll take his own life in jail."

"Are you going to force him to do that?"

Another laugh.

"I am not a spirit who invades the souls of others and forces them to do things."

"No—you're just a succubus."

"A succubus has sex with men while they are asleep. You're very much awake, Harry."

"So all this then is . . . what? When I came here yesterday, the apartment was covered in dust, the concierge acted as if I was a lunatic, telling me the place hadn't been inhabited—let alone cleaned—for years."

"You're not a lunatic. But when you come to visit me every three days, you enter this."

"But what is this? And what about everybody else in the building? Do they go into the same sort of trance which the concierge seemed to be in?"

"Think whatever you like."

"I still don't get it. Why just the three hours? Why just every few days?"

"Because that's all I can do . . . all I can take. I want this . . . our little liaison. But only on my terms. That's why I refused to see you more than our few hours twice a week."

"Because that's all you were allowed?"

"No one controls me. No one."

"But you still loiter with intent every Sunday on the balcony of some dilettante American's salon, picking up idiots like myself?"

"You were only the second man I ever picked up there."

"Who was the first?"

"A German named Horst. I met him there in June of '91. I had just . . . reemerged, so to speak. And I was revisiting places I had been in the past. So, when I found myself back in Paris—eleven years after my death—I decided to try my luck and see what might come of a sojourn on Lorraine's balcony. I must have lurked there for weeks . . . until Horst saw me. Like you, he was a man in his forties, recently divorced, on his own in Paris, sad, lonely. We chatted. He came to this apartment at the agreed-upon five PM time. We had sex. We drank Scotch. We smoked a few cigarettes. He talked about how his wife had fallen in love with another man, his stalled career as a painter, the lycée where he taught art and how it all bored him, and so forth and so on. All our stories are simultaneously unique and desperately similar, aren't they? At eight o'clock, I told him he had to leave—but that he'd be welcomed back three days later. He said he'd show up. He never did. After that, I occasionally 'returned' to Lorraine's balcony, hoping someone might see me. No one did for years. Until you showed up, Harry. You saw me . . . because you wanted to see me."

"That doesn't make sense."

"You must stop talking about 'sense' or the apparent illogicality of our time together. There is no logic to this—except that we are here together because, as I said before, you wanted to see me."

"That's bullshit."

"Then why did you keep coming here, dutifully, week after week? Simply for the sex?"

"That was a big part of it."

"You're right. It was. But there was more to it than that. You needed to see me . . . in every sense of the word. And I needed to put things right for you."

"I cannot accept—"

"Accept, accept. Faith may be the antithesis of proof . . . but you have proof. You. Me. Here. Now."

"You don't exist."

"I do exist . . . as much as you exist. In this room. This moment. This time. This bit of nothingness that is still everything because it's the instant we share now. You can't escape that, Harry. Nor should you. It's the closest you've ever come to love in your life."

"You have no idea about—"

"Love? How dare you? I went out of my mind for love. I killed—butchered—for love. I have far too many ideas about love . . . and I also know it's like everything else in life: it can drive you to the worst extremes, the absolute edge. Yet, in the great scheme of things, it all comes down to a moment here, a moment there . . . and a flicker of connection with someone else. That's happiness, Harry. Nothing more."

"And what about love for your child?"

Silence. Then she said, "That's everything. And you feel you have to kill the person who takes everything away from you."

"Did the revenge help balm the wounds?"

"You mean, do I still relive the sadness and horror of what happened . . . and of what I did? Of course. I still can't get away from it. It will be with me forever. But I have sought redemption . . . through you."

"That's insane."

"Putting things right for another person isn't insane."

"It is when you resort to violent means to do it."

"But look how everything is gradually working out for you. Robson is in jail. So too is Sezer and his nasty henchman . . . and you know they were both gunning for you. Omar tried to blackmail you. He's been eliminated. Yanna's husband didn't deserve a further day of life on this earth. So I cannot really see how you can complain. Because, in time, things will come even more right for you."

I stood up.

"Do you really think I'm going to buy into this madness?"

"You have already done so, Harry. You've been complicit in this from the start."

"You mean, because I visualized you—the invisible woman—whereas others never did?"

"But why did you see me? Because you needed to. Just as you needed me to settle all the scores you so wanted resolved."

"So you follow me everywhere, is that it?"

"Perhaps."

"But why me?"

"What an absurd question. We are involved."

"You call this an involvement? For you, it was an afternoon fuck twice a week, nothing more."

"And for you, it was . . . ?"

"The one thing I had in my life that I looked forward to."

"Don't you think I also looked forward to it? We didn't just fuck in this room, Harry—and you know it. We talked. We told each other our stories. We found some comfort in that. I certainly grew to like it . . . and to need it. I mightn't have always shown it. I might have discouraged you from getting closer . . . but you still did. You needed me—this—as much as I did you."

"Well, if you think I'm going to keep coming back here, slipping into this little twilight zone you've set up here—"

"You can't leave now," she said, her voice quiet, flat.

"Yes, I can . . . and I will. Because this is now dead. As dead as you."

"No, it's not. Now that you know about me . . . now that you come into this place with me twice a week . . . now that I am the person who watches your back . . . this is not ending."

"Fuck you," I said, walking toward the door.

"A stupid response, Harry. But, I suppose, understandable. You will need time to accept—"

"I am accepting nothing. Got that? Nothing. You're never seeing me again."

"Yes, I am. And you'll want to see me . . . or, at least, call out to me at some moment when you're in a situation from which you can't extricate yourself."

"Don't count on that. Stay away from me."

"No, Harry . . . the real question here is: Can you stay away from me?"

"That won't be hard to do," I said and walked fast toward the door.

"See you in three days," she said as the door closed behind me.

I raced downstairs. Once I had crossed the courtyard I stopped for a moment outside the concierge's lodge. He was still sitting there, comatose to the world. I reached the main door. I hit the button to release the lock. This time it opened with a telltale click. I stepped out into the street. Automotive sounds filled my ears as cars drove by. I looked both ways. There were pedestrians on the rue Linné. The old guy in the corner shop was sitting behind his small counter, looking bored. Life was, per usual, going on around me. I returned to the front door of Margit's apartment. Less than a minute had evaporated since I had crossed back into the quotidian world. I punched in the code. I stepped back inside the courtyard. I turned toward the concierge's lodge. He was no longer in an inanimate state. On the contrary, as soon as he saw me he was on his feet, grabbing a large two-by-four by his desk, then stepping just outside the lodge and brandishing this club.

"You again? I told you to stay away. You go. Now."

I did as requested, hightailing it back out into the street. I walked quickly toward the Jussieu metro station. Halfway there I got a bad case of the shakes. Is she with me right now? Does she shadow my every move?

I ducked into a café. I bought a double whisky. Even when added to all the other Scotch that Margit had poured into me, it still did little to dampen down my anxiety, my growing belief that I had lost all reason. I put my fingers to my nose, the same fingers that Margit had pushed into herself. Her smell was still there. I touched the bandage on my hand. *She's dead . . . and she bandaged that hand.* I ordered another whisky. *Think, think. No, don't think. Just run. Go back to the hotel. Get your bag. Hop a cab to the Gare du Nord. Buy a ticket on the last train out tonight to London. But what about the novel? Fuck the novel. Run.*

And then what? Without the novel I have nothing to show for my time here . . . nothing to do when I get to England. At least if I have the disk I can pick up the narrative again. I can give the day some shape by punching out my quota of words. I can tell myself, *You are trying to accomplish something.* So go back to the office and get the disk. There's now nothing to fear. The place has been raided. Sezer and Mr. Tough Guy are locked up in some *commissariat de police,* and the cops are no longer interested in the place. Get the disk. You'll be in and out of there in less than a minute. Then make a beeline for the Gare du Nord and slam the door on this entire deranged episode . . .

By the time I had left the café I had decided that a better strategy would be to go back to the office in the middle of the night . . . preferably right before dawn. If anyone was lying in wait for me—doubtful, but I was still paranoid—they would most likely give up an all-night stakeout by six. More important, I could sleep until five thirty—sleep now being a major need.

I forced myself out of the café and took the metro to the Gare du Nord, where I booked a ticket on the 7:35 Eurostar to London the next morning. I paid cash. As I counted out the notes, I again wondered if she was watching me buy the ticket. I jumped Line 4 back to Château d'Eau and walked into one of the many long-distance phone shops that lined the boulevard de Sébastopol. The place I entered looked like a fly-by-night operation—and was crowded with men trying to get through to relatives in Yaounde and Dakar and Benin and other West African cities. I bought a phone card and took my place at a crude plywood booth and made a call I was dreading, but couldn't avoid. I checked my watch: 8:05 PM in Paris . . . 2:05 PM in Ohio. Susan answered on the second ring.

"Hi there," I said.

"Harry?" she asked quietly.

"That's right. How are you doing?"

"How am I doing? Terribly, that's how. But you must know that already, otherwise why would you be calling after all this time."

The angry tone was the one she always used with me during the final years of our marriage—when I never seemed to be able to do anything right, and when she seemed to have so completely fallen out of love with me.

"The only reason I haven't called is because you barred me from—"

"I know, I know. Rub it in, why don't you. Especially in light of—"

"Susan, I just called to see how you were. That's all."

A pause. I could hear her stifling a sob.

"He hanged himself this morning."

Oh fuck.

"Robson killed himself?" I said.

"His name was Gardner—and yes, he hanged himself with a bedsheet in his cell early this morning. I just found out. Some asshole reporter from Fox News who called me and asked me for a comment. Can you imagine that?"

I said nothing. She continued, "Over the past week, I have lost everything. Everything. My job, my career. Now that it's been revealed I was fucking the dean of the faculty, no one's going to be hiring me in a hurry. Then there's the little discovery that Gardner had a thing for naked seven-year-old girls and boys. I just can't tell you how horrible it was to . . ."

Another stifled sob.

"Is there anything I can do?" I asked.

"Stop trying to sound magnanimous . . . when I know you must be gloating now that your nemesis . . ."

She broke off, crying. I said, "Susan, I want to talk to Megan."

"Megan's very upset right now. The news about Gardner's crime . . . it was everywhere. All the kids at her school . . . well, you know how horrible children can be."

"Will you tell her I want to speak to her?"

"All right."

"Please ask her to send me an email if she wants me to phone her back. And if you need money or anything . . ."

"Are you still in Paris?"

"That's right."

"Working?"

"Not at the moment."

"Then how can you have money?"

"I did have a job . . . nothing much . . . but I've saved a bit. So if things get tight . . ."

"I can't deal with this . . . you . . . right now."

Then, "I will tell Megan you called."

The line went dead.

You've just overheard all that, haven't you? You must be very proud of your handiwork. Another dead man to add to the tally of my adversaries you've rubbed out. And you expect me to be pleased . . . when all I can really feel is sheer overriding guilt.

Stop, stop. You need sleep. Deep restorative sleep. Take pills. Take whisky. Take whatever you can. Just get back to the hotel and hide under the blankets until day breaks and you can flee everything.

So I returned to my grim room in the Normandie. I repacked my bag. I set the alarm on my portable radio for 5:15 AM. I took pills, I climbed into the damp, saggy bed. I clutched the pillow against me. I kept hearing Margit say, "You can't leave now."

You know, don't you? I'm abandoning you come morning and there's nothing you can do to stop me getting on that train. Spook me all you want. Follow me spectrally to London. I'm still leaving. This is over.

The pills did their stuff. I conked out. When the radio snapped on seven hours later, I jumped up, certain that she was in the room with me. Did that mean she inhabited my unconscious as I slept? She watched me sleep, didn't she? Just as she was standing nearby as I sat in that plywood cubicle, overhearing my conversation with Susan. And now she was plotting to get Susan and . . .

It's morning. You've slept. The train leaves in just over two hours. Go get the disk. Go to the station. Vanish. And this will vanish with you. "Faith is the antithesis of proof." She told you that as a way of playing with your head. The cut on your hand? You cut your hand, acting out this delusional fantasy. The concierge is right: you've lost it. Get the disk. Get the train. Find a sympathetic doctor. Get some pharmaceuticals to end this phantasmagoria in which you've been living. Get back to Planet Earth.

I stood in the tiny shower and turned my face up toward the enervated spray of water. I dressed quickly and was out the front door by five forty. The streets were empty, though a few stallholders in the market on the Faubourg Saint-Denis were taking deliveries from assorted vans. I turned up the rue des Petites Écuries, rolling my suitcase behind me, stealing a quick glance at the shuttered Internet café. Au revoir, Mr. Beard . . . and fuck you too. I reached my former place of work. I stopped at the top of the alleyway and peered down. Light was just breaking in the sky, casting a gray-blue tint on its cracked cobbles. No one could be seen lurking in the shadows. I turned back to the street. Empty, deserted, even devoid of cars. I checked onlooking windows. All shuttered or curtained. No one peering out at me. The coast was clear.

OK, here we go. Start counting and promise yourself by the time you reach sixty you'll have come and gone.

One-one-thousand, two-one-thousand, three-one-thousand, four-one . . .

I reached the front door and looked up and saw that the video camera had been prized off its bracket. Probably taken by the cops as evidence.

I had my key at the ready. I opened the door.

. . . nine-one-thousand, ten-one-thousand, eleven-one-thousand . . .

Inside, the corridor was empty, some police tape hanging limply in front of the steel door at the far end; a door now open. But I didn't stop to inspect what was in this once-forbidden zone. I left my bag by the front door and dashed up the stairs, second key at the ready. I unlocked the door.

. . . seventeen-one-thousand, eighteen-one-thousand, nineteen-one-thousand, twenty-one-thousand . . .

My desk had been turned upside down, the emergency door pried open . . . the escape route that I never had to use. The cops had also pulled up much of the linoleum, but they hadn't seen the small crevice above the emergency exit where I had secreted the disk.

. . . twenty-three-one-thousand, twenty-four-one-thousand, twenty-five-one-thousand . . .

I crossed the room and reached up into the crevice. My fingers touched the disk, but they now couldn't gain purchase around it. Shit. Shit. Shit. I tried to pry a finger to one side of the disk in an attempt to push it forward, then started digging at it with my key.

But just as I started to edge it forward, something happened.

There was a large bang behind me as the office door slammed. And this was immediately followed by the sound of the lock being turned twice.

I dashed across the room and started yanking on the door handle. It wouldn't give. I inserted my key and attempted to turn the lock. It wouldn't budge. When I tried to pull the key out and start again, it remained frozen within the lock. I yanked and yanked on the key, jiggling it madly from side to side. It wouldn't give. I kicked the door, two, three, four times. It wouldn't give . . . it wouldn't fucking give . . .

Then I heard another sound. A loud whoosh—followed by an explosion of hot air from the one ventilator shaft in the room. But this wasn't just an overcharged blast from the heating system—as the air that blew out quickly turned into a gray toxic cloud. Within seconds, the room was fogged in, a sulfuric stench enveloping me, singeing my eyes, my lips, my nose, my lungs. I clawed my way through the cloud to the emergency exit. It was already starting to fill up with smoke, but after about ten steps I hit a pocket of fresher air. The corridor was so narrow I kept hitting my elbows off its sides as I ran toward its end.

But when I reached it, I didn't run into a door that would lead me to some sort of freedom. I just hit a wall. A flat brick wall, against which I crashed. I fell down, stunned. The smoke billowed into the tunnel. All fresh air vanished. I began to choke, to gag, to spew blood through my nose. The cloud thickened. My lungs now felt scorched. I pitched over onto the dirt floor. I continued to gag, to vomit. And I screamed, "Margit! . . . Margit! . . . Margit!"

Nothing happened . . . except that breathing became impossible.

"Margit! . . . Margit! . . . Margit!"

My voice was stifled now, my vision fading. And somewhere within all the vaporous confusion, there was one pervading thought: *So this is*

282 · DOUGLAS KENNEDY

what death is . . . a slow choke to black.

"Margit! . . . Margit! . . . Mar . . ."

My voice was fading. I coughed, I sputtered, I heaved. I should have panicked because death was near. Instead, I began to surrender to as-phyxiation. The panic was replaced by a weird calmness: a sense that dying—even in such appalling circumstances—was the most natural of progressions. You're here. You're not. And everything beyond this smoke-filled room simply continues on.

But the moment I accepted that death was nothing strange, the strangest thing happened.

The door burst open and a fireman dashed in. He was wearing a gas mask and carrying a spare in his hand. He grabbed me and slung the mask over my face. As the rush of oxygen hit, he said two words, "Lucky man."

TWENTY

I SPENT THE NEXT five days in the hospital. My condition—I learned later—was initially listed as "serious, but stable." No burns, but I had suffered severe smoke inhalation and there were worries about the lasting effect on my lungs. My eyes had also been badly singed by the toxic fumes. For the first forty-eight hours they were covered with saline compresses until the inflammation died down. I was also attached to a respirator until the pulmonary specialist ordered a further set of X-rays on me and then decided that, though they had received a scorching, the damage to my lungs would be repaired in time.

"But don't even think about getting on a plane for the next six months," he told me. "Any change in cabin pressure could seriously damage the entire pulmonary system, with fatal consequences. You will simply have to stay put for a while, and consider yourself fortunate to have survived such an incident."

Everyone who attended me in the hospital told me how fortunate I was. The police too. Even Coutard—who came by to see me once I was taken off the respirator. As became quickly apparent, his reasons for seeing me had little to do with inquiring after my health.

"Providence was with you," he said, pulling up a chair next to my bed. "The fireman who rescued you told me that if he had arrived three minutes after he did, you would have definitely died."

"Lucky me, then."

"It's not uncommon to feel depressed after such a close escape. But I'm certain the doctors here can give you something for that as well."

"I'm fine, under the circumstances."

"We've charged someone with the arson and attempted murder. I think you know him: a Monsieur Delik, who works at the Internet café on the rue des Petites Écuries?"

"A guy with a beard and a less-than-sunny disposition?"

"The very gentleman. We have reason to believe that he attempted to burn down the building on the order of Monsieur Sezer—who, as you may remember, is still in custody for ordering the murder of Monsieur Attani over a bad debt. Sezer was your landlord and your employer . . . though he never let on that he was the boss behind that charming establishment where you played night watchman. Delik ran the Internet café after his predecessor, Monsieur Kamal Fatel, was found murdered on the Périphérique. Monsieur Delik has confessed to killing Monsieur Fatel over a dispute about a kilo of heroin that seems to have gone astray while in Fatel's possession. Delik was promised half-ownership of the café if he would eliminate Fatel, whom Sezer thought was also trying to muscle in on several of his enterprises.

"Now Delik still refuses to admit responsibility for setting the fire that nearly ended your life. He also adamantly denies locking you in that room and turning on the heating fan full blast and pouring sulfur onto the fire that was started near the generator which runs the building's ventilation system. But a bag of sulfur was found at the Internet café. He continues to deny knowledge of its existence. But who else would have put it there?"

I can tell you exactly who put it there.

"The bag was three-quarters empty—and the sulfur used in the fire exactly matched that found at the café. So voilà, we have definitive proof that he was the arsonist. You should consider yourself fortunate that some anonymous woman—a passerby—phoned the *pompiers* after seeing smoke rise from the top floor of the building. That woman turned out to be your savior, monsieur."

"Did she say who she was?"

"Not at all, monsieur. She simply reported the fire and hung up. Another of your phantom women, no doubt."

No, just my one and only phantom woman.

"We also believe that Delik was responsible for destroying your room. Quite a mess he left there."

"You were snooping around my room?"

"We were alerted to the fact that your room was ripped apart—"

"By whom?"

"Monsieur, it was located next door to a crime scene. Our officers had to return to the place where Monsieur Omar died for assorted administrative reasons, and discovered your *chambre de bonne* in upheaval. Naturally we investigated . . . because we were curious as to why someone would want to so destroy the room of a rather poor writer. And by 'poor' I am referring to your financial state, not your literary abilities . . . though we did commission a translation, *en français naturellement,* of the first chapter of your novel, just to validate your claims that you are a novelist."

"Is that legal?" I asked, my voice hoarse, barely audible.

"You should be pleased, monsieur. You have become a translated writer. Many would kill for the chance . . . though that might be a wrong choice of words under the circumstances."

"Did you like it?"

"Ah, this proves that you are a true writer. Always concerned about public reaction. Yes, I found it very . . . interesting."

"So you didn't like it."

"How can you discern such a thing?"

"Because, despite rumors to the contrary, Americans do understand irony."

"But your first chapter was . . . fascinating. Most fascinating. The day-to-day rhythms of American suburbia. The conservative father, the crazy mother, the sensitive son. Most original . . . and I do presume there are certain autobiographical elements that—"

"You've made your point. Thanks."

"Monsieur, you take me the wrong way. I would have continued reading . . . but that would have meant hiring the translator to deal with the subsequent chapters and as the book is terribly long . . . over six hundred pages so far, and your hero is still not out of university. I presume it's what the Germans call a bildungsroman, *ja*? It certainly has the heft of a bildungsroman—"

"*Heft* is also a synonym for *ponderous*."

"Again, you misread me. But literary criticism is not the object of this conversation. Rather, it's piecing together the narrative of your life on the rue de Paradis. So having ascertained that, yes, you were writing a book and had this very strange job—about which you initially lied to us—we were still curious as to why your room was torn apart. Given that several of your associates—"

"They were never my associates."

"So you say. But given that many of the people with whom you associated—both personally and professionally—were also involved in the sale of illegal substances, we naturally wondered if you yourself were hoarding a kilo or so of—"

"I never, never had anything to do with . . ."

I started to cough and sputter; the agitation causing me to suffer shortness of breath; my mouth tasting of burned phlegm. Coutard stood up and handed me the glass of water on the table by my bed. I sipped it and struggled to keep the water down. Coutard watched me impassively. When the spluttering subsided, he said, "There is also the question of the twenty-eight hundred euros we found in the pocket of your jacket. Wrapped up in several plastic bags. An intriguing way of carrying money."

I tried to explain how I had saved all that money, how it was kept hidden in a hole beneath the sink in plastic bags, and how it was the only money I had in the world, so were he to "impound" it . . .

"You will be on the street?" he asked.

"I won't be able to live. Because I have nothing. Nothing. You can run a credit check on me, search for bank accounts. You'll find zilch. That twenty-eight hundred is my entire net worth."

Silence. I noticed that he had a Zippo lighter in between his right finger and thumb and he was clicking it open and shut. The man was desperate for a cigarette.

"You will get your money back . . . because it has no real bearing on our investigations. Your bags and clothes were clean. We found nothing in your room . . . though I am still intrigued as to why it was pulled apart."

Because she's a mad bitch, that's why.

"It's a strange quartier . . ." I said.

Coutard allowed himself a little smile.

"Of this I have no doubt. Just as I also know that you are a man of remarkable naïveté to have fallen into a job like that."

"It wasn't naïveté, Inspector. It was indifference to what happened to me."

"That's another definition for *nihilism*. But in your case, the nihilism is mixed in with tendencies toward delusion. Or have you finally accepted that Madame Kadar is dead?"

"Yes, I know now that she is truly dead."

"Well, that is an improvement. Did your near-death experience somehow convince you that there is a considerable frontier between temporal life and the underworld?"

"Something like that, yes."

"And all that extraordinary knowledge you had on Madame Kadar's long-forgotten life? Can you now explain to me why you had amassed such detailed information?"

"Does it matter anymore?"

Click, click, click as he opened and closed the Zippo again.

"I suppose it doesn't," he said.

A wave of tiredness hit me. I slumped against the pillows on the bed. Coutard took the hint and stood up.

"The doctors say you will be discharged in a few days. What will you do then?"

"Find a new place to live and try to finish my novel. That's the only reason I was in the office that night, to retrieve the disk that I had left there . . ."

"Yes, I had read that in the statement you gave Inspector Leclerc yesterday."

"Did he also tell you that if you had given me back my laptop, I wouldn't have had to return there for the disk . . . ?"

Click. Click. Click.

"The laptop was part of an ongoing investigation," he said. "Had you had a disk in your room . . ."

I did have a disk in my room. But she took it when she trashed the place. To panic me. To force me back to the office so she could lock me in and set fire to the place and leave me no option but to cry out for her help. Whereupon . . .

"When can I get the laptop back?" I asked.

"In time."

"Might I, at least, get a copy of the novel transferred to a disk?"

"In time."

I shut my eyes. I said nothing.

"We will, no doubt, be in touch," Coutard said. "We will naturally need your new address once you are discharged from here . . . so we will know where to contact you when the laptop is ready to be returned."

And to know where to keep tabs on me.

"Fine," I said.

"You're a free man now," Coutard said.

I am not free.

They kept me in the hospital for a further five days. Leclerc came by on the final day with a copy of a statement for me to sign—a reiteration of my story of how I had been locked into the office as the fire started, and how I had been in the employ of Monsieur Sezer, who had always kept the nature of the activities in the building a secret from me.

"This will lend weight to the accusation that he ordered Delik to destroy the building and yourself at the same time."

They were also buying my story about not knowing what went on downstairs, while framing a man for a crime he didn't commit. But isn't that how all narratives are framed? We apportion blame to some, excuse others, and hope that the tidy package will end the story in a satisfactory way. If I now started talking about how the fire was all down to "her," that would complicate the way they wanted the story to work—and it might lead to me being transferred to the nearest rubber room. Anyway, Delik was guilty of other things. We all are.

I signed the statement. As I handed it back, Leclerc said, "You must feel vindicated after what happened to the gentleman who orchestrated your problems in the States."

So they had continued to track the Robson story. Then again, they were cops. And cops tracked anything that had to do with tracking you.

"I orchestrated my problems," I said. "Whatever I feel about that man, I still pity him."

"You are more magnanimous than I would be, under the circumstances."

Magnanimous. That word again. I wasn't magnanimous. I was just aware of a third party controlling everything.

"You seem to be on the mend," he said as he was leaving.

Nothing's mended.

But they did give me my walking papers the next day. Using the phone directory the day before, I had come across a great find: an actual one-star hotel in the Sixth. The guy on the desk sounded pleasant. Yes, they had a room available—seventy euros a night. "But you say you need it for three or four weeks? Then I can reduce it to sixty euros per night."

I did some fast math. Four-twenty a week and another one-fifty in living expenses. I had just enough to fund the next month and a half.

And then? And then? How will you survive?

No idea.

The hotel was on the rue du Dragon. As I got out of the taxi with my suitcase, I scanned the street. Shoe shops everywhere. Expensive women in expensive clothes. Tidy pavements. Tourists. Businessmen in suits. Good restaurants. Money.

The hotel was agreeable in a fusty old-fashioned way. But it was clean, and the bed was hard, and the floor-to-ceiling windows let in considerable light, and the two men who ran the front desk remained professionally polite. I was also within walking distance of fifteen cinemas. But venturing out was not something I was interested in doing right now. The effects of smoke inhalation were still very much with me. I tried a shortish walk to the Odéon and a secondhand English-language bookshop on rue Monsieur-le-Prince. But after buying four paperbacks, I found the walk home to the hotel a strain—and I collapsed in bed for the rest of the day. The hospital had provided me with three small canisters of oxygen—each with a plastic mouthpiece attached to the top. The nurse in charge of me told me to administer four or five blasts of oxygen whenever shortness of breath arrived. By the end of my first day at the hotel, one of the cans was nearly empty. I could hardly sleep that first night—not just because of my irregular, painful breathing . . . but also because at five the next afternoon, I was due back at rue Linné.

Because I was still attached to a ventilator I had missed our rendezvous three days ago. I figured she understood that—and would excuse it. But as she was following my every move, she also knew I was mobile enough to have checked into this hotel. So I would be expected to show up at her place tomorrow without fail.

I stayed in bed all that day, tiredness still overwhelming me. I left the hotel at four forty. I walked to the taxi rank on the boulevard Saint-Germain. There was—miraculously for rush hour—a single taxi in line. I took it. I arrived at the rue Linné ten minutes later. I crossed into the Jardin des Plantes. I walked slowly, conscious of my breathing. My lungs still felt as if I had been a three-pack-a-day smoker for the last thirty years, but the breathlessness seemed a little less ominous today. I noticed the verdancy around me, the deep blue sky, the hint of heat in the air. Early summer had arrived. In fact it had probably arrived weeks ago—but my head was elsewhere.

Four fifty-five. I approached the door. Five PM I punched in the code. Click. I stepped inside, entering that big silence I now recognized as not being normal. The concierge was immobile in his lodge. I headed up the stairs. Not a sound from a single apartment. Until I knocked on her door. She opened it and said, "You should have been here three days ago."

"A fire delayed me," I said, stepping by her into the apartment.

"Really?" she said, following me in.

I grabbed her arm and pulled it up behind her back.

"Don't bullshit me. You know exactly what happened."

"Trying to hurt me now, Harry?" she said, struggling against the arm. "Because you can't. Pain doesn't have any effect on me."

I pushed her away.

"Well, it does on me—and I nearly died."

"But you made a rapid enough recovery if you're now able to push me around."

"Push you around? You follow me everywhere—"

"You have no proof of that—"

"—you trap me in a burning building. And then, having told me that I would be in a situation where I'd have no choice but to cry out for you and demand your help, I do find myself in a situation where I have no choice but to cry out and demand your help. And what happens?"

She smiled and lit a cigarette.

"You have no proof of that."

"The cops said a woman phoned them."

"Maybe she did. And maybe you should have made more copies of this."

She reached into the pocket of her robe and pulled out a black floppy disk.

"You stole that from my room . . ."

"It's just a floppy disk. One of many millions. And it doesn't have an identifying label on it. Who's to say that it's yours?"

"You knew that the only reason I went back to that hellhole of an office was to retrieve the disk containing my novel because—"

"The cops impounded your computer after they raided that building?"

"There! That's my proof you've been following me—"

"But you still have no actual proof . . . except that you think that I started the fire near the ventilation shaft on the second floor of the building, and added three-quarters of a bag of sulfur, which I later hid in the Internet café to make certain that the entire business was pinned on that bastard Delik—"

"Stop playing with my head."

She came toward me, opening her robe. She had nothing on underneath.

"But I like playing with your head," she said, reaching for my pants. "It's so easy."

I tried to pull away, but she grabbed hold of my belt and forced my crotch against hers.

"If you think I'm going to fuck you—"

"I do think that," she said, popping the buttons on my fly.

"I'm not interested," I said, trying again to push her away.

She reached in and took hold of my now erect penis.

"Liar," she said. "And don't give me any crap about your scorched lungs."

She grabbed the back of my head and shoved her tongue down my throat, then pushed my pants down. I threw her onto the bed. I was inside her immediately. She became violent, pulling my hair, biting into my neck. But I didn't resist, instead drilling into her with angry ferocity. I came fast. So did she. But as soon as it was over, I too felt something close to derangement. Standing up, I touched my neck and felt blood.

"Just think," she said, reaching for her cigarettes. "You've just fucked a dead woman who made you bleed."

I pulled on my jeans.

"Going so soon?" she asked.

"What do you want from me?"

She laughed.

"What do I want from you? *Quel mélodrame*, Harry. You know what I want. Our little rendezvous every three days. Nothing more, nothing less. You come here at the specified time. We make love—or 'fuck' if you prefer. We drink a little whisky. We talk a bit. You leave at eight, *comme d'habitude*. I don't care who you see or what you do when you are not here. Go where you want, sleep with who you want . . . as long as you are here at the times agreed. And in exchange for your visits—your fidelity to our rendezvous—I can promise you—"

"What?" I asked. "Eternal life?"

"Oh, you will die . . . like everyone. That's something completely beyond my power. But one thing I can promise you is that, for the rest of your life, you will have someone watching your back at all times, smoothing the way for you. As I said last time, I cannot manipulate things to give you fame and fortune. Getting your novel published, for example . . ."

"Have you read it?"

"Well, I do have the disk . . ."

"But no computer."

"I have access to any computer I want—as long as the person who owns it isn't using it at the time. Anyway, I read it. It's clear you have talent, Harry. Abundant talent. Your turn of phrase, your sense of place, your ability to describe a character's attributes and complexities. All very admirable. The problem—for me, anyway—is that you cannot simply tell the story and let us discover your cleverness. You have to remind us all the time how clever—and faux-poetic—you are . . ."

"Faux-poetic?"

"Don't take it so hard, Harry . . . but the narrative is swamped by this absurd lyricism, this need to overexplain, this terrible portentousness—"

"Everyone's a fucking critic, aren't they?"

"Are you talking about the inspector?"

"So you were there in the hospital room when he told me—"

"—that he had the first chapter of your novel translated? You have no proof that I was there, but—"

"Can I have the disk back?"

"By all means," she said, reaching into the pocket of her robe and tossing it on the front of the bed. "But honestly, you should either re-work the entire narrative, cutting out all the posturing, the—"

"I don't want to hear any more of this—"

"As you like . . ."

I picked up the disk.

"I'm never coming back here."

A weary sigh as she sat up and closed her robe and reached for her cigarettes.

"Harry, why make trouble for yourself when I ask so little and offer so much?"

"Because you're insisting I be indentured to you for—"

"Three hours twice a week! You call that being 'indentured'? Think of your current predicament. No job. No prospects. And what do you have saved from that awful night job? Twenty-eight hundred euros. All right, you'll eke out a few weeks in that one-star hotel on the rue du Dragon. But then . . . ?"

I put my face in my hands, as again I heard that voice in my head: *She is everywhere . . . she knows everything.*

"I'm not coming back . . . and that is final."

"Fool."

"I don't care what you do to me."

"Yes, you do. And yes, you will . . ."

"It doesn't matter."

"It will matter to you."

"Torture me, ruin me some more, even take my life . . ."

"Harry, you don't know what you're saying."

"I know exactly—"

But I couldn't finish that sentence, as I suddenly doubled over, coughing wildly. Phlegm filled my mouth and, for a few moments, I felt as if I were drowning. Margit stood up and guided me into the bath-room, where she held me as I coughed up black gunk into the sink. Then she led me into her kitchen area and opened a cabinet and handed me a canister of oxygen. Check that: the exact same make of oxygen that had been given to me in the hospital. I took it from her with relief and pried off the cap and clasped the mouthpiece in my teeth and took two deep blasts of the oxygen. It helped. After a third blast, my breathing eased.

"Let me guess," I said. "You got the canister at the hospital where I was recovering from your pyrotechnics?"

"Perhaps . . ."

I stood up, tucking the canister under my arm.

"You should leave that here for the next time," Margit said.

"There's not going to be a next time."

"Yes, there will."

"Don't count on it."

"You'll be here—because you'll have to be here. But Harry—think carefully before you decide to terminate your minor obligations—"

"Obligations? I'm not indebted to you for anything."

"You called out for me when you were about to die . . . and then you didn't die."

"You are not my savior, and you are not seeing me again."

"Don't make me force you back here."

"Do whatever you want to do," I said. And I left.

Half an hour later I was back in the hotel, curled up on the bed, a blanket over me, the plastic wastebasket from the bathroom near me in case I had another phlegm attack. But I now expected to have the roof of my room collapse on me, or to be attacked by a platoon of poisonous bedbugs, or to start spitting up internal organs (surely she couldn't orchestrate something so invasive). I touched my neck and felt the still-moist wound she had made with her teeth. *You've just fucked a dead woman who made you bleed.* I covered my head with a pillow. This can't be happening. I also thought of a lifetime of afternoon liaisons stretching out in front of me—all in service of some surreal notion that I had a permanent guardian angel lurking in my corner, as long as I screwed her twice a week. *You have no proof.* How she taunted me with that phrase. But my anguished attempts at disbelief were quickly superseded by a realization that had taken hold of me in the hospital and had only been reinforced by my encounter with Margit that afternoon: This was all very real. And I did take seriously her threats to bring further harm to me if I didn't meet my "obligations" to her. But I didn't care anymore. Let her take my life. It meant so little to me now.

I holed up in the room until one the following afternoon, finally venturing out for something to eat. I stopped in an Internet café. There was only one email in my inbox: a long missive from Doug, telling me the details of Robson's suicide. He also said that Susan had gone to ground. She had been officially dismissed from the college, and was also now under FBI investigation to see if she was, in any way, involved in Robson's extracurricular "business."

> *I did call her yesterday and she sounded rough. Word has it that she has been suffering from appalling depression— who can blame her—and that Megan is understandably traumatized by what has happened. If you could get back here for a few days, I think it might do Megan some good. If you broach this idea with Susan, I sense she will respond positively to it.*

After reading this, I used a search engine to find all the up-to-date press reports on Robson's suicide. There were plenty of them. Susan's dismissal from the college had also merited a few paragraphs in the news reports, cross-referenced with the scandal that had forced me out of my job. That was the thing about a media feeding frenzy—it engulfed everybody, and I could only begin to imagine the grief that my poor innocent daughter was taking at school for her parents' crimes and misdemeanors.

Switching back to my Internet server, I wrote Susan:

> *I am genuinely sorry to hear of your terrible problems. I just want you to know that I am here to help. As I mentioned in our last phone call, I would also very much like to reestablish contact with Megan, and would be most happy to come back and see her, if she is willing to see me. If you want to contact me by phone . . .*

And I supplied the number for the hotel and for my room there.

I checked my email the following morning and night. No reply. Otherwise I spent most of the day in my room, reading and sleeping and having the occasional bout of hack coughing. The following day there was also no email from Susan. I went to the movies—Hitchcock's last film, *Family Plot*. I managed a fifteen-minute walk by the Seine. At 5:00 PM I returned to the hotel, missing my rendezvous with Margit.

I waited for the sky to fall in. It happened late the following night. The phone in my room rang just before midnight. It was Susan. She could barely talk.

"Megan was knocked down by a car on her way to school today. A hit-and-run driver. She's still unconscious with a broken leg and a fractured pelvis and they don't know if she's suffered any brain damage, but the fact that she doesn't respond to . . ."

She started weeping uncontrollably. She managed to get out a few more words, saying that she'd been taken by ambulance that afternoon to the University Hospital in Cleveland, where they had the best neurology department in the state. "I'm calling from there right now," she said. "It doesn't look good. It doesn't . . ."

She broke off, unable to speak anymore. I told her I'd get the first plane out tomorrow morning. Then I hung up and staggered into the bathroom and fell down in front of the toilet and got violently ill. When I could heave no longer, I started to cry.

Don't make me force you back here.

Do whatever you want to do.

And she had done just that.

I didn't sleep. I wandered the streets all night. I found a twenty-four-hour Internet café near Les Halles and went online and discovered there was a 9:00 AM flight to Chicago that morning, with an onward connection to Cleveland at 2:00 PM local time. Had I been in possession of a functional credit card I would have booked the flights on the spot. Instead I returned to the hotel and asked the night man to book me a taxi leaving for the airport at 5:00 AM. The guy on the desk—his name was Tadeusz, he was Polish—was fantastically kind when I told him why I had to rush back to the States. He said he would hold my room for me at no charge ("It's a quiet time for us"), and was a little surprised when I said I would definitely be back in Paris within forty-eight hours.

"But do not worry, sir. If we need the room we can always pack up your things and store them. If your daughter's condition hasn't improved . . ."

My daughter's condition will only improve if I present myself at 13 rue Linné at 5:00 PM in two days' time.

I was at the airport by six. I paid cash for a round-trip ticket to Cleveland via Chicago, returning to Paris that evening. I phoned Susan on her cell phone from a kiosk inside the departure lounge. It was just after one in the morning in Ohio. She sounded exhausted and stressed beyond the limits of endurance. "She's still unconscious," she said, her voice barely a whisper. "The MRI has shown some bruising to the brain, but the neurologist still cannot determine how damaged it is. The fact that she's not responded to any stimuli is, he admitted, very worrying. The next twenty-four hours will be critical."

"I'll be there by two PM your time. Meanwhile, try to get some sleep."

"I don't want to sleep. I just want my daughter back."

I felt sick. And helpless. And crazed. Did Margit put Megan in the way of the car that hit her? Susan had yet to tell me the details of the accident . . . but in my more rational moments, I couldn't help but think that Margit had set this up as a near-facsimile of the accident that had killed her daughter and husband. But say she hadn't set it up? Say it was all just terrible happenstance? What then? And what if Megan died? *You never get over the loss of a child. Never.*

When the plane took off and I felt my diaphragm starting to contract, I could again hear the pulmonary specialist tell me I'd be risking death by flying. Ten minutes later, as we reached cruising altitude, I felt a crushing pain in my chest. The large woman seated next to me said to her friend, "Oh my God, he's having a coronary!" and rang for a hostess. Two of them arrived, looking very concerned.

"Are you all right, sir?"

I explained it was just a little breathlessness after a lung injury ("You were actually caught in a fire!" one of them said), and asked them if they had any oxygen. One of them disappeared, returning moments later with a canister. I gripped the mouthpiece between my lips and blasted myself three times. Presto. The pain dissipated, but the anguished thought that Megan might die continued to clobber me.

"I think we might be able to find you somewhere more comfortable for the remainder of the flight," one of the hostesses said.

I was escorted to the rarefied confines of Business Class and a seat that turned into a bed. I accepted pillows and a duvet. I went into the bathroom and changed into the sleeper suit they provided. I popped a Zopiclone. I returned to the seat. I hit myself with two more blasts of oxygen and passed out for six hours. It was the first proper sleep I had received in days—and when I awoke thirty minutes outside of Chicago, I felt that, at least, I would be able to function, no matter how terrible the next twenty-four hours might turn out to be.

The landing was tricky—the decompression causing my diaphragm to turn viselike again. Two minutes before we hit the runway, the pressure was so bad I felt as if I was starting to strangle. The oxygen did little good . . . until we were on the ground and I could re-blast myself for a solid minute, emptying one of the canisters in the process.

I had similar problems in the air between Chicago and Cleveland, emptying another whole canister en route and feeling completely breathless by the time I reached University Hospital half an hour after landing.

The Neurological Unit was located on two floors in a new wing of the hospital. ICU was at the far end of a hallway. I was escorted inside by an attending nurse. She said my timing had been good, as the neurological resident was on the ward right now. "I must warn you that walking into the unit always unnerves people the first time, and you might find all the apparatus around Megan rather disturbing. If you find you can't take it—and many people can't—just let me know and we'll get you out of there straightaway."

Her bed was at the end of the unit. That meant walking past patient after patient, all unconscious, all looking submerged by wiring, monitors, probes, drips, and a spaghetti junction of tubes. When I reached Megan's bed, I felt as if I had been kicked in the stomach. There was nothing different about all the apparatus engulfing her. It was simply the realization that this was my little girl, being kept alive by all this medical paraphernalia, including a ventilator that let out an ominous whish as it regulated her breathing. Her long blond hair had been hidden inside a white surgical cap—but her face, though bruised, was, as always, angelic. Susan was seated slumped in a chair, looking more tired than I had ever seen her. Her face was drawn, her shoulders hunched, her eyes sunken, her nails ravaged. A man in a white coat was talking to her in a calm voice. I approached

Susan and put my arm around her shoulder. She reacted stiffly to this—no hello or greeting, and she quietly disengaged herself from my attempt at a supportive hug . . . something the doctor noticed immediately.

"This is Megan's father," Susan said tonelessly.

I shook his hand and introduced myself. His name was Barry Clyde. A guy in his late thirties. Calm, considerate, if a little professionally distanced.

"I was just telling Susan that Megan has suffered what could be described in layman's terms as a deep concussion which has been coupled with a certain amount of brain-stem trauma. The MRI showed considerable bruising on the brain stem. The good news is that such bruising does dissipate and can be followed by a gradual recovery. The more tentative, difficult news is that she continues to be unable to respond to stimuli. Frankly, this has us worried. It could be that the concussion is so pervasive she simply has to heal first before emerging from this comatose state. But—and I must be direct with you about this—it could also be that she has suffered far more profound neurological damage and might be in this absent state for . . . well, it's hard to gauge how long this could go on for."

"Is there a chance she might die?" I asked.

"All her other vital signs are good, her heart is immensely strong, and the brain is getting all the oxygen it needs. So, no, death is not an immediate worry. But—and again I must outline the worst for you, just so you can be prepared—a persistent vegetative state might continue indefinitely. That, I should add, is the worst-case scenario . . ."

I bowed my head and closed my eyes and felt tears sting them. The doctor touched my shoulder. "Please don't give up hope. The brain is an extraordinarily mysterious organ and can frequently recover from serious trauma. Time will tell."

He left us alone. We both stood there, in front of the daughter we made together, saying nothing. When Susan started to break down again and I tried to take her hand, she pushed it away, saying, "I don't want—need—your comfort."

"OK," I said quietly. "How about a cup of coffee?"

"You just got here and you immediately want to go out for a coffee? Spend some time with your daughter."

"I can't bear to look at her like that."

"Well, get used to it. She's not coming out of this. I called my brother Fred yesterday. He put me on to a friend of his—a leading neurologist out in the Bay Area. I was able to get everything about Megan's case emailed to him in San Francisco. He was much more blunt about it than Dr. Clyde. 'In these sorts of brain-stem trauma cases, there is generally less than a fifteen percent chance that the person will make a full recovery, and more than a fifty percent chance that she will never emerge from that vegetative state.'

"Fifteen percent isn't zero—"

"But it's shit odds. And I keep telling myself, If only I had driven her to school yesterday. But I was rushing to see my fucking lawyer, who's doing his best to keep me out of jail as well."

"Surely the Feds don't think you had anything to do with Robson's porn business."

"You've evidently been kept well informed on my downfall. And it must give you enormous pleasure, under the circumstances."

"It gives me no pleasure at all. And let's not fight in front of Megan."

"Why not? She can't hear us. Even if she could, what would she think? How wonderful it is to have a pair of narcissistic fuckups as parents?"

"I'm sure she's been terribly torn apart by what's happened over the last year. But that doesn't mean she hates us. And if we can somehow make it all up to her—"

"Listen to you, Mr. Bromide, Mr. Polly-Fucking-Anna. She's not coming out of this, Harry. We've lost her. And she is the innocent victim in all this. Whereas we . . ."

Again she started to lose it, grabbing on to the metal railings on Megan's bed and crying wildly. The attending nurse came marching down the corridor at speed. She put her arm around Susan's shoulder and led her off back toward the doorway. I stood by the bed and gripped the railings as well, trying not to fall apart, trying to tell myself that I would make this better, that I would get her out of it, no matter what it took.

The nurse returned a few minutes later.

"Your wife is about to be seen by a doctor. He will probably admit her for nervous exhaustion—and we'll find her a bed. She's at breaking point, the poor thing—and who can blame her. If you'd like to see her after the doctor . . ."

"I think I'm about the last person she wants to see right now."

The nurse thought about that for a moment, then said, "Is there anything I can get you?"

"A glass of water, please. And I would like to stay here for a while . . ."

I sat in front of my daughter's bed for the next five hours. I held her warm hand, I watched the undulating beeps of the heart monitor and was frequently lulled into nodding off by the metronomic whoosh of the respirator. I sat there, thinking, thinking, thinking. I put my head in my hands. I started to whisper, *All right, Margit, I'll be back with you tomorrow. I will never miss another of our rendezvous again. You'll have me for as long as you want to have me. Just bring Megan back to us whole.*

I nodded off around midday and woke with a start at three. Megan was still motionless, her eyes stock-still. At five I forced myself out of the stiff uncomfortable metal chair. I leaned over and kissed her good-bye. Then I found the nurse on duty and explained that I had to fly back to Paris now, but to tell my wife that I'd be in touch by phone within the next twenty-four hours.

A cab to the airport, an hour long flight to Chicago, a two-hour stopover, seven and a half hours over the Atlantic: a sleepless night of coughing and sputtering, and I started to have that drowning sensation when the plane made its final approach. Once we were inside the terminal I staggered into a bathroom, bent over a toilet, and heaved up clumps of reddish phlegm. Then I threw some water on my face and headed off to Immigration—an experience I was dreading, just in case the cops at the *commissariat de police* in the Tenth had informed the frontier boys that I was an American whom France could easily do without.

I approached the booth. The cop scanned my passport, glanced at his screen, and said, "Back again with us?"

"I like it here."

"Are you working?"

"I'm a writer. I work for myself. So I'm not holding down a job here."

"And how long will you be with us this time?"

"A few weeks," I lied. "No more."

Stamp, stamp. I was back in . . . with a new three-month visa.

The clerk at the hotel on the rue du Dragon smiled and handed me the key as I came in.

"Did your daughter recover?"

"Not yet."

"Does it look good?"

"No."

"I don't know what to say but 'sorry.'"

"Thanks for that."

"If you want to sleep now, the room's ready."

"Please call me at four, in case I don't get up."

I slept straight through the afternoon. I was out of the hotel by four thirty. I was outside Margit's front door just at five. I stepped inside the parallel world. I climbed the stairs, she opened the door on the first knock. That's when I slugged her, catching her with my fist right in the mouth. She fell backward onto the bed.

"You fucking bitch . . . you punish me by trying to kill my daughter . . ."

She stood up, holding her cheek.

"You have no proof."

"Don't fucking say that again," I shouted and then caught her across the face with the back of my hand. She collapsed back on the bed again, but then turned up at me and smiled.

"You forget, Harry—pain means nothing to me. But pain means everything to you. All you do is live in pain. And you know what you've just demonstrated? You're like every man I've ever known. When you discover you're powerless, you lash out . . . even though the act of punching a woman is nothing more than a testament to your complete pathetic impotency. But go on, Harry. Punch me again. Pull off my clothes and ravage me while you're at it. Anything to make you feel better."

"The only thing that is going to make me feel better is if my daughter comes out of her coma and has a complete recovery with no lasting side effects."

"You ask a lot, Harry."

"You've got to help me—"

"No, I've got to help her. But that can only happen if you play by the rules of the game. Here from five until eight every three days without fail. If you say yes now, and then don't show up for our next rendezvous, your daughter will die. As soon as you are here—"

"I promise I will be here."

Silence. She sat up.

"That's settled then. You can go now. We will start again at our next rendezvous as if this never happened. But do know that if you ever hit me again . . ."

"I will never hit you again."

"I'll hold you to that, Harry. Now go."

"Before I do, I need to know something. Are these rendezvous of ours going to go on indefinitely?"

"Yes, they are. *À bientôt* . . ."

En route back to the hotel, I stopped in a kiosk and rang Susan's cell phone. When I explained that I was back in Paris, her reaction was angry.

"That's so damn typical of you, running away in the middle of a crisis . . ."

"I had no choice. I have a job interview today, and you will be needing money to keep going . . ."

"Don't guilt trip me here, Harry."

"Why, why do you always think I'm attacking you when all I'm doing is—?"

"Reminding me I have lost my goddamn job and am just praying that Blue Cross will cover these hospital bills. Otherwise, it's bankruptcy and—"

"Is there any change there? Any sign of improvement?"

"Not so far."

"Did you get any rest?"

"A bit, yeah."

"Please call me as soon as there's any change."

"OK," she said and hung up.

A day went by. I ventured up to the hospital for a previously arranged appointment with the specialist. He ordered an X-ray and gave me a very hard time when he saw the state of my lungs.

"You've been on a plane, haven't you?"

"My daughter is seriously unwell, and I had no choice but to—"

"Try and kill yourself? I warned you, monsieur, about the tremendous dangers that pressurized environments cause. By choosing to ignore me, you have retarded your recovery completely. The reason you have blood in your phlegm is evident. Take another journey in a pressurized cabin and you might do yourself fatal damage. You are grounded for at least six months. Understood?"

I returned to my room in the hotel. I counted out the cash I had left after paying for the ticket to the States. Around eighteen hundred dollars. Don't think about it. Just take everything as it comes now. What else can you do?

I stayed in the room, trying to read, trying to think about everything but Megan. Eventually, around ten that evening, I climbed into bed. Three hours later I was jolted awake by the ringing phone.

"A call for you, monsieur," said the night clerk. With a click he put it through. It was Susan. And the first words she said to me were, "She opened her eyes."

TWENTY-ONE

THE SAME EVENING that she opened her eyes, Megan began to speak again. The next day she was able to be fed by spoon. Forty-eight hours later, she insisted on getting up out of bed to use the toilet. Despite having a cast on her left arm and leg she still managed to hobble there on crutches. The following morning, the police found the driver of the hit-and-run vehicle. It was a messy story—a recently divorced woman in her forties; a lawyer in a big-deal firm in Cleveland, with "alcohol issues." On the morning of the accident, she had been drinking in her hotel room during breakfast. She was blotto and smashed into Megan around five minutes after leaving the hotel. She panicked and kept on driving, eventually checking into a motel near the Kentucky border, where the cops found her. She was heavily insured—and the lawyer now representing Megan threatened publicity if she and her law firm didn't settle quickly.

"The negotiation was very fast," Susan told me in our daily transatlantic phone call. "Our guy was a complete sonofabitch and very shrewd. Megan will be getting a check for half a million dollars. So that's her college education sorted out—and it will give us a little cushion until I find a new job."

I said, "The important thing is, she will have no lasting physical effects from the accident. The psychological scars, on the other hand—"

"—will be added to the large amount of shit that her parents have already dumped into her lap . . . and the fact that her mother is a slut who slept her way back into a tenured position at the college by fucking a pedophile."

"I really think you should stop blaming yourself here—"

"But I do. I do."

"Well, I blame myself too."

"You're being magnanimous again . . . which is a way of making me feel bad."

"You think that, by being reconciliatory, I'm actually trying to get at you? I just feel very sorry for you . . ."

Silence. I could hear her weeping into the phone.

"I'm sorry, I'm sorry . . ." she whispered. "I've messed up so badly. I've . . ."

"Our daughter is alive and well. That's the only thing that matters right now. And I do want to speak with her again," I said.

"I did tell her you rushed over to be by her side. She seemed happy about that, but couldn't understand why you had to hurry back so fast to Paris."

Because the dead woman who had put Megan in the path of that car demanded her twice-weekly "service." If I had failed in this obligation, our daughter would have remained in her coma.

"As I tried to explain to you in that phone call . . . I had a job interview . . ."

"You could have told them your daughter was seriously injured," she said at the time.

"I did tell them that—and they were very understanding, but also said that they had to fill the post immediately. I have no money. Nor do you. So I really couldn't tell them to wait—"

"That's right—rub it in again that I lost my job. Heighten my massive guilt about—"

"Susan . . . stop."

"But if I stop, you won't have to listen to the truth. And the truth is—"

The truth is: these sorts of conversations are why I started hating this marriage . . .

"The truth is . . ." I said, interrupting her, "I cannot travel anywhere now for the next six months."

"What?" she said, sounding outraged.

I explained about being caught in a fire at the place where I was a night watchman (she had a hard time accepting that bit of information), and that I was told by the specialist who treated me that I couldn't risk air travel now.

"So do you want me to congratulate you on risking your life by flying to your daughter's bedside?"

"Susan, I honestly do not give a shit what you think. What I do know is that, when I got back here I was coughing up blood. The pulmonary specialist has grounded me until after Christmas. This is completely maddening, as where I want to be right now is with Megan. But go ahead and think the worst of me. You always have. You always will."

And I hung up.

Several hours later, as I lay next to Margit in her bed, she said, "I liked the way you handled things today with Susan. Far more assertive than you used to be."

"How do you know how I used to be with her?"

"I know everything about you. Just as I also knew you would do the honorable thing and be here today."

"You call 'coercion' honorable? I am only here because—"

"If you want to carry on with the delusion that you have been trapped into this, be my guest. But you will spend the rest of your life enraged by my alleged ambush of you. Whereas if you are in any way canny, you will see all the benefits our arrangement can bring you. And since you are about to run out of money in two weeks, we need to get you that job."

"But I made that job up."

"So you say."

Three days later, while we were drinking our usual postcoital whisky, Margit said, "You need to go back to Lorraine L'Herbert's salon this Sunday."

"There's no chance of that."

"Why?"

"Because as soon as Madame or her majordomo hears that it's me asking for an invite, they'll slam the door in my face."

"Poor Harry—always thinking that people actually care about him. You didn't outrage Madame L'Herbert when you came bursting in on her, demanding to know if she knew me. Like all self-obsessives, she never muses for a great deal of time about other people, except in relation to herself. So your little scene in her apartment lasted about fifty-five seconds in her consciousness. Fear not—all she and her pimp are interested in is your twenty-euro admission fee. Call them tomorrow and be certain to be there on Sunday night. Then get yourself introduced to a gentleman named

Laurence Coursen. He's the head of the American Institute in Paris, and he's been going to L'Herbert's salon for years to pick up women, as he's married to this very rich nightmare who weighs around one hundred and fifty kilos and spends much of her waking hours giving him a hard time. I know he's in the market for someone to teach film at the Institute. Just put yourself in his path and be charming . . ."

"Fat chance of that."

"But Harry, you are charming . . ."

It was the first time Margit had ever paid me a compliment.

I did as instructed. I called Henry Montgomery, "Madame L'Herbert's assistant." He didn't verbally flinch when I said my name. He just gave me the door code and reminded me to arrive with twenty-five euros ("The price has gone up a bit") in an envelope on Sunday night. This time it was an easy twenty-minute stroll from my hotel on the rue du Dragon to her apartment down the street from the Panthéon.

When I arrived there at the appointed hour on Sunday night, the salon was in full swing. Henry Montgomery didn't seem to recognize me. But he did relieve me of my envelope and glanced at my name (printed as instructed on the front) and then brought me over to Lorraine. As before, she was standing under one of her nude portraits, holding court. Montgomery whispered something in her ear. Immediately she was all effusive.

"Harry, what a joy to see you again. It's been . . . how long?"

"Quite a few months."

"And still here. So Paris has taken hold of you."

"That it has," I said.

"Now you paint, right?"

"I teach. Film studies. And I was wondering if Larry Coursen might be around tonight?"

"Cruising for a job, are we?"

"Actually, I am."

"American directness. Nothing like it, pardner. Larry! Larry!"

She started yelling to a man in late middle age, dressed in an off-white suit that looked around twenty years old and was in need of a good pressing. He came over.

"Larry, you must meet Harry. He's a brilliant professor. Teaches . . . what was it again?"

"Film studies."

"That a fact?" Larry said. "Where do you teach?"

"Well, I used to teach at . . ."

And the conversation was off and running. L'Herbert drifted off. Coursen and I must have talked for around half an hour—largely about the movies (he was a serious film nut), but also about the Institute of which he was the director. As he asked me a bit about the sort of courses I used to teach and my "professorial style," it was evident that he was conducting an impromptu interview on the spot.

"What exactly have you been doing in Paris?"

"Trying to write a novel."

"Have you published before?"

"Plenty of academic papers and the like . . ."

"Really? Whereabouts?"

I told him.

"And do you have an apartment here?"

"I did. I'm between them right now, staying at a hotel."

"Would you have the number on you?"

I wrote it down for him.

"I might be in touch in the next few days."

He started glancing around the room and then locked eyes with a woman around twenty. She gave him a small wave.

"Nice to meet you, Harry," he said.

After Coursen had gone off with his very young friend, I drifted out onto the balcony. It had started to drizzle, so it was empty. I looked over at the spot where I first met Margit. Say I hadn't come here that night? Say I hadn't flirted with her and engaged in that mad embrace and taken her phone number and called her up? But I had done all that because I was lonely and sad and feeling unwanted and lost . . . and because I had so wanted to see her again.

I came into your life because you needed me, Harry.

Yes. I did. And now . . . we are together. In perpetuity.

I turned and headed back into the salon. Lorraine was standing near the food table, talking to a Japanese woman dressed head to toe in tight black leather. Lorraine turned away from her as I approached.

"I wanted to thank you for your hospitality," I said.

"Going so soon, hon?"

I nodded.

"Good conversation with Larry Coursen?"

"Yes . . . and I appreciate the introduction. We'll see if anything comes of it."

"And I saw you out on the balcony. Still looking for your Hungarian?"

"No. But I didn't think you remembered me . . ."

"Hon, you barging in—asking about a woman who came here once in 1980—was hard to forget. But want to hear something rather droll? After you left I did ask Henry about—what was her name?—Kadar? He actually remembered her rather well—because her husband, Zoltan, got talking with another woman the night they were here, and there was a scene out on the balcony with the Hungarian threatening to toss the other woman into rue Soufflot. Henry said he'd never seen such a jealous rage—and one that came out in whispers . . . a sure sign of insanity in my book. Hell, give me a proper screaming match any day. So consider yourself lucky you really didn't meet her. That kind of crazy—when they get their claws into you—"

"I really have to go now," I said, cutting her off.

"Hey, fear not. I won't say a word to Larry Coursen about any of this. Don't want to cost you a job or anything. And y'all come back here again, you hear?"

L'Herbert was true to her word about not telling Coursen about my "girlfriend." There was a message the next day at my hotel from his secretary. *Could I present myself at his office at 3:00 PM tomorrow for an interview?*

The American Institute was out in Neuilly. A sprawling *hôtel particulier* refurbished with classrooms and offices and a large public lecture theater. Coursen was pleasant and businesslike. He had dug out all my professional details. He had googled some of my academic papers and journalistic pieces. As expected, he had read all about the scandal that had cost me my job.

"I'd appreciate hearing the story from you," he said.

I took him through it, trying to be very honest about my errors in judgment and saying that, although Robson went public with the affair, I still felt great guilt about what happened to Shelley.

After I finished, Coursen said, "I appreciate your directness. It's damn unusual these days—and rather refreshing. I also did make a call to one of your former colleagues in your department: Douglas Stanley. He gave you a fantastic recommendation and also said that the entire business with the student wouldn't have turned into the drama and tragedy that it became if Robson hadn't fanned the flames. And hey, that's one hell of a story about what happened to Robson, isn't it? Kind of makes you believe there is some cosmic force out there that punishes bastards."

"That's one way of looking at it."

"Anyway, the thing is, this is France, thank God, not the U.S. . . . so I can't see too many people objecting if I offer you a post here. Between ourselves . . . I completely sympathize. My second marriage ended when my wife caught me in bed with one of my students back at the University of Connecticut. Best thing that ever happened to me, as it got me to France. We're fellow refugees, Harry."

The post was initially for one thirteen-week term. I would teach two courses: "Introduction to Film" and "Great American Directors." The entire total of class time would come to twelve hours a week and I'd be paid eight thousand euros for the term. He'd also arrange the necessary *carte de séjour* with the French authorities. If everything worked out, we could discuss an extension of my contract toward the end of this probationary period.

I accepted on the spot—but with one proviso: none of the courses could run between 5 and 8 PM.

"No problem," Coursen said. "We'll set them up for the mornings and afternoons. But hey, who's the dame? And if you're seeing her from five to eight she must be married."

"It's . . . uh . . . complicated."

"It always is. And that's what makes it fun."

When I saw Margit the next day, she said, "You handled the interview very well. And you were absolutely right to explain the affair the way you did. No excuses. No attempting to apportion blame elsewhere. Very smart. So congratulations . . . though I do think your new patron is *très louche*. And by the way, don't listen to that old queen Henry Montgomery about my deranged jealousy. What Madame L'Herbert failed to mention to you was that I caught that woman giving Zoltan a blow job on the balcony. Now as you well know, I am very open-minded about such things. But to shame me in public like that? So yes, I did hiss a lot at her and I did half-tip her over the balcony. But I was holding her very tightly. A little *salope* like that wasn't worth a lengthy spell in jail.

"But I digress. I am delighted for you, Harry. And don't worry about the one-term probation business. Coursen will extend your contract."

"If you say so."

"I do say so."

"I need you to do something else for me. I need you to get Susan her job back."

"I'll see what I can do. Meanwhile, she's had some more good financial news come her way. Most of Robson's estate went to his children, but he rewrote his will recently, making your ex-wife the beneficiary of his pension from the college in case he died before retirement. It isn't vast—but she will have an income of around fifteen hundred dollars per month. And with your daughter's tuition now taken care of, she'll get by."

Susan gave me this news herself when I called her that night.

"It's about the only thing that bastard Robson did right," she said. "And it couldn't come at a more critical moment."

"I'm pleased for you."

"Benefiting from the pension of a child pornographer—and having to accept it because I am in such financial hot water—now there's dramatic irony for you. And it shows just how low I've sunk."

"You're right to take the money."

"Well, at least the FBI have decided I wasn't the bookkeeper for his little Internet business. They cleared me today."

"More good news. And I have some to add to that."

I told her about the job at the American Institute.

"Lucky you. I so miss teaching."

"And I so miss my daughter."

"She managed to sit up in a chair by the hospital bed for most of the morning. The doctors all say they cannot figure out how she came out of the coma without significant brain damage."

"Miracles can happen, I suppose. We're very lucky. And I'm desperate to speak to her."

"I broached it with her yesterday. She's still very angry at you. I do take some of the blame for that. After everything blew up for you, I really turned her against you. It was pure rage and revenge. A terrible thing to have done. I see that now. And I will try to put it right."

At our next liaison, Margit said, "What an act of contrition on her part. Guilt is such a fantastic leveler."

"Did you organize the pension business?"

"Perhaps."

"And the Feds?"

"Perhaps."

"You really like to keep me guessing, don't you?"

"But look at what you get in return. Emotional tidiness. Wrongs righted. Jobs offered. Admissions of guilt from those who hurt you. Even my services as a real-estate agent. There's a studio apartment for rent in a Haussmannian building on the rue des Écoles. Twenty-six square meters, nicely renovated, and only six hundred euros a month. Very reasonable for this quartier, and you'll be in walking distance of so many cinemas . . ."

"Not to mention you."

"Well, five minutes away on foot is far more convenient than all that travel you used to do from the Tenth."

"And you'll have me almost on your doorstep."

"Harry, you're always on my doorstep. You know that. Just as you know I'm with you even when you don't want me to be with you. But again I digress. You need to get to the estate agent first thing tomorrow morning. Tell them you're a prof at the American Institute—they'll like that. If they make worried noises about your lack of a bank account, tell them you've just arrived from the States and are about to open one. Coursen will supply you with a reference and a two-thousand-euro advance on your contract. That should get you set up. After that—"

"I think I can take it from there."

"Am I sounding like your mother?"

"No comment."

"I just want to get your life full back on track. And this apartment, it's perfect. You won't find anything like it for—"

"OK, Margit. Point taken. I will be at the *agence immobilière* by nine."

By ten the next day I had rented the apartment. Margit was right: it was a terrific little place. Simple, but stylishly done. Coursen was very good about getting the Institute to front me two grand in advance. Within three days I had moved into the studio. After the squalor and dinginess of rue de Paradis, my new apartment seemed pristine and splendidly private. With the balance of money left over from the salary advance, I bought sheets and towels and a stereo and began the process of settling in.

Then the teaching began. I liked my students. They seemed to like me—and I quickly remembered what a pleasure it could be to stand up at a lectern and spout on about movies. The first term passed by with great speed. I got a phone installed in the apartment. I called Susan every day. Megan was back at school within four weeks of her accident. But she was still refusing to speak to her father. "She doesn't talk much to me either," Susan said. "She really mopes a lot. The doctors say it's a natural side effect after coming out of a coma. She's depressed. But at least she's talking to a psychotherapist at school. So . . . be patient. She will come around."

Everything began to fall into place. My contract at the American Institute was extended for two years. I met a guy at a reception at the Institute who edited a weekly magazine for expatriates and was looking for a film critic. The pay wasn't much—one-fifty a column—but it got me writing about movies again and brought in a little more money. I was able to buy a few better clothes. I invested in a television and a DVD player. I purchased a new laptop. I bought a cell phone. I gave my lectures, I wrote my column, I worked out in the Institute's gym, I continued to haunt the Cinémathèque and the little movie houses that crammed my quartier. I had my daily call to Susan about Megan. We were polite with each other on the phone—the edgy anger now abating into a respectful distance. We were no longer enemies; rather, weary combatants who had decided it was now easier to be civil with each other and only had one agreed subject of conversation: their daughter.

Time continued to accelerate. I taught all summer. I loved the vacant streets of Paris in August, and managed a two-and-a-half-day holiday on the beach in Collioure. Outside of my work I found something to "do" every day—a movie, an exhibition, a concert, books to read, magazines to peruse—anything to fill the hours.

One afternoon, I spent the better part of a half hour in the permanent collection of the Pompidou, staring at one of Yves Klein's blue monochrome paintings. I'd seen this one in art books before. But approaching it—in the flesh, so to speak—was revelatory. At first sight, it was just a canvas painted a deep blue—its tint somewhat akin to a late-afternoon sky on a clear winter's day. Darkness was visible within its confines. But the longer I stared at it, the more I began to see the subtle gradients in Klein's shading of the canvas: a complex array of textures and tonal variations, all lurking behind what, at first, simply seemed like a large blue square. But it wasn't just its intricate blueness that held my attention. After a few minutes of direct eye contact, the painting proved hypnotic. The textures disappeared and I found myself staring into a place of spatial emptiness: a void without limits, from which there was no return. Until someone bumped into me, jolting me back to terra firma. I felt a little befuddled. But much later that night, as I climbed into bed and turned off the light, Klein's infinite blueness came back to me. And I couldn't help but think, *That's the void I live in now.*

The floppy disk that Margit had returned to me was put away in a drawer in my new apartment. One evening, toward the beginning of September, I pulled it out and loaded it into my laptop. I spent a long Saturday reading all six hundred pages of my still unfinished novel. When I reached the end, I removed the disk from the computer. I put it back in my desk drawer and resolved never to look at it again.

You're right, you're right, I heard myself telling her. *Overcooked, self-important posturings with no real storyline, no motor to keep you turning the pages.*

I knew she could hear me say that. Just as I knew she was always there, always watching.

"So you finally gave up on the novel," Margit said when I saw her the following day.

"Why ask a question to which you already know the answer?"

"Just making conversation."

"No, you're just doing what you always do: reminding me of your omnipresence."

"I would have thought that, by now, you would have adjusted to—"

"I'll never adjust. Never. How can I, knowing you're hovering over me, making certain—?"

"—that no harm comes to you—"

"But that I also stay within the rules."

"There's only one rule, Harry. Here twice a week from five until eight."

"And in the future, if I want to visit my daughter for four days?"

"Make it three days. Or—when she's ready—fly her over here."

"Can't we negotiate?"

"No. This is the setup. It has its minor limitations. It has its liberties. As I said before, you are free to do what you like outside our time together."

"Even though you're watching over me at all times?"

"And what is wrong with that?"

I said nothing. But a few nights later, I started writing this book. I wanted to get it all down on paper; a record of what happened—just in case something did happen to me—and to try and convince myself that I was not living in a state of permanent delusion. But why should you accept this story as given? It's just a story—my story. And like all stories, it isn't, in the pure sense of the word, true. It's just my version of the truth. Which means it is—and isn't—true at all.

How do you step out of one world and into another? I've no damn idea—but I keep doing it twice a week.

"What happens to you when you grow older?" I asked her recently. "Do you die again?"

"I've no idea."

"And when I die, do I join you in spectral perpetuity?"

"I have no idea . . . but I like the turn of phrase. Are you putting it in your book?"

I met her gaze.

"Yes," I said.

"It's interesting reading," she said. "Not that anyone will believe you."

"I'm not writing it to be read."

"Rubbish. All writers write to be read . . . to have their story 'out there.' But trust me: this will never get published."

THE WOMAN IN THE FIFTH · 317

"Is that a threat?"

"Just a statement of fact . . . as I see it, of course."

"So you're going to make certain it never gets published?"

"Did I say that?"

"You implied that."

"Hardly. Your life outside our hours together . . ."

. . . is my own?

But how can it be when she's constantly there? How can you make a decision when you know there is a third party present, guarding you from the wrong choice? Recently I dashed out into the rue des Écoles, trying to hail a taxi, and unaware that I had stepped right into the path of a motorcyclist. Though less than two seconds away from hitting me, the cyclist flipped over, as if shoved out of my path by some hidden force. He got up, unhurt. But when a cop showed up moments later and asked him if he had swerved to avoid me, he said he was certain someone pushed him.

"Did you see anyone push him?" the cop asked me. I shook my head.

The next afternoon, chez Margit, I said, "Thank you for saving me yesterday."

"Didn't your mother ever tell you to look both ways before stepping out into the street?"

"If he had hit me, it might have taught me a lesson."

"If he had hit you, you would have been dead. The fact that he didn't also taught you a lesson."

"How wonderful to have a fairy godmother," I said.

"How wonderful to be appreciated. Still writing the book?"

"Aren't you reading it as I write it?"

"You have no proof. But I do worry about the way you work so late into the night, and are then up a few hours later."

"I don't need much sleep."

"Correction: you don't get much sleep, but you still need it."

How can anyone sleep when they know there's someone monitoring them all the time?

"I'm fine."

"You should start taking those pills again."

They won't help. Because I will never rest easy with you in my life.

"They didn't do much good."

"Go see a doctor and get something stronger."

"I'm fine."

"You hate this. Us."

"I'm fine."

"You will adjust. Because you'll have to. You have no choice."

But I still clung to the belief that, outside of our hours together, I did have a choice. A few nights after this conversation, I went to a jazz joint on the rue des Lombards and got talking at the bar with a fellow American named Rachel: a woman in her forties, single, something in mutual funds in Boston, attractive, alone in Paris for a long weekend ("The job's so pressured, I only can squeeze a few days off, here and there"), chatty, and happy to match me drink-for-drink over the course of three hours. Around two in the morning, as the place was closing down, she covered my hand with hers and said her hotel was a five-minute stagger from here.

It was all very pleasant and rather romantic. I had to get up early to teach. Rachel wrapped her arms around me in bed and said, "What a nice bit of luck meeting you. And if you're free tonight . . ."

"I'm free tonight."

She smiled and kissed me.

"You've just made my day."

And she'd made mine. I spent much of it in a state of delighted exhaustion, thinking just how smart and lovely Rachel was, and how nice it was to want and feel wanted again.

I arrived back at her hotel, as arranged, at seven that night, a bottle of champagne in hand. But when I asked the desk clerk to call Rachel in her room, he asked, "Are you Monsieur Ricks?"

I nodded.

"I'm afraid Madame has checked out. A death in the family. She left you this."

He handed me an envelope. Inside, on a piece of hotel stationery, was a hastily scribbled note.

Dearest Harry:

Have just found out my mother passed away this morning.
All very sudden and shocking. I so loved our night together.
If you're ever in Boston . . .

And she gave me her number.

I crumpled up the note and handed the desk clerk the bottle of champagne and told him I had no use for it anymore.

If you're ever in Boston . . .

Rachel, I'd come like a shot to see you in Boston—but only for forty-eight hours. Because that's all the time allotted to me.

"Did you kill her mother?" I asked Margit the next afternoon.

"She was an eighty-year-old woman. At that age, a sudden heart attack . . ."

"So if I see another woman again . . . ?"

"Hopefully she won't lose her mother so suddenly."

"Or walk under a bus. You like traffic accidents, don't you? They're your preferred way of settling the score."

"You have no proof."

"You're always saying that."

"See you in three days, Harry. And who knows, you might get a pleasant surprise before then."

The surprise arrived just before midnight that night. I was at home, working on this book, when the phone rang. I answered it.

"Dad?"

The receiver shook in my hand.

"Megan?"

"Thought I'd call and say hello."

We talked for around twenty minutes. I didn't raise the subject of the last ten months. Nor did she. Her conversation was tentative, guarded. She talked about the accident, about school, how her mother was still out of work, how she wasn't sleeping well, and still felt "spooked by stuff."

"This counselor I've been talking to at school—well, he's more of a shrink—he says, 'We're all spooked by stuff.'"

"He's right," I said. "We all are."

She said she had to go. "But maybe I can call you next week."

"That would be great," I said.

"Cool. Catch you then, Dad."

After Megan hung up I sat at my desk for a long time, swallowing hard, choking back tears. Only sometime later did I find myself wondering, Did "she" set that up? Was this the "pleasant surprise" she talked about?

You have no proof.

But I did have evidence.

Inspector Coutard also had evidence. My laptop. Still impounded in the *commissariat de police* of the Tenth arrondissement. A week before Christmas, he rang me at the American Institute to say that I could come by and collect it now.

I showed up later that afternoon. He was wearing the same grubby jacket he had sported when he first interviewed me. His desk was awash with paperwork, his office ashtray clogged up with butts, and he had a cigarette screwed into a corner of his mouth.

"How did you find out I was teaching at the American Institute?" I asked.

"I'm a detective. And I also see that you now have a *carte de séjour* and a new address in the Fifth. I'm pleased that you have moved up in our world; that things are better."

"Yes . . . I suppose they are."

"Well, we no longer have any use for this," he said, pointing to the laptop positioned on the edge of his desk. "Sezer and his associates are still under lock and key. They'll go to trial for Omar's murder and everything else in February. It's a fait accompli that they will be convicted. The evidence is so conclusive . . ."

Because she knows how to plant conclusive evidence.

"Anyway," he said, tapping the laptop, "now you can return to your novel."

"I've given up on it."

"But why?"

"You know why. It was no damn good."

"I never said that."

"I'm not saying that you did."

"But surely you haven't given up on writing altogether?"

"No, I'm working on something."

"A new novel?" he asked.

"Nonfiction . . . though everyone will think otherwise."

I could see him taking that in.

"And your 'friend'—the woman in the Fifth—do you still see her?"

"Every three days without fail."

Coutard raised his eyebrows. He shook his head. He put out his cigarette and lit another, puffing away on it for a good minute while studying me with detached professional interest. Finally he said, "You are truly haunted, monsieur."

Guilty as charged.

The WOMAN
in the FIFTH

DOUGLAS KENNEDY

A Readers Club Guide

INTRODUCTION

Harry Ricks is a deeply troubled man on the run. After a messy affair, a broken marriage, and a disgraced end to his career as a film professor, Harry ends up impoverished and fleeing to Paris, trying desperately to live his fantasy of writing a novel in the city of his dreams. Upon arrival, Harry realizes the city is nothing like the one from his fantasy, and he finds himself living in a virtual flophouse on the wrong side of town. The one light in this bleak world is a chance meeting with Margit Kadar, a mature, beautiful, and charming woman living in the Fifth arrondissement. They begin a torrid, fierce affair. But something very sinister surrounds Harry, as many of his enemies are befallen by sudden misfortune and death. As the bodies begin to stack up, Harry must confront the ghoulish truth about his past, his future, and the one woman who cares for him in this strange city.

QUESTIONS AND TOPICS FOR DISCUSSION

1. Harry Ricks is a deeply flawed individual. We know virtually nothing about his life at the onset of the novel, except that he is on the run from his past. At the outset of the novel, did you think he had any redeemable character traits? How did your opinion of him change as you read more?

2. No one is warm or friendly to Harry upon his arrival in Paris. Harry feels "an ominous sense that I was about to detonate at any moment. . . . The doctor was right: I had broken down." (p. 18) This does not assuage the coldness and downright cruelty he experiences by the citizens of Paris. How much of this instant distaste toward Harry is deserved?

3. Paris is a city that has lived in Harry's imagination for some time. "[It] had been my dream for years; that absurd dream which so many of my compatriots embrace: being a writer in Paris." (p. 24) What do you think the draw to Paris is for writers? How dangerous is it to build up a fantasy for something one has no direct experience with? What are some of the ramifications when fantasy and reality collide?

4. We learn that Harry Ricks has a lot to prove to himself and the world around him. Despite the troubles and chaos of his life, Harry believed he would "find a quiet place in which to get it all down on paper, and finally demonstrate to the world that I was the serious writer I always knew myself to be. *I'll show the bastards* is a statement uttered by someone who has suffered a setback . . . or, more typically, has hit bottom." (p. 52) He doesn't want to write a novel out of inspiration, but out of vengeance against the world he believes has wronged him. Can art be used for vengeance? How productive is this philosophy?

5. The writer Richard Bach comments: "Argue your limitations and sure enough they are yours." Harry Ricks is a man drowning in self-pity and depression. He continually reminds himself he is worthless and deserves nothing. "It no longer mattered what people thought of me. Because I no longer mattered—to anyone else, let alone myself." (p. 86) How much does his initial attitude affect the course of his existence in Paris?

6. Harry Ricks escapes his troubles at the cinema. "The majority of my free time outside my *chambre* was spent haunting all those darkened rooms around town that cater to film junkies like myself. . . . Every day, I'd spend at least six hours at the movies." (pp. 52–53) What do you think the draw of the cinema is for Harry? How does watching films help him to escape life's problems?

7. Harry arrives in the Tenth arrondissement, a seedy, crime-filled neighborhood in Paris, in dire financial peril. After some time, he discovers a secret stash of money, an amount that could seriously change his financial and psychological situation. But instead of keeping the money, he decides to send it to the wife of the one man who showed him kindness, Adnan, who was recently deported and jailed. Why does he do this? What does this say about Harry and his judgment of his own character? Does Harry receive any repayment for his good act?

8. Harry works nights at a very shady job for sinister individuals, but decides he must do it because of his horrible financial situation. He realizes "that I might be landing myself in a situation which could be potentially dangerous, or could jeopardize my future freedom. But I found myself being won over by a bleak but consoling thought: *Nothing matters.*" (p. 72) What sort of freedom comes from this nihilistic emotion? Is hitting bottom really freedom, or just another sign of debilitating depression? How dangerous is this notion?

9. The only breath of fresh air that enters Harry's bleak existence comes when he meets Margit Kadar, a mature, beautiful, and charming

woman. They begin a tempestuous romance full of passionate sex and raw emotive dialogues. But after a few meetings, Margit bluntly pushes Harry away. "Do yourself a favor, Harry. Walk out of here now and don't come back." (p. 145) Why does Margit try to push Harry away? What is she sparing him from?

10. Margit discusses the human desire for vengeance with Harry. "The standard moral line on revenge is that it leaves you feeling hollow. What bullshit. Everyone wants the wrongs against them redressed. Everyone wants to 'get even.'" (p. 147) Do you agree with Margit's philosophy on vengeance? What prevents people from taking such actions into their own hands? Do we deserve our "vengeance"?

11. Right after Harry's sexual tryst with Yanna, he contemplates telling Margit about his encounter. But once he arrives at her front door, she knows about it immediately. How do you suspect she knew of this instantly? What gives Harry away?

12. Ghosts are everywhere in *The Woman in the Fifth*, both metaphorically and physically. All the characters are haunted by their pasts, and in Harry's case, he's haunted by a real ghost. What do these "ghosts" represent? Does it resemble the philosophy that "there are certain tragedies from which we never recover. We may eventually adjust to the sense of loss that pervades every waking hour of the day. We may accept the desperate sadness that colors all perception. We may even learn to live with the loss. But that doesn't mean we will ever fully cauterize the wound or shut away the pain in some steel-tight box and consider it vanquished." (p. 148)

ENHANCE YOUR BOOK CLUB

1. *The Woman in the Fifth* employs a strong narrative style, telling a story rife with human flaws, personal vendettas, and tormented pasts, all spiced with plenty of tension and gritty violence. Harry Ricks is a stranger in a strange land, overwhelmed by the seedy world of the Tenth arrondissement.

   Another author who shares this protagonist-based, fast-action style is famed American crime author Elmore Leonard. Pick up some of his classic crime thrillers such as *Get Shorty, Freaky Deaky, Cuba Libre,* and *Killshot* if you've developed a taste for this addictive style of pop literature.

2. Harry Ricks is comforted by the dark rooms of the cinemas across Paris. Jean-Luc Godard says, "Cinema is the most beautiful fraud in the world," while another famed director, Roman Polanski, comments, "Cinema should make you forget that you are sitting in a theater." Pedro Almodóvar explains, "I . . . wanted to express the strength of cinema to hide reality, while being entertaining. Cinema can fill in the empty spaces of your life and your loneliness."

   Imagine the films Harry Ricks would discuss in his classroom in Paris. Rent some of the great films such as Alfred Hitchcock's *Psycho,* Jean-Luc Godard's *Breathless,* Stanley Kubrick's *Spartacus,* and Akira Kurosawa's *Ran* to see just what these great directors are talking about.

3. The city of Paris is as varied as life itself, each arrondissement representing another form of the city's great cultural legacy. Harry Ricks confesses, "The Fifth was my preferred terrain." (p. 52)

It is also known as "The Latin Quarter," the literary and artistic soul of the city itself. The Fifth has been the home of many artistic luminaries, such as Ernest Hemingway, Paul Verlaine, Albert Camus, Gertrude Stein, and Jean-Paul Sartre. Research the history of this world-famous section of Paris to understand more of Harry's romantic love affair with this unique and creative neighborhood.

A CONVERSATION WITH
DOUGLAS KENNEDY

There are remarkable twists and turns in *The Woman in the Fifth*. When the initial idea came to you, did you foresee these plot upheavals from the onset? What was the process that led you to the discovery of this narrative?

I never plot out a novel in advance. I start with the general premise—the narrator and his or her central dilemma—and the rest arrives during the actual writing. In the case of *The Woman in the Fifth* I was coming out of a difficult juncture in my life when I knew my marriage was failing, and I was beset with the onset of midlife melancholy. One of the manifestations of this was six months of profound insomnia that saw me walking the streets of Paris frequently half the night whenever I spent my week per month in that city. Eventually I was able to put this melancholia and insomnia behind me. And a long-overdue divorce in 2009 rendered me a much happier man. But *The Woman in the Fifth* came out of this strange, bleak juncture in my life. As such it's a novel that reads like a perpetual *nuit blanche*—an endless sleepless night, full of dread and misgiving.

The Woman in the Fifth is a novel of many forms. It applies the psychological narrative of Henry James mixed with the hard-boiled crime-fiction style of Raymond Chandler. It also blends themes of the American expatriate experience with the nineteenth-century ghost story. Could you give some examples of other novels that may have inspired this amalgamation of themes?

There's a brilliant novel by Georges Simenon called *Three Bedrooms in Manhattan*. It concerns a French actor whose marriage has just combusted and who finds himself wandering the shadowy, down-at-the-heels, neon-silhouetted world of 1950s New York. Simenon captures so superbly this nocturnal world of midcentury Manhattan, a time when the city really did wear a perpetual five o'clock shadow. Simenon's portrait of my hometown (Manhattan) as a sinister construct—and of a man grappling with serious emotional demons—began to bounce around in my imagination. And the result was this novel, which is so wildly and radically different from Simenon's, even though it was initially inspired by it.

Harry Ricks finds only coldness and strife in his first days in Paris. As a man who has spent considerable time in Paris, did you encounter any of the coldness Harry experiences upon your own arrival in Paris?

I decided to write a novel against the cliché of the American in Paris. I've read far too many of those sorts of novels, in which the character arrives in the City of Light and inhabits a picture postcard of chic apartments, chic restaurants, chic women, and (God help us) trying to write a novel in his local über-chic café. *The Woman in the Fifth* subverts all these clichés and brings the reader to a very different but profoundly real Paris that is, very much, on the other side of the tracks.

The descriptions of the Tenth arrondissement are so full of life that one can feel the grit underneath one's nails while reading the passages. What personal experiences had led you to write so truly about this "other" side of Paris?

The novel was a huge hit in France—selling more than six hundred thousand copies and receiving largely terrific reviews. But you would not believe the number of Parisians who came up to me after its publication and asked me how I had discovered this alternative Paris. My reply was a simple one: "On foot." I happen to be quite the flâneur—a wanderer of cities (something I developed during my Manhattan adolescence)—and the Paris depicted in the novel, especially the Tenth arrondissement, where Harry lands, is a very real Paris: grubby, tough, anti-picture-postcard. I decided to use Paris as a nightmare landscape, and one in which Harry rarely emerges into the city during the morning. As such, the novel is set in a largely nocturnal and haunted city.

Harry and Margit have an interesting dialogue regarding the modern attraction to the act of shopping and consumerism in general. As Margit says, "It's what people do with their time now. It's the great cultural activity of this epoch—and it speaks volumes about the complete emptiness of modern life." (p. 116) Could you elaborate on this particular philosophy?

Shopping has, alas, become so much of the way we define ourselves in the modern world. We are all enslaved to the idea that buying stuff will make us happier. In the novel, Harry's impecunious state—and Margit's lack of resources as a translator—means they are both outside of the "luxe" aspect of Paris which exists throughout so many corners of the city. Harry is very much living a grubby day-to-day existence until he begins to enter Margit's world, which is not all that it seems.

Infidelity is a continual theme in your works. As Harry laments after his affair with Yanna, "Do we ever learn anything from our mistakes? Not when it comes to sex. That's the one arena of bad behavior in which we are recidivists, over and over again." (p. 157) Harry cheats on his wife, Susan; Susan cheats on Harry. Is infidelity inevitable? Is betrayal somehow sewn into the human experience?

Well, put it this way: infidelity is an essential component of the human emotional palette. As long as the notion of a committed relationship exists, there will always be infidelities because human sexuality is such an interesting minefield of desires, needs, fears, and contradictions. As such, with the promise of fidelity must come the possibility of straying, of betrayal, of seeking comfort elsewhere. Infidelity is so much the third rail vis-à-vis love and marriage—and as all novelists deal with human mess, so infidelity is such a compelling subject with which to grapple.

Another interesting conversation between Harry and Margit concerns the essential nature of American morality versus the French methodology of "compartmentalization." "Accept that— as Dumas said—the chains of marriage are heavy and, as such, they often need to be carried by several people." (p. 138) Margit also criticizes American morality, which she claims as "hypocritical finery." Could you discuss the essential differences between French and American culture in regards to human relationships and marriage?

Put simply: in America we rarely compartmentalize. We also believe there is a price to be paid for bad behavior, especially as you also have to live with yourself thereafter. In France there is far greater compartmentalization—the idea that, within an individual life, there are hidden recesses which need not intermingle with each other. Granted, that's a sweeping generalization. But one thing is very clear to me after a decade of living part time in France: sexual guilt is not the same issue in France that it is in my own country, and I play with this moral gulf throughout my novel.

The parlay between Inspector Jean-Marie Coutard and Harry Ricks is a cat-and-mouse game of information desired and withheld. There is a parallel between these characters' verbal jousts and Raskolnikov's and Inspector Porfiry's interactions in the Russian classic _Crime and Punishment_. Did the Dostoyevsky classic influence these themes of a man wrestling with his own guilt under suspicion?

Of course, anyone who writes a novel about guilt, self-incrimination, and fear of authority must bend the knee in the direction of *Crime and Punishment*. It remains the benchmark work when it comes to delineating the way that the possibility of violent malfeasance is within us all—and how so much of life is lived under the existential fear of being exposed for what we really are.

In the short story "Le Horla" by Guy de Maupassant, a man is physically dominated by a creature bent on ruling over his decisions in the physical world. This is similar to Harry's predicament, as his decisions are dominated by Margit's schedule of meetings that he cannot break, or face the deaths of those he cares about most. Do you have an attraction to these nineteenth-century ghostly tales of men trapped by supernatural creatures? What do you believe the metaphor for these "ghosts" really are?

My interest in ghosts center around a very basic belief: more than anything, we are all haunted by ourselves.

Also by *New York Times* bestselling author

DOUGLAS
KENNEDY

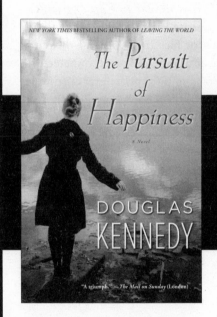

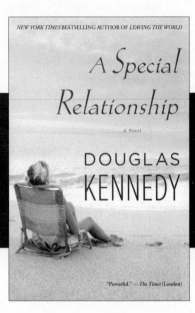

"An engrossing novel that transcends decades. . . . It's a spellbinding but tragic read that you should not miss."
—*The Oklahoman* (Oklahoma City, OK)

"Kennedy's impressive achievement is his narrator Sally, whose turbulent emotions he conveys with an unusual depth of understanding."
—*Times Literary Supplement* (London)

Available wherever books are sold or at www.simonandschuster.com

Also by *New York Times* bestselling author

DOUGLAS
KENNEDY

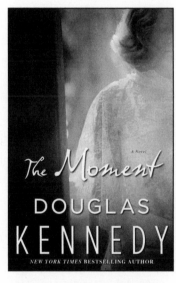

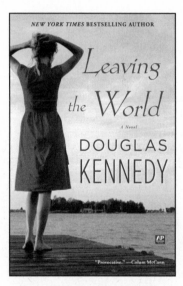

"In his fast-paced, engrossing novels Douglas Kennedy always has his brilliant finger on the entertaining parts of human sorrow, fury, and narrow escapes. Wonderful."
—Lorrie Moore, *New York Times* bestselling author of *A Gate at the Stairs*

"Kennedy's characters embark on long, complex, provocative journeys, and their ultimate strength is that—like the writer— they can throw off bright sparks in the dark."
—Colum McCann, winner of the National Book Award